Weigh Anchor

Book One of:
The Curious Voyages of the Anna Virginia Saga

J. L. Lawson

J. L. LAWSON

Weigh Anchor
Book One of The Curious Voyages of the Anna Virginia Saga
J. L. Lawson
http://jeffreylewislawson.com
jefrelaw@jeffreylewislawson.com

J. L. LAWSON

As a single footstep will not make a path on the earth, so a single thought will not make a pathway in the mind. To make a deep physical path, we walk again and again. To make a deep mental path, we must think over and over the kind of thoughts we wish to dominate our lives.

---Henry David Thoreau

J. L. LAWSON

Table of Contents

J. L. LAWSON

1

Unbroken

"One thus sees that a new kind of theory is needed which drops these basic commitments and at most recovers some essential features of the older theories as abstract forms derived from a deeper reality in which what prevails is unbroken wholeness."
---David Bohm

J ohn ambled back to the house from the driveway. He stood on his porch with an odd expression on his face. He turned and went back inside to rejoin Virginia---his publishing agent and guest.

He regained some of his composure from earlier in the day. "Thank you for your patience. Now what would you like to ask first?"

Ginger looked back to the front door and with an overwhelming sense of curiosity asked, "Who *exactly* were those people? You said distant family? I certainly felt right at home around them; it was a very comfortable feeling."

He looked to the front door and porch; the last several months flooded his memory, *"They* would say that they were just ordinary people. However, I can personally attest that they are in fact: most *extraordinary individuals.*" He let go of his recollections and focused on her. He saw her very clearly for the first time; smiling he offered, "Take that necklace you're wearing," her fingers went instinctively to it from long habit, "I happen to know a story about its little agate pebble that just might surprise you."

"Is this a part of your manuscript?" Ginger was *very* interested now, "We can kill two birds with one stone if you wish to elaborate---I'm all ears!"

He began, "It seldom appears to the casual observer that any *thing* is truly out of the ordinary, save on those rare occasions when the extra-ordinary sneaks into everyday life..."

He added another couple split logs to the fire and they settled into comfortable seats. "To understand the whole context of the story," he reached for the cup of coffee that had grown cold, yet he took a sip and smiled as he continued, "I should begin by explaining: *Wang Fu Kong was the youngest son of a Chinese entrepreneur. He inherited a portion of his father's fortune. In order to avoid losing it or his life at the hands of his greedy brothers, he sailed into the sunrise looking to make his fortune in the New World. Once in San Francisco, he promptly adopted the name of George Livingson...*"

Through the evening, through the night, even throughout the next morning and into the afternoon, during coffee, tea, sandwiches and snacks, he regaled her with the tale of all the generations of Livingsons just as it had been told to him. When he got to the parts that mentioned her own family's roles in the story---the Spelmans, Bessamers and Mastersons---he noticed she closed her eyes as if to etch those histories into her memory forever. The story of 'Papa's Pebble' naturally held her spellbound. They were sitting quietly after he'd brought the story up to the present---omitting the delivery of the watch and his father's medal only minutes before she'd arrived.

"I wasn't even told that I was adopted until receiving this little trinket..." she dangled the pebble at her throat absently.

John then listened to her tell him of how she returned home from the reading of her mother's will with the information of her birth mother's real name, who her mother had *really* been, and of her own *actual* family... *somewhere*. How, when she returned to Indiana and confronted Harvey and Peggie, her adoptive parents admitted what they had done when driving home from an auction the foggy cold night she was born---How they had encountered an overturned bus, a pregnant woman giving birth on the grassy shoulder of the road, and of taking the woman and child into their car with the intention of traveling to a hospital. Then how, since they couldn't have children, their desire for a child of their own overwhelmed them at the cost of the woman's life.

Ginger felt again the anger and vitriol that always arose in her with that recollection, "I am thankful they are now long dead," she admitted without emotion. "That may sound heartless and ungrateful, but it was confusing and difficult while they were still alive." She looked at his face and recognized there was actually what appeared to be compassion behind his eyes.

She demurred, "I don't know why I'm telling you this. I've certainly been analyzed and therapized enough to have gotten through these emotions... but..." He still held her in his gaze without judgement. "Harvey was a nice man, really; he was just spineless when it came to Peggie's whims and demands. Peggie was doting to the point of obsessive and could never understand why I was so rebellious. I was smarter than both of them put together; I despised being trotted out to 'perform' for their family and the few friends they had. She wanted a Barbie; she got me instead---I was a real disappointment. She told me so often enough... She wanted a girl-doll and I was a hoyden with a mind of my own. She screamed at me; slapped me around when screaming didn't work, then sobbed to her husband to 'do something about that tomboy'." Ginger was digging her fingernails into the cushions of the sofa and suddenly realized it. She took a deep breath, tried to smile and sat back with her legs crossed and arms folded.

John was nearly in tears. Her emotions weren't too far from those he'd carried for years, but from different causes. He said softly, "I can't imagine what that must've been like. You see, no one paid *any* attention *to me*; there were *no* parents, *no* expectations, *no one* to disappoint, *no* screaming or abuse at all. I was simply alone: surrounded by other kids; most of them actually *did have* parents--- but parents who couldn't afford to feed themselves let alone their children. So they ended up where I was: in the orphanage. I had all of the same disgust and anger that it sounds like you had. *I* was disgusted and angry at the world at large, or the parents I didn't have, or fate... hell, I didn't even know *who* to be mad at, and that was hardest part I guess: *just not knowing...*" He was suddenly as quiet as she now was.

Ginger's thought, 'Jeez, I had it bad, but at least I had someone to blame and be mad at...' Aloud she said, "The Amoursons were conscienceless bastards, but at least they weren't faceless---I *knew* who to detest and attack: Peggie!" She realized she was saying that out loud because John's head came up and he was looking at her. She softened and sat forward, "When I was finally told the story of my real mother, that I was essentially stolen at birth... I felt liberated and justified---but at the same time I felt *very* alone. After the confrontation with Harvey and Peggie I went on to college and tried to forget. But the realities of my childhood constantly haunted me. There was: what to do at holidays, the stacks of unopened letters from them, and the infrequent messages on my answering machine..." She softened even further, "They *did* provide me with everything they could afford---however misguided and twisted Peggie was. It's just that once I *was* told the truth, I only wanted *so desperately* to have been able to have my *own* mother instead of *them!*"

They both stared out the windows into the lengthening shadows of evening. John said quietly, "...*John Doe* is the only name I have known. You weren't told the truth of your birth and real family until you were eighteen---I am forty this year and was just told yesterday that my name is actually: John *Robert Backhouse* of a remarkable family and startling lineage. That I was---just as you were---lost at birth."

As he showed her the watch, the medal and his 'alleged' birth certificate, Ginger's eyes widened. It hadn't occurred to her for a even a moment that that long story wasn't just for her benefit alone.

Her thoughts flashed, 'Oh my God! What was I thinking?! That this whole tale of the Livingsons was just a salve for *my own* wounds... That all this was about *me*! Ginger-girl! How self-centered are you?! Cripes! Whose daughter are you really? Peggie's girl after all?! *Grow a Conscience*! This guy is hurting too! There *are* other people in the world *besides the great and wonderful Ginger...*'

Aloud she said, "You mean *the* Backhouses... like from the story?! Just as *I am* Virginia Kaitlyn Belle Spelman from *those Spelmans...*"

The implications were boggling. It was one thing to hear family stories and want so badly for them to be real---to be your story too; it's another thing entirely to *know* they are *very* probably real---that one is finally: *not* alone.

John interposed cautiously, "*If* this story *is* true, then there is a large piece of evidence remaining---besides your necklace and inheritance, this watch and medal of valor... *and* this birth certificate. I am supposed to be receiving registration papers in the mail for a yacht! If my guess is correct... I mean if *I really am* the great-grandson of Aaron and Hipolyta Livingson Backhouse... through their son William Henry and Eleanor and son Robert Henry..."

Ginger had one of those minds that absorbed nearly everything; she was way ahead of him, "...Then the yacht in question should be the *Bodhi!*" she said excitedly. "A sixty foot metal-hulled trimaran built in Gotland, Sweden in the late thirties or early forties." They sat quietly for a long while occupied in their own thoughts and speculations---already very weary from the marathon story-telling then fully exhausted after the emotional turmoil relived during the personal confessions.

She mused aloud, "I wonder what my grandparents did with *their* yacht the *Tygress?*"

He was no longer one of her publishing clients at all---*why* she was sitting with him in his house had been wiped from her attention entirely. He was a fellow traveler struggling through the maze of their mutual revelations.

"Do you suppose we could find out?" Her last words were almost incoherent since she was yawning while trying to speak.

John must have been equally exhausted; he asked, "You said you would only be in town these two days?"

She smiled and stretched her full frame across the sofa, "I do have some leeway on that score;" She yawned again, "I'll call the home office and have someone else cover the other few appointments..." then she yawned still again.

He offered something she didn't expect, "You're welcome to stay here if you wish. There is a rarely used guest room on the other side of the house..." now he yawned, "...has its own bathroom and everything."

He yawned again, "I have *got* to go get some sleep or I'm going to fall down right here." He was already heading for the stairs as if her still being there was moot.

Ginger was too tired to think of a reason not to accept the offer. She was a grown woman after all and could sleep anywhere she wished. She heard the sound of a door closing upstairs; she rose and stumbled toward the guest room. She fell onto the bed asleep.

She had been in the publishing business most of her life. Now at thirty-one she still had the habits of sleeping little and working long hours. Rising from the bed before dawn, she found the light switch in the bathroom and closed the door. She took off the clothes she'd been wearing for two and a half days and stared at herself in the mirror. The image that stared back was of a tall auburn-haired woman with lingering freckles across her nose and cheeks, wide shoulders and long legs. Her body was well-toned from weekly trips to any nearest gym---in whatever town or city she happened to be in at the time. She leaned forward and looked more closely into her own eyes.

"Those green eyes are a little redder this morning Ginger-baby, great for holiday decoration but this puffiness is not very attractive at all!" She turned sideways to the mirror and inspected her profile. Putting her hands to her rear end she muttered, "And *this* is not where I need more 'puffiness' either---too much sitting!"

She ran the hot water for a bath and found a fresh bar of soap, shampoo and towels. "At least John keeps his house well supplied for guests." She slipped a foot into the water, "Aah..." then once fully into the tub, she relaxed, "...heaven."

Just as the sun began to turn the morning sky into a rosy promise, she padded into the kitchen in a borrowed robe and was greeted by the cat. "Good morning little one," she smiled and picked up the purring furball. She looked at the counter and range.

"Your pet, John, certainly has proper taste in morning beverages..." and she went about preparing the coffee press for service. While the kettle of water was left to heat up, she went back to the room and retrieved her cellphone. A glance at the time and after a moment of figuring time zones, she dialed her boss to leave a message for him to call her back when he got into the office.

With a cup of hot coffee in hand she went back to the den, curled her legs under her and began reading through John's notes for the book. Mocha followed her every step, hoping for a new napping lap.

"Kitten, it appears the story he told me over the last couple days wasn't *too* far from *exactly* what's written here... good memory!" She picked up another notebook and began perusing its pages as well. "*This* material didn't make it into his story however..." She gazed at the charts, symbols, marginal notations and descriptions as she flipped through the pages.

She looked up when John ambled from his room. "You look like crap, Mr. Doe-Backhouse!" she snickered.

He looked at her and tried to smile as he headed to the kitchen.

She called, "Coffee's made. I didn't know if you had a favorite mug or anything; I just grabbed one and poured."

He took a first sip and answered, "Whichever one I'm holding at the time... and still has coffee in it... is my favorite." He looked at what she was holding in her hands.

Ginger was a little self-conscious at what appeared to be snooping through his things. She covered quickly, "I thought this was part of your story notes... my mistake. Sorry." She wasn't, but she was polite at least, she thought.

John did smile now. "Those are the results of a part of the story I *didn't* tell you," he said cryptically. "You wouldn't have believed me if I had; so what'd be the point of that?"

Ginger was pragmatic. "I am used to judging that sort of thing for myself," she answered calmly.

"But neither am I trying to pry." She changed subjects, "I left a message with my office; they should be calling back..." she looked at the gold watch on the end table, reached and opened it, "...in about half an hour or so." She became all professional, now that she was rested and herself again---that she was in fact sitting in his den, wearing one of his robes, after spending the last three days in his house without leaving for a moment didn't faze her in the least. "Now why don't you tell me how you were thinking of presenting this story of yours. What person, what tone, what voice?"

She knew if she stuck to business her mind wouldn't wander, but it did.

'John's actually pretty good-looking,' she thought, 'Tall, broad shoulders, slightly receding hairline but distinguished looking. Nice hands, strong looking with powerful forearms, and his face was shaven, a couple days ago at least. I wonder if he's ever been married? Is he in a relationship? Forty and single... Is he gay?' She snapped out of the wayward thoughts which she'd tried to avoid; he was speaking...

"...so I figured I'd write it out as it was told to me. Just like a campfire story or something." He sat down and appeared to be waiting for her to respond.

Ginger picked up the watch again. "Well, unless I have been dreaming the last few days... it *is* an epic sort of tale. That *would* seem to be a good approach to take..." she read the inscription aloud. "Time is the uniquely subjective phenomenon. What exactly does *that* mean?"

John stared at a spot over and past her head. She waited for some response to her last distraction. He answered, "Generally you can take it to mean that time is experienced by each person differently. But the meaning that was *intended* by the fellow who inscribed it, I think, was a bit more esoteric than that."

She felt a sudden pang of comprehension and lifted the notebook with the diagrams and charts. "Does it have to do with these other notes of yours?"

He nodded, "Yeah I'm pretty sure it does. But I'm not personally to the place where I can make much more of it than that: Time isn't what we've always supposed it to be..." he shrugged in surrender. Her phone rang and she hopped up and ran back to the guest room where she'd left it.

John ambled back to the kitchen and glanced at the calendar on the refrigerator. "It's Thanksgiving today!" he announced to Mocha who was just taking over the warm place on the sofa so recently made available. He went to the cupboard and looked it up and down, then he opened the fridge and did the same.

Ginger sauntered back into the room and announced, "I'm cleared for the foreseeable future from work..." She had also taken the time to redress. "Look, I don't want to wear out my welcome, but I am *dying* to see if those registration papers arrive... and... I would very much like to travel to Port Isabel and see it for myself!"

There, she had said it. She had argued the point with herself:

that she was a stranger to this guy, that she was just his publishing agent, that all these stories may not be true. But if they were! 'I could never forgive myself for not finding out...' she told herself. 'Besides, I *would* like to know a little more about John...'

John simply smiled and said he'd love the company. "I just realized that today is Thanksgiving! And since *you may* very well be the closest thing to family I have anywhere, except the improbable existence of some extremely long lived relations..."

He stopped abruptly and queried, "Last night, and just now, almost the last thing you said... Did you really say: ...could *we* find out about the yacht?" He put special emphasis on the 'we.'

Ginger felt a little exposed. 'Did I say that? Must've been *caught up* in the moment...'

She answered quickly without looking at him, "Uh huh." Then followed with a rapid patter as she grabbed for her scarf and hat, "I'll just pop into town and deal the motel I *didn't* use. Yay expense accounts!" she turned back and grinned self-consciously.

'Good, he hasn't kicked me out yet. And it appears he doesn't have a significant other; her... or his... name would have come up in connection with a holiday plan...' Her mind raced and before she knew it her thoughts escaped into words... "John are you gay?"

Her thoughts screamed, 'Oh god, I can't believe I just blurted that out!'

John's blank expression said a lot; he answered, "No Virginia, I am not gay. Neither do I have a girlfriend, nor have I ever been married---came close once. So, now that we're acknowledging the elephant in the room... Miss Amourson-Spelman? Is there some lucky fellow... or *lady*... out there waiting for *your* return?"

Ginger blushed, "Call me Ginger. And No! So far no one has been able to stand being around me long enough to appreciate my *finer qualities*!"

'Essentially true...' she thought, 'unless I count the boyfriend I had in college---he stuck around for all of two months.'

John was already speaking again. "...anyway, I have all the fixins for a turkey dinner. It would be my pleasure if you joined me for this holiday meal. *We* can wait for the *alleged* registration papers to arrive. If these folks are as punctual in *this* matter as they have been with the other items, I'm *sure* we won't have to wait long."

Ginger smiled and excused herself and ducked into the bathroom. She came out with her coat, scarf and hat on, "I'll be back before long." John watched her step jauntily to her car and roar out of the driveway.

Ginger was surprised at herself. 'The reason no one has stuck around very long Ginger-baby is because you're too unpredictable... that's what they've said before. And *now* look at you: You're practically inviting yourself into this guy's house and life... Girl, why are you doing this!?' Her feelings were confused but she knew one thing, and answered herself: 'If there is a chance of finding any of my family---John is the key.' That's what she told herself and ignored the rising 'other' emotions just below the surface.

After checking out of the motel, and while she was in town---since the gas station was the only place open on account of the holiday---she filled up the car and bought the only day's papers that were available. When she got back to John's house and pulled into the driveway, instead of blocking the turnaround, she backed in next to the red Land Cruiser.

'This must be his truck...' she thought, 'I wonder if he's the outdoor, rugged camping type? He should have a gun locker and rod racks somewhere in the house...' She hauled her traveling bag onto the porch as John opened the door and lifted it from her hands easily.

"I'll take it to your room... If that's alright?" he announced uncertainly.

Ginger nodded---that was the best she could do. The smells from the kitchen were absolutely heavenly and she was already heading to the pots and dishes for nibbles. He came up behind her while she was 'testing' the turkey, "I don't have 'old family recipes'---for obvious reasons---but I have my own dishes that I have made since I was twenty..."

She blurted out candidly, "I can't cook!"

Odd, she realized she was actually slightly embarrassed all of a sudden; though it had never bothered her before.

"I never learned how to do any more than make coffee and spoon out ice cream... Oh and I can make popcorn in the microwave, or follow directions for frozen pizza. That's it!" She made her best 'Aren't I cute anyway' face.

John grinned and moved close to her; she tensed, thinking he might brush against her or whisper something... He just needed to stir the gravy. She exhaled and chided herself for acting like an adolescent. 'Pull yourself together Ginger-girl! Just because a man asks you to a home-cooked holiday dinner doesn't count as foreplay!'

He was speaking again, "...You seem kinda distracted Ginger. Is there something on your mind? Not that you need to 'bare your soul' to *me* or anything... I just hope you're comfortable is all."

"Oh I'm fine, really," she hedged, "The kitchen smells bring back memories of holidays long past is all. I'm comfortable... I *am* comfortable." She added, almost surprised herself at the truth of it. 'I really *am. Hmmm*,' she thought.

Aloud she added, "Do you have any music in the house?"

"If you open that cabinet over there under the bookcase..." John said pointing with his elbow, "...you'll find all that I still have of cassettes and records. My CDs are in the opposite cabinet."

She was going to find out more about him now. 'You can tell a lot from a person's taste in music...' She looked in the first cabinet:

some classical, some musicals, a few bands from the seventies, a lot of solo artists... same for the cassettes. She went to the newer stuff in the other cabinet. 'Here we *go*...' she thought, 'a bit of new age, vocalists from the forties and early fifties, holiday music compilations, soundtracks, Dylan, the Dead, Brightman, Taylor, Brown, Nelson, Clapton, Enya, Beatles, Stones... Alright John is a good guy...'

Aloud she said, "How about some Christmas tunes?" and she selected the compilation of original recording artists singing the old standards. She set it to playing and adjusted the volume just loud enough to hear---quiet enough for conversation.

"Just in time," John said, "Your dinner awaits," and he held out a chair for her. "Would you like some wine? I have a few choices in whites. Turkey: white meat---white wine---That's the extent of my oenophilic knowledge. Except the word: *oenophile*..."

She heard herself giggle. 'Giggling! Ginger?!'

"Anything white will be grand. I like the sweeter ones..."

He toasted their good fortune at finding their families' identities, and she toasted their 'new partnership,' "...in the book I mean..." she added hastily.

'Geez Ginger-girl! Why don't you just seduce him and get it over with!'

"Mmm. This is great!" she mumbled as she carved bites from the wonderful assortment on her plate. She got to what looked like cornbread dressing and put a large forkful in her mouth. Alarm bells rang, steam shot from her nose and ears. She grabbed for the water glass. Waving a hand over her seared and lolling tongue, she said, "Holy...!"

He chuckled, "In Texas, cayenne isn't a condiment it's an ingredient..."

She contented herself with everything else on her plate and

smiled happily as she dished out a dollop more of potatoes and gravy. "This is all so good!"

"Thank you, ma'am. To top this I will be juggling apples later..." she giggled again.

'Ginger! What is up with you?!' Then she noticed *how* he was eating. Every bite was chewed appreciatively and he made a visible point of taking regular breaths. 'This guy just gets more intriguing...' she mused.

After she helped to clean dishes, they were again settled in the den at a nice fire. The wine was loosening her curiosity and she asked, "Tell me John Robert Backhouse, what will you do when *we* find that the yacht in Port Isabel *is* the *Bodhi*? Are you just going to sail off and write more stories?"

John looked back at her with his piercing pale green eyes, "That depends..."

She sat up a little, "Depends? Depends on what?"

"I *have* sailed before... a little twelve foot Sunfish, but I don't think I have the know-how to just cast off and handle a sixty-foot yacht. Then there are the questions of: Where to go? What else will I write? ...Just to name a *few* things *that* would 'depend' on," and he held her gaze.

"Don't look at *me*: I can drive a car well—and fast, but I've never even set foot on a boat before. Unless you count the ferries in Puget Sound, or the Staten Island ferry..."

He chuckled, "I don't suppose you'd be interested in learning?"

'Alone? In a sailboat with you? For who knows how long?!'

She sat up, "John! Are you making a proposition?"

He demurred, "I can't help thinking that if I am to ever find more answers about my family..."

She interrupted, "And *my* family..."

He continued, "...*And your* family, then I just can't get around

22

the thought that it will probably be at sea... and *on that boat*."

Ginger had known this man for all of three days now. She had *no* idea if he was a wolf in lamb's clothing, if he was nuttier than a fruitcake, or if this was all an elaborate and *amazing* ruse. 'But he couldn't have known *anything* of *my* history before I stepped up on his porch... hell, I have never told a soul. And this story *does* explain all these little tokens: the pebble necklace, the watch, medal, Birth Certificate... not to mention how we *both* had the childhoods we had...'

Taking a deep breath as if ready to accept her fate, Ginger answered, "If that's the *Bodhi, and* if there are lessons we can take: I'll learn." 'What am I saying...' "And what's more, Mr. Backhouse, as long as we're diving down the rabbit hole together, I have a question for *you*!"

He seemed to be uncertain his expression said he didn't know whether he should smile or run.

'Uh oh, I've seen *that* expression before... usually followed by the phrase: I'll call you sometime, or words to that effect. Oh well... here goes:'

"John, I'm terrible at this," she hedged, then plunged in head first, "But do you *really* think you will still want me around after I've asked too many questions, after I've ignored your kindness and generosity for the umpteenth time, after I've yelled at you, kept you awake with my snoring, not cleaned the dishes, come home late without calling---again, taken you for granted and generally treated you like dirt?" She gasped for breath. All that had come tumbling out before she lost her nerve.

'There's that expression again. Damn! why couldn't I just let a good thing alone? Where did that not come home late come from?! Why must I get everything in writing? *What is my problem*?! No wonder no one ever sticks around...' Then he was speaking.

"Ginger, you don't know me anymore than I know you..."

'Oh God here it comes...'

"But what I *do* know is this: *if* this story is as real as it *appears* to be, and *I am* who it seems I am... just as you know who *you are*---then we are from a lineage of remarkable people and I would be forever ashamed of myself and thoroughly regret letting the opportunity to get to know you slip on by, if once you were this close..."

She checked her wince, 'Wait; did I just hear what I thought I heard?!'

"Would you repeat that?" she ventured. He took a deep breath and looked at the ceiling.

'Oh Crap! I've done it again... and I was *so close* this time!'

"Miss Spelman-Amourson, I don't know what 'too many questions' even means---I have a bunch myself. I am used to being ignored---one of the charms of growing up an orphan. If you yell at me, it may be because I exasperated you---something I'd like to not do. I probably snore loud enough to drown your own snores out. I already have a habit of cleaning dishes myself---I don't give it much thought. If you come home late and haven't called---I'll wonder I'm sure, and worry no doubt---but *that* is the kind of suffering I'll take over loneliness *any day*. As for taking me for granted and treating me like dirt---I don't believe it for a second---I *do have* a *few* pleasant qualities which may keep your interest *and* engender kindness from you."

It was Ginger's turn to stare. "Uh... No one's ever said that to me before... In fact, I..." She was instantly lost. This was an unknown frontier. "...What was the question?"

That brought a loud laugh from him, "*Actually* I merely asked if you would be willing to learn to sail! I'm not sure where the questions about snoring, or coming home late came from..."

She blushed to her toes.

He added seriously, "But your instincts are right." He took

another deep breath, "I am *very* attracted to you... In fact I've been trying everything I can think of to get you to stick around longer... to... to stay here as long as you can... with me." He looked for all the world like he would break into a million pieces if she made the slightest move. She was very careful *not* to let that happen.

"Uh, honestly... John... I'm *very* attracted to you too."

'There that wasn't so hard was it? Go on Ginger-girl: Truth.'

"I don't know if it's 'proper' or not to skip the months of 'getting to know you,' but I'm willing to risk it." '

Whew! I'm pretty good at this...'

"I've warned you as best I can---I am *not* easy to get along with..."

He crossed to sit next to her on the sofa and said softly in imitation of her own words, "I am used to judging that sort of thing for myself. I hope you don't mind if *don't* just take *your* word for it..."

She whispered back, "*You* are *so* doomed!" She put her hand to his neck and pulled his face to hers then kissed him.

When he regained his breath, he said "GingerKat, I think *we* are going to *have* to learn to sail!"

The next day was Friday. They woke up in the same room, went down stairs and had coffee, got ready to go out and they went into town. He added her to his own bank account---over her protests.

"You don't have to do this... I am financially *very* sound on my own. I have a little flat in New York... in Chelsea---which I rarely occupy---I have been on expense accounts for the last... *forever*, so my paychecks just go into the bank and pile up. *Really* John, this is *sweet* of you but *so* unnecessary."

John was just smiling all the while. "GingerKat, you noticed the amounts on those few accounts you just signed onto?" She nodded. "When I left the corporate world, I wasn't a Rockerfeller or anything, but I had plenty to get the land and build that house..."

She interrupted, *"You* built that house!?"

"Almost entirely with my own hands, yes. Anyway, I don't have many expenses so those balances don't vary much. *But that wasn't the point of adding you onto them!* I *introduced* you as my *wife* to the Account Manager when we were at the bank."

She smiled in spite of herself, "Yeah, I didn't really think I'd *ever* hear someone saying *I* was their *wife*. It was a *really* nice thing to hear, even though..." It was his turn to interrupt.

"...Honey, this is Texas. That wasn't just a *nice thing to hear*... that was a legal act of marriage in this state. I wasn't being poetic or romantic; I am now your common law husband!"

Her mind raced. 'Wow, and I thought I was impulsive! Ginger-girl you've got a tiger by the tail... Hold On Tight!'

Aloud she said, "Oh."

The weekend was a honeymoon of sorts. She asked question after question, as she had warned him she would, about his whole life and then more and more about the notebook of diagrams and dialogs. "Just give me an idea of what it's about, okay?" she finally pleaded.

He picked up the notebook, flipped randomly to a page and read aloud, "Ah, but therein lies the difficulty... we are subject to a wide world of influences which have nothing whatsoever to do with reason. We are influenced by the form of the things around us, whether shocking or beautiful; we label them and forget them. We are unsettled when they are absent and conversely oblivious when they are present. We are suggestible, hence our closely held notions derived from old wives' tales and urban legends---hearsay for the most part. We are moved by relationship: our friends think thus and such, we think thus and such. Those 'others' *must* think a different way, so we avoid thinking like that---however actually similar to our own thoughts and logical their views may be. We succumb to the superiority of others---No wonder advertising employs so-called authorities and celebrities; it works.

And all of this, while inside of us the turbid roiling kaleidoscope of 'I's persist in their conflicted desires unabated. Our background attitudes and moods lead us to become either inured to, or strangely susceptible to, whatever is coming in through our senses irrespective of our actual needs. And our own inept and uncontrolled gestures and postures, in their turn, elicit a response from the world we encounter---diametric to our own wishes and desires.

These problems and dilemmas arise when a man has not awakened Conscience. So there is no impartation of reason from its objective seat of influence to the Intellectual center and he becomes influenced instead by half-truths, misinformation, hearsay and the rest. This erroneous data so conditions him that he maintains a truly false intellectual model of the world and reality. And just as before, the Emotional center inevitably creates belief structures to support these inaccurate, false and even deleterious constructs. That is the relationship between those centers, whether for good or ill. That is how wrong-thinking, inappropriate attitudes---a false personality---is formed.

Unfortunately it doesn't stop there. These false structures of intellectual models and emotional underpinnings will even condition a man's sensations and movements. This is readily seen when someone has been told repeatedly that, for example: 'snakes are slimy.' Functioning from an emotional belief structure and intellectual construct devoid of any reality, even if that man were to touch an actual snake, he will believe it is slimy although it is certainly not..."

He stopped and looked up her. She was looking out the window and turned to face him when she realized he had stopped.

He ventured, "There are over a hundred pages like that..." Ginger had followed the the words and even created a mental picture of what was being described. She recalled a snippet from a text she had edited not so long ago, and tried to recite it...

"Thought runs you. Thought, however, gives false info that you are running it, that you are the one who controls thought. Whereas actually thought is the one which controls each one of us. Thought is creating divisions out of itself and then saying that they are there naturally. This is another major feature of thought: Thought doesn't know it is doing something and then it struggles against what it is doing. It doesn't want to know that it is doing it. And thought struggles against the results, trying to avoid those unpleasant results while keeping on with that way of thinking. That is what I call 'sustained incoherence'."

John lightened, "That's a good external observation of the internal process I took notes upon... Did you just come up with that?"

She was *very* flattered, and really would like to have been the one to have said it first. She chuckled and admitted, "That was part of a transcription I edited for publication a couple years ago for David Bohm---the mathematician? It seemed you two were speaking of the same phenomenon is all." They sat quietly until she raised another question.

"I don't know how to ask this, so I'll probably ramble a little trying to frame it... Both of these descriptions point to an *actual* dysfunction of the human mind, a *pervasive* dysfunction. I've noticed my own internal dialog will distract me to no end at times; it colors my perceptions of what is actually happening around me... or so I find out later anyway. Is there a 'cure' for this problem?"

John handed the notebook to her and said simply, "I think so. It has proven itself as far as I am concerned... but it's work. I mean frustrating, unrewarding, tedious, humbling *work*. I am only a few steps along this journey and while I've received a boost of sorts, I can see that plainly this is a journey for a lifetime. The good part is that it's practicable---not theoretical or philosophical---but real nuts and bolts, turn of the screw: *work*. I don't know how to answer you any better. Like I said, I'm just a little way along. Does that help at all?"

She took in what he'd said and followed the explanation as far as it went. "You certainly need to work on your sales pitch... No one in their right mind would want to do what you've just described... unless..." And she suddenly had a flash of insight: "But that's the point isn't it! You're talking about losing, or changing what is familiar---comfortable---habitual... *Of course* the process of change would be painful and seemingly futile. How could it be otherwise!" She was rather proud of herself for sorting that bit out for herself.

Then the implications were naked in her mind for that one instant: 'This *isn't* theoretical or philosophical... What *am I* going to do with this knowledge?'

Aloud she said, "John, may I read through this journal *and* ask questions when I'm stuck?"

His smile was comforting, "Darlin' is there any *other way* that you do things that I don't know about?" She chuckled; he *was* catching on faster than she'd thought.

The package they anticipated came in the Tuesday post. It actually *was* paperwork for a sixty foot trimaran yacht. They had a little celebration and talked about how to approach dealing with the facts they were faced with. Then later the same day, just as Alfred had *also* told him, he signed for the receipt of another package: a registered envelope from a British bank.

He woodenly handed the packet to Ginger. "Here GingerKat, you open it. I'm too nervous."

She slit the seal with a penknife and withdrew the contents. Her eyes went as big around as saucers. '

Oh holy crap! Now whose the one who may appear different than what they seem? Say goodbye to dreams of marital bliss

Ginger-girl... He can have anyone he wants now... If he couldn't before that is. Oh Jeez!'

"John, will this make me seem like a gold-digger... just because I haven't got your ring on my finger yet---I mean, just an introduction to a bank manager and a really great long weekend to show that *I am committed* already?"

Before taking the envelope from her, he took off the silver band he'd always worn on his little finger. "I got this from a guy in Santa Fe. He said it was made from silver and meteorite---so it was *very good* for clearing away bad thoughts..." she looked at him incredulously. "That's just what he said..." He put it on her left ring finger. "Now! Did it work? Does that clear away any fears of appearing to be something you're not?"

She grinned and held up her hand to catch the glint of light on her 'wedding band.' "I like it *very* much. All better!" Then she held the check for him to see. "...It's even made out to John Doe!" she said.

He stared at the handwritten amount on the draft; then read the memo at the bottom: 'One time payout of endowment due John Robert Backhouse, aka John Doe'

She said, "There's a note attached," and she read it aloud: "*Mr. Doe, The transfer of these funds has taken place as a result of the sworn affidavit from one George Henry Livingson, a one-time Trustee of this establishment, that you are in fact the son of the last known Backhouse male: Robert Henry Backhouse, deceased: Korea 1953. According to the terms of the Trust, you are required only to acknowledge this connection by legally appending the surname Backhouse to your existing given name. As the only surviving adult child of that lineage---and a single male---this remittance empties the Fund and ends our firm's responsibilities to that family's accounts. Fare thee well, Mr. Backhouse. ---Sincerely, Horace V. Johnson, Director*"

He whistled. "Well Mrs. Spelman-Backhouse, how does it feel to be a *multi*-millionaire?"

Incredibly relieved that he *still* thought of *her* as his mate, she looked from him to the check, to the yacht's paperwork. "I think Mr. Doe-Backhouse, *we* had better get down to Port Isabel and *learn to sail.*"

When they resumed the conversation they were having before *the delivery*, she explained that her apartment in New York City wasn't a real concern. "I've been gone on assignment after assignment and haven't been there for over fourteen months before. That's why I never got a pet, or a plant, or taken up cooking, or..."

John interrupted, "I get the picture! I'm not in the same position by a long stretch, and I could use some objectivity around what to take and what to leave."

She gazed at the appointments of the house and thought, 'Hmm, if I were going to decide what is vital and what isn't, I would...'

Aloud she replied, "If my experience over the last several years offers any guidance: No one needs everything they *think* they need. You saw my little travel bag and my shoulder bag?" He nodded. "I haven't been back to Chelsea for two and a half months now..." Then she saw Mocha lapping water from her bowl. "Mocha-baby goes with us! The rest... well, take your laptop, notes, any favorite books, a change of socks and underwear..." then she shrugged, "You asked!"

He seemed to have a stroke of clarity; his eyes glinted with insight. "Let's just do a little research shall we? It's not like we don't have *anything else* to go on here..." and he held up the journals of the Livingson's tale.

She saw where he was going with this: "Okay... Who of *our* family had to face similar circumstances, and what did they do, take, leave?"

He thought a moment. "They were sailors already, so while we need lessons..."

She interrupted, "Or on the job training! We can hire a Captain to take us... say through the Caribbean as we learn the ropes..." He groaned. "Sorry no pun intended, and voila! In a few months we drop the mentor and choose a destination. What do ya think about that?!"

His jaw dropped and he chuckled at the same time---an odd combination for sure. She could only say, "What? What did I say?!"

"Here," he said and handed her one of the journals already opened to a particular page. "Read this..."

She obliged, hesitant, but she read aloud: *"...Alright... alright. Mule In Rouge it is." Jamie added, "And you shall break the champagne bottle on her prow at the christening.* What do ya think about that?"

That one phrase, uttered by Samuel Allcock upon first meeting George all those years ago had become a part of the family's colloquial heritage, and it still elicited chuckles...when used appropriately, which it always was..."

She closed the journal and remarked, "Oh, I see what you mean! But I never knew my family any more than you did... It's just a coincidence... a common enough phrase."

Neither of them wished to pursue that wild goose. John just had to add: "Samuel Allcock is your great-great-great-grandfather... maternally through the Bessamers, I mean."

Her eloquent response to that was: "Oh!"

"Now as to packing, we *can* get some advice from a couple more of *your* ancestors." He reached for another of the journals and flipped through it until he found what he was looking for, then handed it to her.

She accepted it and asked first, "Which ancestors?"

"Lawrence and Miranda Spelman were your great-great-grandparents... Chloe is the maternal Bessamer connection I mentioned before..." he answered. She read aloud: *"...Chloe mentioned the solution they had arrived at in preparing for the exodus, and Miranda looked at her husband. He smiled, "Already handled my love. I packed your fans and a few scarves. I think you look better in the fans, but on the outside chance you might get chilled, I packed the scarves." She burst out laughing, but Harold and Chloe noticed the flush of embarrassment creeping up her neck at the same time.*

She responded in kind, "How thoughtful you are, a chest cold at my age could be devastating. I hope you packed the tie that matches your tattoo."

Harold and Chloe certainly chuckled with their hosts, but neither of them could for a moment be sure if they were joking to hide their being so unprepared, or making light of their already thorough preparedness. Chloe asked about it.

Miranda smiled, "Lawrence assures me that whatever we pack for this trip, other than a toothbrush and and a change of clothes, will be as useful as..." she giggled, "How did you put it, Lorenzo? It was so apt."

"Pork tenderloin at a Bar Mitzvah" he inserted between sips of wine. She chuckled again. "We face our every day here equally prepared: the few personal effects we rely upon routinely, which go without saying. Nothing more than that will significantly enhance our ability to meet each day. We shall have to assimilate ourselves into a new culture once more. We still have our trunks stored upstairs, in nearly their same packed state as when we arrived here all those years ago."

Lawrence grinned, "We could take them! As sort of good luck charms?"

Miranda batted her eyes at him, "You can carry them, dearest..."

He frowned, "It was just a thought, no reason to get all bossy."

She concluded, "I have a very useful pocket knife, warm clothes for until we reach the Tropic of Cancer, our medicines chest, recipes---the ones we don't know by heart---our purse, and Lorenzo. I promise you, no woman has ever been more well equipped!" Lawrence smiled, "...Two fans and several silk scarves..." She added, "Oh, yes, those defensive items, and further protection against the cold. Thank you dearest."

Harold's eyes showed his obvious merriment and chagrin. "It sounds so simple when you put it like that."

Lawrence decanted the last of the bottle into each of their glasses. "Even before I met George, White Feathers and Belle, I had traveled to the oddest out of the way nooks and crannies of this world---perhaps a few more than yourself---and I seldom packed more than a messenger bag. Why? Because the fewer 'things' I have about me the more flexible and versatile I can be---both physically and emotionally." He smiled warmly at his wife and added, "That goes for uprooting ourselves and being transplanted again as well." He turned back to their guests, "Miranda wasn't kidding, the items of luggage we carried here on that first occasion are still packed with the same 'things' with which we arrived here." He mused for a moment, "Of course traveling with Kaitlyn to Tahoe was a different story, as was traveling with George and Belle, we had so many presents for our friends and family on that trip..."

"Whew!" Ginger announced. "Buddy, we've got some colorful family!"

"So, your first bit of advice seems to be the best. Which car would you like to leave in Port Isabel?"

She thought about the question. 'I love my little Camaro...maybe it will be safer here under the car port, rather than who knows where we'll be able to store it in Port Isabel. Ooh, but maybe he feels the same way about his truck... Nah!'

What she said was, "What ever you think is best," and she crossed her fingers behind her back.

He answered promptly, "Even though we're not taking much, Mocha is used to the truck---if she's used to anything that moves faster than a walk---Besides your pretty teal sportscar will probably be safer here than there. The Cruiser certainly doesn't care where she sits."

She tried not to betray her elation, "Whatever." Then she had only to say, "Shall I get out a map and find Port Isabel? What was the address of the dry dock?"

"Uh..." he fumbled through the paperwork and found what appeared to be the only thing that resembled an address. "It says

'East Harrison St. & West South Shore Dr.' Do you suppose that's an address?"

"Hopefully there are only four corners to choose from..." she answered pragmatically. "Do you think it's warmer down there by a lot or a little?"

He scratched his head, "Up here there's nothing blocking the north wind off the plains but barbed wire... On the Gulf, especially far South Texas, it probably doesn't get any colder than maybe fifty or so... I've only been to Padre in the spring---a few college trips. I don't know, but I bet it doesn't even freeze during January."

She looked around the house once more. 'Now's the time to find out about his outdoorsey skills... first aid, light, tools, weapons?' "John Robert? Besides playing in the sand in College, do you have any survival skills for the great outdoors? Great hunting stories? Maybe you're secretly a fur-trapper? Any SAS training? That sort of thing?"

"I once whittled a spoon from a tree branch. Uh... Oh, and I spent three months in the Pecos Wilderness... alone, with nothing but a tent, one pan, a knife and a 9mm---can't be too careful. *That* sort of thing, you mean?" he answered.

"Yes Jungle Jim. *That* sort of thing!" she quipped.

He threw it back to her, "How about you? Anything more dangerous than crossing Broadway against traffic?"

It was his sudden grin that most irked her. "As a matter of fact, crossing against traffic *isn't* safe. But to respond to the gist of you're query..." she realized her tone was a little snooty, but he had this coming... "My adoptive father, Harvey, was an avid hunter. I learned to hit anything I aimed at and clean it afterwards. I was more at home fishing hip-deep in a stream than with my mother in the kitchen---which explains my aversion to cooking I suppose. I once had to spend the night in a tree because wolves can't climb easily. And last but in no way least: the entire summer before I got the news I was adopted, I spent as a journalist following an Outward Bound group through Colorado. It was a good story and won me a grant for my efforts. *That* sort of thing!"

John knew he must have pushed some buttons because he asked, "Did I do something to tick you off? I didn't mean to..."

She softened, "It was your smug grin that set me off. And that crack about crossing traffic didn't help your case any."

He winced, "Mea Culpa! I'm sorry. I am trying to go against my less pleasant impulses. Like I said, it's a long road ahead. Thank you for being as gentle as you were about it."

She was taken aback. 'So: honesty, patience, calmness, did I say honesty? I may have hit the jackpot at last! Yay Ginger-girl!'

Aloud she said, "I'm sorry too. And you *did* deserve it... Now..." she looked at Mocha napping on the sofa, and whispered, "Does she need to be in a C-A-G-E, or something for the trip?"

He looked like he was struggling with something in his brains--- his face got all wookedy. He composed himself and said, "Ginger, she's smart but she can't understand English. I'm *certain* you don't have to spell words to get under her radar... Yes, I have a pet carrier just to get her into the truck. On long trips, if she goes too, I let her wander around inside the Cruiser."

Ginger eyed the now wide awake cat and announced, "She looks smarter than you give her credit for."

"Maybe there's some projection going on in that assessment; but okay, she's probably smarter than the average feline. I still am not likely to start spelling secrets she shouldn't hear."

It was a ten hour trip to South Padre and Port Isabel. Ginger made good use of the time by reading aloud from the journals. "Jeez, John can you write without commafying every little thing!"

He was satisfactorily chastened, "I can't edit my own stuff easily it seems---I hope it's just a phase. You know 'Early-Writer's-

Syndrome' or something."

It was dark before they arrived. Ginger had called ahead from the road and found them lodging for the night. "Oh boy! Just like a *real* honeymoon! Jonibob, I'm so tickled about this adventure!" And it showed. Ginger was the picture of a happy bride as she let him hoist her over the threshold of the hotel room. He set her on the end of the bed and fell down next to her.

He moaned, "My butt is so tired of sitting! What do you think of a walk and maybe a late evening snack? Does that sound good?"

Ginger was up like a shot, "Sounds great to me buana; just let me change for the warmer air." She unzipped her bag, and pulled out a lighter top and cargo shorts. "Now you get what you need, and I'll be out of the bathroom in no time..."

About fifteen minutes later, she emerged and looked around the room. He wasn't there. "John?" she called suddenly very panicked.

'Crap! Ginger, don't panic... he's here somewhere... check to see if the car's still there...' She went to the door just as it opened and he came back in carrying a cloaked box.

"Just had to sneak our C-A-T up here..." She burst out laughing at his using the whole 'spelling thing'---obviously a little confused about its application.

"Good girl," she said to the unsettled animal within, and she opened the cage door. "Mama's going to bring you back some tasty tidbits. You just make yourself at home and don't soil the carpet, the bed, the chairs..." She realized of a sudden what she'd just done. "Uh, John maybe we should keep her in the C-A-G-E for the time being?"

He smiled, "Good plan."

There was a knock on their door at seven-forty-five the next morning. A voice from outside called, "Mr. and Mrs. Backhouse? I was asked to deliver this..." and an envelope slipped under the door.

Ginger was up and crossed to the door. "Looks like we've been spotted in town! Ah the paparazzi can find us wherever we are!"

John rolled over, opened an eye and muttered groggily, "What's it say?"

She slit it open and read, "Greetings and welcome to Port Isabel. I saw a red Land Cruiser pass the docks last night, and Randy, the front desk guy at this hotel is a friend of mine. I'm Jimmy, the guy with the key to the locked door on your dry-docked yacht's building. Can we meet for brunch downstairs at say ten?"

"That's it." She put the note on the pillow next to his head and went back to the journals she'd been reading since getting up an hour before. "In spite of your horrid punctuation, your writing voice is pleasant..."

He tried to smile, "Need coffee..." he muttered and went to the bathroom.

"Let me finish this one notebook and get the next one, then we can go get my man some java... Okey-dokey?" There was a moan that sounded like agreement from behind the door. She heard the shower come on and decided she would like to rinse off as well; she went to the bathroom door. "Ready or not..."

John got his second cup of coffee just as 'Jimmy's' smiling face greeted them when he entered the cafe. He was youngish, maybe in his mid-twenties, sandy blond wavy hair, steel blue eyes and the frame of a champion swimmer or surfer. He crossed toward their table, said something to the waitress who grinned at him as he passed, and pulled up a chair at their booth. "Good morning again. Sorry to have wakened you, if I did..."

Ginger had a liking for his straightforward manner and charming smile. "No trouble. I was just reading and honeybunch here was nearly awake already."

John winked at her and added, "So Jimmy... Jimmy what?"

The young fellow stood, "Pardone moi, I am James Erikson---keeper of the keys. And you are," he extended his open palm to John, "Mr. John Robert Backhouse, formerly known as John Doe. And this charming lady is Mrs. Ginger Backhouse, formerly known as Virginia Amourson... Does that conclude our introductions?" he added with a smile.

Hackles of suspicion leapt up the napes of their necks.

Calmly as possible, John interjected, "News certainly travels fast," he looked at Ginger, "We've been married for less than a week and the tabloids have already run the story!"

Jimmy's expression changed and he asked, "How's that again?"

Ginger replied in a professional, almost elitist tone, "It's a running joke... But seriously, how *do* you know about our marriage? We had the considerable attendance of *one cat* at the elaborate ceremony."

That friendly grin spread across the young man's face once more. "Would you believe? I just found out from Randy this morning; he checked y'all in. By the way I guessed that Ginger was short for Virginia. Randy overheard you first refer to yourself as 'Amourson.' So no mystery. Oh, that and Alfred called the other day to say that John Doe would probably be here before too long..."

A bit of relief allowed knowing smiles to cross their faces. John asked, "So are you related to Alfred Livingson?"

Jimmy held up his hands as if fending off an attack of patty cake, "Me? I've worked for him a time or two, but he's no blood of mine," and he quickly changed the subject, "Now, when would you two like to inspect the yacht? Which begs the question: What are you going to do with it?"

That question hung in the air as the waitress arrived with their brunch. Once the dishes were arranged and eating commenced, Ginger at last replied, "We thought we'd hire a captain for the boat and learn 'how to sail while sailing' from him or her."

Jimmy swallowed his bite of eggs benedict, "That is an *excellent* way to learn to sail! And there are a number of skippers available for hire down here. Not all of them are actually teachers as well, but you'll know best I'm sure."

Ginger was beside herself. She'd been dying to know about the yacht itself and had tried to be patient. She burst out, "It's really the *Bodhi?* The yacht in storage---it's a sixty-foot metal-hulled trimaran?" Jimmy looked at her with new respect and merely nodded.

He turned to John, "Mister, unless the registration paperwork listed the name... maybe... somewhere. It usually does not---just a registration number---but it *is* the trimaran first christened as the *Bodhi*. I don't suppose you would like to let me in on the secret?"

"Uh..." John began.

Ginger covered, "Well, I was hoping for the *Tygress*, but it is John's inheritance not mine..." That got an even stranger look from Jimmy.

He stared hard at Ginger and asked, "And how could you *possibly* know about the *Tygress?!* And would you elaborate on how that might be *your* inheritance?!"

John and Ginger weren't sure how to respond. 'When all else fails, tell the truth...' Ginger thought fast, "You were close with guessing my name: it is Virginia Kaitlyn Belle Backhouse, nee Spelman-Amourson. The *Tygress* belonged to my grandparents Samuel and Ronia Spelman. The *Bodhi* belonged to John's grandparents' William and Eleanor Backhouse. John's mother's sister, Vera, and my mother, Anna Spelman, were best friends and we're sure they'd have been ecstatic that their children found each other and married. Does that answer your question?"

Jimmy was visibly still sorting out that last bit of family connections on his fingers when she finished, "Fine, sure..." He resolved.

They finished brunch and followed Jimmy to the dry-dock

boathouse. As they rolled up to it and got out of their cars. Ginger said, "This isn't the address on the paperwork!"

Jimmy asked what was *that* address; she told him. He chuckled, "That's where *I* stay when I'm here. I don't actually have room for a yacht in my house..." And he unlocked the three or four padlocks on the large hanger-like doors. As he pushed them open he said, "Here you are, I have a contract with a crane service whenever you are ready to have her back in the water again."

He went to a wall and flipped a few breakers. Lights sprang on overhead and it was as light as day inside. John and Ginger were awestruck. The dichotomy between what you imagine a thing to be like and what it actually is---they were struck by that disparity upon seeing the colossal yacht. Jimmy was walking to the stern and kept up a running description of the modifications he'd made per Alfred's instructions, almost as a tour guide might point out landmarks.

"...Your nav and radar stations are state of the art. The helm is now outfitted with a LORAN, civilian satellite GPS gear and depth finder, in addition to a new compass binnacle with digital as well as the traditional liquid and gimbal. The galley has been refitted with what Alfred assured me were appliances suited to your cooking style... whatever that means. Anyway, there are new sails and back-ups, new mattresses in all the cabins, new freshwater tanks, new heads, new entertainment center in the lower salon, air conditioning, a new freezer with ice maker, new wind generators---yes, I kept the old ones as requested---new sails for the launches and catamaran, new outboards for them as well---the launches, not the cat. And last but not least..." He pulled away a tarp uncovering the steps of the boarding platform and the yacht's name, "She's been rechristened--- Mr. and Mrs. Backhouse welcome aboard the *Anna Virginia.*"

Ginger was so suddenly overwhelmed she nearly swooned. Through her tears, she tried to tell John something but it was incoherent. He helped her to a seat on the boarding platform until she could compose herself a little more. Sniffling all the while she got out: "I have never... been so... honored in my... life... to have this yacht... your... our yacht... named for me... my mother... and me..." and she broke down into tears once more.

For his part John seemed equally surprised, "Jimmy? Was this Alfred's idea as well?" Jimmy could only nod. Ginger's extreme emotions surprised him as well. He was just relieved that she was dripping tears of joy and not revulsion. John mused aloud, "Ginger, I'm getting the impression we're the subjects of a modern-day arranged marriage..." he was quick to add, "...And I couldn't be more pleased with our arrangers' choices for us!"

It was her turn to just nod.

"Okay, I'm better now," she announced unconvincingly, "Lets go aboard and look her over."

Jimmy again repeated the improvements as they came to them. They asked about this or that piece of equipment or appliance and he answered with the calm assurance and knowledge of a shipwright. He went to a panel over the navigation station and flipped a few switches; interior lights came on. "Down either side of the bridge are companionways to the amas and the lower salon."

They were led up and down, around and back up again. They were instructed about the rigging, the decks, the mast, the bridge salon... everything.

When they were once again on the ground, Ginger asked, "John, or I guess I should ask Jimmy, where do we go to solicit for a skipper and how will we know if he or she will be a good teacher?"

Jimmy's eyebrows shot up, "Well that's the sixty-four thousand dollar question isn't it? Hmm. Uh, I didn't want to mention this, because it's really y'all's decision, and I don't want to seem pushy," he added, "or protective," and again added, "or anything..."

Ginger interrupted, "Spit it out James!"

"Yes ma'am. I'm a Captain," he admitted.

"There now that wasn't so hard was it?" Ginger comforted. "We can see why you might not have wanted to spring that on us *earlier...*" Her tone turned more sarcastic, "...better to let us *worry* over it for *ourselves* until we begin pulling our hair out..." She gave him a questioning look. He kicked his sandal toe on the floor.

"You just never know, ma'am... you just never know. I didn't want to seem too eager, or pushy, or anything..." He perked up, "Oh, I almost forgot!" and he herded them back up to the nav station and opened the drawer. "Alfred left this for y'all."

Ginger seemed to be the official letter opener of the two of them and so she slit open the sealed envelope, took out the note and handed it to John.

He read: "*I hope all is to your tastes and satisfaction. If Ginger wishes anything different please don't hesitate to let James know about it. On the subject of James, he is a startlingly good captain should you require the services of one. I have entered a preliminary course into your navigation computer. I believe, unless you have some other pressing destination awaiting you, you will find this one most rewarding. Your servant, Alfred.*

P.S. The launches are now the Agate and the Black Pearl... The catamaran is still the Ariel!

Ginger gasped, "My grandfather's catamaran?! The Ariel?!" She choked up again, "Oh, John!"

John put an arm around her shoulders to steady her and announced to Jimmy. "We appear to be entrusted into your capable hands Captain Erikson. When would you suggest we weigh anchor?"

He smiled broadly, "Great! You won't regret it I promise!" He shook Ginger's hand and then John's. "I can have her in the water by this evening; the mast up in the morning and we'll keep at her rigging until she's seaworthy once more. You'll learn quite a bit about her as we dress her up." He pulled a phone out of his pocket and ordered the crane. "They'll be along in an hour or so. If you want to fetch your things from the hotel; you can take up residence as soon as her hull's wet!"

They did just that. John tipped Randy at the front desk who just stared blankly at him when he was thanked for his role in directing Jimmy to them. Once back at the dry dock, Ginger asked if there would be someplace they would be able to leave the Land Cruiser when they embarked.

Jimmy replied, "Sure, I leave my little jeep at the house when I'm not in the area; I can't see why she wouldn't like some respectable company..."

The crane arrived and in no time the *Anna Virginia* was afloat once more. John handed Ginger aboard then passed Mocha's carrier to her. Once he was aboard with the rest of their things, they made their way below to decide which stateroom to call home. Mocha was nosing around and darting from one cabin to the next as they carried things below. She dashed into the aft stateroom, curled up on the bed and settled down for a nap.

Ginger offered, "We can start in the aft one and move later if we wish..."

Jimmy bid them good evening, recommended a restaurant with a very good menu and said he'd be back in morning before the crane returned to mount the mast. John stood on the foredeck and just gazed around him. Ginger crept up behind him, "Penny for your thoughts?"

"Oh, I was just recalling all the dinners, discussions, showers in the rain and all the children that have played on this deck or one just like it on her sister ships..." He even sounded nostalgic, as if recalling his *own* memories. "And then it struck me---this isn't just any yacht. That story wasn't just another good story, and now *we* are really part of that very tale!"

She put her arms around his waist. "Jonibob, it may be that we'll create our own memories on these decks." She put her head on his shoulder and he lifted his hand to stroke her hair. She continued, "What I *do* know is that I'm almost through your journals and whatever memories we create for ourselves, I think it would splendid to dedicate little niches through the ship to our own ancestors... Our parents we didn't know, our grandparents who grieved us *and* them, our great-grandparents who carved a place for us in this world... but most of all: I want to learn about our families' legacy of traditions and work. Teach me Johnny. You said you have begun. Help me to begin."

They went into the bridge and climbed below to the lower salon. John got out his charts and diagrams and taped them to the walls, describing their significance as he went. They were still talking and recreating more diagrams when Mocha came out of the aft cabin and yowled in hunger. "To be continued..." John announced and they got ready for a late dinner.

Jimmy did arrive well before the crane the next morning. He laid the ship's design plans out on the chart table and described what they were going to do today, *then* what they would need to prepare for once that chore was done. He turned out to be a patient and most thorough instructor. All his directions were clear and he always provided the reasoning and causes for having to proceed the way they were. The crane arrived. They mounted and tuned the mast, made the electrical connections, ran the rigging and hauled out the sails. With Jimmy's careful instructions they raised each one themselves and furled them.

"That's Day One!" Jimmy announced. "I left a list of food supplies in the galley... it doesn't spell out *what* you *have to* take so much as what *kinds* of foods you *should look for*. Everybody's tastes are different, but few people are aware of what the sea air does to some foods..." With that he bid them good evening and said he'd be back in the morning when they could take the *Anna* out into the great lagoon and begin sailing instructions.

Ginger went to the galley and retrieved the list. She and John looked it over. "I think we can restock tonight if you're not too tired." Ginger suggested.

"What? Do I look like I'm beat? I know I'm not in the shape I was ten years ago but I can go shopping!" he replied.

She winked, "You're the perfect shape for me..." and ran to fetch her purse.

He stood looking after her and his eyes settled on the catamaran. When she re-emerged she noticed he was staring at the boat. She walked solemnly over to it and placed a hand on the hull. With tears in her eyes she said, "Oh John. Beside this necklace, this is as close as I've *ever been* to *my* family!" They walked slowly off the *Anna* and went shopping for supplies. When they returned, John fixed up Mocha's litter box and set out her food and water bowls. Ginger put away groceries and went below. She examined the 'entertainment center.'

"John, there's a tape in the video player!"

He crossed to her and looked at the unlabeled tape in her hands. "Well plug it in. Let's see what else Alfred has left for us..."

They settled into chairs and turned it on. The screen lit up, after the static cleared there was a face neither of them recognized. "Turn up the volume, I think she's speaking."

"...and so you're settled on the *Anna* at last! It should come as no surprise to either of you by now that we have been looking forward to this for a *long* time!" Another woman appeared on the screen, both women looked to be nearly identical. "After you've gotten your sea legs under you, we truly hope you'll follow the course Alfred put into your navigation computer. While you no doubt have many places you'll probably *want* to visit... We are *certain this* should be your first stop of choice. No demands, just wishful thinking on our part." The scene cut away to show a white sand beach rimmed with palms. The water was turquoise and the camera panned the lagoon, or bay... it was hard to tell which. "Hopefully your choice for interim Captain has already been made and whoever it is will have been near these coordinates before, if not actually on this island... We wish you good wind and our best hopes for your fulfilling your dreams." The camera bobbled and one of the women was back on the screen. "Oh yeah, Ginger, you should look in the forward cabin locker... We made sure you were properly outfitted for this adventure." The picture dimmed but a voice called out, "They were your mother's..."

Ginger leapt to the forward stateroom door and rushed into the cabin. John stepped to the door in time to see her pulling clothes out of the locker---dresses, pants, saris, swimwear, shirts, shawls and coats and tossing them onto the bed. She looked up at her husband with her eyes so full of tears she couldn't see him. "Mama's things..." she cooed softly and laid on the pile of clothes on the bed, then pulled a shirt over her face, sobbing.

The only question the next morning for Ginger was *which* of her mother's clothes she would choose for their maiden voyage. "Mama was exactly my size!" she announced as she came up for coffee. She wore pedal pushers and a large oxford-cloth shirt opened to the waist to reveal she also wore a Catalina two-piece swimsuit beneath.

John whistled and said, "You look like a million bucks!"

"You couldn't buy these from me for a hundred times that, Daddy Warbucks!" she answered, obviously pleased with her new acquisitions. "Okay I'm ready for lessons; where's our Skipper?"

As if calling him by his title invoked his presence, Jimmy called out from the dock, "Permission to take the helm Sir!"

John called back, "Permission granted Captain."

Jimmy swung his little duffle over the rail onto the deck and cast off the last mooring line. The last act before *actually* leaving the dock was something of a minor ceremony: "Ginger if you will please go to the nav station and bring back the leather pouch from the drawer..." She did and handed it to Jimmy. "John, Ginger, these are your colors---the *Anna* sails under the Swedish civil ensign, always has, always will. If you two would do the honors?" They smiled at each other and went to the mast, clipped the ensign to the pennant halyard and hoisted their colors. The breeze caught it and it unfurled---the first signal to the world that *Anna* was coming out of semi-retirement.

"Mr. Backhouse, if you will be so kind as to start up that outboard the way we talked about yesterday; we can get this fine old girl into more open waters."

"Aye, aye sir!" John answered.

Jimmy turned to Ginger, "Madam Backhouse if you would pour me a mug of that good-smelling coffee, I'll have enough energy to offer you some sailing tips today!"

Again he heard, "Aye, aye sir!" then the outboard erupted.

"Well done John. Now let's blow this burg!" He turned the wheel just enough to clear the piers and taxi the *Anna* through the canals out to the lagoon. "Mrs. Ginger, would you coil the mooring lines and begin unlashing the *Ariel*?"

She was ecstatic. "You betcha!"

The rest of the morning and all afternoon, Jimmy gave pointers for catching the wind, trimming sails, using the tiller for more than just simple steering and naturally all the points of sail. By that evening even Ginger was feeling a little more confident she wouldn't sink whatever boat she was on.

"If you can master the sails of a small vessel like this cat," Jimmy said, "Larger ships like the *Anna* are easy! You see, a smaller craft responds so quickly and is so light, you *have* to know what you're doing to keep her from the deeps. The *Anna* on the other hand practically sails herself by comparison... Does that make sense?" They nodded; after the day's practice they certainly understood what he meant about smaller vessels being more temperamental---They had provided a lot of laughs during the day for all the folks watching from the decks and houses around the lagoon.

John had supper ready by the time Ginger tied off the *Ariel* and climbed back aboard. "Enjoy!" he offered, "Our first meal aboard!" They ate well.

Ginger asked which cabin Jimmy would like to occupy. In lieu of a response, Jimmy pulled a hammock from his duffle and with the fluid movements that must have come from years of the repetitive motion; he strung it to the rings in the roof of the bridge. One end was secured to the forward ring, then he pulled the remainder completely through the large stern ring, doubled it back on itself and clipped it tight on the first one as if the hammock was designed for just those rings.

Ginger commented, impressed, "I bet you could do that in your sleep..."

"Yes ma'am I certainly have." he grinned. "I'll be fine right here until y'all get your sea legs under you and can pilot as well as me."

John asked casually, "Can we spend a few more days practicing on the *Ariel*?"

Jimmy replied, "Take as long as you wish. This is: *The John and Ginger Backhouse Show*! Whatever schedule you'd like to keep is alright with me."

Ginger remembered the video greeting and asked, "Jimmy do you know the island that Alfred plugged into the nav computer as a destination?"

He answered clearly, "Yes ma'am. Most everybody who sails the Caribbean has been by there once or twice..."

"So you think it will be a good maiden voyage for the *Anna*?" she probed.

Again without too much emotion he answered, "Mrs.

Backhouse, hurricane season is mostly passed, the winds are still fresh and it's warm down there. I like the trip, myself. But again: *that is wholly up to y'all.*"

The days of practice were very valuable; when the *Anna* left the intracoastal waterway and entered the Gulf almost a week later, her crew was far more prepared. Jimmy announced as they reached open waters, "We'll let the *Anna* get used to blue water beneath her and wind in her sails at three-quarters. In a day or two we'll give her her head. Then hold on tight---This girl can fly!"

That plan allowed John and Ginger time to become more familiar with all the halyards, sheets, lines, blocks and winches required to hoist and trim sails---which was very likely the reasoning behind Jimmy's announcement. In the meantime: daylight hours were spent learning the yacht, seeing winds and currents and poring over and reading charts. They learned the sea lanes, nautical courtesy and regulations as well as the signal flags. The latter Jimmy insisted upon, not out of malice but as standard procedure.

Four hundred miles from the Texas-Mexican coast they set course for north of Cuba to pass just south of the Florida Keys and into the Bahamas. Each evening Jimmy reviewed what was learned that day, quizzed them on terminology, technique and navigation, until the fifth day at sea as they neared the Keys.

Ginger was first up as usual and Jimmy wasn't at the helm. 'What the...' she thought and looked to the foredeck. There, out on the bowsprit, he was sitting with his coffee, leaning back against the stay and dangling his legs. "Captain?" she called.

He waved absently and called back, "You probably need to adjust course a few points east nor'east... there are submerged reefs coming up on this course before the day is out..."

Ginger's mind raced and her feet followed. 'A *few* points east nor'east...' She made the minor correction just as John came up to the bridge. "John would you trim the main; we just made a minor course correction and it appears she's about to luff a bit."

He responded instantly, seemingly without a thought of hesitation. Finished, he stood looking up at the full sail, now nice and taut, then he looked back to the helm. Ginger smiled, "Nicely done sir, thank you."

John came back to the stern, "Ginger dearest? Where's our captain?" She pointed forward where Jimmy was still straddling the bowsprit apparently napping. "I think we're supposed to navigate the passage passed the Keys on our own." she observed.

John was all grins, "Aye, aye skipper! First Mate Backhouse prepared for duty!"

She thought, 'I love this guy! Let's see... the charts said erratic shallow depths coming up fairly quickly once we pass Havana-Key West... so... we'll make course to split the difference and keep at least thirty miles or so off the Keys...' She looked up at the GPS screen, cross-checked with the LORAN and made a correction of a few more points east nor'east. A subdued thrill of accomplishment flashed through her causing her to shiver momentarily.

"Mr. Mate! Please trim the staysail and forejib, I'll tend to the main... We're at fifteen knots and I think we can get her up to near twenty-five before the afternoon. The forecast suggests fourteen to twenty knot winds with gusts up to twenty-five off the northeast coast of Cuba..."

John happily trimmed the foresails and sat down next to Jimmy who was definitely *not* napping. "It looks like Ginger is catching on rather quickly..." he intimated.

John smiled, "You are a *good* teacher, sir. Thank you so much for your care during our instruction."

Jimmy nodded, "Y'all are doing fine! I figured either of you should be ready for the helm by now... We'll see if you can pilot the *Anna* as well as me yet. Ginger has responded calmly and correctly; the hardest thing to learn is to not 'nag' your ship with too many tiny adjustments when you don't have to. We'll see."

John left the foredeck and went to the galley to start breakfast. "Bangers and biscuits sound good to you?" he called to the helm.

Ginger called back, "You betcha!" and settled into the folding stool on the helm rail. The morning passed without incident. The winds held steadily until as forecast in the afternoon they encountered some serious gusts. The *Anna* tacked close and used every one of them; she ate up the distance along the coast until she was able to be pointed east-southeast and maintain a constant port tack---Ginger brought her sails so tight to her course, she nearly heeled. Jimmy did come back to the bridge after mid-day, poked his head up, glanced at the binnacle to read their speed and raised an eyebrow.

"Near twenty-seven knots... And she's still got both amas in the water. Well done Madam Skipper!"

Ginger was so proud she could sing... "John would you crank up the stereo?!" He did and she sang along with the blaring guitars and bright vocals. She was bobbing and writhing to the lyrics and beat, all the while keeping a clear view of their position and course. As the sun began to slip lower behind them, Jimmy was finally feeling less like an alien youth at an old folks convention and rocked out with them. He flipped on the the ship's lights and came out of the galley with a pitcher of margaritas. John and Ginger were delighted.

"Now this is what I call a Bahamas Bash!" Jimmy announced. He went and untied a line lashed to the mast and raised himself up on the trapeze just thirty feet above the deck.

Ginger thought that was just too cool and had to try it. "John, would you take the helm?"

"Gladly Skipper, I relieve you!" and he swapped places with her.

She called over her shoulder as she bounded for the port trapeze, "I stand relieved..." In a few minutes she was in the harness and pulling on the halyard to raise herself up, far above the deck. She came to level with Jimmy and looked out at the late dusky sky and spreading sea. Her heart pounded, her hair flew and she felt the gentle roll of the great ship as *Anna* sliced through the glimmering waters of the northern Caribbean.

"Thank you, thank you, thank you Captain James! I couldn't have dreamed that it was even possible to experience such freedom!" and she yelled to the winds ahead of them, "Here comes the *Anna Virginia...*"

Jimmy chuckled and replied, "Anything for family, Cousin. Anything at all!"

Ginger was taking a sip from her margarita sippy cup and almost spewed it into the air. "Did you say *Cousin? Family? We're related?!*"

"You were going to find out tomorrow or the next day when we get to Crooked Island... I am James Olaf Henry Erikson, son of Carl Olaf Erikson and Ilsa Rebecca, nee Larrson---the daughter of Kaitlyn Belle Connor and your grandmother's brother Euell Larrson. So, Cousins! Folks have always called me 'Jimmy'..."

"Maybe it's the sippy cup, maybe it's the Caribbean air, but I feel like I've never felt before: I have a husband who loves me. A whole new family who loves me... And *why* was I going to find out tomorrow or the day after anyway?"

John heard a good bit of their chat, "Yeah, why were we going to find out soon anyway?!"

Jimmy was cautious, "They'll *kill* me if I spoil their surprise! Please forget I ever said anything... And *you* absolutely *have to be* surprised!!"

Ginger reached over to him, missed him and began to swing back and forth, giggling the whole time. Jimmy caught her and steadied her trapeze. She promised, "Cuz, we won't rat you out, and you don't have to answer any more questions." She called below, "We didn't hear a thing!"

John called back up, "Hear what?!"

She turned back to Jimmy, "See! We'll be good!"

"It's my turn to thank you... Thank you Ginger." He called down to the helm, "Thank you John!"

John waved back absently, he was studying the GPS and depth finder. "Uh... Guys! We are just passing over a reef area and it drops like crazy after that."

Jimmy let himself down, hand over hand. "Pan out a bit on the GPS screen; if it's getting *that* much deeper, we *should* be passing just north of Nurse Cay!"

As he reached the helm, John could confirm his observation. Jimmy announced, "You guys *really* put some miles behind us today! We're only six hours or so from Acklins Bight! I'll make coffee; y'all will need your eyes and wits about you shortly... I'll turn the stereo back up too. Do you mind if I make a few selections?"

"Feel free!" John replied, "You might not turn it up too loud though..." and he watched Ginger hand over hand herself back to the deck.

"Wow! That was great!" she announced. Then she whispered to John, "What sort of *surprise*, do you suppose?"

John looked into her upturned face, "I suppose... maybe... perhaps another boatload of family?" he tendered cautiously.

Ginger was bobbing up and down, "That's what I thought too... Oh boy, oh boy! But we *have to be surprised!* Remember!" She put her finger to her lips to stress their silence. Then she looked up at the main and back to John, "My head's a little light, I mean I feel light-headed. Don't let Jimmy make the margaritas anymore. I think these were too strong!" She swung around the binnacle, landed on her butt on the bridge steps and crawled to the sofa. "I'm just going to curl up here and take a quick nap..."

John put a blanket over her and returned to the helm. The

'quick nap' lasted until the next sunrise. In several hours as Jimmy anticipated, John navigated the reefs and islets at the entrance to the Bight. As the *Anna* came around the last one, the bay ahead of her was glowing in the distance.

Jimmy grinned, "Well John get ready for a surprise!" They sailed into a circle of four boats: three other trimarans and one bermuda rigged sloop. Jimmy doused their sails, leaving the forejib to ease them into position among the tethered row of ships. All was quiet. It *was* three in the morning after all. Jimmy winked at John as he passed the helm.

He pointed to each in turn, "That's the *Pebble*, that's the *Ananke*, there's the *Hannah Belle* and of course the *Tygress...*" After tying them off to the *Pebble*, he led John over to the *Pebble's* bridge and the only other person up at that hour---his other cousin, Becka Larrson.

She brightened instantly when he came in with John; she whispered, "I saw you approach, but everyone finally *just* got quiet a couple hours ago... quite a party for 'old guys'!" She was holding a swaddled baby and bottle-feeding.

Jimmy looked between them, "Who's the runt?"

She giggled, "I was told that Viola and Portia found her while they were in Iraq as U.N. consultants with Operation Provide Comfort. She was among the wreckage in a village where the second Iraqi plane was shot down in what became two weeks later: the no-fly zone. All the people of that village are dead---thanks to both Sadam *and* to Desert Storm. They *absolutely* checked *everywhere*." She looked to John, "As you might suppose, missing children is a *serious* subject in this family. We take *nothing* for granted. Viola said they even lodged a permanent notice with the consulate on the off-chance some relatives might surface. Vera and Alfred have been taking care of her."

Jimmy stroked the little girl's thick hair, "What's her name?"

"Vera has named her 'Hana Nasrin,' that means beautiful wild rose in Kurdish," she whispered as she smiled lovingly at the infant. "Here, John..." She held up Hana for John to hold. He took her into his thick arms and cooed at her---he was now in love with two females! She reached up a little hand and held his nose.

Jimmy and Becka observed, "It looks like she's found a new play toy! Congratulations Johnny, you are now one of Hana's bobble heads!"

The sun was just lightening the eastern sky as coffee pots and presses began rattling in galleys throughout the flotilla. Jimmy and Becka went from ship to ship letting everyone know about the slight change in plans. On the *Anna*, Ginger was still asleep on the sofa with her head under the blanket. A few people, sipping coffee, came quietly and carefully into the *Anna's* bridge salon and stared at the lumpy blanket on the sofa. John, with Hana in his arms, was sitting at the 'head' of the blanket on the end of the sofa. Hana made a little squalling yelp, John raised a bottle for her and she quieted instantly. There was movement under the blanket. The back of an auburn head appeared and Ginger looked up at John---her back to the rest of the room. She blinked and looked again.

"Jonibob? That looks like a baby!" she muttered and rose up on an elbow.

"Ginger this is Hana Nasrin, it means beautiful wild rose. Hana, this is GingerKat." She sat up and took little Hana into her own arms---her back *still* to the rest of the room.

She cooed, "Hello, little rose..." Once again the infant reached up and grabbed a nose---this time Ginger's---and wouldn't let go.

A woman's voice behind her across the salon said, "Now she has two bobble-head toys---quite a collector!" Ginger's eyes widened and looked at John. He smiled and nodded slightly, then indicated the rest of the room with his eyes. Ginger turned slowly around and her mouth gaped open.

John took Hana back into his own arms as Jimmy announced,

"Ginger let me introduce you to your family... This is your mother's best friend in the world: Vera Livingson, nee Masterson."

Vera came to Ginger's side and whispered, with tears in her eyes and a slight smile, "We've met before... the Tribune Building in Chicago when you were seven." Ginger threw her arms around Vera's neck and the family applauded and cheered. "I'm so glad to have you at last in my arms!" Vera cried and Ginger sobbed in the throes of the greatest joy she had ever known in her life!

The two women whispered together for a while and John rose to walk with Hana around the bridge. Through the windows he spied each of his family making their way to the *Anna---His family*! He was home at last among the dearest people in the world. He had been told all their stories, knew of their accomplishments and even recognized most of them... But they were *here* and *now*---real flesh and blood, not characters in a tale of remarkable people! When he saw Sam and Ronia he nearly collapsed. He waved them over, and met them at the companionway. Ginger's grandparents held him tight.

Sam said, "We missed all your football games, but we've been as proud as we could be at all your accomplishments over the years..."

Ronia added, "You have quite a beautiful wife now, too! Please introduce us..." John walked them over to the sofa where Vera and she were sitting like school girls, holding hands and whispering to each other and giggling.

"Sam and Ronia Spelman, may I introduce my wife, your granddaughter: Virginia Kaitlyn Belle Spelman-Backhouse!" Ginger leapt up and held both of them at the same time... This reunion was just getting better and better! Ronia sat next to her on the sofa, now Ginger was surrounded by the women of her family for the first time in her life. More of their family began to come in.

Two most honored and ancient of the family came forward and stood before John and Ginger, who instantly knelt.

"Get up you two! We're not wearing our halos today... this is an informal gathering of all our family together at last!" Harry turned to the assembled, "Those who were lost, have found themselves among us at last! We are whole once more."

Ginger gaped and said, "But you two have to be..." and her voice trailed off at the inexplicable number.

MamaKat announced, "It's alright, dear... we know how old we are. I think everyone here knows, actually."

Mia and Lena announced, "Mama and Papa turn one hundred..."

"and twenty-five in a few months..."

Ginger recovered, but that wasn't what was so whelming. She had just met these two people weeks before at John's house! They didn't look that old then and they certainly didn't look that old now. "But, you don't look even half that age! I don't understand..."

Olivia, Lila, the twins and their daughters came over to her, "Care to hazard a guess at our ages?" Lila asked coyly.

Katy and Euell who *did* look closer to *their* age of around eighty cautioned, "Just take whatever you imagine and double it!" Katy smiled pleasantly at the women and clucked as she subtly shook her head, "Such show-offs..."

Harry sat down in a vacant chair next to the sofa, Vera gave Kaitlyn her seat and sat at Ginger's feet, now she was utterly surrounded. Ginger held each woman's hand.

MamaKat said, "I understand you and our Johnny had a whirlwind romance... Didn't you two *just meet* under our very noses only a few weeks ago?"

Ginger smiled, "Yes ma'am, but from what I understand of this family's stories, George and Belle still hold the all-time record for strangers-to-lovers in three hours flat... and *they* seemed to turn out alright!" There were ripples of laughter through the room at both her observation and that she knew the family's stories so well.

John sat down next to Vera at Ginger's feet. Alfred approached, took Vera's hand and squatted in front of John and Ginger. He said confidentially, "Vera and I have made up our mind about this precious little girl here..." and he looked into Ginger's eyes and then John's. "She has your eyes!"

Vera said, "We hope that she will be happiest with *you* two as her parents, if you'll have her. Alfred and I aren't as young as we once were---how ever darling our little Hana is..."

Jimmy and Becka announced from the galley on the *Pebble* tethered next to the *Anna*, "Smorgasbord on the *Pebble*! We'll load plates for the honored guests." Jimmy added, "This once!"

The day in the open bay was idyllic. It was yet another surprise when John went below to fetch something for Vera that he noticed the date: the twenty-third of December.

"Ginger!" he called, running up the steps, "It's almost Christmas! This is our one month anniversary!" He came up to find Viola and Portia sitting with Ginger and describing the charts and diagrams beside her. In her lap was little Hana.

Portia looked over to him and smiled, "Johnny we'll have an anniversary dinner for you two later..." and she went back to the discussion. He handed the scarf he'd fetched to Vera; she took his arm and walked with him out onto the deck.

"Johnny, you were seventeen in that orphanage when we found you at last. We had to do some serious soul-searching. *We* knew who you were and we could likely have convinced you. However, Papa Harry and MamaKat counseled us to wait. Can you imagine why?"

John *had* wondered about that, "The best that I can guess is: Knowing *me* at seventeen, I would have been very bitter about the whole situation, whether I was convinced or not."

"That's what MamaKat thought as well. Harry watched

everything you did from that day forward. He knows every place you've been, every person you've known and every single decision you've made along the way. You are my only nephew---my only family---it was *extremely* hard for me to keep 'hands off' and just watch and wait." She looked up at some billowy clouds passing overhead. "Five months ago, when you decided to leave your old life and begin something completely new---as a writer---Harry finally sent word to the family to begin preparations for bringing both you and Ginger home. Ginger already knew who her real family was, but couldn't *possibly* trace us——We keep a pretty low profile. But *you*, you *had* to be approached differently. I *honestly* don't know *how* Harry and MamaKat accomplished what they did---Their methods and abilities are so far beyond most of us it's unfathomable."

John interrupted, "But Olly and the twins, Viola and Portia, George, Lila, Alfie and Olivia...even Alfred...they have been trained and have developed uh... certain remarkable abilities too..."

Vera smiled, "True, but Harry and MamaKat have *a hundred years* of refinement and advancement *beyond* us. John you have been the recipient of a series of miracles---not the least of which, that you have *actually* taken up the work yourself and been a fine example for our Ginger." She sat down in a deck chair and invited him to sit as well. "You remember the Christmas Carol by Dickens?" He nodded.

"You were visited by the last ancestors of our family. The only thing standing between them and being ultimately free of this earth was that their family was not yet whole. They were so completely identified with their family it was an impediment to their passing on. When Harry and Kat *somehow* enabled *them* to perform this one last function---training you and telling you of your family's roots and work---they were at last freed."

She let that sink into John's consciousness. "There are no more ancestors left to guide this family. The greatest achievement of *all our lifetimes* has been to fulfill, *directly*, the true role of man in the

Universe! It is our proudest heritage and our crowning glory. John, without you and Ginger that may *never* have happened. That's not my opinion, that's from Harry and Kat themselves. They said White Feathers and Belle's parting words before they were silent forever were the very same which Harry used to announce your arrival: 'Those who were lost, have found themselves! We are whole once more.' *You* were the necessary 'therapy' those two venerable persons needed. When Harry and Kat decide to leave, they will not linger as all those who came before them had to do---still working out their lasting flaws---they will be gone, beyond hearing, beyond contact and take their rightful and proper place in the ever-growing universe. There are twelve individuals *right now* who are this world's brightest, shining examples of what being a human being truly means. The rest strive ever forward to raise themselves to that level. I am telling you this because, well for one: as my nephew I've wanted to sit and talk with you for ages. The other purpose is this: You have Harry's watch for a reason. Ginger has 'Papa's pebble' for a reason..."

John took out the little golden disk and opened it to read the inscription once more. He looked up to his Aunt Vera. "I'm sorry, I must be the densest guy within a hundred miles... Why do I have this watch and not Alfred? Why does Ginger have Papa's pebble and not Becka?"

She looked back at him lovingly, "I'll answer *your* question with another: Which is more valuable? Knowledge or Being?"

He replied by rote, "First is to know, in order to be able to be and to do..."

"Good. Now: Why is it more powerful to start from nothing and gain everything, than to have it *all* from birth?"

Again he promptly answered, "Because if one is merely the product of a natural occurrence, then whatever is achieved isn't one's own, it's a product of nature---Only what we gain through our own countless efforts and understanding can *ever* be *our* inalienable possession. It is repeatably and objectively ours."

All she did was smile at him. "There's your answer, then. You and GingerKat are this family's new tradition---of the *Objective Way*. Neither of you were born to it, neither of you had the external training---nor do you need it. A new day is dawning for this family. You two *are* our new George and Belle, you might say." He stared back at her, the light of a dawning understanding of his and Ginger's purpose began to smolder in his eyes. His heart was swelling and he could feel what it was to begin growing a soul---the responsibility, the obligation of humble service shouldered with grace and love.

"Auntie Vera?"

"Yes Johnny?"

"I think Ginger and I would like to raise Hana Nasrin properly..."

"Yes Johnny. Viola and Portia are tending to the preparations of that as we speak. She's as sharp as her mother ever was. This won't take as long as with many equally unprepared. You have given her a good head start."

"Auntie Vera?"

"Yes Johnny?"

"Ginger and I should make a little sister for Hana."

"Your family will welcome that, Johnny. You and Ginger will make wonderful parents." Vera stood and walked with her nephew across to the *Pebble*. "Let's make sure you know *all* your family *really* well, shall we? There are a few who are new to you I think... Did you know your mother and I were the only two daughters of Swedish immigrants? And that the Mastersons and Larrsons were *both* from Gotland? You and I have a lot more in common with the crew and passengers of the *Pebble* than just our *work*!"

Ginger came over to the *Pebble's* salon with Viola and Portia in tow. "Johnny, guess what!" she opened. Vera grinned, and John looked up and admitted he didn't know. "Hana is nine months old *today*---on our first anniversary!" Viola and Portia were nodding confirmation behind her. "She can roll over and even sit for a moment or two without falling sideways!"

"Uh... That's wonderful? Isn't that normal for a baby at nine months?" John had to reply; he didn't see where this was going evidently.

Ginger rolled her eyes, "But she's not just any baby! She's *our* little girl..." She held Hana up in front of her and began talking to her. "...and she's the smartest, and most beautiful, and healthiest, and..."

John interrupted, "Sweetheart?"

Ginger moved Hana to her hip, "Yes, my love!"

"Do you know *anything* about raising a child?" His face looked as if he expected to be hit with a cream pie any moment.

Ginger thought, 'A hell of a lot more than you think, and I've got the best mothers in the world right here to turn to for anything...'

Aloud she said, "Not yet... but I'm a fast learner!"

'I am so nice to my adorable Jonibob...'

She looked across to Vera, Mia and Lena. "What do you say ladies? Ready to answer my every question?" They bowed. "There: Settled. Next question please..."

John took a deep breath, "GingerKat, I think we should make sure Hana has backup... As it stands now: it's two against one----that doesn't seem hardly fair to her does it?"

Ginger began repeating what she'd just heard, and the realization of what he was suggesting broke on her like a wave. "Johnny, my wonderful man..." and she turned to the remarkable women around her. "Do one of you want to tell him or shall I?"

MamaKat replied, "It really should come from you, dearest."

Ginger went up closer to John. "You have *already seen* to Hana's backup dearest. MamaKat just told me, and that's why Viola and Portia are giving me the *crash course* in 'How to be a Livingson.' Hana and her little sister deserve all we can give them... Don't you think?"

John looked stunned, "Little sister? I'm the father of *two* girls? And we've only been married a month? And six months ago I'd never heard of the Livingsons? And..."

Ginger passed Hana to her father whispering, "You'll get used to Papa, he's a great man... Really... He just has these *spells*... That's how GingerKat caught him!"

She turned to the buffet, "What is everyone else going to eat?" and she began to load her plate. She muttered, "Ooh, I don't like that---I'll take three. I can't stand that---I'll take four..."

Viola whispered to John, "She's taking 'Like what it does not like' to a new level. That's one fine woman there!"

The men walked with John to the *Ananke's* bridge. Harry stayed with the women. The Larrsons and Eriksons wanted to know if John would bring his family to Gotland for an extended visit. The Livingsons assured him they were also planning a trip there.

Oliver added, "Jimmy has a start-up computer company for which he has to show up at the office... sometimes. I can't say that I know all of the details. Becka has interests of a pressing nature she is anxious to return and pursue. Viola and Portia *just* love Sweden--- more than any other place on earth I think. That goes for their mothers as well."

John answered tactfully, "We hadn't given any thought to travels beyond this. Ginger and I are still *really* inexperienced sailors and are just learning the ropes of our relationship..."

Oliver supplied, "I think Viola and Portia are your new crew... You *really didn't stand a chance* in that matter..." As an afterthought he added, "You're aware that I know *precisely* how you feel?" John smiled and nodded.

Euell and Sam offered, "What you and Ginger *should* be doing then, while we have this wonderfully protected bay all around us, is to get out on the cats and see what a sailboat can really do!"

"I'm sure Jimmy and Becka will love having you two to beat up on... They have been the ones beaten by their elders up until now at least!"

Carl and Nils confided, "We all grew up on the sea too, you see."

"There's no better way to develop communication and trust between each other than to crew a boat together under extreme circumstances..."

That evening everyone gathered in deck chairs on the foredecks of the ships. Harry and Kaitlyn were in the middle. They rose, turned and addressed the family. "A new day has begun to dawn on our little family. Once there was the insistence upon a training from birth leading to the external expression of that knowledge in a physical way. Our last ancestors have left; their parting gift to us was the culmination of all they intended for us---a wholly objective path to fulfilling our birthright as human beings."

"We have been the faithful and humble stewards of this tradition. There can no longer be any doubt of the efficacy and practicable nature of our endeavors. These here are testament to that reality. We have seen the light of true knowledge kindled and burn bright in the hearts and minds of those with whom we have shared this work. It is time at last to pass the torch on to new bearers that they may carry it into this new age of our work." They held each others hands and smiled on their family one last time.

"Farewell. Make great efforts," and they turned their backs to the assembly and took a step towards the prow of the ship. The evening light was dimming, but they grew *brighter* with each step. When they reached the bowsprit they simply turned into pure light and sailed out over the water, climbing higher and higher into the sky. Like shooting stars, they shot off above the last rays of the orange tinged clouds cloaking the western horizon. They were gone.

John held Ginger's hand, she held Hana in her lap and their tears ran down their cheeks unbridled. The rest of the company was looking at them expectantly. Ginger noticed first and asked, "We're surely not the *only* ones who just saw the passing of the two greatest teachers in the world."

While nodding heads looked back to her, she thought, 'Why are they looking at us? I see the gleam of tears in others' eyes. John and I aren't the only ones touched and awed at the spectacle...'

She whispered to John, "Why are they staring at us?"

Vera smiled kindly and answered, "Sweetheart, we're trying to etch this sight into our hearts, minds and souls. As Harry and Kat just pointed out so dramatically, the torch has been passed and we here are the only witnesses."

Oliver made it a little clearer, "White Feathers *alone* was witness to the union of George and Belle---who began the tradition of which we have all been the beneficiaries."

Lena said, "This time around, counting that little bundle you are carrying, now there are *twenty-three* witnesses."

Mia concluded, "Johnny, GingerKat, *you are* this family's new tradition---of the Objective Way. Neither of you were born to it, neither of you had the external training---nor do you actually need it. A new day has just dawned for this family---you are this age's George and Belle... We are savoring the moment."

They all rose then and bowed to the Backhouses, then by ones and twos they went back to their cabins for the night. When only John and GingerKat were left sitting together on the prow of their own ship, John said, "That's just what Auntie Vera told me while you were talking with Viola and Portia earlier..."

Ginger still hadn't sorted out the significance of what just happened and said so.

"...Are they suggesting that we are the..." she searched for the words. "That we are filling the shoes of Harry and MamaKat? Of George and Belle before them? *Johnny*, we're just getting used to being married! And now being parents to our little Hana! I don't think we're ready to lead this entire extraordinary family! Aren't Oliver and the twins the eldest---they're certainly the best qualified!"

John sat listening and nodding to Ginger's very well made arguments. When she finished he laughed and asked, "Do you know why the great blue whale---the largest animal that lives on the earth, perhaps that has ever lived---has a throat that cannot swallow an object wider than a beach ball?"

She looked sideways at him, "No I haven't the foggiest idea why!"

"Because it *just is!*" he replied. "Your arguments are sound, your trepidation is well-founded. I've no doubt that if George and Belle knew what lay in store for them the moment they met, or rather had their first-born: Harry; they would probably would have felt *just as you and I do right now*. GingerKat, it's just like you told me earlier: we've got the best teachers in the world right here ready to answer any question at all, anything, anytime..."

She sighed, "This family doesn't beat around the bush, nor *waste time...*"

It was John's turn to give his wife a sideways look of incredulity. She caught his expression then *realized* how *very much* they *really were* Livingsons after all! She laughed with him.

"Okay, okay! We were confirmed single strangers before thirty-four days ago. It's *our* one month anniversary, we are pregnant, on our own elegant trimaran in the Caribbean, we are multi-millionaires, have an adorable adopted daughter and to top it off we have just been dubbed torch-bearers for the most remarkable family anyone's *never* heard of... Does that about cover it?"

John added, "Just one more thing..." She couldn't guess what else she'd missed, he whispered, "I love you!" She melted.

"Let's put Hana to bed," she cooed.

"Right behind you..." he replied.

2

Embark

"You must live in the present, launch yourself on every wave, find your eternity in each moment."
---Henry David Thoreau

I t was the best Christmas either of them had ever had. And to their utter surprise, even after all the family had done for them already, they had presents! At least Hana had presents, John and Ginger also received gifts but of a different nature. Hana Nasrin Backhouse was presented with her own monogramed burp towels and diapers. She got a little sailor's outfit, her own miniature hammock for a cradle and her own bowl and spoon with pictures of flying sailboats that resembled birds. Then there were the toys: a mobile that played music when it was wound up, alphabet blocks, a doll, a shovel and pail for the beach and crayons. John and Ginger were given a prototype digital camera and all-event passes to the Winter Olympics in Lillehammer.

They rolled their eyes at that one. 'All we need to do now is get to Scandinavia... you don't suppose there's some hints being dropped here... do you?' thought Ginger. This was tempered by her also receiving a leather bound journal and selection of vintage fountain pens. 'Now that's more like it!'

Lena made a sling for GingerKat or John to carry Hana when needed, which wasn't often. Everyone on the flotilla were willing nannies for the little angel. Between Ginger's lessons in objective knowledge and practice on the *Ariel*, every night she put her head to the pillow she was out like a light. That left John the delightful chore of tending to Hana's feedings and diapers and dressing her and playing with her. He slept well too. Jimmy and Becka were very satisfied to at last have competition they could out-sail, for the time being anyway. The *Hannah's* crew were on the phone quite a lot with the directors of the global not-for-profit humanitarian aid corporation they ran from wherever they were. The *Ananke's* crew were conscripted into it many year's before, so they were likewise occupied. Their Gotland families on the *Pebble* and *Tygress* were only too pleased therefore to tend to the day-to-day tasks of laundry, meals, sailing lessons and supplies.

One of the tasks which Jimmy and Becka performed, when not trouncing John and GingerKat on the cats, was to upgrade the software---created by themselves---for the little fleet's Inmarsat equipment. Besides instantaneous global telecommunications, the *Hannah* and *Ananke* kept up their international enterprises and the *Pebble* and *Tygress's* crews maintained their distance-learning instruction contracts. What it meant for the *Anna* was constant open channels of audio-video communications with the other ships in the fleet---one of the perks of having wealthy relatives scattered over the planet.

GingerKat's Journal

The Story of the Living-Sons

1 January 94   I am a journalist by profession but have never been a serious diarist, so this will be interesting if there is actually more beyond this first page. John, my husband---wow, I have a husband!---has journals that describe our family backgrounds well enough---so I won't dwell on that. We have celebrated our one month anniversary, we are pregnant, we're on our own trimaran yacht in the Caribbean, we are multi-millionaires and have an adorable adopted daughter---Hana Nasrin. We have passes to the XVII Winter Olympic Games in Lillehammer, Norway. Euell and Oliver assure us that if we hug the coastline up to the Elbe River, the Kiel Canal will let us avoid the harshest of the North Sea's fury and

70

get us to Gotland with less discomfort. (They should know they've sailed those waters all their lives.) As long as Viola and Portia say it can be done---it can. Our families have been so wonderful to us.

John doesn't know anymore about what we're doing or going to do than I do---and he admits it. What we *do* know right now is: Hana will be one year old on March twenty-third. Our next daughter will be born in mid to late August and we are thinking about names already. We will get to see our first Olympic games *in person* this year. The *Anna Virginia* is our new home and we love her---as much as anyone can love a 'thing.' I know John loves me---even though he didn't say so until a month after we were married---there was never a doubt in my mind. I love him---which is a new experience for me and I am learning... I think I've told him so... that I love him I mean... Harry and MamaKat are gone---they really knew how to make an entrance and exit! I tied Becka in timed races on the cats two out of three times and she won't race me anymore. I can calculate octaves in my sleep, almost notice when I am not being reasonable, and I *know* Hana doesn't cry just to make me crazy---really... I do *know* that.

This work is becoming a challenge. I try to remember to remember myself; I have little dots stuck in places I frequent all through the ship---so I have reminders around me to help. I am still having difficulty not blurting out my opinion about whatever is going on around me. Which is also, I think, part of why I get so frustrated so fast with anything that's not going the way I wanted or thought it should... I'm not standing back and just seeing it for what it is. I always feel like it's a personal assault, a judgement or plot directed at me---Man, do I sound self-important or what! Definitely must work on that---I'll talk to John or one of the others about if they ever had to deal with that... Anyway, at least I have a firm grasp of the structure of things, most especially my own construction---Wow, whoever first figured this out was an amazing intellect... I suspect maybe it wasn't one person with a sudden direct vision of 'everything'... who knows---interesting thought, but my work is here and now.

4 January 94   I hope we do some shopping when we get to New York City, I need *much* warmer clothing than what John and I brought for the Caribbean! We are off the Carolina coast and it's getting very cold! My mother's two cold weather outfits are warm enough for now, but poor John is borrowing things to keep warm; Hana is the best equipped of the three of us. Thank you, thank you, thank you Alfred and Jimmy for refitting a second wheel and instruments *inside* the bridge! I *know* I'd be ready to turn this old girl around if I had to do my watch outside on the helm platform. Our family is so good to us!

Viola and Portia are never down about anything! Whatever occurs, they've got a ready reason for it being a *good* thing... For example: An evacuation hose split from the port ama head while Portia was in there using it. What did she say when she came to breakfast that morning? "Whew I finally got to clean the bathroom floor, it'd begun to smell but I was too lazy to do it before..." (Yeah right, she was lazy!) Or when Viola was feeding Hana and our angel smeared beets all over the back of her down jacket. She turned to John and announced that Hana was an advanced artist: "This is an exact replica of a Jackson Pollack!" Then she drew a frame around the stain and still hasn't stopped telling everyone what a prodigy Hana is!

And they're not the only one's who are able to maintain a reasonable, objective outlook on their own lives... dare I say it? John is amazing too. When I carp about not having 'alone-time,' he tells me a story from *his* years in the orphanage. When I whine about destroying another meal in the galley, he tells me about having six dollars and twelve cents for an entire month's groceries during graduate school. When I lose it over another dirty diaper after just changing her, he reminds me about when I was equally frantic when she was constipated for a week. I've got a long way to go! But I will get better!

7 January 94   I was never much of a shopper. I looked down my nose at the girls in college who would spend entire days walking the malls and boutiques, then offered their 'adventures' as actual conversations of vital interest. That extended to the women in my office later on who did much the same thing. It's *very* different when shopping is 'supply hunting.' Mia and Lena are the world's greatest supply hunters! For them New York City isn't a teeming mass of commercial chaos daunting at best and maliciously intimidating. After we scrounged through the few worthwhile things in my flat and I cancelled the lease, they took me out for hunting lessons.

Rules of Supply Hunting. One---Look at the item's construction: How should it be made if *you* were to design it *yourself* for durability and longevity... Is it? *Two*---Cost is relative: How can a well-made sheepskin coat be the same price as a state of the art GPS unit? (See Rule One) *Three*---Hannah's Law---If you search all week and finally find just what you were looking for *and* buy it; the *very* next place you go, you'll see ten of them for less: Don't obsess over a single item or it's cost. (See Rules One and Two) *Four*---Wind, Water, Fire and Earth can't read labels that say: wind-resistant, water-proof, fire-retardant, or soil-resistant.

That one took some getting used to. Oh, and 'permanent-press,' 'wrinkle-free,' 'pre-shrunk,' 'laboratory-tested,' and 'lifetime-guarantee' are euphemisms for *Gotcha-Sucker!* I was able to haul my 'hunting trophies' home in a knapsack and a medium-sized duffle---which was *Rule Five*---Only kill what you can carry out of the jungle.

John and I are so thankful Jimmy taught us everything about the *Anna* before he let us sail her out of Port Isabel, even having us take things apart and put them back together. Seriously, the more we know---the less we take for granted, the less we take for granted---the more thorough we are, the more thorough we are---the safer and better off we stay. There's a larger lesson in there somewhere... I'm rapidly coming to the conclusion that the work is in everything. It's not just another compartment of my activities, it's life. How often has that enneagram poem been running through my head as I take up even the smallest task now? The line of supervision is a godsend!

"How's the diary going GingerKat?" Lila asked genuinely interested.

"Illuminating," she answered without hesitation.

"Because when George and I, with Ally and my brother went on our first expedition, I *tried* to document every day of our travels. But it became *such* a time-consuming chore, I was ultimately resigned to writing in my journal once a week," she reflected.

Ginger smiled and said she was a week into it and she had only three entries. "I'd really like to read *your* journals, if you let me... I mean if they're not too personal or anything."

Lila laughed pretty hard at that. "Personal yes, but *will* you believe they *aren't* fiction? I don't know!? We saw things, experienced things, hell---we *did* things I still marvel at sometimes..."

Becka came into the *Anna's* bridge. They were anchored on the Hudson within launch distance of Manhattan. The cold winter wind rushed in as the door opened. She was making the rounds of the yachts to set in a new course on the nav computers, again.

"This is the latest and greatest from Euell and Oliver for the voyage. I won't be but a moment and you can offer me some of that cobbler I smell." Ginger passed Hana's book to Lila and crossed to the galley. Hana turned all the pages back to the beginning for a fresh 'reading.'

"John made this before he went out this afternoon. He didn't *say* he expected to have any when he got back. Lila and I have already had some..." Ginger announced as she scooped out a bowlful. "Becka have you ever kept a diary?"

She giggled, "...And I keep it under lock and key in a safety deposit box, under twenty-four hour armed guard with orders to shoot first ask questions later!" she laughed, "Actually it's just a few recipes and notes about a few dates I've had... nothing important."

Lila and Ginger exchanged glances. Lila asked, "What sort of recipes?"

Ginger followed with, "There's a recipe for dating?"

That got more giggles from Becka. She put on a serious face, which didn't suit her in the least, and stated, "Proper dating is an art more than a science, and I'm making significant breakthroughs..." she sighed, "At least I *will* be when we get back home." She entered the final authorizations and stood up, "There you go, all updated. We should be in Amsterdam, three day's sail from Gotland, by the twentieth at the outside."

"And here's your cobbler." Ginger handed her a bowl and spoon. "Do you want cream on it?" Becka shook her head, a spoonful already in her mouth.

"So who's your latest subject for experimentation?" Lila asked casually.

Becka quickly refilled her spoon and got it to her mouth. She indicated she couldn't possibly speak with such yummy food in her mouth.

Ginger mused aloud, "We have all day..."

Becka swallowed and said, "You wouldn't know him anyway, he's *just* someone *I* know is all."

Lila and Ginger shared knowing looks and in a mocking tone, "*Such passion!* Or is that part of the technique?"

Hana made her way along the edge of the sofa from Lila to Becka and held up her book. Becka became instantly maternal and set Hana in her lap and began the book from the beginning once more, of course.

Lila exclaimed, "Saved by the belle!" Ginger groaned.

"Hey there's actually some cobbler still left?!" Viola commented as she entered the salon from the deck and went straight to pull a bowl out and help herself. "Johnny's right behind me, anyone else want refills---last chance?" Becka held up her bowl.

Lila asked, "Will your mothers and Olly be good for this crossing? Fred and Vera are free, I think, to lend a hand."

Viola was already two spoonfuls into the cobbler, "Shoo day gah plenneh helly ears tuhcem..." she answered succinctly.

The confused expressions made her repeat, "Oh yeah they're fine they have plenty of healthy years left in them... say sixty or seventy at least. Look at yourself young lady! They're *only* a few years older than you!"

"It's not the years, it's the miles..." Lila reflected. "I'll just pop over and have a chat them." She passed John coming in, "I tried to save you some but I was over-powered..."

John watched her hop up the steps to the deck and leap over to the *Hannah*. "Wow! Ginger, if I ever need a transfusion just line these people up and run their blood directly into my veins!"

He looked at Viola who had just put her bowl behind her back but wasn't quick enough with her spoon which she was still licking. He made that pained, pitiful puppy look that signaled his disappointment. "Ginger, tell me you didn't tell anyone about the ice cream too!"

Viola's bowl came forward instantly and she went to the freezer, "There's ice cream too?!"

John grabbed her bowl and spooned cobbler into his mouth as quickly as he could before she snatched it back. "Mmm, was that all?"

Viola made a show of cleaning every last crumb and sliver of apple from the bowl and ate it, then said, "Yep."

John went to the oven and took out a second pan of cobbler, "Then you'll be too full for any more... Que lastima..."

Hana went from the edge of the sofa next to Becka and

wobbled two full steps to her daddy's pant leg. John and Ginger gasped at once. It sounded like a vacuum cleaner being switched on.

"Oh my! Where's my camera?! Wait right there darling! Mama's gotta get her camera!"

Hana teetered and plopped down at his feet. He sprawled on the floor next to her. "That was so impressive Princess! Hold Daddy's fingers."

She grabbed on and was back on her feet as Ginger turned on the camera and started snapping away. "Drat! This thing takes so long to click one shot!"

Hana took an unsteady step and then another back to Becka on the sofa.

"I got it!" Ginger yelped, "I actually got the picture!"

Hana looked up at Becka and held out the book again. She hoisted her up and started another 'reading.' Meanwhile Viola had found the ice cream, and dished up more cobbler, now ala mode. Between bites she praised, "Johnny you are such a great cook! Almost as good as Uncle Jean..."

9 January 94   New York City *would* be a dot on the horizon behind us, if we could see the horizon. Fog at sea is very curious: You know you're on this vast expanse---this little speck on the ocean---but all you know of it are your own decks and sails and the sounds of the muted waves. Wow! Another great image of one person's journey through life. All the world around---which we lose attention for and it fades into mere background---and all we seem to see is our own face in the mirror and the chaos around us we are trying always to decipher and reorganize---to make sense of it all. I must remember to pass that one by Lena or Mia, they are the greatest abstract thinkers I've ever met. Just reading John's journals about them really doesn't do them justice. For instance: I verified for myself that every time I did the hands-in-motion exercise there always came a certain point at which I could no longer actually direct my hands' movements with my mind. I wondered, 'How was it that the speed of the Intellectual center was actually, according to the structure, *supposed* to operate at a *higher* speed than the Moving center?'

Lena said that what I was actually using for the exercise was only the most mechanical part of the Intellectual center, and very likely just the two or three of spades---not even the entire Jack. Mia explained that in order to cultivate the *drawn attention* of that center I should engage myself in activities that required drawn intellectual prowess: memorization, the mental organization of material populating my active mind, that sort of thing. Lena said that then I could always slow down the Moving center to a series of deliberate actions---make a slow dance of walking the decks, order every movement of stirring a pot, running up sails, or changing a diaper for that matter... anything repetitive. Mia suggested that after a while although those centers are used to meddling with each other, I will have forced them into the service of my own inclinations of *cooperation*, not the usurpation they were used to. Lena likened it to becoming one with a catamaran. With enough practice, even though you *know* you are *not* the ship itself, you feel every breeze in the sail, you know the precise tension that should be at the tiller, your sense of balance becomes synchronous with the boat's balance---you *are* your boat. You *think* to go left the boat goes left, you *think* right---it goes right. You're body is smarter than a boat, so you have to train yourself to respect it, but it's also better connected to your mind than your body to a boat, so it should learn faster and vice versa.

They went on to say something would be lost in no longer having the external training integral with the objective knowledge. Mia said it wasn't actually a martial discipline, but that it was a passageway to accomplish just what I'd asked about---it had been a very useful tool of integration---not a 'way' in itself. It was a utile cyclical function to address the very real denying forces of our state of disconnection.

Hana took three more steps this morning. This time she walked to me! I can tell she adores her GingerKat. Now if I can convince her that everything she picks up does *not* actually have to be tasted as a vital part of her inspections---Or maybe she's onto something. I am a little jealous that I can't chew on my own toenails as she can. Wait. That sounded weird.

11 January 94   John has been at the helm for hours... I'll go relieve him or keep him company, whatever he prefers. I'm taking this along on the off-chance he just wants someone near. He hasn't ever said so---like so many things---but even though he *says* he got used to being alone all the time growing up, he really *does* like people around---sort of 'alone with company.' Hana's taking a nap and Viola and Portia are asleep, they've been taking night watches.

I don't think he knows I'm sitting behind him. I was very quiet when I came to the bridge and he was looking starboard when I entered from port. He hasn't cut his hair for over a month and it's showing from beneath his wool cap. He has a strong jaw line. He looks as though he's gazing beyond the horizon itself. Do I look like that when I am thinking? His hands seem to go about their duties independently of his direction, like they're his trusty servants just handling the tasks he's left them to maintain. Is that a scar on his neck? I don't remember noticing that before. It's old, just a thin white line from below his ear to the nape of his neck. His back is so straight. His legs look relaxed but his toes are the only parts of his feet touching the deck---like he could leap into action in a split second. I think he's humming... I know that tune... dah ti dum, dah ti di ti dum duhm... The Sun on the Stream! That Celtic tune on the flute or pipes. Wow, he really does have a nice voice and a good ear. I wonder if he realizes he just rubbed that scar, or if it's so habitual that his hands just take care of it for him? Oh! He has Harry's watch open on the console in front of him. I wonder if he treasures that like I do this pebble from Mama... a visual reminder that I'm someone's daughter, that I was thought about and hoped for, that I was once a part of someone's dreams... that I was loved just because

I was there.

"Here's a handkerchief my love. Those are special tears; I'd save them if I were you." John reached out a hand to Ginger with the cloth.

"Did you know I've been sitting here all this time?"

"No. I just heard a sniffle and there you were. How long *have* you been sitting there?" he turned back to the instruments.

She blew her nose and dabbed at a tear. "Not long really."

"What prompted your tears? Regretting ever showing up on my doorstep?" he probed with a smile.

"Absolutely not! You are the best thing that's happened to me since I made the trip to San Francisco for my inheritance!" She clasped the pebble at her neck. "I was actually trying to look at you objectively for once..."

"What's the verdict?"

"Where'd that scar on your neck come from?" she fended.

He laughed, "It's not a great story or anything, really. A childhood lesson in watching where you put your feet."

"It looks like it would have been serious. Did you bleed a lot? Did it take a long time to heal? Were you by yourself? Why do you rub it? Did you know you rub it sometimes?"

He held up his hand, "Whoa. Let me sort those out... Uh, I was by myself. There was this ancient looking shed near the orchard at the orphanage. I used to climb the pecan tree next to it and lay on the roof just staring up at the sky..."

He cleared his throat. "Anyway, by the time I was eleven, I guess I was heavier---just heavy enough I suppose---that when I walked across to my favorite spot, away from view of the big house, I heard a creaking under my feet. Instead of stopping in my tracks I jumped back and my left foot went through a rotted board. I panicked some more and before I knew it my shirt was tangled in a branch of the tree, I grabbed for another branch near my head. My whole leg went through the roof and I felt snared and suspended for *minutes* by my shirt on the branch and my slipping grasp of the other branch.

I fell through the roof and landed with a crash on the floor of the shed. After a moment or two I realized I wasn't dead. I had always wondered what was in there, but it was empty except for a broken old butter churn laying next to me. Then I remembered the noise of the crash when I hit the floor and realized it was my fall that broke the churn. I reached my hand behind my neck and when I pulled it back there was blood on my hand. My shirt was flapping on the branch above the hole in the roof over my head. I used the churn pole to pull my shirt down, wrapped my neck with it like a scarf and went to the door. It was rusted shut. I kicked at it, I beat on it, I threw my shoulder against it. I was starting to feel trapped all over again. Desperate; I ran at it---it fell away in pieces and I rolled across the ground outside from my momentum. I lay there staring up at the sky for I don't know how long. I stood up at last and looked back at my shed and the roof that had been my hidden refuge. I told myself I was too old for kid's 'hide-outs' and I never went back to that shed again."

He looked off passed Ginger into what must have been the vision of that emotionally painful scene relived again... because she'd asked.

Ginger got up and put her hand on that scar, then she kissed it and put her cheek on it. "I love you John."

"Thank you GingerKat." He took a deep breath, "I suppose I rub it sometimes without knowing it. Just before I noticed you were sitting behind me I was thinking about the fog we finally came out of when we left New York City."

"Johnny?"

"Yes GingerKat?" and his voice held the surety once again that she was used to hearing.

"Thank you for talking to me, and answering my questions, and putting up with me." He pulled his head around to face her.

"My love, that's what I live for nowadays: to hear your voice every morning when I get up and before I sleep at night. To try and answer your questions about whatever you wonder about... when I can. Put up with you?! I'd be missing the best part of me without you." He held her eyes until she looked away.

"Really?"

"Really, *really!*"

She wiped her eyes again and sniffled. "I must be up to my ears in hormones. I cry or fall apart at the littlest things lately. Don't let me yell at Hana or anything!"

"Sweetheart you're doing great. You're a lot stronger than you give yourself credit for. I wish I had half your confidence and courage." He squeezed her waist, careful not to crush her.

She laughed and said, "I don't even care anymore if you're shining me on or not. You're good for what ails me Jonibob!" There was the faintest of bleats from below. "Oh! that's Hana!" and she sprang to the companionway and emerged a few minutes later with their girl in her arms.

"Are you hungry now? How about some rice and green beans?" She set her in her dining chair---a hammock chair her size with a detachable tray on the front.

John looked over his shoulder at Ginger. She deftly assembled the meal's components and began spooning the soft foods into Hana's waiting mouth.

"What's this Mama sees?" and she put her finger to Hana's lower front gum. "A tooth! Our princess has another tooth coming in! That explains why you've been drooling and biting at everything... you have a noofie that's been trying to break through. You're *such* a big girl."

82

John smiled, "Shall I order the orthodontist to ready her braces?" he chuckled.

"We can wait for the next one to break through, but put him on speed-dial!" she parried and giggled.

"Did Auntie Viola hear there's a new tooth on board?!" Viola announced and crossed to the munchkin diner.

As she checked the little bud of a tooth herself, Ginger asked, "Did you wash your hands?"

Viola almost paled. "Oops! That's just what I'm doing right now!" and she did. Then Portia arrived and followed nearly the same routine. Viola chided, "Wash your hands first! Jeez, were you raised on a scow?" John and Ginger burst into laughter.

John announced they were holding course and formation. "And we're making good time. If the wind holds without getting too nasty, we'll have already picked up half a day."

Portia replied, "Good attitude. I'm just glad the *Tygress* is keeping pace so well."

"And without us on her sails! That is impressive." Viola contributed and went back to cooing at Hana. "That reminds me..." she shuddered and stood up.

Portia noticed at once. "What was that?!" she asked carefully.

"I just remembered that run to the Suez a week ahead of the others. Anyway, Hana and I made something yesterday evening..." and she went below then came back shortly with tape and a sheet of paper.

"It's a certificate for our Captain!" she announced. "It even has the 'official seal of the Board of Authority'!"

She went to the window above the nav station and taped the 'certificate' to it. Portia smiled and took over feeding Hana as Ginger got up to go and see.

She grinned and read aloud, "*By the Authority of this Board, We hereby confer upon a most worthy candidate, the Official title of Captain, with all of the privileges attendant to that office. Mr. John Robert Backhouse has surpassed all requisite trials and has earned the position of Captain of the Anna Virginia and Commander of our family's allegiance. Conferred this day the Eleventh of January, 1994. Signed: Princess Hana Nasrin Backhouse."*

Ginger held up the edge of the paper, "And her handprint is in bright red paint! This is a treasure!" she was in tears again. "This is so perfect!" She crossed to Viola and Portia and embraced them so hard they actually winced.

"Careful GingerKat, we *are* mortal when all is said and done!" Viola said in mock protest.

"John isn't that the most special certificate you've ever seen?" Ginger asked. John had to wipe his sleeve across his face to answer.

"I'm coming down with my wife's hormones: it seems like every little thing makes me cry or fall apart!" The ladies had a good laugh.

Viola insisted, "We're serious Johnny. You have proven your command abilities and seamanship. We are all most impressed and thankful."

At once John and Ginger turned to just stare at Portia---*she had not finished her sister's sentence!*

Portia said through her tears, "What!? What did I miss? A girl can be touched by things, can't she?"

Hana kicked her foot against Portia's knee and swung around in her dining chair. She made little oohing noises as she spun in circles before Portia caught her chair and steadied her. "Have we decided to have a 'happy meal'?" she asked; the others groaned. "What now!?" she sounded confused again.

Viola whispered that 'a happy meal' was a children's package of chewable objects from a chain restaurant...

"Oh! How silly..." Portia murmured.

Ginger filled Hana's sippy cup; the little girl grabbed it gleefully and washed down her rice and beans. She plopped down the cup and looked at the counter with searching eyes. GingerKat opened a jar of banana and apples. Hana writhed with anticipation and grabbed at the spoon that came toward her mouth. Her mama let go of the spoon and Hana waved it in the air after swallowing the first serving. Ginger put the little jar in reach of her daughter and Hana aimed several times and missed the open top. Mama guided her hand to the inside and the princess pulled out a dessert ridden spoon which she shoved *nearly* into her mouth. She was met with applause from Aunties Viola and Portia who had been watching, holding their breaths.

John turned and asked, "What did I miss?"

"Your daughter is a prodigy! I've been telling you... does anyone listen? Nooo. I'm just a lone voice crying in the wilderness." was Viola's plaint.

"Cheer up Miss Martyr. Everyone believed you the first time," her sister comforted.

Ginger answered the actual question, "Your daughter can find her mouth with a spoon." He grinned and yawned.

She added, "Sweetheart take a nap. I'll relieve you once 'the vacuum' has finished her 'nanas."

"Sank you," he replied trying to speak *and* yawn.

Viola took over the spoon guiding; Ginger went to the helm and checked the instruments. "Any course changes coming up?"

"Nope, not until we pass north of Flores of the Azores in a few hours, and then we set and trim a few points more nor'east," he answered, "I stand relieved" He stood and stretched, then ambled down to the cabin deck and bed.

"I didn't even know there *were* islands out in the middle of the Atlantic..." muttered GingerKat as she panned and zoomed the GPS screen to look around.

"Those are just the one's on the chart because there're people living there," Portia commented, "You might be surprised how many islets and such are scattered throughout the seas... and unless you're careful, watchful and clever, you can miss them completely."

Viola added with a grin, "Or you could be dopey, drowsy and sluggish, and run up on one before you know it---sheer coincidence! Right Sis?"

"It was just that once, don't beat yourself up about it. No harm; no foul," she retorted.

"Portia has found *more* than her share of uncharted, unmapped bits of land where there certainly shouldn't have been even an atoll or reef... Mostly in the South Seas, but her talents aren't relegated to just one sea..." It was hard to tell if Viola was envious or pejorative, so Ginger asked about it.

Portia explained, "Viola has a theory that I tend to tack just enough off-sync with the *entire rest of the sailing world* to venture across stretches of water previously unsailed. It makes no sense nor reason, but there you are. Whatever the cause---I *do* have a curious knack for finding otherwise undiscovered obstacles." She almost appeared to gloat.

Ginger mused, "I'm no marine geologist, but aren't islands and such just mountains underwater?"

"Essentially, yes. What you also would be unaware of is that there are an equally astounding number of submerged seamounts..."

"Places in the middle of the ocean, you can stand on with your head just above water---or if your ship has too deep a draft: ram into," they added.

"The *Anna's* draft is between three and a half and four and a half feet, depending on our lading and passengers, right?" Ginger pressed.

"So the design says..."

"We've done a little more refined calculations in more real world situations and can affirm that..."

"These four yachts actually displace differently than the design calculations insist..."

"The depths of the amas almost always remain between two and a quarter to two and three quarters..."

"The akas are almost invariable between three to three and a quarter."

Ginger was stumped, "Why were Jean and the twins' calculations so skewed then?"

"MamaLena said that drafts *have* to be calculated at maximum load and occupancy *plus a third*, because of the variable salinity of ocean waters depending where you are..."

"If we plopped this girl down in the Dead Sea or Great Salt Lake for example..."

"We could almost polish the entire underside save a squinch along the 'keel-line'."

"Huhm. That sounds reasonable... Is it?" Ginger concluded.

"All we know is what the designs stipulate versus what we have actually measured..."

"Beyond that, darling, is no-man's land!"

Ginger looked at Hana, "Princess, follow your Auntie's example: Verify Everything!"

Although Hana had been watching the conversation after her face was wiped clean, she was ready to be on her own again. Portia set her on her feet next to the sofa. On a directive from his wife, while in New York City, John had searched and found a persian rug that fit the deck space of the bridge salon to a tee. It was huge but ensured that their feet stayed warmer and Hana's head wouldn't bruise quite as badly when she inevitably fell boom-boom. Which she promptly did; rolled to her belly and crawled to a new 'less-rude' part of the floor. She was not convinced, it seemed, that her spills were ever of her own doing.

Mocha came up after tucking John in bed and readied for playtime with Hana. This consisted of mostly staying just out of the girl's reach for as long as Hana had attention for the 'game.' Hana was developing *a lot* of attention. The moment Mocha thought she had time for a quick bath or time to examine a blank spot on the window, Hana was after her again.

15 January 94   From inside the bridge the world outside looks like a nice sunny, even warm day. We are a day or so away from turning to the northeast to follow the northern coast of Spain and France toward the Channel... it's a cold wind out there. The nice part of the clear days is that our little fleet is a visible line of sails fore and aft of us. John and I have been trying to stay in linear formation with them... *they* seem to be able to accomplish this feat easily. When we keep the *Anna* 'just so,' the last ship can't see the front ship---only the one directly off their prow is in sight. Whew! this entry is sounding like a page from a most soggy sea-head!

I took Mia and Lena's advice and have been 'slow-dancing' my way around the *Anna*. I have made almost all of my movements deliberate and after five days I can honestly say: I'm sore. Mechanical movements are easy---I get it! Intentional movements are demanding---boy, does Hana have it... I almost said 'easy,' but is that right? Judging from her efforts at balance and grasping... and how much she sleeps to rejuvenate her energy... Hmmm maybe not so easy. "...become like little children..." that guy may have been onto something.

There is little or no friction among this cadre of individuals, so I haven't had to put into practice any of my active reasoning exercises with regard to persons other than myself. I'm reviewing the plethora of occasions that I know I am susceptible to having my own center of gravity be usurped by whatever is around me at the time. I keep trying to expand my perspective, trying to more readily yield to the benefit of a doubt to belie my preconceived notions and predilections. I won't know if I'm making any headway until someone or something rubs me the wrong way. How does that saying go? 'It's easy for a monk to be enlightened in a cave...' or something like that. I'm looking forward to mingling with 'the masses,' but for a different cause than I once was driven to be among people.

"...To port is Dover, to starboard is Calais... We'll be to Velsen, then on to Amsterdam by evening," Portia announced.

Viola followed with, "We'll lay over for a day or so to re-supply and show you some sights. The trip along the North Sea Canal is pretty---but it's the canal belt around to the Riksmuseum that Amsterdam will be showing her best side."

John asked, "I suppose the launches will reach almost everywhere we need to go in the city? Are there any Coffeeshops along the canals?"

Viola and Portia each cocked an eye at him. "Sure."

"GingerKat you didn't mention that your husband smoked..."

"You two might enjoy the Bulldog Palace..."

"We're going to be at the Leidensplein anyway..."

"Just up the canal from the Museumplein."

Ginger was a little confused and looked to John. "Darling, do people smoke coffee in Holland?" Viola and Portia giggled.

John answered evenly, "For reasons known only to themselves the Dutch call their pot stores: 'coffeeshops'."

Her eyes grew wide, "Oh."

Portia and Viola persisted, "No alcohol, no hard drugs, no kids allowed inside... they're really innocuous,"

"*Harmless* is a good way to describe the the people that go there..."

"Which is why you might find more than the usual numbers of pickpockets and such in the very immediate neighborhoods of almost every one of them."

"A lucrative little eco-industry..."

Ginger put her hands over Hana's ears, "No K-I-D-S?"

John shrugged and replied, "No 'children' under eighteen... Hana isn't a full-fledged shopper as yet. We wouldn't have to leave her outside tied to a streetlamp or anything..."

They settled into an anchorage in Houthhavens and in the morning took the *Agate* into the old canals to Museumplein. John wore Hana's sling, as he was the least likely to become overly weary of carrying her. Neither of them had been in a museum-gallery to rival the museums and galleries around the park. For an early dinner they went back along the canal to a place where Viola and Portia wanted to dine once more. The staff had all changed but the menu was still as great as it ever was. The next day, fully restocked and ready for the short last leg of the voyage they went the couple hundred miles up the coast and entered the Kiel Canal to the Baltic.

18 January 94   Amsterdam wasn't a great trial of my newfound balance---everybody was so nice! Just when I thought I'd really have to bite my tongue over anticipated lines or wholly inadequate service, or unfairness at the markets, shops or anywhere... all I got instead were kind words, genial service, timely lines---with friendly people to chat with---and solicitous market and shopkeepers. As we walked the streets I noticed they even have countdown clocks at the tram stops so riders know precisely when to expect the next tram. I shouldn't neglect to mention the clearly marked paved surfaces for pedestrians, bicycles and motor traffic. How's a girl supposed to work on herself in a paradise like that! Maybe the crowds at the Olympic venues next month will bring it on...

I just reread the initial entries in this journal. I don't remember waking up one morning and being any different, but what I write in these pages doesn't seem to reflect who I thought I was before: there are no mentions of odorous clients, really awful diners, my constant drive to get someplace faster, my smugness---most especially that. Where did my smug, 'I-know-better-than-you-could-possibly-even-in-a-million-years-evolve-to-know attitude go? Not that I'm pining for it---just noticing its absence is all.

John and I are compiling a list of passages, some longer than others, that we are going to memorize. Something to have ready to fill our minds instead of what would habitually squat in the place of real thought. I've already begun with that often quoted statement from Goethe or somebody about committing to do something. I haven't got it word-perfect yet, but I'll write it in here when I do. Uh, if anyone ever reads this, you'll just have to take my word for it that it's written from memory. John said his first selection would be a poem by Rudyard Kipling that he always liked as a younger man: *If.* I like poetry. I especially like the inspiring lines that lift my spirit and offer me a new perspective on my own condition.

Viola and Portia insisted on an obstetrics examination to be sure our next little girl is developing nicely. The *Hannah Belle* has all kinds of equipment most yachts don't carry. For instance what would the average yachtsman do with an ultrasound imaging setup anyway? To cut to the chase here: they delivered my fluids and smears and blood to a lab they've worked with before in Amsterdam---we are supposed to hear back about everything before we even get to Gotland. Have I mentioned how wonderful my family is?

"Except for having to use the outboards a lot more, I *really* like canals," smiled John as they all looked out the bridge salon windows at the passing German-Danish countryside. "It's like flying low over the fields on a very slow magic carpet."

The radio came alive, "This is the *Pebble*. There is a storm in the Baltic just now and we may have to stopover in Rendsburg for the night... We will keep monitoring the situation."

91

A second voice, a woman's, announced, "Ilsa and Eva will treat everyone to dinner at the 'Dalmatien'..."

Viola whispered to Portia, "Easy pickins; you owe me one swiss franc!"

Ginger overheard, "What?"

Portia explained, "Viola spent *one* spring with Ilsa and Carl... and she was so sure she *knew* Ilsa; she bet me that Ilsa would convince Eva to treat everyone to dinner---in exchange they would get to have a shopping holiday. Don't ask me what is so interesting about shopping in Rendsburg, but there you go," and she handed her sister the franc.

Viola flipped it into the air and caught it, "Double or nothing? Call it: heads or tails?"

Portia rolled her eyes, "You're incorrigible."

The clouds were looming as they made harbor below the shops and restaurants of Rendsburg. It became apparent why Ilsa and Eva were delighted for an excuse to anchor here for the night---lots of outdoor markets, loads of great restaurants and then as if that weren't enough: a *chocolate* factory. They made the best of their *forced* layover waiting for a break in the Baltic weather.

The Baltic storm may not have actually been as serious as first thought. It seems Ilsa and Eva were the ones monitoring the weather forecasts and they initiated the fleet-wide warning. 'No harm, no foul,' as Viola and Portia would say.

The fleet made the Larrson cove a day later than expected, but all was well. The shipyards were running at their lowest ebb when Euell, Nils and Carl left them at the end of September. Sometime along the way orders and pending contracts came to fruition. The cove was populated with boats and ships of all sorts and in various states of construction. Many pleasure craft awaited engines or other components, a couple yachts---one thirty meter motor sailor and one thirty-six meter motor yacht---each only waiting on inspection and registration to fill the commissions. There were no less than five military craft for which the yard was contracted to only build the hulls and superstructures. Those were motor cats and one hovercraft. The Larrsons and Eriksons got right to work as soon as their ships anchored and their luggage was transferred back to their houses. The rest of the company disembarked and went to the family cemetery to offer their respects to their interred family.

James Olaf Henry Erikson, Jimmy, made a quick change of clothes and headed off to Stockholm and his firm's offices. His 'sabbatical' from his own firm wasn't really an absence. He was in constant communication and still managed most daily operations while seeing to his familial obligations in the States. It was an internet-web-based software firm just getting off the ground---his long-distance management was actually a worthwhile test of their enterprise solutions.

Becka went along with him, but for different reasons. She was completing graduate studies, also in Computer Science, and Jimmy promised her a position with his start-up after her graduation. Attractive as that prospect was, her main focus was on a reunion with her latest 'experiment d'amor.'

Alfred and Vera planned a little trip up to Gothenburg to see the sights. They even invited John and Ginger to come along. Vera explained, "We know we'll be busy with the Games and seeing the sights of Oslo over the next month, so we thought this would be a marvelous opportunity for us to get away, be tourists and---" with a wink, "---reacquaint ourselves."

GingerKat looked to John, "Could we take them on the *Anna* so they can have even more 'free time'? If you think we could go too, I mean..."

John shifted Hana to his other hip, then decided to set her on her feet which she had evidently been trying to do anyway. He responded with his eyes fixed on his little princess the whole while,

"Sure dear, whatever you wish. This is your decision as much as mine... I'm pretty sure Hana doesn't mind yet where she sleeps and eats."

Ginger grinned and replied to Vera, "That's *my* man! *Would* you and Alfred like to have the forward stateroom and leave the *Tygress* here?"

Alfred spoke up before Vera could get out: 'We'd be delighted,' he said, "As long as it's not an intrusion. You two are still 'charting your own way forward' after all..."

Vera finished with, "We certainly *will* take you up on your most generous offer! Will tomorrow morning be convenient for us to come aboard and weigh anchor?"

During this conversation, Hana made two or three wobbly steps from her daddy's pant leg to clutch at her mother's then back again. She was about to make the round trip once more when she plopped down on the cold ground. It was much less forgiving than her rug-covered 'playroom' on the *Anna* so she set her little face for a protest of the *total injustice* of it all.

Ginger and John both noticed the build up and waited to see what she would *actually* do---as they tried to appear still involved in the 'adult' conversation with Vera and Alfred. Hana bleated out a moment's cry, and when no one instantly rescued her she yelled louder. John put down a finger for her to grab but her eyes were now filling with tears and she'd have none of it.

Ginger observed, "She's wanting all or nothing on this one... Let's see what *nothing* does for her?"

Hana *wasn't* so preoccupied with screaming that she wasn't already trying to stand up again. As she gained her feet her protests ceased abruptly and she started all over to make the round trips between their legs as if there were no interruption. John and GingerKat were so pleased with themselves they each reached down for Hana at the same time and bumped their heads. Inspired, and since Hana was attached to John's leg at present, Ginger plopped down next to her and began whimpering with mock cries of frustration. Hana stood looking at the surprising sight then reached and touched her mother's forehead. Ginger instantly stopped her caterwalling and smiled. Hana smiled back and looked up at her daddy.

"You're so good to us Hana Nasrin!" and he hoisted up Ginger by her hand as he raised Hana to his hip once more. "Shall we head on over to your grandparents house and get ready for supper?"

21 January 94   As hoped, our little girl is growing and so am I. I've begun to put on a little weight. John is sweet and tells me I'm filling out in all the right places. What are the right places for getting larger? I'm not showing much but my appetite is growing. Something that has been niggling at the corners of my mind about our responsibility to a larger world, regarding our sudden wealth, is that I've only ever focused on the plights of struggling writers in North America and getting their stories told. I am thinking that one way John and I can make as great a contribution to our families' humanitarian activities is: to bring the stories and writings of the obscure and outcast in troubled areas of the globe to the consciousness of people in the industrialized world. I need to go over that with Lila and Olivia; they certainly have a flair for finding just the right showcase for the scientific revelations of our human unity.

It's all such a whirlwind in my mind. I am sure my latest musings are spurred on in part by my memory work from Murray and Goethe: "...Until one is committed, there is hesitancy, the chance to draw back, always ineffectiveness. Concerning all acts of initiative and creation, there is one elementary truth the ignorance of which kills countless ideas and splendid plans: that the moment one definitely commits oneself, then providence moves too. A whole stream of events issues from the decision, raising in one's favor all manner of unforeseen incidents, meetings and material assistance, which no man could have dreamt would have come his way. I learned a deep respect for one of Goethe's couplets: 'Whatever you can do or dream you can, begin it. Boldness has genius, power and magic in it'!'" W. H. Murray wrote those lines in his journal later published as: *The Scottish Himalayan Expedition*. Gee, maybe one day someone will take an excerpt from John's journals and it will become as ubiquitous as this one from Murray and Goethe?

It has a two-fold effect on me, to repeat this passage to myself or aloud: I shut down the eddies of thought which might otherwise wind and wind through my mind, constructing nothing and wasting energy. And secondly, I am emboldened to consider carefully any path before setting foot upon it---because once committed, I am consumed with making it so.

John promises that on our trip to Gothenburg he will recite the Kipling poem. I can't wait. He has such a nice voice and even though it takes him a while to get an idea settled fully into his mind... once he does he never looks back. I think that's one of our common traits and why, so far, we have been such good counterparts for each other. That's a tough one to fully work through. If the family arranged as much as they seem to have, where our first meeting is concerned, they certainly took a *big* chance that anything at all might come of it. On the other hand: Were John and I manipulated so deftly that we never stood a chance, as Oliver would say? If that's the case, why don't I feel violated, or used, or resentful, or something? Instead I just feel... gratitude! Try as I might to conjure misgivings, to evoke a feeling of skepticism... I just can't do it. I asked John if he had given this any thought yet. He replied, "GingerKat, I've been wrested and wrangled, and pushed around all my life. At least this time around someone had the courtesy of giving me all the background I could ever ask for and then when push came to shove, left me to my own devices to do with all that information as I saw fit! ...Besides you're the most wonderful woman, the wisest and greatest treasure a man could ever hope to gain on this earth..."

Okay, I added that last bit about being wonderful and the greatest, and wise and all, but a girl can dream! One of my favorite lines from Teddy Roosevelt is, "Do what you can, with what you have, where you are." John and I have a lot to work with; now all we need to learn is how to always be present and be able to do!

"*Oh*!! Sorry, I *really* should have knocked!" John backed out of the doorway and made a face of absolute embarrassment to Hana who just grinned back at him from his arms. Muted laughter from the stateroom wafted up behind him as he tip-toed to the companionway and rejoined Ginger on the bridge.

"I am such a buffoon! You'd think I was raised in an orphanage or something! I didn't knock! I just burst in on Alfred and Vera who were in... uh... very... uh... *athletic* positions..."

Ginger put down her pen and giggled, "John, John, John! Tsk, tsk, tsk... Whatever am I going to do with you? No one said you had to find out this very minute if they wanted to go to the golf course tomorrow! It was just nice of those folks on the yacht next to us to give us their tee-time..."

"I know, but you were busy writing and Hana was through eating... I just... Well, I *didn't think*! Man, I *really* didn't think..." John reviewed.

Alfred and Vera came up and joined them in the bridge salon. Smiling broadly, Alfred offered, "Aren't y'all too newly wed to *already* need advice on sexual postures from us? There must be a copy of the Kama Sutra around here somewhere..." He began to pull books from the shelf as if really searching.

Vera tried to keep a straight face, but burst out laughing. John turned beet red all over again. GingerKat covered, "Forgive my husband. He's not as creative as he at first appears..." If possible John grew even redder.

"Actually, so long as you're accepting company now..." Ginger began, staring at John then back with a smile to Vera, "Those nice

Italians on the next boat gave us their tee-time for tomorrow morning and John was just *that excited* that he *just had* to ask you this very minute!"

Vera grinned and looked to Fred, "How delightful! What do you think, oh slave of love?"

Again John was nearly recovered; then he was once again reddened by embarrassment. He put his face in his hands and Hana pulled a finger away thinking it was peek-a-boo.

Alfred answered, "I can't begin to *mount* a defense against our not going..."

Ginger and Vera were near in stitches just watching the effect of the chitchat on John.

"Alright," Ginger decided, "Just try not to wear anything too *revealing* so John will be more comfortable."

"I'm sorry for barging in! It was thoughtless... I am thoroughly chastened!" John surrendered.

Vera put her hand to his cheek. "Johnny it's quite alright. Actually, thank you for being so excited in wanting us to join you."

"You're very kind." John accepted most gratefully.

GingerKat put away her journal and stretched. "On an unrelated topic... Alfred, I have been wondering about how John and I can begin to contribute to the humanitarian efforts the family is involved in. I was thinking about how many writers and poets there must be in places of crisis who have no wider audience for their experiences..." All three of them raised their brows at the novelty of the idea.

Vera responded, "Do what you know best! That's how the *Hannah* and the *Ananke* got rolling with their projects."

With only about eight hours of daylight, a 'morning' tee-time was ten-fifteen. The Delsjo Golf Club was a very pleasant course with a most satisfactory practice area. Ginger had never taken up the sport and so she just strolled along with the three-some. Hana rode in her sling or, less often, on John's pull cart with his clubs. At three, when they were heading back to the *Anna* from a different direction than their arrival, they discovered the Liseberg Amusement Park. Naturally that was a must for the next day for the Backhouses. Fred and Vera went to the great museum housed in the old Swedish East India Company building. They all gathered for dinner in town that evening.

"This has been a *very* wonderful and relaxing three days!" Vera toasted on their last evening. "Let alone getting to spend so much time with you two, rather you three..." and she reached out a finger for Hana to grab.

John asked, "Has anyone else noticed that there's a distinctive Scottish flavor to this city?"

Fred responded, "If it weren't for the Dutch and the Scottish, this city might not be here at all. It was something of a home away from home for both groups for the longest time. You've noticed all the canals? It's not by accident; the city was modeled to some degree after Amsterdam!"

Ginger added, "Johnny if there were ever a great place to settle down, this is about as good as it gets. I might even be persuaded to take up golf! You three make it seem like a pretty easy pastime to pick up as a hobby..."

The others looked at each other. Vera replied, "Oh, it's a simple enough game: hit the ball, follow the ball, hit it again. Your mother was a natural at the sport by the way. She frustrated your grandfather often enough on the links!"

GingerKat looked to John, "I *could* be a natural! Just like mama... We shall come back here often Johnny! And let's begin looking for port cities with parks, golf courses and great museums. We have a family to raise and I would like our girls to have a taste of all these wonderful places. *Anna* is home, but she can go anywhere, so let's make a list."

"And for their education?" John queried.

Ginger turned to Alfred, "What was your area of study at University?"

Fred looked to Vera, then smiled and answered, "Mostly: Vera-ology! I was an awful student. I took humanities courses---thinking I'd like to teach. I switched to engineering---thinking I'd like to build. I studied architecture, interior design and I even took two years of pre-med... I never graduated. The only two subjects I *was* most thoroughly educated in was golf and Vera."

Vera nodded, "It's true; he was a most persistent suitor. I couldn't believe it at first..."

Alfred interrupted, "'At first,' meaning the initial five years of my ardent and evident interest."

She continued, "Then he managed to get me on the golf course *at least* every weekend, and I was doomed. Four hours of close contact that often... *Even I* realized he was seriously smitten---and with *me* of all people!"

John and Ginger were both stunned at those words, "What do you mean, 'and you of all people?' You're great! That's as plain as the nose on your face!"

Fred added, "Right?!"

Vera blushed, "You should have seen me back then, I was a wreck. Years of anxiety over Izzy and Anna's disappearances, and you two of course. Alone... without my best friend... If it hadn't been for Olivia and Ronia I couldn't have gotten through it at all. I had the work, but I used it to focus my mind on a search for others not so much my *self*. It took Alfred here to gradually loosen me up and take off my blinders..."

She leaned her head on Fred's shoulder. "Then of course he was so much *younger* than I was, and I *couldn't* have imagined in a million years that a young man, who really had his pick of any woman he wanted..." Ginger and John simply looked slightly quizzical.

"Really! You see him now... he didn't get this good-looking over night! But he wanted me. And I was a dowdy, frumpy, lab-coated doctor-person. When Anna left my life I kinda went to seed..."

Neither John nor Ginger could envision how this ravishing beauty, who was closer to nubile than senile by miles, could ever have been called 'dowdy or frumpy.' Her thick blond hair was richly golden, her physique was that of a nordic goddess and her face showed not a crease or wrinkle... In short she was an ageless beauty of clearly divine origins. They said as much and it was Vera's turn to blush beet red.

"What can I say: the work works! Of course it helps to have constant advice from the twins and their daughters, and from Lila and Olivia---they are the root and source of timelessness---I am a mere acolyte compared to them."

Alfred had to nod his agreement at that. "The Livingson men and women are... uh... *special*... there's no getting around it."

Ginger made another announcement, "Johnny, I want to spend as much time with our family as possible! Even though I am only just now recognizing how fu... how messed up I am... I want to live up to the standards our family has set!"

Johnny held up his hand as if writing a list upon it, "One: Find port cities with golf courses, galleries and museums. Two: Educate girls to international cosmopolitan standards. Three: Stay close to family..." He looked at his wife, "Am I getting it all?"

Ginger swatted him on the side of the head, "Four: Don't sass Mama!"

Fred whispered to John, "Can you see the faces of the two men at the table behind me?" John casually looked over his shoulder and subtly nodded.

"Etch their faces into your mind, please..."

At a loss for reasons, John made a mental note of distinguishing characteristics, as if they were screen idols and he would want to recognize them again. Again he nodded. The two men rose and he noted their heights and build. Fred stood up at that moment and reached for his water glass, spilling it on the floor at the men's feet.

"Oops, I'm so clumsy. Please forgive me gentlemen!" The two men smiled faintly and said to think nothing of it, then left the dining room.

"What was that all about, Alfred?" John had to ask.

"I can't be sure because I only caught snatches of their conversation, but when people use words and phrases like: 'there will be lax security,' and 'it will be moved to a place of easier access...' I tend to get my guard up." He responded.

Vera asked, "Security where? Access to what?"

"I only heard 'shriek,' and 'Olympics,' I'm afraid. Ring any bells with y'all? This doesn't sound on the level to me... Of course it could be nothing but two guys reviewing the position of their company's booth at the opening ceremonies---but I don't think so."

Ginger added off-handedly, "Shriek is 'The Scream,' I did a piece on Munch in my undergrad sociology class... then edited a bio on him more recently. The title of the painting supposedly came from his saying, '...*I was walking along a path with two friends, the sun was setting, suddenly the sky turned blood red. I paused, feeling exhausted, and leaned on the fence. There was blood and tongues of fire above the blue-black fjord and the city. My friends walked on, and I stood there trembling with anxiety and I sensed an infinite shriek passing through nature...*' They say it was the eruption of Krakatoa that put so much ash and dust in the sky world-wide, and caused vivid colors in the morning and evening skies for a year or so afterwards. That and his sister was in the insane asylum up the road from the place depicted in the painting..."

That got everyone's attention. Vera asked, "Where is the

'Scream' exhibited?"

Ginger said simply, "Munch was a Norwegian from Oslo..."

Fred suggested, "A gallery in Oslo then? And Lillehammer is just up the road..."

John couldn't help himself, "Those two guys weren't what I would call nefarious, in fact if I passed them on the street I'd take them for yuppies..."

Fred grinned, "Fair enough. But as long as we will be in the neighborhood on the twelfth---at the highly attended Opening Ceremony which will require a great number of security personnel---does anyone mind if I hang out near whichever gallery the painting is? Any volunteers to keep me company?" Three hands went up, then four as Ginger put up Hana's arm. "Alright then, 'and thank you for your support'."

Ginger giggled, "Your welcome Mr. Bartles and James..."

It wasn't difficult to find out in which gallery the 'Scream' was hanging. All they had to do was ask their waitress.

"That's in the Oslo National Gallery. I'm an art history major---our classes have made trips to all the galleries of scandinavia..."

John mentioned, under his breath, as they left the restaurant, "Art History... That's a fru-fru version of an English Major, no wonder she's waiting tables---It's either that or practicing the phrase: 'Do you want fries with that...'"

24 January 94   The weekend with Vera and Fred was illuminating to say the least, and we also have an interesting diversion planned for the twelfth of February, hopefully not *instead of* the Opening Ceremonies in Lillehammer. I hope there's a warm cafe across from the gallery, standing out of doors in a cloak-and-daggeresque melodramatic 'stake-out' is not what Hana and I signed up for.

I was serious about the *Anna* being our new home. Why not, our parents, grandparents and even great-grandparents all lived on these boats at one time or another... they're like mobile estates for us. If John and I can persuade Vera and Fred to live aboard the *Anna* too, then our girls can be home-schooled. Technology being what it is nowadays, they shouldn't ever feel isolated. And what shall our second bundle of joy be called? I'm leaning toward *Sonia Isabel*, I wonder what John's thought of... I must ask again. Last time he just shrugged and said he'd find a book of names. Find a book of names?! Honestly, sometimes he can be so thick! We have all our family history, all the ports of call and interesting people we've met... and he wants to pick names from a book. Okay GingerKat... Let's give him a little more credit than that. A broader selection allows for more options---look at *Hana Nasrin*, now *that* wouldn't have crossed my radar. I should ask Viola and Portia, they have like twelve languages in their heads to choose from...

John and I had better also begin gathering something more than just English and a little Spanish and French. One thing at a time Ginger-girl. First 'wake up' then learn to speak. Exercises, exercises, exercises. This week I have practiced 'Not-say-I,' 'Picking a Center' a day, my on-going 'Memorization' to occupy the place, also 'Active Reasoning,' and I have studied and studied the diagrams and charts for clues and new insights. Not surprisingly, every time I pick a different center to observe and exercise, I see something I'd never noticed before. Like yesterday, I picked my moving center. I have perhaps thirty habitual postures that my body simply moves between. I know because when I slow down there are definitely harder transitions which always arrive at easier positions---the harder transitional movements are the ones between postures---I'm convinced. I asked John to observe me all afternoon, when he could, and he picked out my usual postures---the very ones that were the easier stations I'd noticed.

Active reasoning is still not second nature for me. I can't say how much I get wrapped up in my own view of how something is and ignore the chance to take a look from a different perspective of it. When I decide someone is such and such a way, as far as I am concerned, that's it. Not accounting for the fact that *they* are likely under influences to which *they* mechanically react, that *they* have their own most used leaks; that *they* are the product of the impacts of their society, family and friends---Sounds too familiar. How can I possibly keep making accounts against people when they aren't responsible for their own reactions---they are programmed, mechanical and essentially in the world of illusions all their 'waking' days---exactly what I am trying NOT to be! I *am* trying.

27 January 94   Fred and Vera are seriously considering moving aboard! Yay! Sam and Ronia are settling into Euell and Katy's home and so they are making a gift of the *Tygress* to Jimmy or Becka, whichever one would like it. They actually consulted me first. I am so honored to be a part of this family! Have I mentioned that lately? Anyway, Jimmy has his own good-sized motor boat. Becka has always loved the *Tygress's* lines and ease of sailing. I bet she has an engine installed if she takes possession. Oh, her 'experiment,' must not have ended up as she'd hoped. She's been wearing black a lot more lately, and I don't think it has to do with fashion... I must find time to have a girl-to-girl with her.

The *Anna* will be mooring in Killengen off Bygdoy Island in Oslo beginning the first week of February. Ilsa was so excited that she and Nils were invited to consult for the Swedish Biathalon teams... Yes, 'teams.' Women began competing two years ago! Of the six sports at the winter games, biathalon and figure skating have to be my personal favorites. When I was little, sitting in front of the television and watching as many of the events as the network covered was a very special time, and it only came around every four years---very special. After the broadcasts I'd get out my twenty-two rifle, take the scope off, then ski through the fields outside of town. I pretended I was: 'the first and greatest woman biathelete in the world!' I shot cans off fence rails, and skied around in a giant circle (putting the cans back up along the way) and then do it all over again... Those were the days. I wasn't much of a skater, but I always thought it was beautiful to watch.

This will be so exciting---after we do our little stake-out at the National Gallery thingie with Alfred. (John and I aren't putting much stock in the whole bogey-man art thieves thing, but we do want Fred and Vera aboard the *Anna*---so the twelfth is 'stake-out day'!) Ilsa and Nils have trained up at Lillehammer with their teams in the past and spent enough time in Oslo to assure me that there are a number of warm cafes and restaurants across the streets from the Gallery. Fred has already decided each of us will take a side of the building to watch if we can not locate where in the gallery they are displaying the painting. Vera suggested they could get in anywhere regardless of the painting's location... so, we cover the whole thing.

It's been twelve days since I began my repetitive movements observations that the twins suggested. I tried the 'hands-in-motion' and to my surprise I think a different part of my mind has kicked into gear---two parts actually: one for one hand and one for the other. Too Cool! I want to get a metronome and check this objectively... so I'll really know if there is improvement. On a related matter, physically speaking, Viola gave me another ultrasound and the sonogram is conclusive---there is a creature growing inside me! Fortunately human---thankfully female, according to Lena and Mia anyway. No one has challenged their judgement in... well: Ever... so here comes Sonia Isabel. John came up with Vera Virginia: Vee-Vee or Viveka for short (meaning: small woman, coincidentally) NOT. Then he offered: *Miranda Linn*. It means 'Flower of Admiration'--- keeping up with our little wild rose and all... Hmmm. MirandaLinn Isabel Backhouse. Sonia Isabel MirandaLinn Backhouse... Decisions, decisions.

30 January 94   Sonia (Wise) Isabelle (God is Bountiful) MirandaLinn (Flower of Admiration) That should cover all the bases. The spelling of Isabelle is tribute to the woman who started it all for us, I know Izzy wouldn't mind in the least. So 'The bountiful wisdom of God is a flower of admiration'---A lot to live up to, but always aim high! HanaRin and MirandaLinn, I think we've got some winners here. It was pretty well cinched when Vera pointed out that Myra is a nickname for Miranda... Two names of our revered women in one! How cool is that?!

We head to Oslo soon. The *Pebble* is already there. Nils and Ilsa are involved in the teams' preliminary on-site training at the Birkebeineren Skistadion in Lillehammer itself---so many of the venues are spread across the countryside. The ice skating is supposed to be in Hamar, between Lillehammer and Oslo. Oh boy!

Viola and Portia will be on the *Anna* for the trip. They have promised to expand some of my exercises to include even more integration of my centers. John has begun a similar regimen under Fred's tutelage. Anyway, I'm not supposed to give it a moment's thought, no anxiety, no expectations... I'm trying.

Even though we no longer have any ancestors to hear, Hana, John and I have made little niches around the *Anna* for some of our own forebears---it just feels right somehow to remember the giants' shoulders upon which we now stand---And they're good reminding factors. I wish to remember myself! Always easier decided than done, but we must have a wish. Okay, the six leaks are: unnecessary movements, uncontrolled talking, lying, negative emotions, inner considering and uncontrolled imagination. The influences are in two categories---inner: emotional background-attitudes, my physiological processes, unbridled thoughts and ever-changing desires; outer: power of suggestion, associations of form and relationship and the perceived superiority of other people. How am I doing? Movements? I have noticed that I have tensions in my body that don't have any obvious cause... just a huge overuse of muscles there. Talking? I need John to estimate that for me... I think I'm doing really well with that one. Lying? I am failing miserably at this one. I haven't completely owned the fact that I am not *one* particular individual but am an amalgam of Gingers and they all claim to be 'me.' Negative Emotions? I may be getting better at not showing them, but I sure know they are there! Uncontrolled imagination? Yep. I want to follow a thought through to its conclusion *but* off my mind wanders through associations that just pop up as one and another facet of the topic gives rise to them---like a dog chasing a squirrel. Identification. I had to ask several times of several of my teachers to define this for me. The explanation I understand best is: 'When something has me, and I no longer have it'... I took that to mean losing myself in an account against someone, or dwelling on a thing, activity or expectation to the exclusion of all reason. Mia put it like this: 'Thinking goes in a direction, identification goes in circles.' That makes sense.

So how about the influences---I am not free of myself yet. I know I am still pulled this way and that by the external ones. The internal ones? I know I have conflicting desires---that little episode at the dinner table the other night was a good example of that dilemma. I think unbridled thoughts, or ineffectual thinking is a root cause of my identifications---so yep, still have those. As far as physiological processes go, I'm a sea of hormones just now---thank god I haven't killed anybody!

"Bygdoy is the Museum Island! This is great!" Vera announced as the *Anna* sailed almost into Oslo proper.

Since Ilsa and Eva's families were all on the *Pebble*, the *Ananke's* crew transferred to the *Hannah* to minimize the number of moorings we require---so that's why Viola and Portia were aboard the *Anna* once more.

Viola reiterated, "And, you may be interested in knowing that as property goes, this is the most expensive real estate in Norway. Thankfully we've permission for just using the fjord..."

Portia added, "I don't want to think about what a lease would be ashore!"

"That's sobering," John commented. "Can we stay in this anchorage for the duration of the games?"

"That's what Oliver says... and daddy knows best!" Viola responded.

Once they anchored and got settled for the weeks ahead, Alfred and Vera went onto the foredeck. He looked out over the fjord and islands. "We have seen some of the most beautiful places on earth, and this certainly rates as one of them. It's so much like Puget Sound and the San Juans---even the climate and weather!"

Vera put her arm around his waist. "It really is. It reminds me so much of the first sailing trip you took me on up to Orca's Island---and our first kiss..." she sighed. A smile spread across his face at the recollection; he sighed too...

Inside the bridge, Portia carried Hana on her hip; Viola looked out at Alfred and Vera. "Those two are such a cute couple, and our great nephew Alfred is such a force of nature---it really took someone of Vera's power to keep rein on him."

Portia remarked, "And to get him to maintain a domestic life in Tahoe for as long as they did---Whew! What a woman!"

That piqued Ginger's curiosity, "...Force of nature? Powerful woman? Are we talking about the same two gentle people?"

Portia handed Hana over to John, "Oh yeah. Like clouds are gentle..."

Viola added, "...Until the storm breaks, then they don't seem so cuddly!"

John had to ask, "Huh?"

Viola related a 'little' story. "It was maybe three years after Vera moved to Tahoe. Alfred was home from University---not graduated mind you---just done with it for a while. Anyway, Alfie suggested that he stay in Tahoe and tend the Mercantile, which Alfred did. There was a blizzard that winter and no one could get out and about for days. Vera had been receiving newspapers from the Chicago area and scanning them every week. The snow gave her an opportunity to catch up on past issues, and Fred helped. Years before, he had been involved in the search across northern Indiana and Illinois--- inquiring at clinics and hospitals until he had to return to University. He didn't participate again with that phase of the quest.

On this new go around he was dutifully looking through the various news articles and just asked off-handedly how the search of orphanages in *New Mexico* had gone... Vera stared at him blankly...

"We didn't check them..." she muttered.

Alfred bounded for the telephone and began assembling lists of orphanages in a five state area around the accident site. When the snow abated, it was Alfred who flew down to New Mexico to begin making the tedious inquiries of every single institution. He called back daily with updates for Vera. She wanted to have gone along, but with Olivia and Ronia away indefinitely, she was the only physician in town. There was a rash of flu and other ailments following the harsh weather that kept her tied to Tahoe. Once that subsided she made the decision to fly down and assist on weekends. Nearly every weekend Alfred flew up to fetch her and every Monday returned her.

It was a long and seemingly insurmountable task making visit after visit and poring over the records of every *possible* haven for orphans. In the first months, Fred eliminated New Mexico. Vera joined him when she could and over the rest of that year they eliminated Oklahoma and Arkansas. Alfred kept up the task in Louisiana until it too was proven to be absent the one child meeting their specific criteria. Next came Texas. It had been two years and Alfred was still indomitable. Vera began to have a whole new respect for this man who once wished her 'Pappy Burstday, Beera' as a toddler.

He started south and worked his way north. As always, beginning with cities or towns with V.A. clinics or hospitals and then covering the surrounding areas. At the end of that year, on a weekend with Vera at his side, they drove up to an orphanage in Ft. Worth. They didn't even have to ask to search the records---as they approached the main building some boys were having an informal scrimmage on the front lawn. There was Robert's face on a young man with the near exact build and height as their lost cousin. Alfred stood staring at him as Vera went on inside and verified just this *one* young man's files. The football landed at Fred's feet and when he picked it up to return it to the boys, there was John looking him in eye.

"Here you go buddy," Alfred said and handed it to him. John took it and threw a *long* pass to one of his friends.

"Nice arm!" Fred commented.

"Thanks mister..." John replied, "All-State quarterback three years running! Next year at this time I'll be at Rice, maybe in their starting line-up," he said proudly.

Vera emerged from the building with a grin wider than her face. She nodded to Fred and he took her by the arm and led her to the car.

"Take a picture or two of him, that's all the satisfaction we'll get today." He repeated the gist of his brief encounter with John, "...and he's gotten a scholarship to Rice---all on his own!"

They returned to Tahoe and passed around the photos. It was a bittersweet celebration. Vera gave all the credit to Alfred, who gave it right back to her. Fred picked up one of the newspapers among the stacks of them from the upper midwest and said, now for our other cousin. Amazingly, on the second page of that very issue, he saw a line that changed Vera's whole demeanor. She had really let herself go over the last several years and looked to be ten years older than she was. When Alfred handed her that paper, folded to the article he'd just found, those years dropped from her like a dress seven sizes too large.

"Virginia Kaitlyn Belle *Amourson*!?" She cried for hours. It was probably the tears, but maybe the swelling of hope so soon on the heels of finding Robert and Izzy's boy---whatever it was, when she emerged from her room dressed to fly to Chicago, she looked like a million bucks. Alfred flew her to a small airfield outside the city proper and they went to the Tribune building.

Well, you probably know the rest: How Vera saw you with your so-called parents, how you looked exactly like your mother at that age---which coincidently was about the same age at which Vera first met Anna---when they were both gawky out-of-place girls in the Tahoe school. Fred flew her to Etna Green and she cleared up all the mysteries surrounding Anna's disappearance. Fred has been the one to follow everything you two have done since John was eighteen and Ginger was nine. Over *all* the intervening years they kept house in Tahoe---Vera at the clinic and Fred at the Mercantile."

John interrupted, "Kaitlyn and Vera said it was Harry who had followed our every move, and decision, and pursuit..."

Ginger stared out the window at the couple on the deck, "But it was *Alfred*...?"

Portia answered, "Far be it from me to contradict either of those ladies, but *we know* as a verified fact that it was Alfred who made the flights, took the pictures and kept the journals. He was certain to have kept Harry and MamaKat informed. But *it was always* Alfred and Vera."

Viola interjected, "It was Alfred who set the timing and made the arrangements for Ginger's 'inheritance meeting' in San Francisco. Ginger, you likely don't remember the man who greeted you at that office, and then conducted you into the 'reading of the will'... That was Alfred---he was also the one who wrote the script for that little drama.

And John, when you were at Texas Instruments after graduation and made that breakthrough in micro-circuits, didn't you find it odd that the *Vice-President* of your department got news of your discovery before you had told *anybody?* Or: when you were at Cisco Systems and came up with that truly innovative enterprise solution that saved so much manpower, money and time to implement---*and again* it was on your director's desk with your name on it by the next morning? Or when you decided to distance yourself from the hectic pace of the city and buy some land up north---You probably don't remember the real estate agent who led you to the property and closed the deal without your having to do anything but sign the paperwork?"

Portia added, "Or more recently, you certainly won't have realized that when you mailed out your abstracts for publication to all those publishing houses---how it was *only* Boundary Press who actually received it---and how the *only* 'available agent' was our Ginger?"

The Backhouses stared back at Viola and Portia as if in shock or trauma. Ginger almost whispered, "That was *all* Alfred's doing?!"

Viola answered, "Alfred *and* Vera---the dynamic duo!"

John was overwhelmed, "Those particular discoveries and innovations are what got me promotions, raises and offers that ultimately landed me enough money to consider leaving the corporate world entirely... and decide to be a writer... *that* decision brought..." and his voice trailed off into silence. John and Ginger stared out at the two 'gentle people' on the foredeck."

Portia had to add, "I don't suppose he mentioned that he's: a registered nurse, a licensed pilot, a sea captain, an incredibly successful entrepreneur who also has his own detective agency--- which is routinely contracted by Interpol, or that he never actually finished any one degree plan while at University---he's tested out of everything he ever wished to add to his repertoire."

Viola remembered, "Oh! And he passed the bar exams in New York, California, Illinois and Texas just on the off-chance he *might* have to manage *any* legal matters on your or Ginger's behalf! No small feat there..."

Outside Alfred corrected Vera, "No my love, our first kiss was right here on this very foredeck, while anchored in Kaneohe Bay on your sixteenth birthday..."

Vera kissed his forehead, "Unfortunately you leapt off my lap and ran away from me on that occasion. Mmmm, the first kiss *I* was thinking of was on the *Tygress* in the East Sound, after which you *didn't* leap off my lap and run away..." she winked.

He put his mouth close to her ear, "No I certainly couldn't have run away on that occasion. You have amazingly strong legs... I almost couldn't move, let alone get up or flee."

They ambled back into the bridge salon and were greeted with stares of awe from John and Ginger, looks of respect from Viola and Portia, and the toddling steps of Hana toward them. "There's my princess, come to Auntie Vera, munchkin..."

Alfred noticed the stares, "What?! Are my antlers growing back or something? What's with the looks?!"

Ginger just rushed up to him and hugged him tightly, "I love you Uncle Alfred, I really, really do..."

He smiled and patted her back. "I love you too, GingerKat..."

John followed his wife's lead and while hugging him whispered, "You and Auntie Vera are *so* amazing!"

"Thank you Johnny, thank you very much..." and Alfred looked inquiringly over John's shoulder to Viola and Portia who just shrugged and played innocent.

Vera stood with Hana in her arms, "Ah I see what this is about!... You two *have tried* those postures John espied us in the other day..." The room erupted in laughter.

Ginger looked to John, "Not yet, but what about that Johnny? Don't tell me you've already forgotten how to imitate what you saw!

I will be *very* disappointed if you have..."

John was well passed embarrassment over that mistaken encounter and volunteered, "Just say the word, vixen, and we'll see if you're as flexible as Auntie Vera appears to be!"

She grabbed his hand, "Uh Huh! Come on ya big galoot, before *you* forget and *I* get as big as a barn!" Over her shoulder she said, "Auntie please watch Hana for us..."

Once the young couple were out of sight below, Alfred crossed his arms and looked Viola and Portia up and down. "Alright Aunties, what have you two been up to in here?"

Viola protested, "We thought they should know just how they 'happened' to be here and what it took for that to occur..."

Portia supplied, "Just the truth, buddy, just the truth!"

Vera looked at Alfred and said softly, "You know dear, they were bound to hear the story sometime. Harry and MamaKat only gave them enough to whet their curiosity after all..."

Alfred sat on the sofa and took Hana onto his lap as Vera handed her to him. He cooed to the girl, "Next they'll be telling your folks about how *you actually* came to be in our little family..."

She just cooed back and put both her hands on his ears and pulled. He made a show of 'chewing' her little neck and she squealed with glee.

Vera looked to Viola and Portia and commented, "Oh, I'm sure there's no reason for that story to be repeated... Do *you*, ladies?!"

Viola and Portia put on their best innocent faces. "If you really want them to always think *we* found this little cherub, so be it!"

"But don't come crying to us if you let *one little bit* of information slip and have to answer GingerKat's barrage of questions---she's a good journalist, always has been and you know it!"

Alfred smiled back, "Vera and I are just too old to be parents---

it wouldn't be fair to Hana! She deserves these two kids... Besides, who'd believe Vera and I could have had children at our age anyway!"

He turned back to Hana, "You're Vera's little miracle you are..."

Turning back to his Aunties, "So what if Hana doesn't look the least bit Kurdish... stranger things have happened!"

Vera sat down next to him, "I got to nurse her and we doted on her for the first eight months of her life... *our* little girl is in good hands with John and Ginger."

Alfred added, "That she's a Livingson will prove itself soon enough... by then they'll be further along the path..."

He looked up to Viola and Portia again, "John and Ginger will be the ideal parents for both *this* little prodigy *and* their own delightful armful! *You'll* see..."

Vera sighed, "I was never so tickled as when *they* came to *us* and *insisted* we live on the *Anna* with them! How perfect is that?!"

To Hana she cooed, "*Auntie* Vera and *Uncle* Alfred will always be here for you darling one."

Viola and Portia remarked in tones of deepest respect, "You two rival our mothers in absolute selflessness."

"Going from Hana's *real* Mama and Papa, to being her Auntie and Uncle is the sort of thing we always thought *only they* could have done..."

"You two are our new heroes!"

"After Papa, MaMia and MaLena naturally..."

Vera smiled, "That means an awful lot to us coming from you two. Thank you very, *very* much."

Hana wiggled off her *Uncle's* lap and got to the floor. She teetered for only a moment and was off on her own two feet to explore the bridge.

Vera's beatific smile made her face positively glow. "You go girl!" she whispered.

J. L. LAWSON

3

Which Way

"I've always been in the right place and time. Of course, I steered myself there."
---Bob Hope

February 94   This yacht is so fine! We have Auntie Vera and Uncle Alfred in the forward stateroom, Viola and Portia in the starboard ama (their preferred cabins on any of the sister ships), Hana in her little hammock in the aft stateroom with us, Mocha---wherever she wishes to be---and it still doesn't feel like the *Anna* is crowded in the least! John and I are now able to sail her on our own if need be, although it is truly a blessing to not have to at present. I mention this because when John and I used our 'babysitters' the other day for a few heavenly hours, it was as if we were the only two people on the ship... on the ocean... in the world! John certainly *did* remember what he'd glimpsed by mistake in the forward stateroom that day. *And* if he *didn't*... if he merely *improvised*---well more power to him! I'm one happy GingerKat!

Now that we have some background on our Alfred and Vera, and that he really knows what he's doing, it's a lot easier to decide to follow his inclinations about the alleged Scream theft. Hmm. Is that like verifying? Uncle Alfred has asked that at least one of the crew go with him everyday to the National Gallery. We all have taken the tour and found that painting. He secretly attached miniature tracking devices to the frame---Why don't galleries and museums do that anyway? Oh well, I guess they don't; or if they do: thieves would know that and simply have to remove them or disable them. If John's impressions of the two guys we saw are even close, they certainly aren't on Interpol watch lists or anything, so not world-class

119

art thieves. What does a 'world-class art thief' look like? I am so out of my depth!

I am getting my first taste of friction. John and I took the *Agate* to the harbormaster's office---just to pay our respects and pick up local regs and such. We were all smiles and Texas-friendly but the office manager person was a Cold Prickly. A dour young man with delusions of mediocrity, greasy hair and thick glasses. I took him for someone's nephew or something because he certainly wasn't the aspiring sort. Here's a bit of the exchange: John said, "Howdy, we are from the *Anna Virginia*... part of the fleet with the *Pebble*... she's been here over a week..." The nameplate on the desk said *his* name was Abigail Hansen. *Abigail* didn't even look up from *his* book---he *had* to be a disinterested relative just filling in... I said, "Mr. Hansen, are there any local regulations that we should be aware of during our stay in the fjord?" Still nothing. Then I noticed the earphones... I waved a hand in front of his face and he looked up over the top of his glasses, still no smile. John and I repeated our greeting and question. Sean reached to a rack of forms and pushed several toward us and said, "Temporary moorings information, write in your purpose for being here, where and how long you will be anchored, home port references, contact information and your ship's registration info..." and he put his earphones back on. I thought of a few interesting devices to shove up his... I took a deep breath and waved my hand in front of his face again. Then he actually showed an emotion... perhaps his only one. In a whiny voice of outrage he said, "Was *I unclear* about the requirements? 'Please' fill out the forms and submit them!" He pointed to a box labeled 'Form Submissions' in five or six languages on the wall opposite. I took another deep breath and forced myself to smile. John was simply filling in information---as demanded. I thought: 'Our family never does anything halfway; I'm sure that Uncle Nils already submitted all the data for our fleet when he anchored.'

I set Hana on her own feet on the floor and ambled over to the harbor postings board behind Sean's desk... pretending that I was just following Hana. It looked to have all the moorings and anchorages that were occupied in this section of the fjord. In big print there was Nils's 'submission' clearly indicating all three yachts, locations... everything the little grease-ball had asked us to rewrite. In my best dumb blond voice I said, "Oh John look! Uncle Nils has already registered our yachts! Isn't he a dear!" John stopped writing and crumpled up the forms in his hands after making sure they were the same forms as those on the board. "Excellent!" John said, and turned to Sean. "It appears all we need are copies of any local regulations specific to this harbor... wake generation, generator-motor noises... that sort of thing..." Sean stood up slammed his book on the desk along with his earphones and stomped into the back office. We could hear his whiny screeching through the door. He emerged a moment later and plopped back down in his chair, not once glancing in our direction. By now I was ready to slap his little face until my hands bled. Through clenched teeth he said, "The captain of one of your other boats has all that!" and he put on his headphones, cranked up the music and swiveled his chair away from us. I must have tensed for a lunge at the little snot, because John put his arm around me rather abruptly and scooped up Hana in his other. "Let's go see the pretty swans Hana princess," and shuffled us out the office door.

That's what I meant by at last encountering friction! Why did my first real exposure to sleeping people have to become confrontational? But that wasn't the end of it for me---Oh no. I berated *John* for cow-towing to the greasy runt, accused him of being *spineless*, and generally went on for half an hour or so ranting at the inhospitable people of Oslo, and if it were up to me we'd blow off the whole trip and go home! Needless to say, I have a long way to go yet. How *utterly* embarrassing. I have some serious remorse of conscience over that little episode. 'Easy to be a saint in a monastery...'

Viola was doubled up in laughter and Portia had trouble getting her breath. "What did you want to shove up..." John interrupted, "Hana dearest let's go look at the swans and ducks some more." She was smiling already at the suggestion.

"I don't know what came over me?! I guess he just caught me *so* off guard... well you can see what I have to overcome. I am a total bitch——and I never even noticed until today! God, how asleep have *I* been?!" Ginger moaned.

Portia and Viola could offer only, "Gaining even a modicum of self-awareness is illuminating, *if* one is sincere with oneself. You certainly seem to have honestly seen yourself for once."

"Most of what we have to 'do' in this work is 'undo' so much that is useless in us."

"The real pain and misery of the work isn't in the exercises or the tedium of great toil..."

"It's what you saw today: the terrifying reality of our own state."

"That's the source of all our pain, sorrow, and now *you* can even add 'remorse' to that list."

"Congratulations, GingerKat!"

"Uhgh!" Ginger replied. "It doesn't feel like an accomplishment..."

Viola was quick to say, "But it is! It's great! You can't work on something you can't see! But now you can see! Isn't that grand!" her voice was cheerful and enthusiastic.

Ginger protested, "But it's like the first time you take a tour of a slaughterhouse! When you realize there are a lot of things no one *really* wants to know or see. I can't look at bacon or sausage anymore without hearing the squeals..."

"Yep," Portia added, "It's just like *that*. The dysfunction of man's inner state *can't* be anything *actually* beautiful to behold---It is mis-wired, unorganized, chaotic and ugly. But until one actually has eyes to see, he will go on thinking bacon comes from the store in plastic wrappings and *never* suspect the awful truth... to use your analogy."

Viola encouraged, "It won't get any better than this! And this was just the 'ogre of your frustration and disgust,' just wait until you encounter some of the other little beasties of your inner world: Prejudice, Envy, Greed, Ignorance, Slavishness..."

Portia buffered the 'encouragement,' "You'll be just fine. One moment at a time, one step at a time, effort by effort, you'll be right as rain in no time..."

Ginger added sullenly, "Oh good! I have something to look *forward* to on my *Eightieth Birthday!*" Sarcastic... but still sullen.

"Self-deprecation doesn't become anyone; really dear *do* keep some perspective..." Portia enjoined.

"What would have been the proper perspective in *that* situation? What would you have done?!" Ginger pleaded.

Portia replied easily, "Hmm, I wasn't there but I suspect I would have scared the crap out of him, then threatened him to within an inch of his life..." Ginger's eyes rounded.

Viola simply commented, "When *you* can *choose* your response, you learn what may be best for a given situation: Sometimes you turn the other cheek; sometimes you make them forget their grandmother! But neither of those actions are of any worth if they are simply your mechanical reaction to the impression---and *not* your intentionally chosen response. Do you see what I mean?"

Ginger nodded, "So you could slap the tar out of him, without rage or fury... just because you were sure that was what he needed at that moment..."

Portia replied, "Something like that. But you always get more with honey rather than vinegar... It may sound trite, but giving someone what *they* perceive to be their 'due,' more often than not lets *them* give *themselves* license to help you if they can..."

Ginger sat up straighter and tried a smile. "Back to work for GingerKat! I'm going to start dinner."

Both ladies announced, "*You cook now?!*"

"I'm learning... I can boil water, read a recipe and follow it honestly---because I know the language of recipes now too..." she said.

When Alfred and Vera returned to the *Anna* once the gallery closed for the evening; he had a few things to say about the administration of the institution.

"They are actually *moving* the painting to a *less* secure floor! They don't insure several of their works---because 'none of them can possibly be resold'---too recognizable, they presume. I don't know the director personally but I have a suspicion he's never heard the terms: 'ransom,' or 'intentional collectors'."

Vera intervened, "Alfred thought *he* ought to take the thing just to show them how foolish they were being."

"They *are* being foolish!" John interjected, "Texas Instruments had better security for their *parking lot* than these guys have for their valuable collections."

GingerKat suggested, "I'm not a security expert or a public relations person, but wouldn't a film of the anticipated robbery be the be all and end all of the caper? Don't they have surveillance cameras all through the gallery... I'm sure I noticed a few on my walk-through yesterday."

Vera wondered the same, "...But I suppose masks would be sufficient to foil interior video, and unless they strike in broad daylight, outside video would likely be too dim for recognition." She thought a moment longer, "When would *you* pull the caper; *if* you were doing it Alfred?"

"When no one was around..." He answered quickly, "...early

morning, perhaps when just garbage-collectors, street-sweepers and newspaper delivery people are the only ones on the streets. People who go about their jobs nearly oblivious to what else is happening around them..."

Viola opened her mouth to point out the obvious. Alfred continued, "...Meaning generally even *more* oblivious than others in different occupations..."

"Alright," John listed, "The twelfth, early morning, lax security because of the Opening Ceremonies are a little later, and what was the motive again? If it's 'ransom' the painting won't be taken too far away... but if it's an 'intentional collector' it could be on the other side of the world before the next morning."

Alfred said, "If the two we overheard at the restaurant are it, I don't think they are the 'ideal' *tools* of an intentional collector, so I think it's safe to say: ransom."

"So it won't ever be too far away. What's the range of your locators?" Ginger asked.

"Up to five miles or so... not far really. If I were the thief, I'd remove the object to a familiar locale, still in the country naturally---border-crossings will be a little tighter for a month or so. Those two didn't look like competitive yachtsmen, and a puttering dingy or even a motorboat wouldn't be an ideal 'get-a-way' vehicle on a fjord that can be blocked---so: overland travel. Figure a range north up to almost the arenas for the games: forty miles or so... and south up to an hour's drive---They have to consider: ease of transport, drop-offs, collections, get-in, get-out etc."

Vera mused, "Okay, it'll be for ransom then. But couldn't it also be to make a statement---an attempt to rub someone's nose in something? Why the 'Scream'?"

Viola ticked off, "It's famous, it's iconic, it's a national expression, it symbolizes..."

Portia suggested, "helplessness, futility, angst..."

Vera tallied, "So perhaps a statement on behalf of a group that typifies any of those things..."

Alfred had to remind them, "Again, those two were, as John observed, more yuppie than nefarious, I would add 'non-activistic'... Just a couple of opportunists."

"Money?!" GingerKat announced. "*Just* for money. How much can they *expect*?"

Alfred had that one too, "The painting's estimated worth is seventy-two million... so figure they could ask for a lot, but they can only get what the Gallery can afford---not what the market will bear: the Gallery can likely come up with a couple million..."

John asked, "Something's been nagging at me Uncle Alfred, why did you spill your water when they got up from the table?"

Alfred grinned and reached into his pocket, "Hoping to find something like this..." and he held up a crumpled receipt.

"What's that?" Ginger asked for all of them.

"A receipt for:" and he read off the slip of paper, "four apples, a half dozen eggs, a loaf of bread, frozen pizza, and beer."

Vera had to roll her eyes, "You picked that boy's pocket, and all you got was a grocery list!"

He looked hurt, "From a market in Asgardstrand, actually..."

Viola and Portia deduced, "Home base for our duo?"

He nodded, "Perhaps... that was all that was in his jacket pocket. It's dated nineteen January so perhaps so. It does at the least place him in that town on that day... but does he live there? The other tidbit I picked up..."

Vera raised her eyebrows again, "Really Alfred, you're incorrigible!"

He continued, "Was to notice his shoes..." and he stuck his tongue out at her.

He sat back and explained. "You can tell a lot from a fellow's shoes. For instance, his were brown, but his slacks and shirt were navy blue. They were scuffed just as John's are there..." and they all looked at John's shoes. "See that worn abraded crease and the scuff below it?"

John looked down and explained, "That's from tying off and untying the mooring lines. I put my foot on the line to the ship to take off the tension as I unwind it from the dock cleat... Oh! I see!"

Ginger understood, "Our grocery shopper spends a lot of time closer to the sea than up in the high country. He's not fashion conscious, and... where's Asgardstrand?"

Portia answered, "About *forty* miles down the coast, across from Bastoy Island!"

Alfred continued, "Does anyone recollect what the gentleman said when I apologized for spilling the water?"

John said, "I didn't understand it, it was Swedish..."

"Not English anyway," Alfred encouraged, "Norwegian. Although they had been talking in Swedish and English during their conversation... the parts I overheard that is..."

Vera wondered aloud, "And..."

He accommodated her, "And when someone is surprised, as he was with water spilt on his pant leg and shoe, they lapse into their native tongue... more often than not---so he, at least, *is Norwegian*--- likely from Asgardstrand, on the coast just about an hour's drive south of Oslo off the main highway!"

Viola and Portia clapped, "Well done Sherlock, but why are we just now being regaled with this fount of insight?"

"You've had these bits of information since... when was it? In Gothenburg, eleven days ago?"

Alfred accepted that, "But until I'd seen the 'lay of the land' and understood the feasibility of their plan... What was the point? If you'll forgive me... While I took their dinner conversation seriously enough to take the minor steps we did at the time, it wasn't until we arrived here and saw the situation on the ground, as it were, that any credibility could be allotted to their alleged scheme. So *now* your hearing about what I know, or have surmised. Otherwise I'd just have looked like a paranoid, or worse: a stalker..." and he added with less bravado, "...That, and I *just* found out this morning from a supply rep: that the mom and pop grocery I have the receipt from is in: Asgardstrand..."

GingerKat took her casserole out of the oven, "So in a few weeks we can sail down to Asgardstrand, use your little locator thingy, take the painting back and return it---no muss no fuss. Dinner's ready."

6 February 94   I was in tears yesterday. Lila and Olivia invited me to the *Ananke* for tea and cake---very British, but *why* they invited me wasn't for the tea ceremony. MamaKat left all her wardrobe with them. That included what she traveled with when away from home, *and* all the rest of it since she and Harry left Tahoe *several* years ago. They took me down to the lower salon, and everything was spread out along all the walls and over chairs. Lila pointed out several winter outfits, and fur coats, hats, gloves and such. Olivia hoped the shoes and heavy stockings would be a fit. I got to play dress-up with two of the grandest women in the world---I felt like such a little girl. I didn't play dress-up when I was young, so it was a rare and wonderful treat. I *now* have some *very* elegant clothes, but better than that for me is the knowledge that MamaKat, Mama and I were the *same size*. We wore the same size shoes too, even though she had *much* better taste than I *ever* did. What a woman! I am taking every opportunity to wear a different outfit as often as possible---No 'pearls around the house' or anything, but I'm making an occasion out of otherwise ordinary events. I still am more comfortable in jeans and a sweater---but get this: MamaKat liked to wear jeans and sweaters around too! She just wore silk shirts beneath the sweaters and deluxe leather pumps instead of sneakers... Classy, *always* such a classy lady!

At least we haven't had to keep up the 'surveillance' over the last several days and so we could just be tourists. The maritime museums here on Bygdoy are instructive. George and Lila really spent time in the Heyderdahl Museum. Oslo proper is so cool. The city covers about two hundred square miles and more than half of that is forest! Really!... not just parks... which are everywhere, but forest. Vera and I have made the walk into the city up Bygdoy Alley several times together and each time we pick a different side street to explore. At the same time I have been picking a center and observing without judging what is around me. I *will* become more objective... I will!

Regarding that wish---I have been re-evaluating my encounter with that kid at the harbormaster's office and I am realizing my identification sprang from his ignoring us... actually: *me*! I didn't receive proper acknowledgement from him... that's putting it mildly... I was ignored! That snowballed into my finding *all* his manifestations offensive. Then my own emotional state was so disconbobulated that I attacked John too! My sweet John! Whew... it certainly doesn't make my responses any less palatable, but it gives me hope that I can begin sorting through my own crap! Yay, Ginger-girl! Let's go find some more friction...

Note to self: I don't know if Auntie Vera realizes I have read all John's journals, or how detailed most of them are... but I think she's taking me through a form of external training?! She keeps reminding me to keep my shoulders back---keep my posture 'just so.' Not that I have any problem with that, I just don't want her to be too disappointed when I don't ask: "What was the point of that?" as almost every student has always eventually asked... Or will I, without realizing I am when it happens? I have so far to go and so much to sort through in my inner world I refuse to dwell on 'what ifs' and 'maybes.' What will be, will be.

"John, I just don't understand why if Auntie Vera and Uncle Alfred are with me, you still don't want me to go and see Lillehammer before the games start? I'll be totally safe..." Ginger was almost getting vexed with him.

He looked out the windows of the bridge and across the harbor. He didn't answer... and appeared to be gathering his thoughts. "I don't know why I don't want you to go... I think it's more that I want you to stay. I just had this overwhelming feeling of abandonment when you mentioned it and it's not going away. *Sure* Hana and I will be just fine here. *Sure* you are in good hands with Vera and Alfred. But since I didn't want to go... I guess I wanted you to want the same as me." He looked at her, "How dumb is that?!"

The hackles that *were* rising in her before about his irrational response melted in light of his confession. She held him close and whispered, "That is totally irrational, but cute. I am deeply touched that you are so attached to me that you can't stand to think of being apart. No one, and I mean *no one* has ever been attached to me like this before---I am honored. But, I *do* want to go and see the town before the crowds descend enmasse. And I *really* wish you'd reconsider going along... think of it as a favor to me---I'll owe you one..."

He gave her a little smile, "I feel like a kid, pouting and stamping my foot, just hearing myself put words to the feeling..."

She kissed his cheek, "There now, that didn't hurt so bad, did it?" She tried again to persuade him. "I don't want to talk you into something you really don't want to do... at the same time I kinda expect the same from you in return. But if you won't have it any other way: I'll stay here and not go..."

He rolled his eyes and stiffened in her embrace. "No, I'm just being unreasonable. Hana and I will certainly go with you. It's probably better that she see the place with fewer people there too. And we can get the lay of the land before having to deal with crowds *and* figure out where everything is..."

She grinned, *"That's* just what I thought *too.* Great minds thinking alike?"

He had to smile then. He went to the windows and began pulling down shades and curtains. Then he turned abruptly, "You just played me! Didn't you! And I folded like an army cot!" His shoulders slumped a little.

She gave her best, *'but aren't I cute anyway'* look, and replied, "Nonsense John, we just had an adult conversation and you changed your mind---that's what *I* heard anyway."

He relaxed. "You really *are* smarter than I am, *aren't* you... God I hope MirandaLinn gets your brains!"

"Don't be silly, M'Lord! You are the brightest, most determined, thorough, understanding, compassionate man of integrity that I have personally ever known. But no offense, I *would* like our MirandaLinn to get my figure not yours!"

He smiled slightly, "Amen to that! So... I'm *not* a mindless follower or a *spineless* freak?" he muttered with the sound of uncertainty in his voice.

She crumpled onto the sofa, *"Oh John.* I am *so, so sorry* again, for venting my anger on you after that episode. I don't *now,* nor have I *ever* thought of you like that! My mouth just formed words around my fury over *personally* being mistreated by that boy."

She reflected a moment, "Is *that* why some of your feelings of abandonment came to the surface again over this excursion?"

He nodded slightly. She continued, "Johnny, I *know* I have a fearsome temper. And I *know* I have a *long way* to go to overcome it. *And* I know you are going to be the victim of it when it raises its head again... But *I am seeing it now,* and *I am trying* to put something against it. *Please* don't give up on me John..." Her heart nearly exploded from remorse all over again, tears were really beginning to roll down her cheek.

He crossed to her and knelt before her, "I'm not yet as strong as Harry, or George, or Alfie, or Alfred... In fact I don't know if I'll *ever* be *that* strong. But I am working on myself too. I just have a lot of preconceptions---*misconceptions*, I realize---about what marriage is and what *we should* be like together. Long years of being alone and *imagining* what it might be like I suppose."

He gathered his resolve, "*I love you.* And I *will* endure whatever is required of me at your hands... I just can't promise that I won't feel hurt, nor guarantee I will be able to separate you from *your state* when something like that happens again..."

She really sobbed this time. "*I don't want to hurt you...*" she cried. "I want you to be as happy with me, as I am being married to you..." She wiped her eyes and tried to clear her throat, "This has all happened so fast... and I have been dealing with everything the way I *used to* deal with things, and *now* I am learning my old ways aren't very good for *anyone!* I'm not making excuses for myself: I know I'm mean-spirited and selfish---But that you love me... that you *actually* love me gives me hope that I can learn to love you too... *really* love you, not just what I *thought* love was," and she couldn't speak anymore. He held her close and stroked her hair, kissed her forehead and rocked her gently in his arms.

"We'll get there. I *know* we will!" he whispered.

She tried to laugh through her tears, "I love it---say it again---*WE!*"

"*We* are on this journey together, and *we* will work through everything that comes at us, or arises from us..." he promised.

Alfred and Vera came in with Hana in Vera's arms. "...It's just a train trip up into the mountains..." Alfred opened, "It's not a parting of ways or anything; you'll see each other this evening..."

GingerKat finally did laugh, and John's hearty laugh at what they must look like joined hers. "Yeah, we're just goofy kids in love..."

Ginger answered, "And John's decided to come along after all."

They rose and John took Hana into his arms. "GingerKat if you'll get munchkin's travel bag---I already have it packed in the lower salon. I'll get the picnic bag---also already packed."

She hopped down the companionway and emerged with the bag and an odd expression on her face. "You *already* had her bag *and* a picnic lunch made? *You were planning to go along all this time anyway?*! And you made me try and trick *you* into coming?!!"

She marched right up to him and looked him fiercely in the eyes, "John Robert Backhouse! Our children had better be *everything* you are!"

She turned to Vera, "God I love this man!!"

Even though the opening Ceremony was still days away, the little town was bustling with athletes, the media was setting up, the athletes' families, and folks like themselves were trying to get their bearings before the real crowds showed up. Hana had a little fur coat, hat and little fur boots that made her look like a little Inuit or Laplander---very cute. She contrasted only slightly with her mother's legacy sable coat, boots and ushanka. Alfred, Vera and John were well dressed against the cold, but still looked more like GingerKat and HanaRin's *entourage* rather than family. No one minded in the least---especially John, he was so proud of his little family---that they looked like a million bucks was icing on the cake.

They had their official event schedules and and followed the Venue maps per the schedule, as a guide to visiting the various arenas and stadia. The Olympic venues were actually spread over a wide swath of that region, so they focused on the accessible ones near the town. They also took in the local attractions: the Maihaugen (a huge open-air museum) and the Garmo Stave Church, the art gallery and generally just wandered through the picturesque wooden buildings of the town. To get the full tourist experience they went to visit the

Skibladner, the paddle steamer of the Mjosa river, and even though it was in winter storage they walked the pier and headed to the train station to have their picnic lunch and enjoy the view.

"In four more days I bet we can't even do half of what we've done today---in the same amount of time..." John pointed out.

Ginger smiled and gave Hana her sippy cup before shoveling more rice and brussel sprout baby food into her mouth. Vera leaned back against the station window and turned her head to look out at the hustle and bustle of the snow-covered little hamlet.

"This is so much like Tahoe in January, except the Tahoe doesn't freeze over like that river out there has. The same looking folks, the same beautiful mountains. If it weren't for all the signs in Norwegian, I almost feel that I could step out of here and turn the corner for the house on the hill..."

The glint in Alfred's eye belied his distaste for heavy winter snows. Just seeing his Vera so happy was worth all the snow in scandinavia to him. John must have had the same expression for his own reasons, because Vera commented.

"Johnny, you seem very at peace with your world today. Any insights you'd like to offer?"

He stretched and smiled even broader, "I'm just enjoying having my family around... it's still so precious to me; I hope I never take it for granted."

Alfred agreed, "Big guy, you have a heart of gold and a family of precious gems there..." he nodded to Ginger and HanaRin. "We'll get you up to speed with your external training---now that you've decided to pursue it anyway---knowing it's not entirely necessary..."

That got GingerKat's attention at once, and she turned to Vera.

"Have you been guiding me along that path too? Because I could swear some of your suggestions while we are on our walks sound amazingly like what I've read are the family's traditional methods..."

Vera tried to sound nonchalant, but didn't pull it off, "Oh, really... Hmm, I was just... uh..." she was a *terrible* equivocator. "Yes, dear. I have. But you are in no way bound to follow a single scrap of my advice. You are your own person with a great head on your shoulders. You will do exactly as you see fit."

"Relax Auntie, I am glad of it," and she turned to John, "Especially as it appears my husband is taking on all comers for advancement of his aims---I'll surely not be left behind at this junction."

John tried to explain quickly, "I *was* going to mention about that; I just got so involved I didn't *think* to... Well that's it isn't it!---*I didn't think*. I'm sorry. It wasn't meant to be 'behind your back' or anything."

"You people!" Ginger announced, "Chill! I'm not jumping down anyone's throat today. It's my day off from being the dragon lady. I'm just trying to keep up with my own family is all."

Noticeable exhalations were simultaneously released around the little circle. She rolled her eyes and went back to feeding Hana. "Really Hana darling..." she whispered to her daughter, "Your family worries too much..."

10 February 94   We were approached by some anti-abortion activists on the return train to Oslo. I have spent most of my career in publishing, that is to say among the community of professional or aspiring professional writers and authors. I had not until now had a direct interaction with Christian Fundamentalist Evangelicals. I've seen the blurbs in the news, heard their tirades as I've scanned cable channels in hotel rooms, but never had a personal encounter. Now I have. Probably because we clearly used American-accented English, we were approached as fellow followers of their mission. It appears many of their compatriots are descending upon these Olympic games as a platform from which to launch a global message. When it became apparent to them that we were not affiliated with their cause, we became targets of their 'witness to the power and grace of God through Jesus Christ.' I have been naïve to suspect there are innocuous well-intentioned people behind the placards and Bible-thumping rallies that make the news. Those five people on the train functioned under a dogmatic umbrella of 'faith' so myopic that it excluded any possibility of counter-point on the issue of abortion. Since Vera has been a physician throughout her entire adult career and has firsthand experience of circumstances and seen the emotional repercussions of the situations leading to and including abortion, she offered her perspective as a trained and experienced professional. She made it very clear that there were extenuating circumstances which made abortion in some instances not only conscionable but emphatically necessary. Even understanding that our little party were adamant about the responsibilities of parents toward children---They spent the rest of our ride to Oslo making our journey miserable. In their opinion we were mistaken to the point of being deluded; we were doomed to eternal damnation should we not repent our aberrant 'beliefs,' and finally---and I think I understood them correctly to say that---God loves everyone and waits with open arms for his children to turn from sin and return to Him...

The self-referent arguments and circular logic with which they assailed us left me in utter confusion. It turns out that since John was raised in the Bible Belt, he hadn't really ever given the unreasonableness of 'literal fundamentalism' even a second thought---they were there; he ignored them---he simply had no time or use for the hypocritical and self-serving representatives of that movement. He explained away my confusion this way: 'If you were accosted in an airport by a group raising money to send representatives to the United Nations, and their espoused mission was to legitimize the 'flat-earth' world view... Would I: Donate to them? Ignore them? Pity them? Avoid future encounters at all costs?

Or, Join their delegation?' I had to say that I would likely have a bit of pity for them, and wish to ignore them if possible. He said that's how he had gotten along during his youth---being raised around those sort of 'Christians' in Texas.

Alfred's only comment was regarding his own experiences and observations with those sort of 'Christians.' He said that more and more of them nowadays are couching their 'outreach' efforts, whether in their own communities or in foreign missions, in the guise of *humanitarian assistance. But* that in order to 'qualify' for that assistance the subjects were *required* to submit to their evangelism in the form of classes and workshops. No submission, then: No assistance. "Their 'Christianity' *does not employ* the unconditional love *they preach.*" Very informative. I'm thankful to have my family and the work.

The opening games were the next day and a good night's sleep would have been a great thing---except for the early morning stake-out protocols.

"Yes, I got the vehicle license plate number and a good look at the two men..." John insisted and held up the slip of paper on which he'd jotted down the number. "They *were* our diners from Gothenburg, but they were gone so fast, there wasn't anything I could do to stop them."

Alfred had out his laptop and was watching the little blip move north toward Lillehammer then cease blinking... "Out of range. At least we are going that way today," he mused, "We'll likely pick up the signal somewhere along the way..."

Vera reminded her husband that, "We will most certainly *not* interrupt our enjoyment of the day's activities with side-trips trailing *blips* on screens..."

"I didn't suggest that we should. I just find it curious that they headed north toward the Games rather than south and certain refuge," said Alfred in defense.

She countered that, "It may very well be that as unlikely as it may seem, these two are in fact stooges for some intentional collector. And while you *are* a marvelous detective, darling, unless you are asked to take up the case---*please drop it!*"

He closed his laptop and smiled, "Absolutely. Now shall we head up to the Opening Ceremony?"

That is just what they did. Along with the crew from the *Ananke*, the Gotland delegation made their way up north and enjoyed the Olympic Village in Lillehammer, now in full swing. John and Alfred took turns carrying Hana, while the ladies mostly cleared their way through the crowds and found seats for everyone in their group. Interestingly, they were seated just below the royal box and so King Harald V and Crown Prince Haakon Magnus, who both officially opened the games and lit the flame, passed by them to fulfill their duties. Hana reached out her hand at an opportune moment and the Prince smiled at her, he even shook her little hand. GingerKat and Vera were on cloud nine the whole rest of the evening and night---their little girl!

The next Tuesday was the only day so far on which there weren't competitions they wished to attend. They took a break from what was now their routine trek to the train station and journey north, only to return very late in the evening exhausted. "Hana is cutting two more teeth and she's not so easy-going about all this commuting as she was a week ago..." Ginger explained.

"That's good enough for me," John confided, "We'll stick around here and relax. What do you think: maybe go up every other day, or every third?"

"We'll see. We can still watch the events on the television right here..." she answered.

Vera sat down next to the girls on the sofa and sighed. "I am certainly ready for a day or two off the pace we've been keeping."

She faced Ginger, "How have your active reasoning exercises

developed?"

Ginger was silent for a moment as she gathered her response. "I have come up with 'reasons' from the sublime to the ridiculous to keep myself from dwelling on the seeming affronts to my *self-importance*. But what I'm wondering now is: Why am I actually protecting that fixture of my inner world by doing this? I mean shouldn't I be dismantling it instead of just giving it excuses not to become engaged?"

Alfred chuckled and looked to Vera waiting for her response with the same expression Ginger wore as she also waited. Vera took a deep breath and began. "You have heard the expression: 'Use it or lose it...' Whatever we don't regularly utilize, or exercise or practice gradually atrophies, withers and becomes useless. Just as a muscle atrophies, a mental exercise we no longer engage does too. I'll give you an example. Your phone has an address book feature..."

Ginger nodded.

"And when you wish to speak to someone, do you use that feature or your speed dial?"

Again Ginger nodded.

"Before that invention, didn't you once have a slew of numbers memorized---the ones you called most frequently and, I suspect, even some you only called every now and again..."

Ginger nodded and said, "I had a bunch of numbers in my head, or rather in my fingertips. I could more easily recall a number by punching it in than recite it from memory..." she recalled.

"Precisely. And now: What was your home phone number, the one at your New York apartment in Chelsea for the last four years?"

Ginger looked thoughtful, then admitted she hadn't a clue.

Vera pursued, "Alright how about something closer to the present: What was your boss's number?"

Again Ginger looked thoughtful and about to recite it, "Uh, I don't know... but it's speed dial four!" She giggled getting the gist of the example.

Vera smiled, "That is an example of what I'm trying to describe. You're not *protecting* your self-importance, you're letting it languish into obsolescence through disuse. As you well know, everything we encounter has the capability of 'rubbing us the wrong way.' By putting something against it---practicing active reason, preparing ourselves for our day, 'directing our day,' even trying to remember ourselves as continuously as possible---all these exercises steal back the energy which our *false* personality... our notions of self-importance... have usurped over our lifetime."

Alfred and John wagged their heads, very impressed with Vera's analogy and explanation.

She continued, "You see darling, due to our abnormal upbringing and the state of multiplicity in our inner world, if we were to attempt to transform each 'I' individually as each rears its little head and presents its own desire... we'd never finish the job. It would be like trying to cook one pea at a time in the boiling water to feed a table of sixteen---very impractical. We must be sly about it; we must *rely* on our *already established* tendencies toward the habitual and mechanical---We are trying to use the false personality's structures *against itself*. In that way, we transform whole servings of 'peas' rather than one at a time... Does that make sense?"

Ginger's forehead was furrowed in thought. She opened her mouth to respond and shut it again. The room was quiet save for Hana's pushing a rolly toy across the rug.

GingerKat answered at last, "Let me see if I have this: Even though my inner world is a chaos of multiplicity, there are bands or gangs of 'I's' which are used to coalescing in reaction to a given external impression..."

Vera nodded.

"...And by seeing each of those ahead of time, how they leap to the foreground when I introduce an excuse that undercuts their habitual or routine manifestation---I am essentially breaking the glue that has cemented them together? But how is that *transforming* anything?!"

Vera replied, "We are constructed such that: the part of you that *wants* to do this work must have allies amongst the other 'I's' of your machine---the more allies, the greater the strength of your conscious wish to continue this work. By detaching 'I's' from their former 'allegiances' they become candidates for conscription into that conscious effort---enmasse, rather than singly."

Ginger's hand went to her chin and her eyes sparkled. "I think I get it... It is the *nature* of our 'I's' to coalesce. We are using that facility to our own advantage. But this takes so much constant vigilance and attention. It is such..."

Vera responded instantly, "...*Work*?! Yes darling, it is called *work* for a reason---not just because all the other four-letter words were taken..."

John asked Alfred, "So based on Vera's explanation, how has the external training fit into the scheme of things over all these generations? I mean what has been the point of, at some juncture of development, focusing solely upon the physical side of our existence? Why..." Alfred held up a hand.

"Let me see if I understand what you are asking. Your wondering: If the work is a struggle to reorganize our inner world into law-conformability, then how can the seemingly purely physical traditions of our discipline be of any assistance or use? Does that catch the gist of your query?"

John nodded, as did Ginger now that the subject had been broached.

It was Vera's turn to chuckle, and she looked to Alfred waiting for his response with the same expressions John and Ginger wore as they waited.

He cleared his throat. "While we generally speak of each center as if it were an entity unto itself, distinct and separate---and they *are* in one fashion---they are *not* in another fashion. All things are connected. I realize that may sound a little trite, but it is the reality in which we exist: Interconnectedness.

Movement is born from Instinct, Intelligence from Meaning... and each of these centers have within themselves an inner structure that is a fractal of the whole in which they themselves have existence. Are you with me so far," he asked.

Three heads nodded back.

"Very well. An aroma can evoke an attitude or background emotion. A posture can elicit a memory. An emotion evokes a change in body chemistry and even a posture. A thought provokes an emotional response, a movement and sometimes a sensual perception. All examples of: Interconnectedness." He paused again to be sure they were with him... they nodded once more.

"Once the *understanding* of the structure has pervaded a person's intellect and begun to reorganize the data there... In order to make *that* understanding ubiquitous throughout the *whole* of the machine, certain disciplines of a seemingly entirely physical nature may be employed to weave that understanding into the Moving center where our postures and triggers for memories reside, as well as into our Instinctive center where many of our emotional preferences have their roots. You must remember that for all intents and purposes man lives entirely in his lower story throughout the length of his life with only haphazard interactions with any other of his centers."

He waited for that to sink in then said, "Let me illustrate. If our inner structure is likened to a house, we actually live our entire life in the basement. The *vast majority* of our manifestations come from the Moving center exclusively, a tiny fraction from the Emotional center, then manifestations from the two of spades---seat of the formatory apparatus---account for the rest. It is, therefore, the Moving center that *must* be addressed and re-calibrated. This is important---We can objectively sidestep it through right-thinking and by creating the proper emotional constructs to support those thoughts---*But* to *transform* it!... *that* requires objectivity of a different nature. It was the practice of this family for uncounted generations to employ *both* approaches. The discipline *forces* a change in the postures, emotional connections and instinctive demands of the machine through a calculated process---objectively conceived and implemented. Objective reality is almost forced into those centers, so that they will *finally* correspond with the objective mental construction *already* present in the intellectual center." He relaxed and examined their faces for evidence of a glimmer of understanding.

Vera was most readily impressed with his exposition. John and Ginger seemed to be satisfied as well.

John asked, "But both of us..." he indicated himself and Ginger, "...know the purposes behind that training now, how could that discipline work out if *we never* go to the place of questioning its practicability?"

Alfred had to laugh out loud. "You mean neither of you would ever get to the point of saying: 'what's the point of that'?" and he continued chuckling. His response was unexpected and John merely nodded.

Alfred answered, "Will the sun come up tomorrow?" and his eyes expressed an indication that he expected a response.

Ginger and John nodded.

He continued, "Have you ever read the same book twice, or even more times?"

Again nods of agreement.

"Will you eat, again, something you've eaten before *and* enjoy it?"

Nods once more, only this time it was dawning on them where

he was going with these questions; he concluded, "Although a person may *know* what lies ahead of them---simply knowing it versus *experiencing* it are vastly different critters. My grandfather, George Lawrence, was instructed by his father about this interrelationship *before* he entered the training of the discipline. So, *he understood it beforehand* and thus *never asked* the question: 'What's the point?' That *did not* translate into a recognition of what he'd *also* acquired during the long training process. In fact it enabled for him the *possibility* of transcending himself to a degree wholly unanticipated by the mere knowledge alone." He paused to allow that accomplishment to register.

"That is why those of us, Livingsons in the direct lineage and our mates, *know* that: the purely objective approach to the work *is completely viable*. Yet we *also* know it will be a somewhat longer road without the addition of the discipline. Knowledge *and* Being must become objective. The discipline isn't necessary in one sense, yet in another sense it facilitates accelerated growth and unity."

Vera smiled and added, "My sister's and my grandparents always told us that we were special. We once asked, 'Who are we really, *why are we special*?'"

She went to put on the kettle for tea and began the tale... "Grandmother said that before the age of technology, before the industrial age, before there were even empires in Europe, there was the legend of a little kingdom: a Prince on a quest who was presumed dead, a peasant girl and her mother the healer, and a prophecy of the release from sorrow. The story went like this:

It seems that while the King and Queen were on an official visit to a neighboring kingdom, their son was left as regent in their absence. He was used to sport and his favorite was the hunt. He had been trained by the greatest trackers and woodsmen of the age---so he was very good at hunting. It was said that he could track a the flight of a bird on a cloudy day, that he could track a fish through a river to the sea. And because he was also handsome, he was arrogant, rash and overly satisfied with his accomplishments. One evening he disguised himself and went to a tavern, seeking a diversion from his duties. An old storyteller related to those gathered there the tale of the of sorrow that loomed over all kingdoms---that so long as the great dragon of destruction dwelt on the earth, there would always be desire and death as the inheritance of mankind--- and the power of peace and wisdom would not return to the land... but that there was the prophesy of release.

While his parents were away and he was supposed to be managing the affairs of the kingdom, he decided instead to go on a special hunt... a quest. His advisers cautioned him against such impulsive choices, but he ignored their counsel and mounted his horse. 'I shall find the lair of the dragon of destruction and tame the unicorn of purity and wisdom, only then shall I return,' he announced and rode off into the wilds.

When his parents returned and heard how their son abandoned his administrative responsibilities and went instead upon a noble quest to secure peace and prosperity for all kingdoms, they were torn between disappointment and hope. Disappointed that the Prince left before they returned, and hope that he would truly succeed in his quest. After long days in the saddle, the Prince did at last pick up the ancient trail once left in the earth by the great dragon---ages ago. He followed the faint traces through a dense forest, over a barren desert and under mountains in the dark places none dared to venture. He was in a glade beside a pool where his horse could refresh itself, and he could catch a moment's sleep. When he awoke, standing over him was the great dragon---he was paralyzed with fear at the sight of the ancient one. The dragon asked, 'Great Hunter Prince, you have found what you have sought, what is it you would have done with me?'

The Prince gathered his wits and replied, 'Oh ancient one, long has your influence of destruction loomed like a cloud over the kingdoms of the earth. I set off on this quest to find you and implore you to leave this realm---leave us that we may have that peace which we have not known for uncounted generations.'

The dragon cackled at the prince's naivete. 'What could possibly entice me to depart so rich a land as the earth, where I may at any time dine upon the fear, despair and anger so easily evoked in its creatures? I will surely need a most persuasive reason to do such a foolish thing.'

The Prince was ready for this, 'Oh great one, the reason is this: I have sought you out first to offer you the opportunity to go of your own free will. Next I shall find and entreat the unicorn of purity and wisdom to bless this realm and thus deprive you of your sustenance.'

The dragon pondered his words solemnly. He made a casual retort, 'Young Prince, do you know how to find this unicorn?' The Prince admitted he did not know as yet---but that he would seek until he found her. The dragon said, 'I happen to know exactly where she resides, but now that I know your mind, I do not believe it would be in my best interest to tell you...'

The Prince was undaunted by the information and refused to despair as the dragon hoped. He rose and mounted his horse, 'I shall find her without your assistance ancient one. Are you then resolved to remain? For you shall surely starve and die if you do.' The dragon smiled and said he'd take that risk. The Prince spurred his horse at a lope out of the glade. Many, many months he searched. There seemed to be not a trace of the unicorn in the whole vastness of the world. At long last he happened to return one day to the glade where he first encountered the great dragon. The scent of the wildflowers and the soft afternoon shadows worked like a spell upon him and he fell asleep. He dreamed that he met the unicorn. She explained that she was held prisoner in the great dragon's mind. That only the purest and most impartial heart, incapable of malice could hamper his violent lust long enough to release her from his thoughts. The

Prince slept on. He had been away from his kingdom for so long now; he was weary to the bone and he was sure his parents had given up hope of his ever returning.

A young girl from a nearby village, searching for special plants and roots in season, happened upon the sleeping young man. She carefully made not a sound to disturb him. With her eyes so wholly focused on him, she did not see the limb across her path. She tripped over it and fell with a splash into the pool of water. The Prince awoke at her cries for help. He fished her out of the water's tangle of weeds and set her on her feet once more. He looked her up and down and saw that she was both beautiful and unafraid. 'Tell me from whence you have come,' the young man demanded. She was too awed by the young man to speak and so just pointed in the direction of her village, up the valley beyond. 'Come I shall take you home,' he said and lifted her to his own saddle. He led his horse as she directed up into the valley beyond and at last they reached her village and her mother's little house.

The girl related to her mother all that she had seen and gave to her the plants and roots that she had gathered. Then she told about how the young man had saved her from the water's tangle of weeds which was pulling her under to drown her. For his part the young man told of his long searching quest---what the dragon had told him, his ultimatum in return and his futile search for the unicorn... then he told about his dream.

'This is most illuminating,' the woman replied. 'I am a healer, as my mother was before me, and her mother before her... back through time. We have developed our skills to counter the great dragon's sway over men and so attempt to cure the ills of man. If you can find such a one as has a pure and impartial heart incapable of malice, all our knowledge of plants and of nature may be turned to improving the lot of man and making the earth more fertile than ever it has been.'

All the while they talked, the girl hummed a tune to herself as she went about her duties in the house. The young man watched her as she moved about and thought: 'Here is one with a pure heart, I shall test her...'

He stuck out his foot suddenly as she passed close by him and she tripped, letting the bunches of dried plants in her hands fall in a mess to the floor. She rose and apologized for her clumsiness and went about picking up the mess. The young man asked the healer woman if her daughter had always been so impartial of spirit and without guile or malice. She admitted that she did not know. 'This girl is my daughter because I have trained her. She was left with me only a few years ago by a dying man who said she was his only treasure in life and would I take her in and train her. He knew his days were numbered and wished only the best for his treasured girl.'

The young man said, 'Truly she is a treasure, for I cannot descry any malice in her heart!' The woman realized what he suggested and called the girl to her side. 'Little Treasure, would you be willing to go with this young man and face the great dragon?'

The girl looked from one to the other of them and shrugged. Then she finally spoke, 'I will meet the great one, but I can't imagine that one such as I, who is so small and insignificant, could be of any help to you in this.'

They rode off that evening and reached the glade where the pool of water still lay quiet and undisturbed. The young man said, 'The great and ancient dragon may not show himself as he once did if he suspects you are near me. Go there up into that old oak tree and situate yourself for a long wait in the branches.' She did as he bid her and he laid upon the ground and feigned sleep. They did not wait long before the great one was again standing over the Prince.

'So you have returned at last young Prince. But I do not see the unicorn accompanying you...' he smirked.

'True you do not see her, but she sees you plainly enough.' He knelt before the dragon and said, 'And so I ask you again to depart of your own will, before you meet starvation and doom.' The prince did not wait for the dragon to cease his laughter at that and motioned for the girl to climb down and kneel near him before the great one. She did as he bid her and the great dragon then stared down at her as well. 'This is not a unicorn, this is but a girl... and a very deliciously tasty looking girl she is too!' He put his face near to her expecting to evoke great fear and so revel in dining on her despair and trembling. However, she was firm in her resolve and was not troubled in the least by his menacing overtures.

While the dragon was thus vexed and preoccupied with the girl's nonchalance in his presence, the Prince wasted no time---He called forth the unicorn, as instructed. From out of the ancient and great dragon's head, as if riding from a great distance, the unicorn emerged and stood before them. She defied the ancient one and declared, 'Long have you held me captive in your thoughts. I am free once more upon the earth and shall travel to its ends---from my every footfall shall spring prosperity and from my breath shall issue peace. You shall surely starve and wither!'

Knowing this to be true, the great and ancient dragon took to wing and sailed straight up to the sky, passing out of sight on his journey to the moon---his most ancient of lairs. There he remains, ever watchful for the opportunity to once again descend to the earth and sate himself.

The Prince knelt humbly before the girl and the unicorn and swore his absolute allegiance to them both. 'Whatever you require of me I shall do or die attempting...' he exclaimed, 'I have been arrogant and sure of my own strength. Now I see that the power of calm and pure impartial reflection, as shown by this small and beautiful girl, is greater than my powers. I see my own true worth and only wish to serve you.'

The unicorn spoke to the girl, 'Will you have this man as your husband and equal? Or would you ride with me upon my journey of healing? The choice is yours alone.'

She replied, 'I can't imagine that one such as I, who is so small and insignificant, could be of any help to you in your great journey. I will bind myself to the young man and be his helpmate. For although he is brave and a great hunter, he will need me to become greater than he is.'

The unicorn blessed them and they returned to his kingdom. His parents had died of broken hearts since he was absent for so very long and the kingdom was open to usurpers. He and his Princess led their horse into the walled city and went directly to the palace. The Prince removed his cloak to reveal the royal crest and he held up his ring which was the seal of royal command. The guards showed obeisance and proclaimed to the court that the Prince was returned. The rascals who had begun to pillage the royal coffers were brought before him and his Princess. He turned to her and asked, 'My Princess instruct me. What should best be done with these who have been so errant and unfaithful?'

She stood and walked over to them. They cowered on their knees before her. 'Assign them the task of distributing the grain at the storehouses to the poor and needy of the realm, should they prove themselves faithful in that, they shall earn your clemency.' The Prince directed it to be done as she commanded. And thus went all of their decisions for putting the kingdom aright after it had been so long in disarray.

A new era dawned upon the earth and there was peace and prosperity for an age of man. The Prince and his Princess ruled as King and Queen and had many children---mostly daughters. The healer from the faraway village was summoned to train them and at last the healing arts were used to more greatly improve the lot of mankind and further the health of the earth itself."

Vera took a deep breath, "Before you ask: What does this have to do with my sister and I, I'm way ahead of you---that's what we asked as well. Grandmother said: 'My little girls, *you* are the true daughters of that long lost kingdom. It is *you* who will one day vanquish the ills that plague all of mankind.' I needn't tell you what an impact that had on Myra and me. We determined to become healers that very day and so begin the journey to peace and prosperity for our fellow man."

Hana was asleep in John's arms and Ginger's head was on his shoulder. Their eyes had been fixed on Vera as she told the tale, but their minds saw the events as if they actually unfolded before them.

Ginger asked, "That's a wonderful story, but what does it mean?"

Alfred, sitting at his wife's feet, smiled and replied, "It is a parable of our inner world---the union of Knowledge and Being---of personality and essence---which opens the door to peace and prosperity in our *inner kingdom*. Vera's grandparents never forgot and so passed along all they knew to their grandchildren. The Livingsons aren't the only lineage of mankind to keep the truth of man's birthright alive... There isn't a secret handshake or anything amongst those who bear the truth to recognize one another. We all seem pretty ordinary, actually---because *we are* 'ordinary,' at least as men *should* be ordinary. The Mastersons are a nordic lineage with their own methods and traditions. My grandfather and grandmother encountered other lineages on their expeditions." He mused to almost to himself, "It's just that we are all so few and far between---and not all of them are a single family, some are actually havens or schools where the great knowledge is merely kept resident. Sometimes it's in fragments, sometimes it's so allegorical it's unrecognizable---as the Mastersons' almost is."

Vera raised her eyebrows and sighed, "Too true. Neither Myra nor I understood the meaning of the tale beyond its superficial directives---so we decided to pursue careers in medicine, *not the work.*

It wasn't until I was with Anna on holiday in Hawaii all those years ago that Oliver, George, Lila and the others explained to me what I was *supposed* to have understood from that tale and the others my grandparents sometimes told..."

Both John and Ginger could only say in soft voices, "Wow..."

Alfred asked, "Have we satisfactorily answered your questions about overcoming self-importance and about the discipline?"

Ginger and John both nodded. John continued, "Will we be ready in time, from our own work on ourselves, to train HanaRin and MirandaLinn as we should?"

Vera replied, "Who can say? You are in an 'immersion' sort of program. What with all your family around you as reminding factors and guides... You two may outstrip even our greatest adepts... Who knows?"

Alfred added, "What we *do* know is that: you get out what you put in, and you two are making efforts. No effort is ever lost."

GingerKat asked, "I think what John was getting at was: since we are supposed to be some sort of 'poster children' for this new era of the family's traditions---an objective tradition---should we even consider pursuing the discipline as well?"

Vera and Alfred were careful not to chuckle. "Only a fool doesn't take advantage of help that's available," he remarked.

Vera added, "There is no line of demarcation across which you may not pass... Harry and MamaKat simply recognized that you two represent a break with the past. That does *not* mean you aren't allowed to learn what *was* once required... it means it is now your *choice*. It has *always* been the choice of the seeker. In this case: You shall train your children in, and with, reason; provide them with the objective knowledge regarding the structure of the world and man, and always be there to guide and direct where possible---There is simply no longer the *imperative* to follow the discipline... as there once was."

John and Ginger were both visibly relieved. John explained, "...Because we both want to learn all that our family can teach us!"

Ginger added her enthusiastic voice to his, "We want this for ourselves and our children. We want this so we may become as effective as possible in our lives. Who knows? There may actually be people out there seeking and who also would *actually* wish to follow this path of losing and sacrifice..."

Vera and Alfred rejoined, "We can only hope..."

16 February 94   John and I got an earful of information yesterday from Alfred and Vera. We are going forward with our wish to incorporate the discipline into our training. First, of course, I need to get to the place where I can be more objective about myself and the world around me before I subject myself to the rigors of a discipline that are built from that foundation. Vera is taking me along at baby steps because of that. The more I see of myself, the more convinced I am that John is either a saint, or has been so enamored of me for some strange reason, that he has continually over-looked my egregious short-comings. It's hard to believe *I am so very different* in reality than I thought I was---as recently as a few months ago!

I am learning to hold my tongue before saying whatever pops into my mind to say. I can recognize, better each day, from where my impulses and manifestations come from in my machine. Oh and about that---'my machine.' I really struggled with referring to myself as a machine until Lila made a very good observation. She said, "Of course we are not machines in the sense of a complicated arrangement of nuts and bolts. We are machines because we are so completely mechanical---driven by external forces and always reacting in wholly anticipated ways subjective to ourselves alone." I'm sure that's been said before, but that time I heard it. Yay Ginger-baby... Your ears are opening!

Another little technique one of my family has passed along to me in my struggle to liberate myself from myself, was this: "Try and imagine that the person next to you is exactly like you. He or she has the same dislikes and likes, the same hopes and plaints. Now also realize that that person will die, just like you will die. Doesn't their state merit compassion? Isn't pity and compassion precisely what is evoked in you when you *really* see them for who they are? When you can learn to love yourself---you will instantly accept them and love them also. Not because of some precept or some commandment---but because that is the only reasonable response to their existence." I said 'wow' then, and I say 'wow' as I recall it for these pages. Naturally the difficult part of all of this is to remember to try... or rather to *remember* to remember to try...

John found a book, in English, at the secondhand bookstore the other day. It's a compilation of talks by a guy named Gurdjieff. I think I remember reading his name in John's journals... Anyway, it is titled: *Views from the Real World*. How about that for pretentious? Since he has begun reading excerpts from it and telling me about them, I read a bit from it also. There was this one passage I found to be so apt for me at this place in my training. It said, in so many words: '...If a man *were* deprived of his illusions, and all that keeps him from seeing reality. If he were deprived of his interests and cares, his expectations and hopes---all his strivings would collapse, everything would become empty. There would remain an empty being, an empty body only physiologically alive. This is the death of I, the death of all that it consisted of, the destruction of everything false collected through ignorance or inexperience. All this will remain in him merely as material, but subject to selection. Then he will be able to choose for himself and not have forced on him what others like. He will have conscious choice...'

I thought that was a very good description of what's happening to me---actually, what I am doing to myself. I think I'll read some more of that book, he seems to have a good way of saying things that otherwise aren't easy to say at the best of times.

"I *know* Hana is completely adaptable to many situations,

ordinarily. But right now she's dealing with changes in her body too, I can understand that... What I want to do is simply spend the next five days or so at the figure-skating arena. I can have Hana with me, we'll sit nearly in the same place everyday and she will have some stability---at least in her surroundings---while she goes through this teething thing."

John scratched his head. "Alright GingerKat... as long as Vera or someone is with y'all in case both of you need assistance for some reason. I'll tell Jimmy and Becka that Alfred and I will join them." Ginger actually smiled.

"Now that wasn't too hard was it?" she cooed. "I think Vera wanted to see figure-skating also... I'll ask her first thing in the morning."

They settled in for the night now that that was out of the way. Hana was swaying gently in the hammock above the foot of their bed, asleep. John put his arm around Ginger and whispered, "Thank you. I feel better about it now..." and he drifted off to sleep.

In the morning Ginger did in fact ask Vera about the event, "Spend time with my two favorite girls? You Betcha!" and they made plans to spend the next several days at the figure skating arena.

They took their time getting Hana ready for the outings, having a bite to eat and packing a picnic basket. They ambled rather than strode to the train station every morning. Finally it dawned on Ginger that she was NOT the same woman she had been.

"I actually *prefer* a slower pace. I *like* having the time to *think*. I *like* not having a phone at my ear all the time... and I definitely like being a responsible *parent!* How strange is that?"

Vera looked at her askance, "Are you suggesting that you can see a real and perceptible difference between who is looking out from the mirror in the morning now, versus the person who once met your gaze?"

Ginger said simply, "Yes." She waited then added, "That's not all

I can see more clearly..." She had Vera's undivided attention with that statement. "Vera? Will you train me to do everything I *know you can do?*"

Vera hesitated. "Sweetheart, I can show you the way, but I can't give you my understanding---and that understanding is what leads to the 'doing' to which you refer. And it takes a great deal of trust and submission of your will to even be shown the way..."

Ginger said promptly, "I trust you implicitly!"

Vera asked candidly, "Even though I have been one of the one's to manipulate you over at least these last several months?"

"I have been manipulated *all* my life: From what other people said about me, through simple suggestibility, or through persuasive arguments intended to get me to do one thing or another. What is different now is that I *choose* to accept certain manipulation and ignore others..." Ginger would have said more but she noticed Vera was looking far away. "And at least *you* love me," she finished.

Vera looked at her straight in the eye, "How do you *really* know that?" she demanded uncharacteristically.

Ginger adjusted Hana on her hip and straightened her little hat as they walked. "Because you trust me with your only daughter," she said clearly. Vera stopped walking.

"What?!" she balked.

"Because you trust John and me with your..."

Ginger began to say again, when Vera interrupted. "I heard you. What makes you think *that*?!"

Ginger pulled just a fold of Hana's cap away from her ear and she reached up to Vera's ear and ran her finger along the outer ridge. "Because you and Hana have exactly the same ears. Because Hana's once darker hair is now showing streaks of paler blond. Because her eyes are the same tint of green and shape as Alfred's. Because her fingers and toes are the same length and proportion as yours... But appearances aside---and she is obviously NOT Kurdish---it's how *you* look at *her*. How you are almost a puddle of butter when she cries. The way you have the slightest glint of restraint when she starts to walk and you won't let yourself rush to keep her from falling---*You are her mother. And* you have entrusted her to me." Ginger repeated, "I *certainly* trust you implicitly! You believe in me---I *absolutely* have faith in you. I trust you!"

Vera sat down on a nearby bench, still looking into Ginger's eyes. "It's not that Alfred and I didn't want a child. We just know we aren't 'young.' When Hana's a teenager, we'll be... Well, talk about a generation gap! Hana deserves you and Johnny. Only Viola and Portia---and now you---know the truth of it... And she really *was* born in that Kurdish village. Alfred and I were on that mission with them when my water broke."

Ginger was playing with Hana's little gloved hands playing 'peek-a-boo,' "Auntie Vera, I don't know if John has put two and two together yet, but on behalf of both of us we are *truly honored* to be chosen as her parents." Ginger stood up again and made ready to continue on to the station. "Now. Will you train me?"

Vera held her shoulders back, wiped a tear from the corner of her eye and said, "I've *been training* you for two months now... Our little girl deserves ONLY the best!"

When they returned home that evening, Alfred and John made an announcement through their laughter. "Remember those anti-abortion folks we enjoyed so much on the train?"

Ginger rolled her eyes and played along, "Yes."

"Well the local association has just announced that *they* were the ones to steal the painting *AND* they demanded that the Olympic broadcasters show a film they are sure will further their cause---*The Silent Scream*! Can you believe it?!"

Vera answered, "That's likely the *only* thing that prompted their move---a mental association to the *title* of the painting. They're no doubt kicking themselves that *they* didn't think of the theft first!"

Ginger was incredulous, "But they are *supposed* to be Christians, fighting on the side of good? You know 'do the right thing and all!' How can they conscience lying about responsibility for stealing a work of art? Lying? Stealing? Aren't those still on the 'No-No' List?!"

Alfred let John take that one. "GingerKat, there's an aspect of the progress of an octave that I haven't mentioned. If the necessary forces, or pushes don't enter at the proper time and place, the octave does not follow a consistent line; it deviates. In fact it deviates to the point that it ends up diametrically opposite to its intended destination. You've heard the expression, 'The path to hell is paved with good intentions...' That's actually an observation based on this reality."

Alfred only added, "If I were God, I'd get a new public relations company. The ones he's contracted to at present are worthless to the point of being dangerous..."

Ginger absorbed the octave information and it caused her to have some serious self-reflection over her wants and desires and how she was approaching them. When she was finally satisfied that she wasn't in peril, she asked Vera, "Wouldn't that apply to raising children, too?"

"Oh my," Vera responded, "It applies to all things that progress through steps or phases... so, it would have to apply to raising children as well."

She mulled over the implications and added, "Now if you and John were to decide on an agenda for raising your children and followed it explicitly throughout their development... And if, for some odd reason, you neglected to take into account the inherent needs of the children at each juncture, or pushed them beyond their actual level of development at those times... Yes, the results might very well become nearly opposite of your intended outcome for them."

She considered what Ginger's concerns might actually revolve around and interjected, "By the same token if you and John did nothing at all, children will still grow up into adulthood anyway. They will be inculcated by their environment and fully absorbed into their society."

John and Ginger chewed on that last bit and shuddered. Ginger was first to respond, "Jeez, parenting sounds like a tightrope act! How do people do it?"

Alfred said blandly, "They don't. Look around. The power of suggestion through advertising---misinformation; the constant barrage of 'expert' opinions always contradicting each other, and on top of that: just sheer laziness has produced what you see. And those parents who do genuinely *want* to do right by their offspring don't know how humans are *actually* constructed and develop, so inevitably their children may *appear* more capable, but they will *still be* spiritually handicapped---objectively speaking."

John muttered, "Grim..."

Ginger concurred, "John? Are we up to this?"

Vera's laughter actually felt soothing rather than mocking, "Would you ask Hana to clean the dishes---now---at her age?"

Ginger answered bluntly, "No, of course not..."

"And when she *is* big enough to be able to do dishes, will you promptly nag her to get a job---since she can clearly do dishes?" asked Vera.

Again Ginger replied, "No!"

"Ah, but what if she shows a gifted command of how a kitchen works and is a better cook than you---but still only five or so years old? Wouldn't you want her to put those talents to use and make an income?" pressed Vera.

Exasperated *and* relieved, Ginger answered, "No. I see where you're going with this. Are you suggesting that what was once called 'common sense,' or 'mother wit' is sufficient to avoid most of the heinous mistakes we fear?"

Alfred and Vera nodded. "Don't borrow trouble from a tomorrow that isn't here. Today has it's own challenges---Don't you think?"

John asked, "Do you suppose what we just went through, on a pretty small scale, is what most parents lie awake fretting *all* the time?"

Ginger said, "No wonder people age so quickly---that's a lot of stress on a daily basis!"

"Indeed." Alfred agreed. "John, you are doing quite well absorbing your training. Ginger, Vera says you are coming along very nicely with yours. You two *really* needn't give your parenting skills a second thought... Really!"

Ginger announced, "About my training... Vera you told me this morning that you have been training me for the *last two months*?!"

Vera nodded, "Yes, dear?"

"Was it like how you were always reminding me to keep my shoulders back and posture 'just so'?" she recounted.

Vera laughed, "Oh no sweetheart! You just had crappy posture---truly horrid. I couldn't abide you schlepping around like a knuckle-dragger; you have such wonderful broad shoulders. You hold yourself much more beautifully now."

Ginger's rosy cheeks were the only sign of her embarrassment. She inclined her head to her Auntie and asked, "Then what have I been doing that's part of my training? I don't get it?!"

Vera seemed to have hoped she wouldn't have to answer that question. "Very well," she said calmly, "set your daughter on the sofa and stand up."

Ginger's expression clearly conveyed her confusion. Vera

continued as she approached her, "There are certain repetitive tasks in which you have engaged over the last months... yes?" And she set Ginger's hands on her right hip, "Is that about the position of your arms when holding Hana?"

Ginger nodded, uncomprehendingly.

"Please shift 'Hana' to your other hip."

Ginger did so.

"A little quicker, dearest." Vera encouraged.

As Ginger sped up the motion, Vera made an amazingly quick jab at Ginger's solar plexus which was deflected instantly by Ginger's 'shift.'

"Again, please," Vera requested, and once more her lightning jab was deflected.

Ginger's face was still a mass of surprise. First that she deflected the punch and second that Vera seemed so capable of such extreme damage.

Vera said, "Every single time you walk with Hana, you set her down the same way and pick her up the same way. Please set 'Hana' down."

Ginger dropped into a squat with her arms and hands in front of her.

"Now pick 'Hana' up." Vera demanded.

Ginger did so, rising from the squat in a fluid motion with her arms and hands in front of her and slightly to the side.

"Now, more quickly please."

Ginger complied and Vera's leg rose like striking snake in an arc aimed at the place Ginger's head had just been.

"And pick up 'Hana,' quickly."

Ginger rose again into the accustomed posture as Vera's other leg swept from the opposite side and was blocked instantly by

Ginger's arms.

Vera continued, "You recall I have, 'it seems,' always been across the room from you when I've needed a rag to wipe Hana's chin as she's eating or burping or whatever, remember?" Ginger nodded.

"Please toss me a rag."

Ginger's right hand flew up from her side and her hand flipped up palm forward at the the end of the 'toss.'

"Yes that's it. Now the other arm, please."

Ginger repeated the motion with her other hand and arm.

"Please 'toss' me a rag, but more quickly," Vera intoned, and she made a roundhouse kick at Ginger's chest. Ginger's arm blocked the kick and her hand flick pushed Vera's leg away.

"The other arm, please," Vera requested, and she aimed a stiff-arm swipe at Ginger's face. Once again the blow was deflected and the hand flip became a grip on Vera's forearm.

Vera bowed and said simply, "John, Alfred... Take Hana below."

Alfred was already moving to pick up Hana and John followed after him quickly. Ginger waved to Hana who was smiling and waving to her as she went down the steps. Ginger turned back as Vera's fist caught her in the solar plexus.

"Oomph!" she gasped.

Vera said, "Let's try that again." They did. This time Ginger deflected it easily and Vera made a leg sweep to her body, Ginger dropped with her hands out which caught and followed Vera's leg across to the other side. Ginger rose back up as Vera spun from the momentum to deliver a straight-arm punch. Ginger countered it and held Vera's forearm. The rapidity of the assault was such that Ginger had no time to consider which counter move to engage---from wherever the attack came; her body responded smoothly and efficiently. Alfred and John were peeking up into the bridge salon at the sparring match and saw firsthand how Ginger had to begin improvising: 'squats' became also sidesteps and rolls, 'tossing rags' became the initial movement of spins carrying Vera's momentum away from her, 'shifting' became pivots and spins. After fifteen or twenty minutes, without a break and without damaging the appointments of the bridge salon, Vera ceased her assault and bowed.

She asked simply, "Now... What *don't* you get about your training thus far?"

Ginger was speechless.

Vera added, "We'll strengthen your flexibility and expand your facility at improvisation, but I think you're coming along nicely, dear."

Alfred and John came back up to join them.

Alfred said to Johnny, "You'll notice that for GingerKat, not a thought stood between her need for a response and that instant response---which accelerated even into improvising."

John nodded at Ginger who simply sat quietly on the sofa with Vera's hand in her own.

Alfred continued, "The discipline is designed to take repetitive ingrained movements and wed them to the senses and emotions--- sidestepping the intellect. Because they are trained in a person through emotionally positive acts---constructive activities of care, repair, assistance and such---the disciple's movements are recorded positively in several centers at once. Any tedium which may begin to infect an activity and thereby cause it's rejection, or worse still: the arising of negative emotions, is repeated until even that tedium and negativity has long been 'worked' out of the task through exhausting its force. *That* is why some training takes longer, some shorter."

He smiled to Ginger, "Vera chose all your encounters with Hana for the express purpose of not allowing *any* tedium or negative emotion to have the least opportunity to rear its ugly head---thus accelerating your training."

He turned back to John, "That Ginger was able to translate what must have seemed to her wholly unrelated movements into a defensive pattern of activity so easily---well, that's a tribute to both teacher and student!"

He bowed to the ladies and shook little Hana's hand, saying "Well done young master; you have taught your mother well!" The quiet of the bridge was broken; they all laughed at that *and* Hana's response. She truly appeared to be bowing in return!

Ginger collected her thoughts and tried to compose herself to say, "Auntie Vera, thank you for manipulating me so masterfully. I am humbled and honored that you have devoted so much of yourself to me."

Her tears were streaming down her cheeks unheeded. Hana reached up and touched them then put her finger to her mouth---as she did with most everything these days.

Vera kissed Ginger's forehead and whispered, "All that I do is for you, my love---for you and *our daughters*."

Alfred announced, "Who's hungry? MamaKat, you look like you have worked up an appetite! Shall we catch up to the *Hannah's* crew? They are headed over to Lille Herbern by launch."

They bundled into coats and set off at as quick a pace as possible through their part of the harbor. Once passed the buoys Alfred opened up the outboard and brought them to within sight of the *Nina* and the *Golden Hind*.

"Oh, the whole of the *Hannah* and *Pebble* are out for dinner... It's a family night on the town..." Vera clapped.

22 February 94   After five days with Vera and Hana every waking hour, I think I am becoming a 'family woman.' And I like it! Vera and I kept secret ballots on the men's figure-skaters and the ice-dancing we watched over those days. All of hers and all but one of mine made it to the finals. That was fun. Hana has developed a taste for pikekyss, that's a baked meringue---literally translated it means *girl's kiss*, and also she's begun to suck on Jarlsberg cheese. Vera and I have a lunch of either smoked salmon or rakfisk---essentially fermented trout---on flatbread. The sauces make the meals in my opinion.

For a whole week now I have been aware of my training in the discipline. For the two months before this, Auntie Vera had been conducting my training completely without my knowing it---Wow is she good! I'm no adept or anything, but I can keep myself and Hana safe from most of life's little happenstances: jostling crowds, runaway objects, all the sudden bumps and collisions of modern life and the like. More importantly, I am remembering myself more often and for longer periods of time, and the depth of those experiences is becoming more pervasive. I'll offer an example from this morning: Uncle Alfred and John went with the other men to watch the cross-country relays and they left really early. Hana slept through her father's leave-taking and *then* slept on until about seven. I stayed up with Vera in the main salon after the fellows left. We didn't hardly speak a word between us for maybe an hour and a half. During that time I sensed the warmth and texture of the rug under my feet, heard the sounds of the shorebirds and gulls, watched the sky gradually glow brighter and brighter and enjoyed the warm bitter taste of the coffee in my mouth. I kept my posture straight and my muscles relaxed but poised. I held a state of compassion and gratitude in my heart for where I was and who I was becoming, as well as all those who have had a hand in that development. I mentally reviewed the day ahead and chose an exercise which I knew would sync with those activities---and all of those centers' activities occurred in me at the *same time*! I actually began to feel as though I was nearby watching me sitting there doing all that---how crazy is that?!

After Hana got up—she has been sleeping through the night for eight days now!---I fed and dressed her and we went across to the *Hannah's* salon where *all* the other women of our family ended up. I was thrilled. Then something amazing occurred: one by one each lady told her story of how she had developed in the work---how she was trained, how the discipline was introduced and progressed for her and, most importantly of all to me, how they held Auntie Vera in such high esteem! My Auntie Vera! Naturally she remained as modest as ever in the face of the extraordinary accolades they showered on her. Then it dawned on me: Vera is the *only* one of the women who trained and developed in the work without either being born into the family or having *first* married a Livingson. She is unique. Naturally she *is* married to Alfred, now, and that brought her the additional 'special' instruction and discipline each of the other ladies has acquired. After Becka and me, Vera is the youngest of our women, but even our eldest---Lila, Mia and Lena---don't actually look any older than she does---And I know for a fact that the twins and Lila are over a hundred! I am such a child...

"But I want to see both of them!" Ginger made a mocking stamp of her foot and pouty face... then just as quickly she had to laugh. "I don't care. What does everyone else want to do?"

"I'm pretty sure it's going to be back to the snow fields and tramping from viewing point to viewing point tomorrow." Alfred commented.

Vera protested, "There aren't any enclosed areas for viewing the events, so Hana won't be able to do anything but play like a mummy in her winter wear."

Ginger held Hana up and asked, "Do you want to go play like a Mummy, HanaRin?"

Hana burped up her last rice and apples meal just then. Ginger averted her face just in time, but the rest was now decorating the front of her sweater.

"Isn't MamaKat's little girl clever! You kept your mess completely off the sofa! You're the cleverest little girl in the world!" she praised as she began pulling off her sweater and tossed it to the sink. "I suppose Hana and I will grin and bear it *just* watching the finals of the ladies singles in Hamar..." and she sighed as if making a loathsome surrender.

Vera let out her breath and relaxed, "Good, and I'll join these ladies. Sitting in the Arena in Hamar is much more appealing to me than shuffling through the ice and snow all day in Lillehammer."

Neither Alfred nor Johnny really expected any different. "I'm guessing if any of the other ladies of our entourage are going out, they'll likely be joining you two." Alfred prophesied.

Ginger added, "Oh boy, *another* Ladies Day Out... Yippee!" Now in just her thermal underwear top, Ginger was at last beginning to show signs of MirandaLinn growing inside her. Johnny put his hand on her belly, then lowered the side of his face as if listening for talking or something.

"Johnny, dear, she's not moving so as *you* can feel it yet, and she's definitely not singing yet." Ginger remarked. "I feel her swimming around every now and then, but nothing sudden or drastic."

It was when John's head was at her belly that Ginger looked at her husband for the first time as *her* man. Her own devoted and loving man. She'd called him that often enough, but at that moment it became an emotional and very physical reality to her. She put her hand on his head, and directed, "Over here just a little more... There---Can you feel her pushing back?"

His face lit up and he pulled back looking into Ginger's eyes, "I felt her! She's a strong girl..." He reached over for Hana and picked her up. "Just like her sister! Strong and clever!" He 'ate' up Hana's little tummy and she squealed with glee.

Vera and Alfred were just that pleased at the scene. She offered, "Would anyone like to play Trivial Pursuit until bedtime?"

Alfred added, "I'll serve the cake and ice cream..."

They settled into armchairs around the table and set out the game. It was another pleasant evening on the *Anna Virginia*.

In the morning, most of the women of the three ships went to enjoy the skating in Hamar. An interesting thing happened after their arrival: Vera, Ginger and Hana went to the seats they had occupied for five days previously and the other women were in the box seats directly behind them. Next to the trio were two women and a child who had also been to the previous five days of skating competition. The elder of the two women got Vera's attention and opened a conversation.

"Do y'all speak English?" she asked as politely as she could.

Vera smiled and answered, "Yes, we are from the States originally. Are you three from the U.S.?"

The daughter, as it turned out, answered, "Memphis! We saw you almost everyday for days but we couldn't ever hear you speaking... She's a lovely little girl," she announced smiling at Hana.

Her mother introduced them.

"I am Dorothy Perkins, this is my daughter Ellen and my granddaughter Chelsea..." Ginger smiled and reciprocated.

"This is Vera, I am Ginger and this little cutie is Hana Nasrin." Hana was nodding a little and didn't exactly look her brightest and best at the moment.

Dorothy focused her attentions on Vera and continued, "Did y'all fly over? Do you have relatives in the games? Where are you staying? Have you eaten at the..." and she slaughtered the pronunciation of the place so that Vera didn't know what restaurant she meant.

Vera tried to take each question, "Um, we sailed to Oslo; we're anchored just off Bygdoy and that's where we are staying. We do not have relatives *in* the games but two of our family assisted in *coaching* the Swedish Biathalon teams..."

168

While Vera and Dorothy kept up their banter, Ellen looked to Ginger and asked, "You sailed here?! It seems awfully cold for sailing... aren't you freezing at night?"

Ginger giggled, "No the *Anna* and our family's other boats are quite cozy. We are *very* comfortable, thank you. What about yourself? Where are you staying?"

Ellen replied, "We're at the Royal Christiana. My husband Edward is in international trade...that's where he always stays when he's in Oslo. All your family is on boats in the harbor? I hope you all have plenty of fur coats! Yours is lovely by the way... Is that *real* sable? We flew in from Atlanta through London; it was a bumpy flight..."

Ginger was slightly caught off-guard by the non-sequiturs being tossed her way, "Yes, this was a gift from one of my relatives who passed on recently..."

Meanwhile Dorothy was confiding to Vera, "...So I have to make sure Norman and Edward remember to get reservations every evening otherwise we'd starve... As a grandmother it seems I have to be the one to organize everything and keep it all together!"

Vera smiled, "Yes, the burdens of command!"

Dorothy tittered. "That's what it is: command. That's a good way to put it. Vera I'm liking you more and more... Are you and your husband trying for children too? ...To keep up with your sister, I mean... Your mother must be soo delighted to at last have a grandchild to spoil..."

The rest of the ladies in their family were sitting quietly, listening to the conversations and desperately trying to hold their tongues.

Vera smiled wanly, "I'm afraid our mothers passed on quite a number of years ago. It's just us two now." Vera slurred 'mother's' intentionally to avoid bursting Dorothy's perceptions.

Dorothy consoled her, "Oh! What a shame. Every little girl should have a grandmother to dote on her and spoil her!"

She kept insisting on the 'spoiling' thing. Ginger was ready to ask: 'Exactly what do you mean by that phrase...' When: Chelsea---Ellen's little girl of about three who was clinging to her stuffed animal, perhaps a reindeer, it was hard to tell---had been oohing and aahing at the skaters warming up on the ice, she turned and announced, "Mommy, I want a dress like that one. I want to go and skate with the prettiest lady over there. I want some hot chocolate. Mommy, I want a dress like that one. I want to go and skate with the prettiest lady over there. I want some hot chocolate..." ad infinitum.

Ellen told her that she was as pretty as any of them, and if she took lessons she could be in the Olympics someday, and yes she would get her some hot chocolate very soon... "Mommy is talking to the nice lady right now. Don't hold Rudolph by his horns, you'll tear them off; and Mommy *will not* buy *another one again*---this is the last one!"

She turned back to Ginger and said, "When Chelsea came along, Edward and I were sure we'd still be able to maintain our normal life at the club and such, but now it's only Edward who gets to go out and about. I have to take Chelsea to dance lessons and her play dates and her soccer practice and her doctor's appointments... We never get to go anywhere!" Ginger was beginning to understand what Dorothy meant about 'spoiling.'

Dorothy was just telling Vera, "...So when Norman and I turned fifty-eight last year we decided we would finally do some traveling. He was able to stop going into the office everyday... computers and networking and that sort of thing... it's all technological and beyond me, it seems like just so much magic or something... Anyway, we just had to go to an Olympics for once and see scandinavia... All his folks are from around here somewhere... Your sister's daughter is just precious! You must've been very proud when Ginger had her! I certainly love being a grandmother, at last I can spoil a little girl and hand her to her mother to change the diapers and to feed her and such... the privileges of age! Your still young now, but *you'll see* when *you* get to be *my* age... there are definite advantages!" She moved her head closer to Vera's, "Although confidentially, truth be told, I don't miss sex one tiny bit!"

Vera was still woodenly smiling and nodding while Viola and Portia were nearly in stitches behind her. Every now and then one of them would snort from holding in her laughter and she'd try and compose herself enough to apologize for 'sneezing.' Ginger's face was an interesting mask of smiling incredulity. At last the first of the competitors in the finals was announced onto the ice and they got a reprieve from their vociferous neighbors.

Ginger turned to Vera and said softly, "Norman and Edward had the right idea..."

Vera cackled and said, "But they missed seeing my precious *niece!*"

Ginger snorted so loud and hard at that one, she had to blow her nose to also disguise it as a sneeze. Hana was waking up to the spectacle on the ice and watched the gliding and spinning ballerina with a focus that made little Chelsea's distracted tantrums look... well like the distracted tantrums of a three year old.

Olivia leaned down and whispered to Vera, "Did we hear her correctly? She's only fifty-eight?! ...And looks like *your* grandmother already?!" Vera nodded.

Olivia looked to either side of her at the other Livingson ladies then added, "Cripes, we must look like cheerleaders on a field trip to her! Please introduce us!"

Vera wagged her finger at Olivia and whispered, "Tsk, tsk, tsk... be nice or 'Auntie' will have to give you a whipping!"

Between the skating blocks of competition there was indeed time to socialize some more and it was naturally Viola and Portia who *just had* to introduce themselves to Dorothy. Vera nearly held her breath as one after the other of them chatted frivolously with the lady from Memphis, hoping neither of them would insinuate anything dreadfully embarrassing or difficult to explain. She needn't have worried.

Dorothy gave each of them some 'sound advice' on hunting for a good husband---after she had determined they weren't lesbians, that is. They listened thoughtfully and thanked her profusely while their mothers had to avert their faces to keep their obvious amusement concealed.

Then Portia said, "This is my mother Lena Livingson-Bessamer. Mama this is Dorothy Perkins from Memphis---that's in Mississippi."

Dorothy corrected her, "Tennessee! It's a pleasure to meet you young lady, your daughter is charming... you should expect the pitter-patter of little feet around the house before another year or two I should think! I have been told my advice on love is seldom wrong... if it's followed that is!" and she wagged her finger at Portia to stress the point.

Lena extended her hand to shake Dorothy's, "It's a real pleasure to make your acquaintance. Imagine meeting fellow Americans halfway around the world! And thank you so much for giving Portia such good advice... it's good that she hear it from more than just her father and me!"

Dorothy was quite satisfied with herself and truly enjoyed the praise. "Not at all, not at all." She brought her face a little closer to Lena's and whispered, "In fact, I have a nephew here at the games. He's a little old for Portia, but he's a banker and very rich---would you like me to arrange a meeting? It would really be my pleasure... I have a sixth sense in these matters---I think your daughter would be a good fit for David, he's a bit of a playboy---he just needs a real woman's touch is all." Lena looked back at Dorothy with a blank expression.

Dorothy added, "I'm sure when you get to be my age you'll develop a *better sense* for these things as well... I'm sure it's *just a matter of time*. You'll just have to trust my judgement on this one..."

Lena's vacant gaze was interrupted as Mia elbowed her in the ribs, "Aren't you going to introduce me to your new friend?"

Lena made the quick introduction and excused herself, "I have to find a restroom..."

Lila rose with her, "I'll go with you!" When they were several steps away, they burst out in giggles that nearly led to tears of hilarity.

Mia received much the same 'advice' from Dorothy as Lena had, and also received an invitation to set up Viola with her nephew David, the banker. Mia thanked her and then also had to excuse herself to go to the restroom. Viola, Portia and Olivia rose to go with her. Vera and Ginger were left with Hana at the mercy of the Perkins matriarch... alone.

Then Vera said *she* needed to take Hana to the restroom. As she rose to go, Ginger held her arm and pulled her back to her seat, whispering, "You will *not* leave me *alone* with these women!"

Vera whispered back, "Just kidding! I wouldn't dream of it. I love you GingerKat!"

Vera smiled and kissed her cheek, "You're a good woman Mrs. Spelman-Backhouse; you *could* manage alright alone, but there's no need just yet!"

When the other ladies returned they were more composed. Perhaps not surprisingly a little way into the second block of competitions, a dapper young man found his way to the Perkins box of seats.

"David!" Dorothy announced as if shocked, "What are *you* doing here?"

Viola whispered to Portia excitedly, "*That's* the mouth-breather from *our* bank in New York City! The one who couldn't tear his eyes from your cleavage..."

Portia replied quickly, "Really? Do you think he'll recognize us? Does he know how old we are?"

Viola answered, "I doubt it, he never looked us in the face... And no, age is not a requisite for changing gold into currency..."

That little conversation was interrupted by Dorothy announcing her nephew and introducing him to them.

"Davy, this is Portia and Viola. They're from America too! Isn't that a coincidence?" David extended a hand and smiled a toothy grin.

"A great pleasure to meet fellow countrymen so far from home... that is American girls rather..." and he guffawed at his little humor. Portia and Viola looked to Ginger who was nearly in tears holding back her laughter.

Viola said, "Say haven't we met before?"

Portia played along, "Your right sis," she turned to David and asked, "Were you in Manila last autumn?"

Viola corrected, "No not Manila, it had to have been Singapore!"

David's grin was faltering.

They continued between themselves, "I'm almost positive it was at the market in Mumbai..."

"No it couldn't have been, it must've been at the Marina in Monaco..."

"Or the casino... that's it: the casino!"

"No, *his* name was Ralph not David..."

"Then it must have been at the Copa Cabana or on the beach in Rio, two seasons ago..."

"No those were Ricky and Chuy, not a David at all..."

The whole while Viola and Portia went through their routine, Dorothy just stared at them with her mouth hanging open... giving the obvious indication that David was from her side of the family as he had resumed that same apparently 'normal' expression. Vera interrupted them and asked David if he traveled often. He nearly didn't hear her and only turned his open-mouthed gaze upon her at hearing his name.

"Huh?!" he uttered.

"I asked whether or not you travel extensively?" Vera repeated.

"No, ma'am. This is the first trip I've made since graduating NYU seven years ago," he finally formulated.

Vera turned to Viola and Portia, "Ladies, stop it! Young David here doesn't travel... Be nice!"

Dorothy squinted at the two of them and asked timidly, "Do you two travel for pleasure or business?"

Portia replied as gently as she could manage, "On business mostly, our family runs an international humanitarian non-profit..."

Viola added, "But we try to mix business and pleasure if we can."

David regained some of his composure and commented smugly, "Oh, an international firm! Maybe I've heard of it---I'm in finance after all."

Portia replied simply, "The Gotland Freedom and Humanitarian Aid Society."

His jaw dropped, "Uh, That's the GFHAS? *The most* prestigious and *most highly funded* IGO in the world!?"

He looked to the other women on either side of Viola and Portia, to inform them perhaps that, "The GFHAS has an operating budget that surpasses most industrialized nations' GDP!"

Then he looked more closely at Viola and Portia, "It's rumored to be run by the same family since 1935---I mean literally---*the same family*!"

Dorothy couldn't follow, "David! What did she say? *What* are you saying?"

David answered her without taking his eyes off the women behind him. "They work for an Intergovernmental Organization started in the thirties..."

He turned abruptly and asked Portia skeptically, "What do *you two* do with that organization?"

Portia answered directly, "Run it."

David's eyes turned to saucers; he whispered to his Aunt Dorothy. She looked up at the women behind her and turned back to him, "Use your *eyes* Davy! These women aren't *even my* age *yet!*... What *are* you going on about!?"

David insisted, "I'll prove it," and he turned to Viola. "How old are you?"

Gasps from all around him met his ears. Dorothy swatted the side of his head.

"What in the name of... Have you lost your mind!?" She turned to all the ladies and made a general declaration of apology for her idiot nephew. Viola was unruffled and opened her mouth to answer his question... Lila put her hand on Viola's shoulder and she closed her mouth at once.

Lila replied to Dorothy, "It's quite alright. Some things simply cannot be taught to the younger generation and therefore cannot be avoided. David dear, it is *wholly impolite* to ask a woman's age... no matter *how young* she may be. Therefore, my niece is *not* at liberty to answer that question... and judging from your *tone*, I don't blame her in the least. That was simply *rude*."

Mia and Lena had to turn away to keep from laughing aloud and undercutting Lila's solemn response.

Dorothy swatted his head again; he excused himself and left.

Dorothy turned and apologized once more. The Perkinses weren't quite so sociable the rest of the afternoon. Needless to say, when they all got back to the yachts that evening, the number one topic of conversation were the Perkins women. But not in the way one might have expected. The tone of the conversations had more to do with how *they* had responded to the ladies from Memphis and less about those ladies personally.

"I don't care how badly you wanted to tell that young man off for being a lecherous imbecile... that is simply unacceptable and you know it!" Lila chastened Viola and Portia.

They did indeed know it well, "But it's just so damned frustrating to constantly be at the mercy of people's illusions," Viola protested.

Portia continued, "You *know* we are *most* tolerant---even understanding of *just about* everyone with whom we come in contact..."

"Either through business or pleasure..."

"But this kid really irked us! When we were at our New York bank and first met him..."

"...All he did was stare at our breasts and make insinuations and innuendos..."

"No respect whatsoever!"

"Totally unprofessional in the first place..."

"And degrading in the second..."

Mia and Lena put the kibosh on their ranting. "Sweethearts, if we dealt with *every* person accordingly..."

"Wouldn't we ultimately be no better than your young man back there?"

"Myopic..."

"Devoid of apparent conscience?"

"Pejorative..."

"Shallow of spirit..."

Viola held up her hands. "We get it... really!"

Portia added, "Thank you, Auntie, for not adding 'Unlady-like' to the list..."

"We already feel remorse for taunting him..."

"And it was a poor example to set for HanaRin..."

"Or our GingerKat, for that matter..."

Ginger spoke up, "I was more surprised at how those ladies could jump from topic to topic with such fluency *and* expect an honest response to each query they rattled off. *Then* to have the audacity to force advice on Auntie Vera *and* match-making schemes on Viola and Portia... Well, I guess I just never noticed... I mean I never really actually perceived how ridiculous people can be. I probably seemed, or rather likely *still* appear, just as ridiculous to you all."

Vera sat bolt upright. "Stop that nonsense this instant! GingerKat, you have not at any time been so utterly asleep as our new friends from Memphis. Of course you have your peculiarities, which of us do not? *All* that is being said here and now is that we walk a fine line just being who we are!"

She turned to all the family assembled there, "Show of hands please! Who amongst us has a birth certificate?"

Each person looked from one to another; after a moment or two only Ginger and John had their hands up.

Ginger asked, "Huh? How can you *all not* have a birth certificate?"

Vera smiled at her odd question, "But Ginger dearest, you don't have one either. That country doctor couldn't verify your birth because *he wasn't there*. Now perhaps your birth *was* registered in *that county* afterwards, as an Amourson---but *you* are missing those personal documents just as we are. Whether it was because we were born at sea..." Several heads nodded, including James and Becka's. "...Or that documentation was lost in disasters: fires, or earthquakes or floods..." Several other heads nodded.

"Oh, and Johnny dearest take your hand down. You *do* have *your* birth certificate as John Robert Backhouse, but I'm afraid my Alfred is over-zealous when it comes to procuring things---you have the *original* and *there are no copies or records*---we certainly checked."

John smiled seemingly gratified that he was in the same position as the others for all intents and purposes.

Vera continued, "In this age of information and technology where everything is electronically recorded somewhere---and several times over---We, ourselves, are not in those electronic files as a 'modern citizen' ought to be." Then she took another tack to illustrate her point.

"Who has a passport?" She asked of them. Most all of them raised their hands.

She stipulated, "...other than the ones actually and legitimately from Sweden?"

Hands went down and she continued, "...A drivers license?" That got chuckles; Alfred raised his hand proudly with the youngest four.

Vera turned back to Ginger, "You see dearest, even if Viola and Portia hadn't been restrained from blurting out their ages or their direct connection to the families' organization, they couldn't have proven it. Sure they could recount their life stories or perhaps have introduced still living persons who 'knew them when' but the only paper trail for us is the one we've *made* for ourselves---which do *not* reveal our actual ages. We are essentially undocumented persons in a world of identification badges and papers. We are able to perform our responsibilities in our own organization because we mostly sail where we need to go; we function under the aegis of the U.N. for the most part, wield a substantial economic power and *we do not force people to know who we are*---quite a contrary attitude to most every other person on the planet I'm afraid."

That last was aimed at Viola and Portia, as if they hadn't been sufficiently chastened already.

"So let me see if I have this rightly..." Ginger followed, "You have passports, but they are 'Swedish' or you use your United Nations identifications as sort of international identities and all of *those* represent you as younger than you are---So you *can* fly if you wish. You pay taxes in Sweden, then?"

Some of them nodded.

"You manage, as young Davy said, the largest IGO on the planet with an operating budget larger than most industrialized nations. Yet with all of that, we all own a sum total of five yachts, four cars... do we own houses besides John's, the Port Isabel house and storage and the homes on Gotland?"

Oliver answered first, "We still hold title to two houses in Tahoe and two in Berkeley, and our plantation in Sri Lanka..."

Olivia added, "Ginger owns the Inn in Venice... and Alfie and I have the Francesconi houses there too..."

Ginger's eyes became round as marbles.

Lila contributed, "We still own my parents' compound in Hyderabad..."

Alfred looked around the room, "I think that sums it up for you darling. Yes we do wield great influence, but we are not actually well propertied, and we *do* function under the radar of society for the most part. Carl and Nils at least have a very visible and very profitable business in Gotland that allows us a somewhat *normal* presence in the world---beyond that..." and he shrugged.

Ginger recovered, "The Inn in Venice?! The Concession? It still exists?"

Olivia smiled, "*Sure* it does. And it's still a Spelman property. Sam and Ronia asked Alfie and I to manage it in their stead... uh... a while back, but it's there alright. It's not an income generator for the family... it's more of a safe house or a retreat..."

John asked Ginger, "GingerKat, what do you think? We don't have a destination per se after the Olympics are done. Would you like to go to Venice and see what was your great-great-grandparents' home for so many years? If you like we can stay as long as you wish..." He glanced over to Olivia to see if that were feasible.

She smiled and nodded encouragingly, then added, "Actually the owner's quarters are nearly just as they were when Lorenzo and Miranda left. Even the room where Miranda gave birth to Jean Baptiste---with Mama Belle there as a midwife."

Ginger was in tears just thinking about it. All she could do was look up into John's eyes and whimper a little "Uh-Huhmm," and nod her head.

26 February 94   The Closing Ceremonies are tomorrow and the spectacle of the seventeenth Winter Olympics will come to an end. I am beginning to appreciate the position my family is in with respect to the societies in which we find ourselves. It's true what John wrote in his journals: the Livingsons save everything. The thing is, they just don't acquire much to start with. We are going to Venice in a week or so and I am going to have our little girl in the same room our ancestor, Jean Baptiste, was born. Alfred and Vera have promised to stick with us... although Alfred said he might need to make a few short trips during our stay. Before a few months ago, I had been to London once and all around the States, but never really traveled other than that, and *never* as a tourist. Now it seems John and I are permanent travelers---Citizens of the planet---We really are becoming real Livingsons!

Speaking of that... Auntie Vera was very kind today. She said I had a few peculiarities---a *few*!? I know I am more screwed up than that, but it was very sweet of her to say it none-the-less. Perhaps she was seeing me as she hopes I will be someday. I hope so too. More importantly I am working toward it, every hour, every day, week after week. I'll be more than I am now, and then I'll strive to be more than that. That's all I know to do. And once I can actually 'do,' I'll find some way to contribute to my family. I'm reminded of when Harry rode back from San Francisco with his father, hoping he would somehow find a way to contribute to his family that had done so much for him. He succeeded. MamaKat succeeded. Oliver, Lena, Mia, Viola, Portia, the Larrsons and Eriksons, Sam and Ronia, George, Lila, Alfie, Olivia---even James and Becka are succeeding. John and I have our work cut out for us!

All that aside, today is today---now is now. I must keep my eyes set here in front of me---now that I at last have an inkling of where I'm going.

"You've been gone three months... You might just ask for another sabbatical, or whatever they call it in your business." John answered.

Ginger was trying to decide whether to sever her ties with Boundary Press entirely and start over with another company later if need be.

"They call it 'extended leave,' but I don't know if they'll go for it." Then it dawned on her, "Jeez! I still have to get *your* journals into publication! Talk about falling through the looking glass---just call me Alice! I'd nearly forgotten all about why or how we met in the first place! Whew, this has been an amazingly fast-paced few months," she paused in reflection, "But still, I don't *feel* as though I have been rushed or hurried through anything? Hmmm..."

Alfred asked casually, "Have you ever considered starting your own Press?"

Vera looked up from feeding Hana and waited for Ginger to respond to that interesting notion.

Ginger was a little caught off guard, "Uh, not exactly... although I do know what it takes. I have been doing it for years. Now everything's going toward digital. It wouldn't surprise me if in less than four or five years, print on demand pushes out off-set for good!"

Alfred's interest was piqued, "How's that again? What is 'print-on-demand'?"

Ginger's voice went into recital mode as if she were giving a spiel she'd given many times before... in fact she had. She outlined how books have *traditionally* been produced and how, with the advent of far-flung networks---predominantly the internet and web, "...there's a movement afoot to cease warehousing the thousands of titles produced *each year*. It's environmentally sound as well as economically favorable..."

Alfred asked a few more questions, mostly about who were the players at present, were they public companies, are there any 'up-and-comers'? Ginger gave out what she knew in response to his queries.

"But, you really should find a listing of them and contact them directly. I haven't dealt with the back-office administration of any of the presses or publishers with whom I've worked."

Alfred was tapping his foot on the deck during the whole of the conversation; Vera noticed and was fairly sure what was going through his mind.

John turned a page of the newspaper---in English---he'd picked up. "Hey! The Gallery has a ransom demand from one of those groups claiming responsibility... probably the anti-abortion bandwagon folks... hmm, 'see section H, page two'..."

He flipped through the sections, "Here it is," and he read aloud: *March Third, Oslo (AP) ...A lawyer connected with opponents of abortion said today that one of his clients would arrange the return of "The Scream," the Edvard Munch painting, in exchange for $1 million. A statement on national radio by the lawyer, Tor Erling Staff, was the second time that Norway's small*

183

anti-abortion movement has been linked to the theft of the painting last month. Mr. Staff said he had faxed the client's demands to Culture Minister Ase Kleveland on Wednesday. "The man who contacted me is not the thief, but someone who has the possibility to produce the painting," he said. Mr. Staff is a well-known lawyer whose large clientele includes members of the anti-abortion movement. He filed a court appeal in an unsuccessful attempt to halt the deportation of 12 American anti-abortion campaigners on Feb. 11, the day before the painting was stolen from the National Museum. On Feb. 17, the Rev. Borre Knudsen, a Lutheran minister, who has invited the American campaigners to demonstrate at the Winter Olympic Games, said on radio that the painting would be returned if national television broadcast "The Silent Scream," a film showing a fetus being aborted. The police have expressed little public interest in the statements by the minister and Mr. Staff.

He put the article down, "So now it's a million bucks to boot! These guys are priceless!"

Alfred sneered, "They really need to grow a pair, 'Not the thief but someone who can lay their hands on it?!' Why don't they just come out and say: We haven't got it! I've a good mind to..." and he looked over to Vera. "Darling, the games are over; may I please take care of this little dilemma for the Gallery *now*?"

Vera wiped Hana's chin, "If you feel you must, but please don't make us too delayed for our trip to Venice?"

"Hardly any time at all... Although I will be inviting you all to a little tour of Asgardstrand..." he added cryptically.

4

Now...

"In these matters the only certainty is that nothing is certain. Home is where the heart is."
---Pliny the Elder

4 *March 94*   All I know for sure is: that in less than twenty days Hana Nasrin will be one year old and John and I will have been married four months. I will have five and half more months of carrying MirandaLinn, and the *Anna* will be nearby if we aren't on her already after her birth. I am closer everyday to becoming the *real* Virginia Kaitlyn Belle Spelman-Backhouse. John *is* John Robert Backhouse---Author, and is fast becoming the same 'force of nature' that are our Uncle and Auntie. Alfred and Vera are our constant companions and we are making plans to visit all the families' homes... All of them! I have resigned my position at Boundary Press. I don't know who is going to publish John's journals---but I still have editing to do over the next several months, so that decision can wait for now. We are sailing today for Gotland, with a stop along the way for Alfred in Asgardstrand. Just as when we arrived, as the last of the fleet, we will be the last ones back to our cove in the Baltic.

I made a comment yesterday about feeling as though I'd fallen through the 'looking-glass' like *Alice*, but this doesn't have any of the qualities of a dream. I know John feels much the same way. Neither of us have had a moment's regret or a look back over our shoulders. The sun still rises in the morning, the rain still falls, the wind still fills our sails... we are wholly blessed and we know it. I notice I say 'we' a lot more... it seems so natural and I have difficulty thinking it could be any other way. It's almost like Dickens's *Christmas Carol*, or Capra's

...*Wonderful Life*, except we're not seeing what *might* have been---we're living it here and now! Although I haven't said so for a while, I love my family!

"Good morning GingerKat. Is that your journal? Have you actually become a diarist?!" Alfred inquired as he came to the galley for coffee.

"Actually my first entry was the first of this year and I return to jotting down notes every few days or so. It was a thoughtful gift and I wish to make good the intention behind it," she replied, closing the leather-bound book and tucking it into the shelf above her.

"Noble, very noble... My hat's off to you. I haven't developed that knack as yet. I might should though, the thoughts in my head must be slipping out my ears or something---I don't have the capacity to hold twelve things in my mind so clearly as I once did." He stirred his cup, "Although otherwise I'm bright as ever I was!"

Ginger giggled and kissed his cheek, "You are a bright and shining star in our sky..." she lowered her voice to a whisper, "Your daughter shall be proud of you too---We'll see to that!" She winked; he understood and not another word on the matter was spoken. "How long do you plan for us to be ashore in Asgardstrand?"

"Not terribly long. While my compadres were watching the last of the events the other day, I did a little checking in Nittedal..." he began.

She interrupted, "Nittedal?"

He continued, "Yes it's on the way up into the mountains. My little locator blips have been showing on the screen there this whole time; I thought that was very odd, so I went to see about it. I found them---the frame of the painting in a waste bin. It seems they weren't so inconspicuous as I'd hoped. I removed them and sent an anonymous note to the Gallery regarding their whereabouts."

"What's that to do with Asgardstrand then?" she wondered.

"Only that I also ran down the vehicle license John was good enough to remember and two days ago I finally made the connection to our boys in the seaside village. It was a rental car and not *un*traceable, just clogged with red tape. All we have to do when we arrive is make a search for Mocha-baby---it seems she's run away somewhere near this address..." and he handed her the results of his investigation.

"But Mocha is below waiting for Hana to wake up; she's not lost?!" Ginger countered.

Alfred looked shocked, "She's not?! And I've already had flyers put out around the village with her picture and everything! Oh well..." he grinned.

His scheme became clear. "Uncle Alfred! You are a treasure, aren't you---and I thought Auntie Vera kept a tight leash on you because you were dangerous---but it's actually because you're so valuable!" John came up with Hana in his arms and set her on the rug with a few toys.

"She'll be ready for something more than her bottle in a little bit. She went through it like lightning this morning..." He stretched and went to the nav station. "Weather looks good for several days, we can be in Asgardstrand after mid-day or so. Well Uncle Alfred, shall we weigh anchor?"

"Just give the word, Captain," he replied.

"Consider the word given," John turned back to the computer screen, "...at your leisure then. Viola and Portia have a 'Do not Disturb' sign on the access to their cabins... Auntie Vera was rustling around in y'all's stateroom, so we should all be ready to embark. The *Pebble* and *Hannah* will be in Copenhagen by this evening, the seas are friendly and the wind is steady."

The short voyage down the coast was pleasant enough, but more importantly for John, he actually appeared comfortable at the helm... like he belonged there. Ginger watched him as she fed Hana her 'solid' food. 'He's certainly more himself and less John Doe everyday...' she mused, 'I think he's gotten taller, too! Must be my imagination---that can't really happen, can it? I just remember his head being just shy of the companionway lintel and now he ducks as he passes through it...'

Vera worked a crossword and looked up as Viola opened cabinets and drawers looking for something in the galley. "Lose something?" Vera asked.

"I want to lose my hunger..." she mumbled, "I thought Portia hid a slice of cake in here..."

Ginger laughed, "Oops! Sorry, I was up with Hana late last night and found a piece of cake..."

Viola shifted to the fridge and turned on the stove to begin making eggs and sausages. "Then breakfast food it is... We can blame the missing cake on Mocha; she likes cats."

The smells of the galley, the fresh sea air and a clear sky made the morning invigorating. Although still cold they were sailing again and it felt grand to be at sea. Vera took a rag and began methodically cleaning one of the bridge windows.

Ginger asked, "Vera? Let me do that, you go back to your crossword and keep an eye on Hana please..."

Vera replied, "You saw *how* I was cleaning?"

Ginger caught the nuance, "Yes Auntie, I saw *how*."

Ginger began with the same window Vera had begun: left hand counter-clockwise applying the cleaner, right hand clockwise removing and polishing. She took her time, trying to allow her mind to keep up with the movements. She whistled as she toiled and soon Portia recognized the tune: Dylan's, *Boots of Spanish Leather*, and she tried harmony. Not to be left out, Viola took the fifth and Vera hummed a bass line. When that was over they began *Time's They are a Changin'* and then some other, more obscure ballads. By the time the insides of all the windows were cleaned, and Ginger was ready to bundle up and clean the outsides, they were just finishing *Story of the Hurricane*. Meanwhile Alfred had been composing a letter or something at the desk.

John announced, "We'll be at Asgardstrand in less than an hour. You might wait on the rest of the windows, for a little while at least."

Ginger looked over to Vera, who smiled and nodded her assent. Hana had fallen asleep during the 'concert' and Alfred said, "I hope our littlest angel is up when we get to town, I am counting on her winning smile and native charms to lubricate y'all's door-to-door search."

Portia said, "What?!"

Ginger explained what she'd understood from the early morning chat with Alfred, and smiles rose on all their faces. "Clever! Very clever, Alfred!" Portia admitted, "Okay, we'll play along..."

Alfred pulled out a map of the village and pointed along the street they would focus on during the search. "Hopefully, one of the two of 'our boys' will be home... if I had a valuable artwork in my house, I'd be sure someone didn't steal it from me after I'd done such an effective job of stealing it myself..." He covered the approach again, "John you will have to carry Hana, since you're the only one who can recognize them; you'll be less intimidating just standing 'nearby' holding the baby. Well ladies, are you ready for a good stretch of the legs?"

Ginger protested, "Why can't I go with them?"

Alfred, put out his lower lip, "I'm sorry sweetheart, but don't you have the *outsides* of the windows to finish?"

She muttered a soft, "Urgh, a girl's *work* is never done!" In a brighter voice she said, "Hana, be a good little spy for MamaKat, won't you?"

Hana burbled something and they were away. Ginger put on her coat, hat and gloves and went to begin her chores.

A while later Vera brought out a cup of hot tea for GingerKat. "...And the windows are looking better too... how delightful!"

Ginger smiled and accepted the warm mug. "What's Alfred going to do once we locate our rascals?"

Vera looked up toward town, "He has friends in interesting places. I suppose he'll be sending one of them an evocative notice and his thoughts on how to both: recover the painting and capture the goofs... He loves this sort of thing. I'm so glad we stay on his good side! Anyway, he's promised this is as far as he needs to take the 'case'."

"There they come! That didn't take very long..." Ginger commented.

Vera looked at her, "Darling they were gone almost two hours."

Ginger looked surprised, "My how time flies when you're on a yacht in a strange port, cleaning windows that are already clean!"

Viola and Portia were obviously tickled about something. "Guess what Hana did?" they began when they were within earshot.

"Our little angel has the instincts of a sleuth! We walked to every house on the street Alfred indicated... and zippo, nada..."

"Then as we turned a corner to go down the next street over, HanaRin practically twisted Johnny's head off making him turn around and check two of the doors that looked to be just alley entrances."

"They weren't! And at the first door we knocked on to give our sad tale of woe once more..."

"Hana squealed and Johnny nodded that was one of our guys!"

She held up the address for Alfred and grinned, "Mission accomplished Sir Alfred Conan Doyle..."

They arrived near Gothenburg by late evening. At least the air was no longer freezing as they made anchor off Branno, a sheltered

Island with a good harbor. Alfred had sent off his missive by email to an old friend at the 'Yard,' and was ready to celebrate the recovery of 'the Scream.'

"Shouldn't we hold off on parties until they *actually* have it back in the Gallery?" Vera asked gently.

"We could, but we'll probably be in Venice by the time they get their act together enough to follow through with a very simple plan. Meanwhile we are close enough to Gothenburg to make me feel as though we are full circle---from the first hint of the theft to the first ray of hope at its recovery---Partytime!"

Alfred stomped the deck with his foot. In answer, from his well-timed signal it seemed that the speakers 'stomped' back at him; the strains of 'We will, We will Rock You...' came blaring over the ship's sound system. They had a party.

John weighed anchor in the wee hours of the morning and they were passed Copenhagen by mid-day with the sun on their backs as they sailed northeast toward Visby. By around midnight the lights of the Larrsons' Cove glowed off the starboard bow and they were home safe and sound. They spent a few days visiting and making last minute arrangements and repairs. On the ninth of March they were heading for the Kiel canal and the coast down to Amsterdam---then it would be seven or eight days on to Venice.

9 March 94　　　　I've cleaned windows, scrubbed the inside decks, dusted, cleaned bathrooms and rearranged our stores. Tomorrow I get to start all over! It may sound at first blush like I'm a servant on my own ship, but that's not the case. This is a list of my credits---not my burdens. I'm getting wonderful training and the *Anna's* getting a most thorough going over to boot. Win-win. You can't imagine how much I'm looking forward to the Inn in Venice---I hope it needs repainting or all the floors cleaned. I know at least I will get to learn to row a sampan... How cool is that?!

I'm looking out at the sea, Hana's asleep and I keep thinking: our girls will be raised on this ship for the better part of their young lives. What will they think of the world? Then I remember that at least they will have a head start in knowing how it's *supposed* to be in reality. They will know the whys and the hows John and I didn't know at their age. What will they want to be when they grow up? What new technologies be available to them that aren't even imagined right now? What challenges will they face? Where will they want to live? I know I'm just imagining, and I don't have enough information to follow after answers, but... we're parents now and I'm beginning to understand life from a whole other perspective than I had not so long ago. Thinking is good. I should however think about things I can actually come to some resolution over. Like: what will I do when they ask to go to Amsterdam, alone? Or what will we say when they bring home odd creatures in boys' disguise? Or how will they know we love them?

First things first---John and I need to get the journals edited. Alfred seemed interested in print-on-demand technology, I wonder if he has ideas to make that a reality as another business for our family? Actually that's a very good idea. We can make a difference by what we choose to publish and distribute... I wonder if anyone else, besides Auntie Lila, has kept journals over the years? It's a small start, but if I know anything by now---it's that *everything* starts small.

11 March 94   I don't know if John realizes it but he's been humming a lot. Do I hum? I asked Vera and Alfred if either of them played the piano or any other instrument. What I discovered is that it's difficult getting a straight answer out of Alfred when he'd rather not divulge something. What could be so sensitive about admitting to playing the piano? At least Vera said outright that she never learned an instrument. I want to learn the piano and I have just a few years to learn enough to teach the girls... I need to get busy as soon as we reach Venice. I think we need to learn Italian and Swedish also... I think they speak English in Sri Lanka.

Amsterdam was beautiful---that is to say the galleries and museums held beautiful things. Well, also Amsterdam is a pretty place, we took a bike tour and we didn't even get sore! More importantly neither of us got 'sore' when the *Agate* appeared to have been stolen. We docked her near the Rembrandt House and took a walking tour of that end of the city---the Old Kirke, the red light district and other notable places. When we returned to where we all knew we tied off the boat, it wasn't there. That was an odd sensation. After retracing our steps and verifying once again that that was in fact where we left her, one of the boat people on the canal waved a greeting and mentioned that she'd seen a launch taken down the canal that way, and she pointed. We didn't have much else to do otherwise so we followed the street along the canal in that direction. We nearly made it all the way to the harbor again, when Vera saw it tied off next to a Coffeeshop two blocks over on another canal. Now that may seem strange, that she could spot *our* launch amongst all the boats on the canals, but then you haven't been to Amsterdam. Almost all of them are houseboats converted from longboats; they are a very uniform shape and size. The few other boats to be seen are a different design from our launches, so it wasn't as much searching for a needle in a haystack as it may seem. When we got over to that canal the *Agate* was gone again. Alfred saw it turn into the Leidsegracht canal, so we split up to check the both directions it could go. When John and I emerged at our end we spotted it further down to our right and waved for Vera and Alfred to follow as we headed towards the newest mooring. Fortunately this time it was still there when we arrived.

We made sure it was the *Agate*. A fellow and his girlfriend came out of the house above it while we were inspecting it. She says, 'Their taking your boat Jerry!' and he answers, 'Nah, you must be confused, that's not my boat.' And she says, 'Yes it is; it says *Agate* on the back and everything.' Then she drags him over and demands to know what we're doing with *his* boat. John smiles and explains our whole day to her. By then she was fuming mad and she punched 'Jerry' in the ribs and kicked him in the nethers then stormed off. Jerry chased after her but we decided he was on a fool's errand at best. Anyway the point of this little tale, beyond getting our launch back with very little disconbobulation on our part, is to say 'Jerry' and his *ex*-girlfriend left a large quantity of Amsterdam's best in the launch, and neither John nor I had ever tried it before. So we did. Note to self: Don't smoke and edit or write---Otherwise: pretty harmless. What's the fuss about?

"Mont Saint Michel within the hour!" called Ginger from the helm, "And it appears we're coming in on a high tide. We're going to dock at the island!"

The others turned to the windows with binoculars in hand. Sure enough, the sea reached all the way to the waves lapping against the island monastery-fortress.

"What an occasion!" Alfred exclaimed.

John looked at the depth finder. "Uh, we are rapidly moving into our draft zone... How long is the tide in?"

Alfred replied, "It's a new moon... so figure... three or four hours. Then in twelve hours it should come in again. So even if we are stranded on this go around, we'll be floating again in relatively no time."

Ginger looked at the others then to Johnny, "It's your call Captain. Shall we sail right up to their gate, or we can heave to and take the *Black Pearl* in... she has the slightly shallower draft of the two..."

John didn't hesitate, "I'm not stranding the *Anna* anywhere if I can help it. We'll anchor a mile or so out, where she'll even float at low tide and take the launch in." Ginger pointed the *Anna* north of the island as he said it.

"Oh boy!" Ginger and Vera were both excited, "Dinner on Mont Saint Michel. Can we stay overnight?" John and Alfred looked at each other with straight faces.

John broke the news... "Uh, yes we'll definitely be staying overnight. And if we aren't up and in the launch at high tide tomorrow morning, we'll be there the rest of the day tomorrow as well..."

Ginger blushed, "Oh yeah, I see what you mean... Oops..."

John smiled "No harm, no foul my love. Uncle Alfred will you give me a hand with the launch once I drop the anchor?"

"Aye, aye sir," he answered and handed Hana over to Vera. "Was that fun munchkin? You got to see through binoculars..." Actually Hana hadn't given up 'seeing through binoculars;' she was most fascinated by the phenomenon and Vera had to keep holding her up to the window until she was quite satisfied that the 'pictures in the magic glasses' wasn't going away.

Once in the *Black Pearl*, they motored across the mile of surf leading right up to the fortress walls. There was a watergate on the southeast side where the channel was deepest. They moored and set off up the steep lanes and steps to secure a room. That accomplished, they selected a restaurant for the evening. John was grinning like a Cheshire cat all the while.

Vera and Ginger had to ask, "What's up with the idiotic grin?"

"Wait until we are seated and have a glass of wine; I'll be delighted to tell you," he hedged.

They were offered a choice of tables as it wasn't the height of tourist season, and word had already made it through the village of Montois that *this* group had arrived by yacht. John selected a table at the bay window looking back up to the mainland over the still tidally submerged saltmarshes---effectively they were on an island.

Glasses were filled and John raised his for a toast. "As the only one of us who evidently knows precisely where we are and exactly which rooms we have for the night..."

Vera interrupted, "Johnny, we all know where we are and which rooms we have... numbers three and four right across the lane there..." and she pointed.

"Very well," he grinned broader if that were possible, "then you evidently know that at *this* moment we are sitting at the *exact* table, and are lodged in the *precise* rooms in which Harry, Kaitlyn and the rest of their entourage stayed on their trip here one hundred and seven years ago nearly to the day! 'To love and to all those who bear it'!" He clinked his glass to each one in turn as they woodenly gazed back at him.

Alfred and Vera were the first to break the spell and say, "You've *got* to be kidding!"

Followed quickly by Ginger who held Hana tighter and in a hushed tone said, "Oh my God... and Hana is sitting where *another* baby Hannah once sat at *that* dinner!"

Vera and Ginger were tearing up fast as the implications swept over them. Alfred wasn't so far behind them in dabbing his own eyes. John just sat and looked out over the sparkling sea and pastel sky as sunset drew across the bay.

Alfred muttered, "All our great-grandparents were right here..." and he rubbed his hand across the table as if perhaps being able to sense them directly. Vera's ancestors weren't apart of that gathering, but her long personal relationships with almost all those venerable folks certainly gave her cause for heartfelt reminiscence.

John finally commented, "I *thought* y'all would like to know that little historical tidbit..."

The next morning, John took them on a tour of the island monastery-abbey-fortress. He had not only recorded the history of the Livingsons---their story had become his own---the history of his own life and ancestry. He knew it as well as his own memories. Everywhere they walked that day he had an anecdote, another tale or a conversation that marked a new direction in what would become the hundred year journey of George Henry Livingson and Kaitlyn

Elizabeth Spelman-Livingson, their family and their impact on all those that followed. When they reached one certain place along the eastern wall, Johnny stopped and held their hands.

"Just as Belle said when she once sat on this parapet on this very spot and looked out to Tomberlaine," and he pointed across the marshland, "We know we are on hallowed ground just as she felt it that day a century ago."

They boarded the launch and reached the *Anna* while the tide was in late the next afternoon. Once all was secure once more, they made sail for the northwest point of Spain and on around Portugal for Gibraltar.

16 March 94   I know it is not possible to actually sense or feel the emanations of a person from long ago. And I know stones don't actually hold onto a trace of a memory of those who once trod them. But, there was something so instinctively and emotionally overwhelming about being on that island that was so completely outside my experience. Yes, I know that having John tell us about each spot and vantage point evoked those experiences in us... but that's the point---the island made the history *real* and *tangible* to me and to Alfred and Vera as well. We shall most certainly return there when our daughters are older and they will be able to have that living memory of their forebears as we now have. Thank you John for deciding to be a writer, thank you for listening and recording every word, thank you for sharing yourself with me. I am blessed.

Sailing down the coast of Portugal, the air is getting warmer and the nights aren't so chilling. I hope it holds all the way to Venice. Since the change in temperature, Vera has moved my scrubbing activities out onto the whole of the *Anna's* decks. I am still supple enough to wash and apply a brazilian teak wax. I know I must look like a combination water bug-giant inchworm out there, but the deck looks more than fabulous and I am gaining new postures and movements, new connections between centers, greater attention and focus, and best of all---I remember myself more often than not. How does that go: *A sleeping man might notice moments of conscience, a conscious man recognizes his moments of sleep...* I'm 'sleeping' less and less these days.

Hana did another in her long series of amazing feats: she outsmarted Mocha this morning. One of the cat's favorite pastimes is running across the bridge between companionways to go below, across the lower salon and emerging at the other companionway again... sometimes repeating the circuit like a race car around a track. Hana was playing at the sofa next to the galley and tossed one of her poof toys where Mocha could grab it, which she did. The cat ran off with it through the far companionway, but instead of following Mocha, Hana went to the *other* companionway and stood there beside it. Sure enough, in a moment there came Mocha and Hana pounced on her. They tumbled across the rug and Hana came up with the poof toy--- and a few scratches. Did my little girl cry? Not one tear! She held up the toy out of Mocha's reach and twirled around in what we decided was the 'Hana Victory Dance.' Too cute!

"This evening we'll be anchoring in the harbor at Favignana, off Sicily..." John announced and yawned as Vera came to the galley for coffee.

He and Alfred were up most of the night---John at the helm and Alfred at the computer. They maintained a conversation of sorts, sometimes talking about two different topics, but it kept them awake and attentive.

"So... two days from Venice, then?" she asked.

"'Bout that. Remind Ginger she can use the outside helm and wheel. The weather is beautiful and if she hasn't had enough of the outdoors by now, the fresh air will do her wonderfully I should think..." and he yawned again.

"I heard her singing to Hana as I came up, she should be along in a moment... you can remind her yourself." Vera replied.

John chuckled, "That's if I can remember all the way until then.

What were we talking about?"

Hana came crawling up the steps and squealed what sounded like 'Mordie,' which they took for 'morning.'

"Good morning Princess!" John answered in greeting, "Where's mama?"

Hana looked at him and looked at Vera, then she raised her arm and pointed behind her down the companionway from which she'd just come. She turned and squatted down---as if she really needed to duck the lintel---and looked down the steps. She clapped and stood up as Ginger emerged.

"I'm for bed!" John exclaimed and passed the helm to his wife.

Ginger looked at Vera, "He was up all night again! It's like he's determined to get up to Venice as soon as possible---likes it's a race or something."

Vera smiled-sighed-shrugged in that expression of 'what's a girl to do?' look. Ginger nodded and checked their heading and sail trim, looked at the forecast and made a tentative course plot for the day.

"There. May I have some coffee please?"

"Coming right up..." Vera announced. Alfred entered whistling a merry tune.

Instantly suspicious, Vera remarked, "Well you certainly are chipper this fine morning... What are you up to now?"

Alfred tried to look hurt, but he couldn't manage it. "I'm looking forward to catching tuna this afternoon is all... really!" Vera was uncertain. He added reluctantly, "...*and* last night I made some inquiries into what it would take to begin a start-up print-on-demand operation..." Vera crossed her arms, but Ginger was ecstatic.

"Uncle Alfred! How great..." she caught herself and asked, "...Uh, is it feasible? I mean do we have to have a factory or a plant or something to make it go?"

He took a sip of coffee and went to the computer at the nav

station, "See for yourself..." and he pulled up his data, then relieved her at the wheel. Vera went to look at the preliminary information also. The two women scrolled down through the data, and got to the last few entries: paragraphs of projections and setup costs.

Vera commented, "Alfred dearest, it doesn't say what *size* building or *square footage* estimates or anything... Did you get sleepy?"

He chuckled, "No... well yes I did, but that's not the issue. A person could start up their own print-on-demand operation in their living room if they wanted to. Beside the expense of the computers, and the large format inkjet printers, the only other expenses are a bindery machine and commercial paper-cutters if you wish to work in bulk..." Ginger and Vera looked at the bottom lines again.

"Uncle Alfred, is *this really* the whole cost?!" Ginger uttered.

"Yes Punkin, that's the whole cost---for start-up. The next page outlines overhead and weekly, monthly and annual expenses in materials and supplies. I estimated low: at fifty titles and a few hundred printings per title. Once that was accomplished, it's just like a recipe for pancakes---a proportional increase determined by desired quantities of product." He went back to whistling.

Ginger relieved him at the wheel and thought, 'John and I could use the Inn... it has enough space---without even intruding on the living and dining areas. We could set it up on one whole side of the upstairs and dedicate one room to printing, one to binding and one for warehousing materials and product. I know my industry contacts are viable for distribution...' She was staring out at the glistening morning sun on the Mediterranean ahead of them and reached for her sunglasses. 'We really need to learn a couple more languages... or find reliable translators... and how was *I* going to find these *obscure* poets and writers? Put an ad in the local newspaper?! Where there are no newspapers? Get with it Ginger-girl!...'

Her musings were interrupted momentarily by Mocha shrieking and bolting from the bridge cabin. Hana was still standing next to the sofa and table with her sippy cup upside down and a cherubic expression on her face.

"HanaRin? Were you *feeding* the cat?" Ginger asked evenly.

Hana nodded her head and grinned, waving the sippy cup in front of her so that drops were splattered by the motion. Ginger added, "Let Mocha-baby have a *choice* of whether she *wants* to 'eat,' okay darling? You *might* get scratched if you hold her down to feed her!" Hana held up her elbow and then pointed at her knee and made a most sad face, "yeah yeah..." she agreed. There were little scratches where she indicated, but still not a peep of complaint escaped her lips.

The only two things Favignana had going for it in the short time the *Anna* was around the cove, were the one beach, Lido Burrone and *really* good tuna fishing. John and Vera took Hana to the beach where she got to use her little shovel and pail at last, while Ginger and Alfred fished for tuna and continued their discussion of the print business.

Alfred cast and added, "You know the rest of our family *do* speak several languages and very likely come into contact with just the clientele your seeking..." Ginger had one on the hook and her reel whirred as the fish took out the line. "Use your gloved hand to slow the spool!" Alfred cautioned. She got it under control and began fighting it in. Alfred reeled in his line and fetched the gaff. "Even if they were to send along a hand-written manuscript, we could type it up and have it translated, return both the original and translated copies to the writer and leave it to him or her to verify them... Keep the line taut, but don't yank on it. Good." The fish was a tuna, not a great whomping monster, but a good size for their dinner. "Oh boy, grilled tuna tonight!" he announced.

The beach wasn't warm but it wasn't too cold either. Hana found all kinds of uses for her 'tools' that weren't envisioned by the manufacturers. Who'd have thought they could be such an effective scepter and crown, or boat and warehouse, or... well catapult and reloader had probably been done before.

John asked, "Did I get that right? Ginger's idea of a publishing business may be a 'go'?"

Vera answered while removing the last barrage of sand from her hair, "It would appear that not only that, but you may have to ramp up your own writing and editing to keep up..."

"Whew! I'm glad we'll have a home base for a while then. Vera? Is this how the other 'family interests' began---An idea that got fleshed out and then plunged into whole hog?"

Vera chuckled, "I don't know about *all* of them, but once all the denying forces are evaluated and reconciled, it is just a matter of 'doing it'."

Hana left her pail and shovel and began toddling along the beach searching the sand for... something. She squatted down and picked up a piece of iridescent broken shell. One would have thought she'd found the treasury of Solomon. She soon had so many pieces that she kept dropping them as she went to gather another and another. John was watching her carefully on the off chance she veered into something harmful or into the surf. What she did then was surprising rather than scary though. She made a little pile of her 'treasures,' made a mound of sand around them then ran back to get her pail and shovel. When she found her mound again, she began 'sorting' her shell pieces and depositing them in the pail. Well 'sorting' is an odd interpretation, regardless of each item's merits or demerits it was tossed into the pail anyway.

Even after everyone had their fill of tuna that evening there was enough to store away for snacks and another meal. With the scirocco behind them up through the Adriatic, they arrived in the lagoon and entered the lanes to go around to the moorings just outside Sacco Della Misericordia and the Misericordia canal that led nearly to the Inn.

"We couldn't actually purchase these docks, so we had to settle for ninety-nine year leases on three of them---I guess they qualify as income generators too, but most of it goes to maintenance..." Alfred explained as the *Anna* came close enough to cast her mooring lines.

Vera announced, "Seldom do our ships actually tie off to a dock... so Mocha shall now earn her keep. Ginger you might want to find an assistant for her."

Ginger looked momentarily confused until she remembered the point of having a cat aboard a boat to begin with, "Ooh. Mocha-baby get busy! No more lazing about!"

The short ride down the canal to the Concession was over before they knew it and Alfred handed Ginger the keys. "Vera and I, along with Portia and Viola, were the last ones here..." he looked at Vera, who finished, "three hundred and fifteen days ago..."

John looked at her and remarked, "Auntie? Are you sure about that 'estimate'?"

They all laughed, while only the other three understood the implication. Ginger unlocked and opened the front entry area, then crossed and unlocked to open the main doors proper.

She called in a loud voice, "We're Home!"

Her voice echoed around the front room. Vera and Alfred went to open the louvre doors around the courtyard, while John carried Hana and opened drapes and blinds. He set her on her own feet and she toddled off toward the registration desk. Ginger walked to the wall where Miranda's sampan was mounted, and just stared at it. Vera and Alfred noticed, then John saw her too.

"Sweetheart, shall Alfred and I make an inventory of the kitchen and go out for supplies?"

Ginger turned her face away from the boat on the wall and through a few tears of joy she just nodded. Vera went into the courtyard and turned on the water to the Inn.

Then called, "GingerKat, let me show you the rest of your house."

They climbed stairs until they reached the back of the upper floor. "Here are the main switches and fuse box..." she opened the panel and Ginger reached in and threw the main breaker. Nothing happened. "Excellent!" Vera intoned and closed the panel. Ginger's questioning look brought the response, "It's *good* because it means we *did* turn everything off before shutting her down last year, and it's good because: no loud popping is a good thing!"

Vera then guided her and Hana to the owner's apartments. She opened the unbolted door and held it for Ginger and Hana to enter. Ginger crossed the room to the drapes and pulled them back. Sunlight flooded the salon and the many-colored carpets and rugs sprang to life. She turned slowly around looking at the wall hangings and tapestries, then she went to the hallway. She opened the doors to the guest room, to the bathroom and finally to the master bedroom.

Vera asked, "Can you see everything clearly, dear?" Ginger looked back at her, tears in her eyes.

Vera smiled, "I thought not..." and she flipped on the light switches in each room. Ginger picked up Hana and they sat on the big bed in the master bedroom---her and John's bedroom---her great-great-grandparents' bedroom. She was obviously whelmed.

"When Alfred and I are here we sleep in the guest room. I am not aware that anyone has slept in here since Lorenzo and Miranda left the last time. We'll need to change the sheets and air out the comforter and quilts."

She picked up a bundle of the bedding and took it out to the balcony. As she was spreading them along the railings, Ginger came out with a bundle of her own and soon the upper balcony around the courtyard began to look inhabited once more.

"Shall we go through and uncover the rest of the furniture?" Vera asked as she headed down a side stairwell.

Ginger called, "Come along Hana, we've got some work to do here!"

Hana toddled out of the apartments and followed her mother to the steps; she reached up her little hand.

Ginger smiled, "You might as well get used to the stairs sometimes..."

She took the girl's hand and they slowly descended into the great room once more. Vera was already removing and folding sheets from off the chairs in the sitting room near the fireplace. They finished that room then moved to the dining hall. When that was done they went to the kitchen.

"We will do some potting and planting..." she said as she opened the back door, "On our other shorter visits it hasn't been practical to have plants---only to just leave them behind..."

The greenhouse was bright, humid and warm beyond the door. Ginger followed Hana out into the long room. The toddler put her fingers into every pot of soil within reach and plopped down on the tiled floor to pull at a few of the worts growing up through the joints between tiles.

"I've never grown plants. Except when I was little, my adopted parents had a garden patch behind the house. I only remember weeding it, Peggie did the growing and harvesting." Ginger remarked.

"You should get some experience now!" Vera commented, "It's very rewarding... and some varieties of plants might be nice to have on the *Anna*---herbs, and such. Oh! That reminds me. You and I will need to get you up to speed on medicinal plants. MamaKat was very thorough with augmenting my medical training with her own vast knowledge of natural remedies---We'll build you your own Medicines Chest... very practical."

The gentlemen returned and came to the kitchen loaded with sacks and bags of staples, perishables, and to Ginger and Vera's delight: seeds!

Vera grinned, "Do we have good men or what!"

John and Alfred put away everything and laid out bread, cheese cold meats and a bottle of wine on the kitchen table.

"Wine in moderation is just fine... for a 'growing' girl," Vera told Ginger when she balked at a glass. "Alright George Alfred Nils Livingson, it's time to retire for a while to the music salon..." and she gave him a 'look.'

He understood implicitly and headed for the salon. The others carried their snacks and glasses to sit around a coffee table near the fireplace. Alfred took a seat at the Steinway and ran his hand along the ivories to test its general tuning. Satisfied, and with Ginger staring unbelievingly, he placed his fingers to the keys and began the first movement of the Moonlight Sonata.

For several minutes neither John nor Ginger breathed. The magic of the melody, the light through the windows, the warm tones of the rugs and Hana standing at his elbow as he played had utterly mesmerized them. The piano reverberated through the Inn, into the courtyard and filled the space around them like the smoky vapors of an incense burner. They were soothed, inspired and in a revery each of them only seldom experienced. Vera's eyes were closed and she hummed with the melody line. When the last strains faded into the air of the room, she opened her tear-filled eyes and asked softly, "Would you play the other one I like?"

John and Ginger were still in awe of what seemed an impromptu concert held just for them. Alfred began and the 'Ode to Joy' resounded in the room. His adaptation for the piano held the beauty of a full orchestra with the light high notes of a choral rendition. It was magical. When all the room was quiet once again, Ginger asked in a very small voice, "Uncle Alfred, will you help me to learn to play?"

He smiled warmly, "Of course, come on over here."

Ginger's eyes opened wider, "Now?!"

"Is there another time?" he responded. She rose and went to sit with him on the bench. He set Hana in his place next to her. "Now let's simply begin with some fundamentals, shall we..."

John and Vera went upstairs to the conservatory above the owner's apartments. She opened the louvres and the late afternoon light flooded the room. "Johnny, you shall have several months in which to complete your edits and begin a new series while we are here awaiting your next daughter..."

"Auntie Vera, about that," and he tried to find the words he wanted, "I don't know if Ginger has noticed yet, but Hana *isn't* Kurdish. In fact she's so much more like you and Alfred it's spooky. Have you noticed how her eyes are exactly like Alfred's and her hair is lightening to closer to your shade, and her little fingers look amazingly like miniature versions of your hands and when she stands up to walk she straightens herself and her shoulders precisely as you do..."

Vera held up her hand. "Yes, Johnny, Ginger has noticed. We have had a lovely chat about those very observations."

After she removed the sheet covering it, she sat down on a settee and patted the seat next to her. John sat down with her.

"You see, my dear one, Alfred and I really had no idea we could have possibly conceived, but we are not the sort to shy away from a challenge. I carried her to term, even while we tramped through villages and across the country sides of Georgia, Azerbaijan and the Kurdish homelands of Northern Iraq with Portia and Viola. Hana *really was* born in a bombed out Kurdish Village just as the girls told you. What we asked them *not* to tell you was that that's where my water broke and I went into labor. Those two women were a godsend---I've delivered I don't know how many babies into this world, but it is another matter entirely to be the one doing the pushing!" She giggled, "Alfred was a dear, he had been trying to think of names for weeks, but when Hana emerged he greeted her by her full name and she yelled at that instead needing to be slapped for her first breath of life. He looked at her and said, 'Young lady, your mother is tired and you should rest too---besides it's a perfectly good name!' Anyway, we came straight back to this Inn...''

John said, "Aah, so that's why you knew to the day when you were last here---and Hana's birthday is approaching... That reminds me of the other question that had been bothering me: How could y'all have known *for sure* what her birthday actually was... Now I get it!"

She continued, "Quite so. Anyway, the longer we gazed at our little miracle the more we began to recognize the repercussions of her birth, our ages and a normal life... so we rejoined the family in the Caribbean on the *Hannah* with Viola and Portia and made them swear to keep to the story we'd prepared, which you heard. Now six people know the truth of Hana's birth... and we'd *really* like it to remain an exclusive story." She looked at John earnestly and he nodded solemnly.

"I am just so honored, and I'm sure Ginger is, to be selected by y'all to raise her..."

Vera smiled, "And imagine how tickled we were when you two 'insisted' we live with you on the *Anna!* It has been a dream come true!"

John stretched out his feet in front of him; the sounds of scales and a few chords from the piano wafted up to their ears. "Just one more thing," he turned to Vera and asked, "Has Uncle Alfred told you how my training is going? Because he doesn't say anything to me except that 'You're progressing nicely, very nicely indeed...' anytime I ask him. You knew my father, and... well... Am I anything like him?" A tear rolled down one of his cheeks.

Vera put her arm over his shoulders and whispered, "Robidob would have been most proud of you, not just because you look just like him, but because you are his son through and through. You have the same cautious, but friendly manner, the same disarming grin that puts others at ease, and most of all: you have that amazing memory and recall. Ginger let me look through your journals---you have an unparalleled ability of recollection and you *definitely* inherited his heart of gold. That you were so good to Ginger when she turned up on your doorstep, told her about her family so thoroughly and let yourself fall in love with her... it takes my breath away..." She had to compose herself before continuing.

John commented, "Well I don't know about 'letting myself fall in love with her,' she's just about the greatest thing that ever walked through my door... and she's... well, she's..." Vera took over when he faltered for modifiers.

"Anyway, Alfred doesn't ask *me* about *Ginger's* progress and I don't ask *him* about *yours*---that's all between master and student--- but what I *can* say is that he is more happy and satisfied now than he ever was, and I know it isn't all to do with my... how did you put it?... 'Athletic' activities?" and she laughed out loud. John could have blushed but he was too happy to be self-conscious over anything.

"Thank you Aunt Vera that means more to me than you can imagine," he stammered and rose to look out over the rooftops and canals.

The westering sun over the far lagoon made it appear that the island was bounded by a cordon of fire instead of sea. He took deep breaths and let his tears trickle down his face unchecked.

21 March 94   If I wake up in my flat in Chelsea and this has all been a dream---I'm heading directly to a little house in north Texas, down a winding road outside a little town I know, to find a man named: John Doe! Seriously, no matter how wonderful one day is, the next day brings something even greater. I don't know, but if this goes on I may expire from an overdose of bliss! But here's the job: some slight repainting on the outside, all the courtyard and in the rooms we want to keep for more guests---John and I are thrilled---how strange are *we*?! The other neat thing about being me is that this is *my Inn*, so I get to choose the paint colors for the outside, inside, any and all the rooms, you name it. Me! The girl who never stayed in her own apartment, or grew houseplants or had a pet... that girl with the tempest of a temper and such a foul mouth... the sworn-to-be-single woman, the fast-paced, get it done yesterday businesswoman, insecure and brazen enough for two women... ME! I looked through my knapsack when we grabbed things off the *Anna* to have with us in the Inn for the next several months and I found my appointment book. That was an eye-opener. How did I do it? What was I running from? It's a wonder I hadn't burned out young.

We went out yesterday and shopped for toys appropriate for a one year old. The selection was disquieting. What ever happened to alphabet blocks and wooden trains? To rag dolls and tinker toys? We ended up buying materials to make some toys for her. Hana will encounter the modern world soon enough---the cell phones, laptops, CDs, grunge, rap and the ever-growing world of Barbies... Until then she'll have a full dose of reality and the soundness of a healthy home life. John is making posters of some of his favorite diagrams from his journals, I couldn't be more pleased---talk about instructive wall décor! We also have found an assistant for Mocha-baby---two actually. Now she can leave the *Anna* in good hands, I mean paws, for a while and follow Hana around the Inn. She was used to sleeping with her, either just under Hana's hammock or in it when Hana helped her up. Speaking of that... Hana is taking a little while getting used to a normal bed. John volunteered to hang a hammock for her, but both Vera and I agree: she's going to have to get used to different things---it's just part of life!

Vera has arranged my schedule so that early mornings we are out in the sampan and afternoons are for painting. John's schedule is just reversed from mine. It's not that we actually need the 'shift' and 'just so' of the routine in the boat, but it so makes us feel like part of the family; we just can't help ourselves. It's a modest identification we can both live with.

"Happy Birthday to you, Happy Birthday to you. Happy Birthday dear Hana, Happy Birthday to you!" they sang and placed a cake in front of her with a solitary candle on it.

"Blow it out!" Ginger coaxed and showed Hana what she meant. Hana puffed out her cheeks in imitation of her mother and then they collapsed again, clearly not catching the nuances of 'blowing.' After a few more tries, she caught on and the candle was extinguished by a mixture of exhale and spit.

"Whatever works..." Ginger commented, and sliced off pieces of cake for everyone. Hana's was smaller than the others and her little brow furrowed in confusion.

"Eat that much and then there's ice cream too... We'll try and avoid a tummy ache if we can..." John consoled her. The wrapping paper shredded all over the floor behind her was testament to her being anxious to try new things. The toys were naturally secondary to ripping the paper and playing with the empty boxes. Many of her notions of 'playing' she'd obviously picked up from the cat.

"One year old!" Alfred repeated. "Our princess is just getting bigger every moment! John you might as well start rehearsing your spiel to prospective suitors now... they'll be lining up at the door any day now!"

Vera and Ginger held up the new little outfits Hana had received. "She'll probably wear the nicest dresses to play in the greenhouse and demand to wear her play rompers out on special occasions... if she's anything like me as a little girl..." Ginger remarked with a grin. "I was never a 'little lady'!"

Alfred made a comment in mock surprise, "You! A tomboy! Who'd have thunk it! You mean all those hunting and fishing trips with Harvey---you actually enjoyed those?! So only owning two dresses wasn't from a shallow bank account?!"

"Ha, Ha, Ha." Ginger retorted and stuck out her tongue. Hana thought that was elegant and promptly imitated her. Ginger saw it and rolled her eyes. "I am such a *great* role model for my daughter! She'll be scarred for life from my ridiculous behavior..."

Vera squatted on the floor with Hana and began making faces to go with her tongue out, until they were both able to make the most inane expressions. Vera looked up at Ginger, "She's going to pick it up sometime, might as well have her do it really well!" Hana practiced her new look on John and Alfred, who tried to respond in kind. "We'll get around to 'when' she should employ this talent when she's old enough to choose... right now all she wants and can do is grow and imitate everyone and everything around her. Those are the centers that develop first..." Vera assured her. "Remember darling, few parents even know their own construction let alone its actual development. Many of the child-rearing notions people carry around with them aren't thought through, and those that are still don't have an actual basis in reality. 'Someone said to do this and they did it, another person said do that and they did it'... ad infinitum, ad absurdum."

GingerKat sighed and looked at her little angel still making her odd expressions, "We'll learn together little one; we'll learn together."

24 March 94   Four months into this pregnancy and I see more elastic waist crinkle skirts on my horizon. As the weather warms I think dresses will be a comfortable alternative to cargo pants and shorts---which is all that's in my spring and summer wardrobe now. Who knows I may even shop for some of those poofy peasant tops---if my breasts continue to grow at this rate, I may just need to shop for a tent! And my hips are broader, my belly is noticeably rounder, my feet are more sore at the end of the day and I swear I'm growing hair where there wasn't hair before... Ah the joys of motherhood! I've been telling Hana she has a little sister coming; I think she's catching on. Yesterday she carried her rag doll under her shirt and kept plopping it on the floor or yanking it out and holding it like a baby---yeah I think she's getting the picture.

After rowing and painting during the day, Vera and I are getting the greenhouse in order. We have flats of germinating herbs and some vegetables. I do like to water things, it's very restful, but makes me want to pee all the time... another one of the endearing qualities of pregnancy. I've seen most of the canals on this side of the grand canal... We are in the Cannaregio neighborhood, there are loads of families around here because this is where 'regular' Venetians live. The rest of the island is cafes, restaurants, stores, shops, galleries, museums and more churches and plazas than one would think you could cram onto and island this size. The best part is: no cars... I haven't seen any bicycles either. Boats. Loads and scads of boats, but no land vehicles---heaven. I realize I'm rambling, but I think I am succumbing to weariness these days. The Inn is looking good though.

"The rooms for the equipment are cleared and ready. Just have the delivery men put the crates in them; we'll open them up and get it all organized when we get back." John clarified. "Uncle Alfred assures me we won't be gone more than three days. Just over to Liechtenstein and back."

Ginger was feeling separation anxiety and it was a completely alien experience. "Call when you get there, and call every morning and evening... and anytime during the day that you think about it..."

John was holding her hand as they walked back from the fruit and vegetable market. "GingerKat, if I didn't know better I'd say you've grown attached to me!" She swatted him with the bag of carrots and cabbages.

"Don't make me come after you is all I'm saying, you big lunkhead. And of course I'm getting attached to you; I can't even sleep well without your sonorous tones to lull me to lalaland."

"My love, it's just some banking and paperwork matters that *have* to be handled in person. If I could do it by email I certainly would. You and Auntie and Hana will just have to bolt the doors and keep a sentry on duty until we return... No problem, right?" She swung the bag of veggies at him again.

"It's hormones; I know it's hormones. But Johnny, I mean it! Call me all the time, or I shall be very vengeful! I'll let out the Ginger-bitch and she'll rip your heart out..." she insisted.

"Nonsense! You've hidden my heart somewhere only *you* can find... there's only an empty space in my chest these days..." he smiled and she relented.

"Alright, call me twice a day and I'll make do," she finally agreed.

By the late afternoon, once the day's painting had been accomplished, Vera surprised Ginger with a special treat. The brick oven was heating up and four pizza crusts lay on the prep table waiting for ingredients. Hana was covered nearly from head to toe with flour, and she seemed to revel in her 'costume.' Mocha was not so pleased as she'd tried to 'decorate' the cat as well, albeit unsuccessfully.

Vera greeted her with, "Have a shower and you can decide how we shall finish these off and put them in the oven." Ginger was still laughing at Hana's ridiculous appearance; she went up the stairs with Hana on her hip, "You are the silliest girl in the world, you are. Let's go have a bath together and we'll come back and 'cook' some more, okay?" Hana nodded her consent.

Refreshed and cleaned they came back to the kitchen where Vera had made up a scrumptious looking salad and had glasses of wine on the table waiting. "What'll it be?" and she waved to the bowls of possible ingredients. "When the pizzas are done, I have another surprise for you two..."

"Oh do tell! This is such a welcome change of pace," Ginger cooed and looked at the clock on the wall.

Vera noticed and remarked, "Is your phone charged? I thought I noticed it was almost dead..." Ginger grabbed it and checked the screen---'full charge.'

"Very funny!" she retorted. "I am *such* a wife. It sure didn't take long for me to transform into a nagging millstone..."

"Oh, don't be so hard on yourself, GingerKat. No one thinks you're a millstone..." and she sprinkled mozzarella on the one dressed so far.

"I *am* a nagging wife..." she moaned.

Vera laughed, "No you're a pregnant woman. We get a lot of latitude when we're carrying the future. I think men are the ones who actually get naggy and obsessive when their mate is ballooning all out of proportion..."

"I'm ballooning out of proportion?" Ginger moaned again.

Vera giggled, "You really do have it bad... No you're not out of proportion for a pregnant woman. You're divine."

That helped some, she thought, and finished decorating another pizza. Hana was concocting one of her own... "Young lady if you even eat a bite of that beast you're building, I'll be very impressed," her mother commented.

Vera said, "I hope you like Cary Grant?"

"Who?" came Ginger's plaintive response.

Vera's jaw dropped, "You've got to be kidding me! 'Cary Grant' THE Cary Grant---sexiest male film star of all time? Witty, debonair, romantic, suave, romantic...."

Ginger's eyebrows shot up, "Auntie Vera!"

"Well, who do you think of when *you* think of great looking leading men?" she countered.

"I don't know? I hardly ever go to the movies... uh, Harrison Ford?" she offered.

215

Vera rolled her eyes. "We're going to take you to the movies tonight and you can see what a real leading man is!"

The pizzas went into the oven and the phone rang. Ginger twirled it around on the table without picking it up to answer it. Vera watched her and almost doubled up with giggles, "You are a terror!" she uttered through her chirps of laughter. Hana clapped and Ginger picked her up and held the phone to her little ear. Hana's eyes got round and she smiled, pulled away and looked around, then pulled the phone back to her ear, backwards. Ginger turned it around properly and said, "Do you hear daddy?" Grinning, Hana pushed it away again. Ginger held it up to her own ear and walked to the courtyard.

Vera picked up Hana and held her up to look in the oven. "Their cooking... Mmmm pizza!"

Hana made the yummy noise too and wiggled to get to the floor. She grabbed Vera's hand and pulled her to go to the piano in the salon. She tried to climb to the bench on her own, but that wasn't working out. Vera gave her a boost and the little angel began to play a scale. Finger over finger, note by note, she got through an octave, then she went back down that octave. When she reached the bottom she started up at the next key as the beginning of a new scale. Vera sat enchanted and proud as she could be.

Hana went through four iterations of octaves before Ginger came in and announced that "Johnny and Uncle Alfred have gotten to their hotel and are going out for dinner. They send their love to each of us..." and she crossed to Vera and kissed her, then did the same with Hana. "There; those are from our men... They really do love us!"

Vera replied, "There was never a doubt. Now, you make the couch all comfy for us and pick out which of the movies you'd like to see first. I'll go check the oven."

Ginger held up each one of the five in turn for Hana to inspect as well. "Sweetheart, you know as much about this guy as I do... Which one shall we humor Auntie Vera with first?"

From the kitchen Vera called, "I heard that!"

Hana held onto one longer than the others, Ginger read the title and turned it over to read the blurb on the back. "Hmmm, it says 'you can expect the unexpected when they play: Charade'... This can't be terrible... Good job HanaRin. Now let's spread out this quilt and comforter and get snuggly for a 'girls night in,' shall we?"

Vera came out with the salad and bowls, then returned again with a selection of pizzas. "Alright, 'Ladies Night' has officially begun," and she hit the remote 'play' button.

Two hours later and Ginger had a pillow to her chest and a very happy smile on her face. Hana had dozed off between them and Vera asked, "Ready for another?"

"I know how Reggie felt. Thrust into a world she didn't know existed after her husband wasn't who she thought he was and then there was Cary Grant always with a different name... Brian Cruikshank, Peter Joshua, alias Alexander Dyle, alias Adam Canfield... I think I would have taken the stamps and run! What's next?"

Vera slipped another one into the machine and said as she sat down, "This one's a little different. It's called: 'An Affair to Remember'."

A couple hours later, Ginger was convinced. Dabbing a tear from her eye, "And she bought his picture and he found her wheel chair..." her voice trembled. "Oh Vera that was so romantic! What's next?"

Vera grinned in spite of herself. They watched 'Father Goose,' 'Philadelphia Story,' and 'North by Northwest' before Ginger was as sound asleep as Hana. Vera covered 'MamaKat' and carried Hana to bed. When Ginger awoke in the morning it was to her phone ringing. She answered quickly and began filling John's ears with the tales of the marvelous Cary Grant.

When John got off the phone and told Alfred what the conversation consisted of, Alfred howled. "Vera has another convert!"

When Vera came downstairs with Hana in tow, Ginger said with her mouth full, "I love cold pizza in the morning! Do we have any ice cream?!"

Vera asked, "You haven't perhaps made coffee yet?"

"Oh, yeah sorry..." and hopped up to fetch her a cup. "I told Johnny all about our movie night. I had so much fun, and you were right: Cary Grant IS a most handsome leading man---even as an unwashed drunk sea captain, he's charming. That was great!"

Vera smiled and yawned. "The video rental fellow only had those... but we can go and see if he has something else that strikes our fancy. You need to get dressed; the sampan awaits!"

"Yes ma'am!" and Ginger rushed up the stairs, took a cold shower as usual and came downstairs. Vera and Hana were already on the quay waiting.

With Hana bundled up and nestled in her lap, Vera sat in the bow of the sampan as Ginger rowed them through the canals toward a destination Vera had already specified. Vera gazed at nothing in particular then as if merely thinking out loud, asked, "What could provoke a person into ignoring reason so completely that they ceased to have any control at all over their thoughts and emotions?" she took a deep breath, turned her head to Ginger and called, "Shift." Ginger made the required movement fluidly and with poise.

She reflected on Vera's question: 'Who *has* any control over their thoughts and emotions. I can think of something that makes me angry, or sad, or happy or anxious... That's the only way *I* know of, so far, that I can 'control' my emotions. Even in order to do that...'

Vera called "Shift," and Ginger shifted once more. '...I have to choose a thought strong enough to evoke that emotion. More often than not however my emotions show up automatically from someone or something rubbing me the wrong way, or flattering me, or impeding me, or disrespecting me...'

Vera called "Shift," again. Ginger did so. '...There's no reason in any of that. What little I have is only enough reason to choose my thoughts ahead of time... to prepare myself so that I don't have such a knee-jerk reaction in my emotions to whatever comes up around me. That in itself is a relief---something truly worthwhile to maintain...'

Vera called "Shift;" Ginger shifted. '...and if I were able to constantly maintain that, what then would provoke me into ignoring that little bit of reason I have acquired? It will inevitably be something that I have habitually reacted to in the past...'

Even though she was thinking hard about the question, her senses seemed heightened and her body felt like a tool that she could command at will.

Vera took a breath as if to speak, Ginger shifted in anticipation of the command. '...something which I have not yet examined and prepared against that brings up an emotional reaction from me. I want to avoid losing the emotional balance that reasoned thought provides...'

Vera turned her head in Ginger's direction; Ginger shifted. '...To do that I must know myself more completely, observe all my reactions... Observation itself brings an emotional background with it which preempts another emotion from becoming suddenly stronger. Intentionally observing myself will increase some thoughts and emotions and cause *any* others to decrease.'

Vera blinked; Ginger shifted. She said aloud, "Anything *can* cause a person to surrender what reason they have so that they are left with uncontrolled thoughts and emotions. *Never* having the

219

intention to use reason in the first place *will always* cause that result."
She shifted once more, and looked at Vera and Hana.

Hana looked up at her mother and said a new word: "S i f!"
Ginger smiled and shifted. Vera looked Ginger directly in the eyes,
then bowed her head. Ginger stopped rowing and bowed deeply in
return.

When she rose again, Vera said, "Welcome to the real world.
Now you may take us wherever you wish." GingerKat rowed them
to the *Anna* and then back to the Inn---shifting at will.

"What just happened this morning?" Ginger asked when she
came back from putting Hana down for a nap.

Vera replied, "Our work demands our constant vigilance over
our own machine. Most of the time when we *do* make a
breakthrough---transform something in ourselves---we are the only
one to notice and acknowledge the realization. Once in a while it is
useful to have feedback from those around us---from *some* source
outside of us---that a threshold has been passed---a rite of passage,
if you will."

Ginger's heart swelled from her teacher's reply. At the same
time she remembered: '...It's true worth will be shown in time.' So
instead of abandoning herself to the gratifying pleasures of self-
satisfaction, she dedicated the emotion she now felt to lifting her
spirits should she ever need that potent an emotion to balance some
future state.

She embraced Vera and said simply, "Thank you for caring for
me and guiding me; I love you so much Auntie Vera."

"I love you too GingerKat," Vera whispered. "You're a good
woman, a good wife *and* a good mother."

They worked together painting the interior walls of the
courtyard. "A couple more days and this old Inn will glow again!"
Vera encouraged while they cleaned brushes and roller pans.

Ginger said, "Would you listen for Hana? I want to clean the outside windows... the shower the other day left spots..."

Vera smiled, "Certainly, I'll finish up here..."

28 March 94   I have graduated from Work Pre-School! Yippee! It's not exactly a 'graduation' per se, but Auntie Vera has graciously let me know that I am making progress---I still feel so accomplished. Even though there is so much ahead of me, it is really gratifying to receive her offer of esteem for my work so far. Johnny and Alfred get back tomorrow morning and we have put together a little surprise for them: The Peggy Guggenheim Collection at the Palazzo Venier dei Leoni is opening a new wing. I think it's just for a shop and cafe... but here's the thing: Vera and Alfred are old friends of the last curator and we have been invited for an evening at the Museum---dinner and a private showing of the new exhibits! Now, if I can just get Hana to wear a dress without lifting the skirt over her head, we can be as haute couture as anyone... She will, we aren't, and that's just the way it is.

If all goes as planned, when John Robert and Alfred finish their business today, the Spelman-Backhouses will be the proud directors of *Voyager Press*---a specialty publisher, incorporated in Liechtenstein, based in Venice and run from this very Inn. I have some ideas on how to make this a going concern and still maintain our intended tour of *all* the Livingson holdings world-wide---not to mention raising our girls at sea as much as possible. Aim for the moon, land among the stars... AND make great efforts!

"I didn't know Rudolfo still had any pull with the Collection after that fiasco over the leaky roof?" Alfred commented.

He and John were delighted about the soiree and considered it a fitting celebration for the inauguration of the 'Voyager Press' enterprise.

"Evidently some other poor schmuck got the blame, leaving Rudy still in their good graces. Anyway, tell us how beautiful we look, adore us and dote on us---we finished the painting and fired up the brick oven while you were off playing monopoly." teased Vera.

She was unusually high-spirited this afternoon and Alfred had to do a double take when she emerged from their rooms looking for all the world like Princess Grace on holiday, and he said so.

Vera was demure; she stood at the base of the stairs, "And to introduce the lady of the Concession: Mrs. Spelman-Backhouse!"

GingerKat descended the stairs and both gentlemen's eyes popped out of their sockets. Ginger was dressed in a black satin dress, cleverly concealing her pregnant state and flattering all her feminine assets. She joined Vera, with Hana in her arms---dressed just as beautifully as her mother and Auntie---and the two ladies smiled coquettishly to their men. Hana wriggled and stood teetering in front of them, then as if cued, she lifted her skirt over her head. Vera and Ginger were prepared for this eventuality. Hana was wearing a little polka dotted body suit---very cute!

"Well it appears your training may be required this evening, Johnny, just to keep away the fawning admirers..." commented Alfred.

"I may be only able to handle six or seven at a time... you should be prepared to deal with the other forty or so!" Johnny responded.

Vera tossed her head back in a laugh, "Don't worry your little heads. GingerKat and I can most certainly fend for ourselves!"

Alfred and Johnny looked at each other; Alfred said, "We were talking about protecting HanaRin... What were you talking about?" Vera swatted him with her clutch and took his arm. They gathered into the launch and in less than half an hour they arrived at the Palazzo Venier dei Leoni canal steps.

Alfred asked, "Oh... did the equipment arrive in good condition?"

Ginger replied that the delivery had not yet been made. John handed her and Hana up onto the step of the watergate and she took his arm with her free hand. Vera and Alfred were behind them as they ascended the steps.

Alfred whispered to Vera, "How did you convince Ginger to don a dress?!"

"Don't be cheeky," she replied, "Our GingerKat has more taste in her little finger than most of the women you see tonight... she just needed a little encouragement to reveal her insights and flare is all..."

Alfred's eyebrows rose slightly as he looked up at their niece, "Yes, 'revealed' is a good way to put it. I hope she doesn't catch a chill... that's a lot of uncovered tanned skin to keep warm."

Vera smiled. Ginger had assisted her to dress as well and she knew she looked better than she had in a number of years. Alfred's hand always at her arm or waist all evening was the simple proof of that. It was good to be adored---every so often at least.

They were 'fashionably late' and John held Hana for the first several minutes until she squirmed to be 'free' and investigate the gallery on her own. He set her down and she held his finger, pulling him from room to room. The guests were a mix of the avant garde, old and new money. Hana was a reminder for all, it seemed, of their own grandchildren somewhere else. Ginger tried to keep up with them, but found herself increasingly distracted by the art and sculptures displayed on every wall and floor through which she walked. She was academically familiar with the modern art movements through books she had been instrumental in publishing. To have so many works surrounding her was a little overwhelming. The modernists and abstractionists captured her attention the longest; especially the vivid displays of color and fractured presentations of the cubists. Alfred and Vera were mingling, perhaps catching up with old acquaintances. John was wherever Hana wandered for the time being; leaving Ginger to herself appreciating a new world that she only had a brushed passed before.

'...This has *such* a technical substructure,' she thought as she gazed at *Contre Jour*, Counterlight by Umberto Boccioni, 'How could someone evoke so much emotion and curiosity from a pencil drawing! Her hair, the scene through the windows, the knit of her sweater---those eyes and her stare...' She took a couple steps back from it and then moved in closer once more. She glanced over at the painting: *Elasticity*, and then *the City Rises*, but her gaze kept coming back to the 'simple' drawing of the girl in front of the window. 'Is it the play of light? ...the subject? ...the masterful execution? What is it that holds my attention to this girl's reflection...'

She gasped. 'She's a reflection of the viewer! It's *my* gaze, my own curiosity peering back out from the pencil strokes... *Me*, standing in this gallery with the lighting and the indistinct backgrounds... *How* did he *do* that?' Her thoughts and reveries carried her to amble through the rest of the collection and out into the fresh evening in the courtyard.

The 'dinner' wasn't a sit down affair or formal in any sense---it was more of a smorgasbord. Platters of hors d'oeuvres, cannolis, 'wraps,' finger sandwiches, stuffed vegetables and fruits were on tables in the courtyard, and in the newly opened cafe-gift shop building was an open bar with more substantial dishes. When she passed a set of french doors that looked out into the sculpture garden, there were Hana and John with an admiring little group of patrons watching Hana investigate one of the more massive abstract pieces. From the smiles on their faces, it was apparent she was already establishing quite the fan base. GingerKat circled around them to get to the new wing without being observed; she truly wanted to try and see her family from an objective perspective she hadn't perceived before. As she lingered near a pair of bronze statuettes, her position offered her just that vantage she'd hoped to obtain: she could see Vera and Alfred on the patio amongst a very odd gathering of individuals and across the space she could hear the little squeals and chirping laughter of her daughter. People milled around, ambled in twos and threes, debated, ogled, laughed, listened or chatted all around her. The sense of being alone in a sea of people was a stark impression that was both novel and a little unsettling——as if she was one of the statuary or art pieces and no longer a member of the tribe of humanity about her.

"...Mama!" came a cry from across the courtyard, and Hana toddled toward her as fast as her little legs would shuffle. Each of her steps, at that pace, looked to be the one to send her sprawling... Ginger's knees became weak just watching her. GingerKat knelt down to receive Hana and pick her up into her own arms in one fluid motion. Hana babbled about something---something which had evidently very much impressed her---Ginger would have to have John interpret as best he could imagine from what he'd seen of her 'adventure.'

"I think she's certain those stone ball-looking things will roll if she could just push them from just the right place..." John attempted. Hana was pointing and her eyes were a little wilder than usual.

Ginger observed, "I think our munchkin is also very tired. She didn't have much of a nap this afternoon, with Auntie Vera and I playing 'dress-up' in the next room. She just couldn't miss a moment of the 'playtime' we were having. I'll carry her for a while and find you when she nods off. Would you trade off with me every so often, lugging her around?"

He grinned and straightened his tie. "It is my honor and duty to your majesties!" He grinned and bowed. "Do you want me to find you a selection of tasty treats? Or a seat, perhaps? Our angel is getting heavier everyday... or maybe it was just being away for three days that I'm only just noticing it now."

Ginger oomphed as she shifted Hana to her other hip without disarranging her evening gown. "No, she really is growing fast. I think I would like to find a place to sit for a little bit." And she followed him up onto the cafe patio.

225

Vera excused herself from the knot of people she and Alfred were attending and came over to where Ginger rested. "What do you think so far?" she asked as she approached.

Ginger smiled and told her about the few artists she'd admired and others she'd viewed in the modernism wing, about her sense of detachment... "Oh, and I'm really glad we had that Cary Grant-a-thon the other night. This is just like one of those parties in the movies; it feels like I got a little 'party-training' ahead of time."

Vera cocked her head, "You've never been to one of these sorts of things before? You're in the publishing business---I just thought this sort of thing was part and parcel of your industry?"

Ginger giggled, "...No, no, no...I have always been more of a front lines sort of employee. The galas and book-signing parties and the rest weren't my cup of tea. I was the one on the plane, on the road or otherwise out of the limelight. This is a new world to me," and she waved her arm across the still ambling, chatting, serious and comical crowds around them. John set a little plate of assorted yummy looking things on the cafe table at her elbow.

"There's more where this came from. I'll replace whatever bits of this you actually like." He stroked Hana's hair. "The princess didn't take long to nod off."

Alfred walked up to them with a nice looking couple at his elbow. "Vera, Ginger, John this is Mr. and Mrs. Pantaleoni..."

Ginger rose up smoothly from her chair, in spite of her 'burden' and extended her free hand.

Alfred continued, "Edward, Miriam this is Virginia Backhouse of Voyager Press... the publisher I was just telling you about."

Miriam Pantaleoni held Ginger's hand and, smiling warmly said, "It is so good to meet you Mrs. Backhouse! My husband and I are in the publishing business also. Oh! What a darling little girl!" and she caught herself when she noticed Hana was asleep.

She lowered her voice, "Alfred has told us that you produce specialty books. Edward and I may have need of your services."

Edward shook her hand also and added, "I have made the mistake of biting off more than I can chew---there have been a flood of 'coffee table' books accepted by a few of our more ambitious agents and we are just not in a position to fit them into the production schedule for many months."

Alfred explained, "The Pantaleonis oversee the graphic arm of EBS in Great Britain..."

Miriam acknowledged, "A 'flood' is a slight exaggeration. It would likely be four or five titles over the next seven months. Alfred says you have a print-on-demand branch with large format color capabilities?"

Ginger shifted into 'professional' mode and she pursued the conversation as if she had an entire publishing house behind her ready at a moment's notice to answer to her every settled agreement. Vera disentangled Hana from Ginger's shoulder and dress and covered her with her own shawl at her own shoulder as Ginger engaged in the 'business meeting.' John was just that pleased and delighted to listen to his wife hold her own in the dialog that ended with the Pantaleonis assuring her they would be forwarding to Voyager their 'overage' clientele.

"...We can set up a contract that will give Voyager enough leeway to accept or deny submissions, naturally..." Miriam was saying. Ginger accepted their terms.

Edward beamed at his wife and glanced at Alfred, "Excellent. I will have a Director contact you on Wednesday, if that's convenient Mrs. Backhouse?"

Ginger smiled and nodded, and after parting handshakes all around, the Pantaleonis excused themselves. "Miriam, we still have a few minutes to look through the west wing there if you wish, before the gondolier is supposed to be here for us." They strode across the courtyard in a lively and good-humored conversation.

"Well that went well…" Alfred suggested to his family who were looking after the couple they'd just met.

John clapped him on the shoulder, "Uncle Alfred, I don't know how you do what you do… but you do it really well! Thank you…"

Alfred allowed himself a grin. "It's nothing, really. Anyone with some gumption and a keen ear for people's needs can do it." he demurred.

Vera turned and kissed his cheek. With a sigh she mentioned, "I think you can allow yourself to say 'your welcome' dearest."

GingerKat had put her arm around Vera's waist and her face up to Hana's head, kissed both of them and turned to Alfred. He said, "You're most welcome."

John went into the cafe and came back with glasses of champagne. Once each of them held a glass, "Here's to Voyager Press. She's hit the ground running and we just need to hold on tight!"

They drank to the toast.

"GingerKat, I haven't been around you when you were wearing your 'professional hat;' that was so impressive!" He turned to the courtyard and announced, in not too loud a voice: "Virginia Spelman-Backhouse will not be accepting any more audiences this evening; thank you for your devotion."

Ginger giggled, "Once a publisher, always a publisher, I guess. Maybe it was hearing the 'buzzwords,' it's still second nature for me---I have been in the business for my entire adult life after all."

Vera rejoined, "And at your *first gala*, you gathered up some business for a company that only became a real entity day before yesterday---see what you have been missing?"

Ginger rolled her eyes, "If I can always bring the munchkin and play dress up with you all, I could get used to it. Uncle Alfred? Had you and Vera met the Pantaleonis before? How did your conversation turn to their business? Did you tell them that we were just getting new equipment, or that we were just getting started!?"

Alfred's expression was the same as every time Ginger began a barrage of questions; he waited patiently for the shower to subside, just nodding until he had a chance to respond.

"Uh, Yes. That's what they like to talk about. Yes. And Yes. Honesty is always the best approach; the alternatives only cause more work and trouble in the end." John and Ginger sorted back through his answers against the order of her questions and finally smiled.

"Thank you again," Ginger replied with a sigh. "I didn't want them to have the impression that we were anything other than what we are: A wannabe printing shop on the second floor of my house!"

Vera had to say, "Sweetheart, you are more than that. As you just said a moment ago: You've been in the business all your adult life! Don't underestimate your own abilities nor those of your 'assistants'!"

John grinned, "Yeah! Hana, Alfred, Vera and I are completely able to take direction. Lead on!"

Ginger blushed in humility. While she accepted the support her family was willing to offer, at the same time it was more than that. She realized she had just 'assumed' it before---as if it were just a part of her 'dream life'---*of course* everyone would take a role. But now it was *actually* happening and their poignant pledge of support resonated in her heart with the devotion she now truly felt from them. This *wasn't* her imagination or her fantasy any longer---These were real people, *really* her family and *really* giving her their admiration and devotion! 'Ginger-girl you've lived in your imagination and illusions too long. This is one more wall that has had to fall. *All* of me has to be real or none of me can be. There's no such thing as a *little bit* conscious!' she thought.

With a tear glistening in the corner of her eye, she replied, "Well the first thing we need to do is get HanaRin to bed. Do we need to offer our regards to anyone before we go, or anything?"

"I would like to find Rudy, if he's here and thank him for the invitation." Vera confided, as they disposed of their empty napkins and little serving plates.

"I asked," Alfred replied, "He wanted to be here, the assistant director told me, but his youngest daughter is having her third baby just now---he's in Milan."

John took Hana into his arms from Vera, "Alfred, if you'll get the coats, I'll head to the watergate with sleeping beauty here."

Ginger and John followed Vera toward the end of the patio, and John went on across the courtyard and through the main house. In a little while they were in the launch and motoring back to the Inn. Each of them sat silently as the lights of the Venice palazzos glittered across their wake.

The smells of the fireplace and the last meal from the kitchen in the Inn lingered after them as they went up the stairs to the apartment above the great room. Ginger got Hana into her jammies and nestled her into bed. She put on her own pajamas and a warm house robe and went down to the kitchen.

"She's one tired little explorer tonight..." she said to the others who were sipping hot chocolate around the table. Vera ladled out another cupful and handed to her.

"The equipment should have been here already; I'll get the tracking numbers and find out where the shipment is in the morning." Alfred offered.

John yawned and asked, "Will we be able to actually get it all up and running pretty quick? I mean is it pretty much 'plug and play' sort of stuff, or do I have a learning curve ahead of me?"

Ginger commented, "Some of it should be ready to go once it's plugged in and connected. It's the software and internet connections that may take a little attention."

She turned to Alfred, "Does the Inn already have an adequate dial-up account locally, or should we look into a commercial contract with a bigger server company?"

Alfred replied, "You know? I'll have to look through our house records. I haven't tried to log-on since we've been here, and last time we were here..." he looked at Vera and smiled, "...we were otherwise occupied. I didn't check then either." He looked around at them, "Odd, don't you think, that none of us have gone on-line since we got here? Four astute and technically connected people such as ourselves?"

Vera giggled and yawned, "Yeah, that's me: Miss Technocrat. How *have* I gotten by these last couple weeks without checking my email!?"

Ginger chirped a little laugh, but then paused to think. She said, "Actually---How *have* I gone without staying connected for so long? This is a record! Am I so compartmentalized that once John and I started this odyssey, the door to that part of my world simply closed without notice or anything?!"

Alfred comforted, "Perhaps, but you'll remember your world has been in a kind of 're-formation' these last several months. Even though you've *talked* about your previous life and world, hasn't it seemed just a little 'foreign,' or at the least: far less *urgent* to maintain those habits and patterns? Like you were discussing the life of someone you knew *really* well, but wasn't too close by?"

Ginger thought about it. She posited meekly, "Do you think I'll just slip back into that 'persona' again when Voyager Press is up and going? Do you think my real life that I have now will fade into the realm of distance just like my other life has? Am I going to just forever wash from one thing to the next---the most recent experiences gradually dissipating with the new experiences overwriting them...?"

Vera cautioned, "Take a deep breath GingerKat."

Ginger did. She took several calm deep breaths.

Vera continued, "What you have been describing is nothing more than the anxiety and worries of a weary mind. You are stronger than you know---that is to say---you are stronger inside than you have known yourself to be. Your presence *will* absorb *all* of your experiences and gradually make your every 'real' memory integral with it... You are growing. What you are thinking now, how you are feeling now... all of what you have been---*really* have been, not the false bits---will *always* be a part of you."

John commented, "I never thought of it like that! But it makes sense."

Ginger recited, "...'All this will remain in a man, but subject to selection... He will have conscious choice'."

Alfred smiled, "*Views from the Real World*... the title sounds a little off-putting, but the messages conveyed in its pages are certainly appropriate---as we gain more perspective on our own views of reality."

Ginger said, "John, I thought you just found that book at a bookstore... a random happenstance while we were in... wherever we were."

John replied, looking between her and Alfred, "It *was* in a bookstore, but Uncle Alfred found it and recommended it to me."

Alfred sat back and sipped the last of his cocoa. He volunteered, "There are a number of people who have come to something in themselves---actually, a great many down through the ages. Some of them *have even* written of their understanding. What is difficult is to find, however, are those writings that resonate with you---right from the outset. Paradoxically: the ones that 'speak' to the fewest number of people often have the most comprehensive perspective... whereas those that 'speak' to the masses *actually* have only a *partial* viewpoint to convey---a superficial observation in the guise of a Universal Perspective---Yet they remain just platitudinous hogwash. Then take parables; they can be taken on *many* levels---To the literalist, they are 'informative;' to the philosopher, they are 'deep;' but to the practical man of knowledge they 'speak' volumes about the realities of both his inner world and the greater world in which he finds himself. It's a matter of discernment to distinguish one writing from the other, and *that* must be developed in a person---no one is born with discernment." He yawned and admitted he was exhausted from the day's activities as much as they were.

Vera gathered the empty mugs and set them in the wash basin for the morning. "Alright my loved ones, off we go to bed."

J. L. LAWSON

5

Every Day

"Real worth requires no interpreter: its everyday deeds form its emblem."
---Nicolas de Chamfort

3 April 94   The equipment arrived two days later than was scheduled. Welcome to Italy... of course that takes the sting out of contemplating having to meet deadlines in our new venture---'it's Venice, what did you expect?' Anyway, John has taken it upon himself to install our management software. I keep forgetting that he was someone else before he was a 'writer.' In fact he was a very successful someone else at doing what he did. And then there's Ginger... the clever girl with the publishing life background... oh so glamorous and thrilling. The girl I've almost forgotten how to be! Hopefully what Vera said is true---about my being able to integrate all the real parts of me into this new person that is growing more real everyday---still with the same face and body I notice.

We have new sprouts coming up in the greenhouse and Hana hasn't pulled all of them up yet, so we may have some herbs and vegetables after all! Note to self: Keep trays on upper shelves and hang the step stool in the closet---out of sight out of mind... I hope. Vera and I built my own medicines cabinet and she has begun helping me to stock it. There is a wonderful little shop across the grand canal that keeps dried plants and roots and things. I'm learning a little at a time. It's just like how I'm learning piano under Alfred's tutelage---a little at a time.

I installed the upgraded page layout software I'm already familiar with; thankfully it was one of the packages this equipment was

235

designed to utilize. We made a test run of a few of John's not-fully-proofread-or-edited journals. I reformatted them from his files and picked out a reasonably attractive cover. The resultant book was as good a quality as anything on the shelves at our local bookstore, Libreria Internazionale Marco Polo. I know because Vera and I took Hana to that store and let Hana pull books off shelves while I made the comparisons. It's not that I don't know what a quality book is 'supposed' to look and feel like, that was my job after all, it's just that I couldn't trust my own memory and the fact that we *made* our book from scratch with our own equipment---no offset presses, no bells and whistles. It looks good!

The Pantaleoni's business director contacted us just as promised. I dubbed John our Vice President of Systems so that we sorta appear to be a little more 'corporately professional' than we are at the moment. He wanted to be Grand Chief of Can Do, but I told him: 'You must work your way up from senior management first, and prove yourself...' We had a good laugh. Vera wanted to be Vice President of Pretty Things. Alfred chose: Vice President of Figure It Out. That naturally left me with the vaulted title of Madam President, translated as: 'Go ask Ginger'---I was hoping for Admiral of Print.

Alfred ordered our first major batch of supplies. Hana made the first marginal notes with crayons in our first book. Vera catered our first staff meeting (dinner two nights ago) where John brought our first semi-official annual projections from the Pantaleoni contract and the Journal printings. I made my first executive directive: Voyager Press shall be wherever we are at the time; so I asked Alfred to figure out the viability of converting one of the *Anna's* amas into a version of the printshop we have set up at the Inn. That went over well; at least Vera and Hana clapped.

"You know," Alfred remarked as he came into the kitchen with estimates for the Anna's refit, "Venice was once the center of fine paper manufacturing. There are still commercial enterprises and even small shops that make everything from marbled paper to excellent rag papers."

Ginger's brow furrowed a bit, "What are you suggesting?"

"Only that: Since we want to keep the Voyager Press operational even when we are away, one way to do that would be to have a couple local employees, who knew the business and could make the print runs in our absence." He tried to sound nonchalant, but it was clear he was offering some advice.

John commented, "If we were to do that, and I mean *if,* there's a technical side to this venture that would take a novice a substantial learning curve to get up to speed."

Ginger considered the notion. "Let's see---there's the receipt of the orders, the confirmation of specifications, formatting and cover design, proofing, distribution and billing---all of which we *could* handle on the *Anna* without being here. What we wouldn't be able to do is the actual production, quality control, packaging or shipping. What am I leaving out?"

Vera offered, "Resupplying the paper and binding stocks, the inks and glues, remedies for technical glitches..."

John added, "Back-ups of production files and inventory monitoring..."

Alfred shrugged, "It was just a thought."

Ginger countered, "Actually, it is a very good thought. The things we've thought of so far that we wouldn't be here to do, aside from what John said about learning the software applications and running the scanners, printers, cutters and binders---that does sound like a viable alternative to refitting the *Anna.* Anyone we take on to learn the ropes will have to become adept at those aspects of the enterprise as a matter of course." She thought some more and followed with, "We'd need to train maybe four different people all the same tasks to be sure *someone* would be here and knew what they were doing..." She looked at Vera. "How would you like to be a guinea pig, Auntie?"

Vera thought she saw what Ginger was getting at, "Do you want *me* to learn *all those things* so that we know how long it takes to train someone *and* what kind of questions will arise?"

Ginger nodded.

"Well that's pretty sound thinking. I'm game," she responded and turned to John and Alfred. "Gentlemen, teach me the publishing business!"

Johnny and Alfred writhed their hands like melodramatic villains anticipating a scheme.

"Igor, we have a 'victi'... that is, a 'volunteer' for our experiments! Prepare the laboratory!" said Alfred.

Johnny's left shoulder rose perceptibly and he drug his right foot behind him as he turned for the door. "Yes, Master... May I use the cattle prod this time? Oh please..."

Vera and Ginger giggled at their improv. Then Hana toddled around the table dragging one foot as best she could without falling down.

She repeated, "Eedoor, Eedoor..." That was priceless!

Vera asked, "What should be my first project... something that will familiarize me with all the doohickies in the print shop?"

A smile grew across Alfred's face, "You could start with your scrapbook and notes from the seventies... I'm sure you'll use the scanner and the formating software enough getting those in shape for a book..."

Ginger and John were instantly alert.

"What scrapbooks?! What notes from the seventies?" Ginger hesitantly asked.

John was even more curious, "What were you documenting during the seventies? Weren't you and Uncle Alfred in Tahoe working and playing golf on the weekends?"

Ginger followed with, "Do you have pictures and stories of your growing relationship? Now that's something I would like to read and see pictures of. What did you two really look like back then?"

Vera had remained noncommittal as the questions came at her, and Alfred folded his arms to see how she'd respond. After a pause, Vera got up from the table and said she needed to go to the *Anna*.

Ginger said promptly, "John, would you watch Hana; Vera I'll come with you." They left the kitchen, grabbed scarves at the front door and were off to the Anna.

John looked at Alfred, "What was that about?"

"Your Auntie Vera didn't bring everything to the Inn when we moved in for the long haul." he responded.

John wasn't put off, "Yeah, I get that! I mean, what did she keep a scrapbook of while y'all were in Tahoe just taking care of business?"

"Well if I told you that, it wouldn't be a surprise; now would it?" Alfred countered.

John saw the he wasn't going to get anything from his uncle. Anytime Alfred wanted to be cagey about anything, no amount of cajoling or wheedling would drag out even a hint or clue.

Alfred followed with, "We should think about installing an outside entrance to the printshop upstairs. It's probably not a good idea to have the hired help traipsing through the Inn just to go in and out of those few rooms on a daily basis. Besides, we can put up a sign over the door, *Voyager Press, Inc.* and gain a little visibility in the community." He raised his hands and spread them as he said it, as if he were envisioning the 'marquis-like' signage.

"Changing the subject, AND making sense at the same time... Very clever, uncle..." Johnny sighed. "Okay, yes. It is a very good idea; if it's really more economically feasible to have employees here while we are on our tours. I suppose you've calculated the wages and benefits costs already for retaining four or so?"

Alfred's expression dropped into serious mode, "Hmm. I sorta thought we'd recruit from the ranks of the apprentices or students---make the work at the press a kind of 'internship'."

John picked up Hana before she actually got all the way into the oven on whatever 'fact-finding mission' she thought she was on.

"An internship? Interns with *a lot of responsibility...* You don't think they'd catch onto the fact that they were being used as full-fledged staff and demand to be compensated as such? And wouldn't we be more secure, knowing that our shop was being run by people invested in it's success rather than essentially seasonal workers?!"

Alfred brightened suddenly, "*Invested...* now that's a *very* good insight. Would you suggest that instead of a 'full benefits package,' our interns would go for an actual stake in the company? 'Employee-owned and operated' is a real trend nowadays... How would you set that up?"

John looked back at him blankly. Not because he was stumped, but because his mind was also racing to fill in the blanks for pursuing this tack.

"Um... Six months: training on the job after successful completion of the probationary period perhaps an incremental investiture---say, share options or some such arrangement?"

"Since we're not going to go public, I suppose you're suggesting that we decide what our company's worth after, I guess, maybe a five year projection of income? Divide the 'shares' so that we always retain control and dole out blocks of them to our 'partners' with profit checks handed out at the end of every fiscal year---a profit-sharing program?" Alfred was carrying the idea through to its logical end just as John was doing---at least they were on the same page.

They sat quietly as they each were forecasting a 'five-year' revenue stream and trying to calculate apportionments. Hana, in John's lap at the table, began pouring salt on the table and making abstract designs in the scattered crystals. John played along and sorted out two 'piles' of the salt, as Hana pushed his hand away and spread it back out into chaos again. John tried once more to sort out piles and Hana grabbed his hand and held it away as she returned the piles to their scattered condition again. Alfred was watching the interaction as he thought about the puzzle they posed for themselves.

John chuckled, "Hana's the smart one!"

Alfred looked up, "Huh?"

John continued, "Who's to say that what we dole out in profit-sharing is 'actually' proportional to our revenue income?"

"Say again?" Alfred responded.

John explained, "I mean: let's say every year we take in... I don't know... twenty thousand---just for having a number to work with. On top of the satisfactory wage each person is allotted, they receive a profit-sharing check at the end of the year---proportional to their vestment."

Alfred nodded.

"Whose to say 'we' have to see *any* profits for ourselves at all? Their wages, profit-sharing and bonuses... all come from the proceeds of the contracts they are toiling to fulfill. We only need to be re-imbursed our first few year's outlay of start-up funds and a stipend for our part in setting up the work from the *Anna* while away."

Alfred squinted at him, "You're describing a non-profit... Right?"

John did a double-take on his own explanation and conceded, "Yeah, I guess that's a non-profit... I don't know much about how corporations are structured financially... I just see how *this* can work."

Smiling, Alfred added, "That's all this family has actually been doing for the last half century or so... even the Mercantile stopped showing a profit back in the thirties and never actually regained profitability. We kept products on the shelves, kept records and made the transactions, but not much came in more than was necessary to keep the bills paid for the store and wages for any seasonal employees. And I don't need to mention the GFHAS. We wield vast financial influence, but the entire sum---save salaries of actual employees and stipends for volunteers---is redistributed into the lives and communities we serve. That 'community' just happens to be, at last estimate, two and half billion people in eighty some odd countries world-wide."

John responded concisely with, "Oh, I see." Then when the concept sank in a little deeper, he added, "This is a *working* model then... You have done this before! So, why bring up the question in the first place if you already had the solution?!"

Alfred responded clearly, "But *you* didn't have the solution yet... Don't you think it's better that *you* thought of the resolution, rather than someone else *telling* you how to do it?"

"Alfred. I hope I remember how you do what you do when I'm there to see it! So I can pass along your most excellent model of teaching to our children..." John commented humbly.

"I suppose you'll have ample opportunity---I hope you remember too. This pattern of mentation was taught to me by my mother and father, who were taught by their mother and father who were taught by theirs... Vera and I want so much for you and Ginger to have all the opportunities to see these patterns that we know we can provide..."

Tears were forming in Alfred's eyes. John hadn't fully understood until *that moment* just how *pervasive* the Livingson family upbringing was, or could have been. It of course *seemed obvious* that conscious people *would* raise their children differently... but until this moment, the depth of *that difference* hadn't fully dawned on him.

"Hana? What have we here?" John asked.

The 'salt spread' on the table had circles and squiggles and lines running through it.

Hana looked up at him grinning, "how do it..." she said triumphantly.

Alfred and John stood up to get some perspective on the 'design.'

"What are you three doing?" Ginger asked as she and Vera came back to the kitchen from there walk.

John looked up, "Hana's made another work of art---mixed media this time!"

Vera looked at the 'design' in the salt and the shakers' arrangements. "What a clever girl! Once she gains a bit more control over her small muscles that enneagram will look more like it should!"

John did a double-take... Ginger squinted, as if that would assist her seeing what was before her eyes three feet away.

"Oh my..." they said almost as one voice. Alfred patted John on the shoulder and looked to Vera.

"We knew it wouldn't be long before the Livingson in our little girl would come to the surface. At least it's not as shocking as Mia and Lena's 'talents' when they were Hana's age," he commented.

Ginger muttered, "John are we up to this?"

Vera put her hands on their shoulders as well, "Of course you are. But you will have to abandon whatever you 'thought' parenting entailed. Remember darlings, you *must* make the knowledge of *your own* inner structure and its development clear in *your* minds before you guide the development of another person. Your understanding is growing all the time... you'll be fine. We have faith in both of you."

The looks of skepticism on each of their faces showed clearly the depths of their misgivings about their confidence in her words. Ginger sat down and put her face in her hands. John sat next to her with Hana in his lap. Hana reached over and put her fingers in

Ginger's hair and pulled some away. Ginger peered at her through her fingers and smiled.

"Johnny why does Hana have soot on her chin?"

"Oh... uh, she was going to explore the oven before I pulled her out of it a while ago," he answered readily. "I *guess* she was exploring... maybe she was checking it out as a summer residence... I don't know what goes through her head these days."

Ginger chuckled and the dark clouds of uncertainty that had reduced her to fear and trepidation vanished. Her chuckle became a laugh. "Nor do I, my love, nor do I!" She turned to Vera and Alfred. "Any insights?"

Alfred offered, "The 'summer residence' idea was as good as any as far as I'm concerned..." Vera nodded.

John said proudly, "See honey? I don't know what goes through your mind and I'm sure you haven't any clue about what's rattling around mine. *But*, the next time we can't find Hana around the house, let's not dismiss even the most *unlikely* of hiding places. Options! More options!" he called as if he was a floor manager calling his employees to ramp up production.

"Speaking of options..." Alfred began, "John figured out how to set up our print shop salaries and benefits packages, all in the space of time it took you two to fetch scrapbooks from the *Anna*! How about that for efficient use of time?!"

Vera and Ginger looked at John with admiration. John's expression was enigmatic. "Yeah just me---and Socrates here..." he waved to Alfred, who chuckled at the reference. "So, what did you document during the seventies?!"

"If I told you now it wouldn't be a surprise now would it?" Vera answered coyly. "Would you show me how the doodads upstairs work please; I might as well get started."

"Right this way Madam Author..." and John led her up to the

print shop leaving Alfred and Ginger at the table in the kitchen.

She turned to him and asked, "Uncle Alfred, can you give me the gist of what you and John have come up with for the hired help and will it be more feasible than outfitting the *Anna* with a mobile press room?"

Hana was utterly uninterested in the discussion and pulled on her mother's hand to go to another room. Ginger waved for Alfred to follow them until Hana found a more 'exciting' arena in which to explore and play. She dragged them to the sitting room and tried to climb up on the piano bench. Ginger helped her up and raised the keyboard cover for her to play. While Hana played her scale, Ginger absorbed the proposals about the profit-sharing, the outer entrance and the signage. They talked for an hour or so and Alfred explained the pros and cons of the situation as best they knew them.

6 April 94   I think Vera's scrapbooks have to do with John and me somehow. She's been up there in the print shop from before dawn until after dinner the last two days now. Whatever it is, it's going to be exciting to see. All she's said so far is that the equipment almost does the work for her... that's encouraging for our prospects about hired help picking up the tasks readily. I have been continuing to edit John's journals while Uncle Alfred and John have begun to erect a very attractive stairway up to the second floor of the Inn. Hana can sit for over an hour playing scales on the piano. Her attention span is longer than mine was in college! I do trust Vera and Alfred, I do trust Vera and Alfred. They said John and I would be good parents... but we have our doubts.

Instead of dwelling on my perceived inadequacies, I am trying to fend off preconceptions about what's going on in our little Hana's mind and instead, just responding to her with the knowledge of what is *actually* supposed to be developing in her at this age. I bought a 'Caring for your Child' book at the libreria and looked up the stages of development for one year olds through three year olds. According to *that* book's criteria, Hana is a fricking genius-plus! She's so far ahead of 'normal' development it's like she was dropped off by a spaceship of an advanced race from a distant galaxy or something. So much for guidance from the 'so-called' experts! I just wish her hair would grow in a little; I want to put her in little ponytails, maybe even braids.

Jeez Ginger-girl! She's not a Barbie doll! Now wait... let me think this through... Yes, she's 'advanced,' but that's according to an *average* picture of a *sampling* of *average children* her age. That does not take into account any data specific to the actual structure and real development of a human machine. Yes, their models physiologically follow the development of a child's body, but their extrapolations about the mental and emotional capacities of a child are experimentally obtained---meaning they began with a hypothesis and did or did not evaluate their results candidly and sincerely. Hmm.

I reviewed John's notes about the development of life on earth and the correspondence of that paradigm with a single individual's development. What I see there is that Hana is a perfectly normal child at one year old. She is exercising her instinctive and moving centers and daily expanding their capabilities---adapting to her environment and manipulating it experientially. She is gradually absorbing real data about that environment and storing it in her emotional and intellectual centers. I know that because I tested it. When Mocha runs away from her after her attempt to do 'something' to the cat that the cat wants no part of, I tried to mimic her attempted 'something' on the cat by doing the same thing to her. She didn't like it---and those attempts stopped. *She made the connection* that she and the cat don't like the same thing---at least as far as *that* 'something' goes. That's a small example of the emotional center beginning to function... it may be modest now... but she's only one year old---it's appropriate and corresponds to what I am observing about her *proper* development, not what the 'book' says.

I wonder if that's what Vera and Alfred meant when they said John and I will be good parents; that they have faith in us. I'm feeling better about his. Something else I noticed as I read through the journals was how our family's parents seldom, if ever, tell a child 'no.' Rather, and they are masters of this, they redirect and offer alternatives. When Belle's twins were small she never reacted with shock or over-the-top emotions either. She seemed to always address whatever inanity the girls created with a calmness that allowed the twins to assess their own foolishness. She really hammered them with the adverse repercussions of their acts in the light of reasonableness——how the world actually works, not how we *want* it to work *and it doesn't.* I mean she reiterated their errant actions with those 'expected' results and reminded them of those instances until the girls couldn't help but always remember the consequences for themselves. A reinforcement: both the good things *and* the goofball things---All without constantly berating them with 'no, no, no,' or 'see I told you so.' Essentially Belle *took herself out of the equation.* She didn't have to vindicate her own advice; she didn't feel the need to have 'the power.' She actually allowed her children to develop their own power, reasonably, rationally and consistently. So that when she asked them to do something: a chore, a task or an errand, they had no 'background' resistance to her wishes. 'Mama wants this, it's reasonable,' 'Mama does what I ask that's reasonable,' 'I'll do what Mama asks...'

Anyway, that's the subtext I read.

"Except for all the time transcribing my written notes and such, this could have been done even quicker. I can see how having electronic files of manuscripts that can be readily formatted and printed with such great speed and efficiency will be a vast improvement."

Vera praised the setup in the print shop as she handed Ginger and John the culmination of her seven day project.

"And those machines almost do everything for you! I wish I had

had something similar in my practice in Tahoe---pulling up records, entering the information in one place and having it available in a variety of formats depending on the application..."

Ginger held the coffee table sized book in her lap. HanaRin was even more eager, if that were possible, to see the 'new' book. Naturally at her age the world *did* still revolve around her wants and desires. She reached over to open the cover and begin 'her story.' Johnny smiled and sat down next to them.

"Okay. Let's see what the mystery was all about..."

On the first page was the title: *The In-between Years of Ginger and John Backhouse, Volume One.*

Ginger gasped and John gulped. "Auntie Vera! Is this what it sounds like?"

Vera and Alfred laughed, "You sound like little kids yourselves... READ!"

Hana turned the next page and there on the left were two pictures: one of Ginger at nine years old, freckles across her nose and hair in pigtails, standing in the lobby of the Tribune building in Chicago. The other picture was of John at seventeen, in blue jeans and sweatshirt, his arm up with the football poised to throw a pass. The background was the facade of the orphanage in which he'd grown up. On the facing page was a brief account of their real parentage and how they happened to be where they were in those photos.

Hana turned the page and the title of the first 'chapter' was entitled: Ginger age Nine. There were pictures of her at school, newspaper clippings, Vera's notes about her accomplishments and pictures of Ginger with her friends and of her walking home through the empty country roads to home. Ginger couldn't even see the words or the pictures her eyes were so clouded with tears. John was thoroughly rapt with reading every article and note about his wife.

Needless to say Hana kept turning pages, Ginger or John would laugh or cry, point to the pictures and describe the backgrounds for Hana. She would have gotten through the 'book' in about five minutes if left to her own devices. As it was, the reading took well into the night. Alfred put Hana to bed after Vera fed her and gave her a bath. She was just tired enough to drop off to sleep without asking for a bedtime story.

Alfred and Vera rejoined John and Ginger in the sitting room as they were just finishing 'their' book. John looked at them and asked simply, "How did you get some of these pictures?! I mean like when I was in the Pecos wilderness; there wasn't another person within twenty miles of my little camp, but here is a picture of me sitting at that very campfire!"

Vera answered simply, "Your Uncle Alfred is a very capable person."

John insisted, "But really! How?"

Alfred admitted, "Remember when you had just set up camp and were off searching for firewood or something and you ran into some old guy that claimed to be a park ranger? He asked you how long you were intending to stay, where were you going to be hiking, did you prepare properly for the elements, did you have the permits for your stay... and all that..." John looked closely at Alfred as he held a tress of Vera's hair across his face like a moustache. John's eyes nearly bugged out of his head. "THAT WAS YOU?!" he said incredulously.

"How else could I have gotten those pictures? You weren't always just sitting in your cubicle at TI, or dining at a restaurant with friends or playing golf... Sometimes I had to... be creative..." Alfred acknowledged.

John's brows furrowed, "How do you know about my office space at TI?"

Vera answered, "My Alfred has had an amazing array of

seasonal jobs: janitor at corporations and schools, press agent, park ranger, tour guide, gas station attendant, HR rep, electrician, telephone repairman, cable guy, mechanic, apartment rental agent, real estate agent... the list is too long to enumerate."

Alfred countered with, "And you haven't?" He turned to John and Ginger, "Your Auntie is a most versatile actress... and she enjoys disguise quite as much as a stage diva. I personally liked her as 'the harried dumb blond in the university counsellor's office'."

Ginger's eyes focused on Vera, "My university? When I had to keep coming back over and over again to sort out exactly how many hours I still needed for graduation? You were in *that* office?!"

Vera demurred, and Alfred replied, "In that office? She was the counsellor! She even tried to get you to come back a fifth time, just to have one more opportunity to chat---of course you were so put out with the whole situation that she was more afraid of eliciting a physical confrontation than a pleasant 'talk' so that was that. But do you remember the cleaning lady on the third floor of that magazine..."

Vera interjected, "Conde Nast..."

"Thank you... the one that kept running the vacuum cleaner near your desk seemingly every time you had a deadline to meet and couldn't abide the interruptions?"

Ginger was rapidly becoming inured to the breadth and depth of the undertakings their Aunt and Uncle had gone to in order to watch over them through the years.

Vera was hesitant but asked, "You don't feel violated, we hope, that we essentially stalked you two over the years. It's just that if we'd left everything to chance and happenstance, we might never have been able to know when would be the right moment to step in at last..."

Alfred made a different defense, "It could have been *anybody* in those places at those times, just because *we* happened to be *them*...

250

Does that actually make a difference in the long run? We did stay in the background for the most part... We just added a helping hand every now and again..."

John looked at Ginger's expression to be sure he wasn't alone in his whole-hearted admiration for their 'involvement.' Ginger was the one to respond first.

"Auntie Vera, Uncle Alfred, I speak for both of us when I say: We couldn't be more grateful, or feel more loved and cherished than to know just how much... how far... how devoted you were to us that you stayed so close to us over the years..."

John asked simply, "And how did you decide what would be the 'right moment'?" Ginger nodded and waited for an answer to that as well.

Alfred replied, "There was no set criteria, if that's what you mean... But when John decided to turn his hand to writing, even though that had never been an activity he'd engaged in before---And you were already in that field, so to speak, it seemed to be the closest we were ever going to get, short of directly arranging an encounter, to bringing you two together. Not that we were trying to make you a couple, we just wanted to you both to know your actual roots at the same time is all. We weren't trying to be matchmakers or anything, just trying to kill two birds with one stone, if you see what I mean?"

Vera enjoined, "That you two did, in fact, hit it off and become so close is completely your own doing---In truth, that hadn't occurred to either of us or anyone else in the family that I am aware of..."

Ginger looked at John, "I wasn't 'in the market' for a mate when I came to your house on assignment that afternoon..."

John answered, "And I was pretty certain of my bachelorhood already. Alone was what I was used to, and I had even convinced myself it was alright to be permanently single..."

Ginger continued, "But when your 'distant family' was there and they were so... so comfortable to be near... I guess I became softened to the idea of just spending time with you---although I was nominally there on business. Of course your telling me the history of this pebble certainly put me under your spell..."

John admitted, "I would have tried to come up with *any story* that would have kept you coming back. If there is such a thing as love at first sight... I had it bad... I mean chronically, terminally, never-get-over: bad! I just happened to only know that one story."

They were holding each other's hands throughout the exchange and Ginger kissed him. "True Confessions? I thought you were hot for an older guy! That you wanted to have *me* there in *your* house telling me a story---a really *great* story, to boot---It was all I could do to stay in my own room that first night; that and I was whipped, and dog-tired..."

John repeated, "For an *old* guy?"

Ginger blushed, "Oops. You know what I mean. You were single and forty something. Uh, am I gonna regret this?"

John laughed and dispelled his wife's momentary disquiet. "No that's cool *baby*, I'm as *hip* as I can muster for an 'old geezer.' I'm just glad you took a chance on me!" Ginger laughed out loud.

They looked over at Alfred and Vera who had tactfully remained quiet through that dialog. Vera was in tears and Alfred's smile transcended language---it was the look of a man experiencing the satisfaction and gratitude for their years of watchfulness vindicated at long last.

All he could say was, "Good, you're not angry with us."

Everyone laughed at that understated observation.

Ginger asked, "So there's a Volume Two?"

Vera blew her nose and replied, "Actually there is a Two: that covers the Eighties. And a Three: that comes up to when you first held Hana, and I, at long last, was free to embrace you after thirty-one years of waiting..." She was in tears again.

Alfred explained, "Our emotions around this topic are still very close to the surface. We'll be just fine again in the morning..."

At the kitchen table in the morning Ginger pointed out that Vera would still need to go through a 'workshop' on troubleshooting the equipment. They were certain now that any intern could get up to speed in a week to just run the 'presses,' but if anything went wrong, if there were any glitches, they'd need to know at least where to begin in order to figure out a solution. While John sat with Hana and Vera in the Voyager offices going over exigencies, Ginger assisted Alfred in the final touches to the outside entrance: the doorway and sign.

Ginger hadn't spent much time in her life working with tools and such, so this was an eye-opening experience. Alfred was very patient and answered each and every one of Ginger's myriad questions about every little thing they did and why. They accomplished in four days what could otherwise have been done in one, but Ginger came away from the experience more confident in her own abilities, and the entrance looked very impressive as well.

The 'staircase' up to the second floor 'door,' was actually designed and installed in such a way that it looked for all the world to have *always* been a part of the Inn. The double doors were a very good likeness of the main entranceway to the Inn, and the staircase was even tiled along the sides as the rest of the walls of the building were tiled. It was a very good installation.

"Now we just need to install deadbolts on the interior doors so that this area is sufficiently separate from the rest of the building... and 'voila'---Voyager Press has a brick and mortar home!" Alfred announced. "And that it's a second floor establishment... very Venetian, molto Italiano!"

Ginger giggled, "All I know is that it looks really good! And it is functional. What more could someone ask of an office space?"

19 April 94   I've been a little too busy to journal the last several days, and it felt as though a little part of my life was absent. Voyager Press is a real thing and we've been given heads-up that the initial installment of the Pantaleoni contract is on its way to us--- good timing. Vera and John have proven that within two weeks we can train interns at least enough to marginally function on their own for the tasks we might require of them. Alfred is formulating a program to pitch to our target schools and guild members that should insure a dedicated workforce for the Press. We'll see.

I've been taking Hana to a local playground. It's not much right now---I'd like to arrange for improvements to it---but the other children and their parents who frequent it are friendly and the kids are well-behaved. Hana has been trying to run. She toddles as quickly as she can and spends a lot of time falling down. It's torture to watch and not really be able to protect her from the scrapes and bruises she's inflicting on herself. It's another aspect of parenting that's a real challenge for me. John's the same way. The first time he came with us, he was nearly as exhausted as Hana. He chased, I mean, 'followed' her around the entire time trying to keep her from falling down. I had to physically restrain him after half an hour to just let Hana do what toddlers do when they play: go boom-boom!

We had some rain a few days ago just after the new doors were installed. Vera and I went to the docks and did some cleaning on the *Anna*, taking advantage of the 'free' freshwater. The sails and rigging, not the stays and shrouds, have been stowed so that they needn't be unnecessarily weathered when we're not actually sailing her; she gets enough exposure when we sail her. Mocha's two 'assistants' have been doing a pretty good job, judging by the number of headless rat carcasses littering the decks. Between their 'trophies' and the bird poop, we had our work cut out for us on the cleaning detail. The *Anna* has been scrubbed clean, waxed and polished. Everything we could put a cover over has a cover over it now, and she looks like a well-dressed lady again.

I am five months into this pregnancy and I just *thought* my back hurt a few weeks ago. Now my center of gravity is really changing and the stress on my lower back and knees is definitely showing---I am sooo looking forward to getting to term and the real discomfort awaiting me when I'm twice this size! Joy, joy...

"I am so glad we went all out and got the highest resolution scanners we could lay our hands on..." Ginger commented. "We couldn't do *this* job or any like it without this capability... How much will they cost to replace if something goes terribly wrong?"

John repeated, "Probably less than we laid out for them... we got them as first generation, every time they come up with another iteration, it seems the price drops a little on what we are already satisfied with using..."

"That's counter-intuitive, but then I don't know technology, I guess." Ginger concluded.

Alfred came in and announced, "Okay I have two potential candidates coming by tomorrow: one from the College of Print Arts, and the other is a lady who has spent the last four years at a small local bindery..."

Hana sat on the floor arranging and rearranging the reject scan sheets of the latest project. It was a book on the elements of neo-classicism in the Modernist movement, some sort of overgrown master's thesis project or something, but Hana thought the pictures were pretty---just out of 'proper' order. They were contracted to produce a master proof and an initial fifty copies once the proof was certified by the author. The other project that was running simultaneously was a little more relevant: a photographic essay on the relief efforts after a five point five earthquake and subsequent tsunami that hit Sumatra. Alfred was pleased that although neither the *Hannah* nor *Ananke* were there personally, the GFHAS led the 'first-in' setup and organization efforts.

That comment led to a lengthy discussion about the other global incidents their organization had been instrumental in over the last several years. "Job security is a given so long as the people of this world ignore the humanity and basic needs of their brothers and sisters..." Vera added.

Alfred insisted, "Whether it's civil strife and war, inadequate housing and construction, inequality in the distribution of resources, or the lack of preparation for inevitable natural disasters, anyone who turns their attentions and efforts to filling the void in the unreasonableness of mankind will always have a job to do. We just hope there will come a day... someday... that that job is unnecessary at last."

Vera cautioned, "Don't hold your breath..." Her expression changed and she added, "I don't like to fall into cynicism, but *sometimes* it *can* be overwhelming..."

John told Ginger, "I am so glad you had the idea for an independent publishing company. Whether we publish stuff like these two volumes, or our families journals, or the stories and poetry of obscure artists in regions of conflict... It really feels as though we're advocating a change in the right direction." Ginger raised an eyebrow, and John added, "I know, I know... *We* can't change anyone, they have to want to change themselves... but it's good to put real information and sound thoughts and ideas in front of people, isn't it?"

Alfred rejoined, "That's about all we *can* do."

Hana pulled on her mother's hand to see her 'work.' Ginger and Vera looked over the rearranged images and they both had to take a second look. For the most part, Hana's arrangement wasn't as random or arbitrary as one might have expected. In fact, Ginger commented, "I'd like to run a separate version almost just as Hana has laid out. Look at the movement of color and geometry..."

Vera thought, "...And who would have conceived of juxtaposing these three images..." Johnny and Alfred had to see what the girls were admiring in their little angel's diversion.

Both of them agreed with Ginger, "We should make one copy, at least, in this new arrangement. Hana didn't really know what they were saying but she understood they approved of her little project and so she wandered off to do something else. Alfred followed after her and they ended up in the apartments sitting amongst Hana's blocks and building an abstract configuration of walls and little towers. Ginger fetched her camera from the office and snapped a few pictures without either of them noticing---or *apparently* noticing at least.

There was a knocking at the main doors downstairs. John went to answer it. A little while later, there were gasps and peels of laughter coming from the Voyager rooms. Alfred and Hana went to see what caused the commotion. Becka was sitting on the settee and telling Ginger and Vera all about her journey to Venice. John brought in refreshments from the kitchen as Alfred was asking, "So what prompted you to leave before the semester was over?"

Becka grinned and held up her left hand. A glittering diamond said it all.

"Okay, so your engaged! Who's the lucky fellow and where is he?!"

Becka chirped excitedly, "He's on his way; I came ahead to give you all heads up and tell you what we are anticipating for the next few weeks..."

Vera asked, "And *who* is he?"

Ginger asked, "When will he get here?"

John and Alfred said, "You *will* be staying here won't you?"

Becka giggled that they were so interested and seemingly as excited as she was. "He's the man I was 'working on' before going to the Caribbean last winter..."

Ginger asked, "I thought that fell through, didn't you say he had a change of heart or something? You sure moped around in black long enough afterward..."

Becka countered, "Yeah it did and I was down, but we ran into each other a month ago and it seems he's learned his lesson: Nobody's better than Rebecca Lara Belle Larrson for sheer reasonableness and determination!" She giggled again. "That, and he explained what was so disenchanting about me the first time around..."

Vera urged, "Which was?"

"His fragile male ego had difficulty handling the knowledge that my family is so incredibly accomplished and that I have been literally all over the world on so many different missions with the GFHAS and all..."

She held up a finger and let it curl down, "He was... uh... intimidated."

John asked, "How did he overcome it that now he's apparently so completely on board?"

Becka lowered her voice, "Uh, you should probably get him to explain that part. All I know is that after one long weekend with me in Gothenburg, he proposed and I said yes, absolutely!"

"When will he be here?" Ginger asked.

Becka answered, "Tomorrow or Saturday... He's coming by train from Brussels."

Alfred asked, "What did you do about your classes?"

Becka's happiness was indomitable, she replied, "This semester I only had one 'course,' my thesis committee... it was mostly a check-in thing. When I told them the news, they were willing to reschedule it for a later semester."

Ginger had to ask, "Why the surprise visit? I mean we're delighted, but did you lose your phone or something?"

Becka's giggling was infectious, Hana was even chirping little giggles. "We weren't planning to come and visit until next month. I was going to call, then I thought I'd just email, but then he had business in Brussels this week with the European Union Council of Ministers, so I hopped on a train and said I'd meet him here when he was done in Brussels. I hope I'm not interrupting anything..."

"No, no nothing... We're very excited that you thought of bringing your fiancee to meet us!" Vera insisted.

Ginger reinforced Vera's enthusiasm, "We've just been getting this publishing thing off the ground and playing houses... You know: taking Hana to the playground, going to the market, hoping for family to come and visit... that sort of thing!"

John asked, "May I move your things to one of the suites? You pretty much have your choice of rooms at present..."

Becka hopped up, "Oh yes, please. Let me help," and they carried her duffle and shoulder bag across the courtyard and she selected her rooms.

"Ivy will love this place, I know he will..." She pulled out a change of clothes and John excused himself. When he went to the office to pick up the glasses and bottles he'd brought up, the others had already cleared them away and were still in the kitchen.

"Well, do we know more about him than that his name is Ivy and he's had an epiphany about our Becka?" he asked.

Alfred repeated, "Ivy? That's more than I heard."

Vera pointed out that, "Oh... then he *is* the same fellow I remember her speaking of when we were in the Caribbean... he's a graduate in political science and finance, Ivar Johannson. I think she said he was working as the liaison, or with the liaison committee for Sweden's bid to enter the European Union... That also explains his being in Brussels..."

Ginger had only to say, "She looks so much happier now than a few months ago..."

Vera added, "Nils and Eva thought highly of him... until she came home in tears after their 'temporary breakup,' anyway. No doubt if Becka loves him, they are reconciled as well."

Becka popped in at that moment, "My ears are burning! And yes, Papa and Mama think he's great. Even Jimmy likes him, and that's saying something. Jimmy's always been a little over-protective of me," she confided.

Alfred smiled, "When's the big date, or have you set one yet?"

Becka reached for a slice of cheese for her cracker, "I don't know for sure. We have talked about having a little ceremony in Gotland, or just a civil thing in Stockholm. Who knows where we'll end up being when the notion strikes us to just not put it off any longer. I know this sounds impulsive..." and she looked at Ginger and John, "...but look who I'm admitting to being impulsive! The 'oh-we-were-married-after-knowing-each-other-for-three-days-and-now-we-have-a-one-year-old-girl' people! And Hana's growing really fast... she's actually talking a little now!"

As if to emphasize it, Hana babbled something that sounded like: 'I'm a big girl.'

John announced, "We've been meaning to try this little ristorante just a few bridges over toward the school grounds... Shall we have a pre-meeting-Ivy-celebration this evening?"

It never took much to encourage anyone in the Inn to go out to eat. Venice could probably boast of two restaurants per person; there was always another 'nice little ristorante' to try. The goal seemed to be to never eat in the same place twice. Hana walked as far as the playground and when she realized they weren't going to play, she opted for being carried. Alfred hoisted her up on his shoulders and she rode the rest of the way. Becka had cut her hair since they'd seen her last. Instead of the long strawberry blond tresses that she used to keep pulled back or up in a french braid, it was now cropped in a block cut with her bangs long enough to push behind her ears. She was as tall as her mother, nearly six foot, and she'd inherited her father's sea blue eyes and broad shoulders. When they settled at a table and were sipping their wine, she made another announcement.

"Oh! I must be in the throes of bliss... I just remembered the other thing I wanted to tell you." All eyes turned to her. "The *Tygress* is my ship! Jimmy didn't want her, since he loves his little motor yacht, *Valkyrie*. So, Ginger, thank you, thank you, thank you for giving me the best ship in the waters!"

Ginger was speechless. She had no idea that Sam and Ronia would *actually* make the presentation of the yacht in *her name*. Becka continued, "I asked Grandpa to fit her out with twin Elco drives. She'll be ready in May for her first voyage sporting her new power plant... if she makes it up the queue by then that is. I probably won't need it except for getting around marinas and lagoons---anywhere I'm in tight quarters---but it's great to have in a pinch... like a tattered main, broken mast, you know: the bad stuff..."

Ginger composed herself, "I knew you'd love her, and I rather thought you might make that addition. So, might we be seeing you and Ivy here in Venice this summer as well?" She heard herself ask that last bit. 'Whoa Ginger-girl, you are definitely starting to sound like a mother!'

Becka brightened even more, if that were possible. "That's exactly what we were hoping to do!"

John asked, "Does Ivy sail then?"

Becka's crisp response was confidence personified, "He'll be a better sailor after I'm done with him. He didn't have many opportunities to sail while growing up. But I've taken him out twice... before I put her in for her 'surgery,' and Ivy really loved it. He picked up the basics quickly enough, he'll be sea-worthy before long."

Their dinner arrived and it was another very satisfying meal at a new place to eat. Alfred commented, "So far, we haven't found a place that I didn't like! Is that because I have a plebeian palate, or is there no such thing as a 'bad' ristorante in Venice!?"

Vera and Becka agreed, "After hundreds of years serving visitors from all over the world, how could the Venetian cuisine be anything but wonderful?"

"Good point, well taken." Alfred acknowledged. "And how do you like your gelato, young lady?" he asked Hana.

She smiled, maybe because she was included in the conversation, maybe because she had a bite in her mouth at that moment. Either way, Hana liked desert best.

Ivy came in on the afternoon train the next day. Since he wished to surprise Becka, his unannounced arrival caused a lot of excitement. When he knocked at the front doors the ladies looked at each other with expressions of jubilant anticipation; Becka's face was transparently ecstatic.

"It's Ivy!" she exclaimed and leapt up to get to the door as quickly as she could.

'A good sign,' Ginger thought. 'Can't stand to be apart from our Becka. A very good sign.'

Ivar Viktor Johannson was three or four inches taller than Becka, which put him an inch or two taller than either John or Alfred.

Vera remarked, "Wow, he's a *gorgeous* viking!" Ginger was careful to not stare, but it wasn't easy.

John overheard the whispered awe and commented loud enough for Ginger to hear, "For a *young* guy..." Ginger looked at him, and rolled her eyes.

After Becka disentangled herself from their embrace she made introductions, "Ivy, this is..."

Ivy interrupted, "George Alfred Nils Livingson and Vera Elizabeth Masterson-Livingson..." and he bowed taking Alfred's extended hand and clasped it firmly. He held Vera's hand and kissed it. Alfred's eyebrows shot up and Vera's expression was close to that of a spoiled little girl.

He continued, "And these are John Robert Backhouse, his beautiful bride Virginia Kaitlyn Belle Spelman-Backhouse and their daughter Hana Nasrin. I am honored to meet you all. Becka has told me perhaps too much about you each; I feel as though I know you quite well already," and he knelt down to look Hana in the eye on her own level. "But nothing prepared me for meeting this most beautiful young lady..."

Hana peered from behind her father's leg, grinning like the Cheshire Cat. She reached out her hand and held his finger. He made a show of 'shaking' her little hand and she giggled.

Vera cleared her throat, "Becka hasn't been as forthcoming with stories about you... and now we see why. What ever she might have said would not have done you justice, I am sure."

Becka's grin was as broad as Hana's, "This is Ivar Viktor Johannson, Special Attache with the liaison team from Sweden to the Council of the European Union for Sweden's accession into the Union. His grandfather was one of the seven men who met with Papa Harry to form the Gotland Freedom Society..."

Alfred warmed to him instantly. He put his arm around his shoulders and said, "Welcome Ivy, let's get you situated." John reached for Ivy's travel bag and went to put it in Becka's rooms. Vera and Ginger led them all to the kitchen where their afternoon snacks of breads, cheeses, fruits, meats and wine had just been laid out on the table.

"Special Attache... what does that entail?"

Ivy chuckled, "After struggling to the top of my undergraduate class in political science and business administration, then working through a Masters in International Relations and Global Finance, I am now a glorified librarian, essentially. But it's for a good cause, I think."

John rejoined them and offered, "You should feel right at home here then. Only Ginger is actively using her education at present. The rest of us are just filling in the gaps." They carried the trays of food to the sitting room and Alfred softly played at the piano with Hana on his lap, her hands trying to stay on his hands as he played.

Becka bragged on Ivy, "Librarian! pshaw. Ivy has drafted every article, proposal, regulatory document and agreement that has passed between the government of Sweden and the Council! And once the accession is finalized he will likely be installed as the chief assistant for the Swedish Representative to the Council of Auditors." If her pride in Ivy were any more apparent she'd have them addressing him as his majesty.

Ivy deflected the rising appreciation in his hosts, "Like I said, glorified librarian: long hours, tedious details, sorting, amending, shuffling and shuttling. It's a truly *glamorous* position," he added facetiously. He turned the conversation away from himself and candidly admitted, "Mr. Livingson, you were the cause of Becka and my breakup last January."

Alfred balked. "How's that again?"

Ivy smiled, "Perhaps not you, completely, but you were the icing on the cake. You see when Becka returned from the Caribbean she told me as much as she dared about why she went down to the tropics, about each of you and your roles in your family and more to the point, a bit about each of your backgrounds. I felt such a deep sense of inadequacy over comparing myself to her family, of my own history versus your amazing exploits... what's the phrase? I shriveled up like a walnut!"

Vera consoled, "Becka may have exaggerated our activities for the sake of impressing you. We are really very ordinary folks."

Ivy and Becka spurted out laughter. Becka explained, "No, Auntie, I *understated* your activities and he still became dejected and distant."

Ivy added looking at John and Ginger, "Becka told me of your family's determination to find you two and then to keep up with you over the last twenty some odd years---that story alone would have been enough." He looked to Alfred and Vera, "But she also told me of your family's global involvements from the founding of the Gotland Society, the enfolding of your family's already long established Humanitarian Aid projects into that Society and the various projects through to the present. Facts are facts; there's no room for exaggerations. It was however you, Alfred... if I may call you Alfred?"

"Call me anything you like; *Uncle* Alfred is used a lot." Alfred interjected.

Ivy smiled, "Thank you. It was when Becka told me about you, sir, that was the icing on the cake for me. All your accomplishments, everything you've done for not only your own family but so many others... and without any regard for having your own participation acknowledged at any point---I was reduced to impotence and extreme feelings of inadequacy."

"And what turned that around for you? Because, well, you're here." Ginger inquired earnestly.

Becka had not stopped beaming during the entire interview, she held one of Ivy's hands in both of hers as he answered this last question. "Actually it was because of a talk I had with my Grandpa. He remembers most everything, still, even from before the war. Anyway, he told me a story about a young prince, a peasant girl and a prophecy..."

Vera's eyes widened and she interrupted, "Was your grandmother a Masterson?!"

Ivy's expression was pleasant shock, "Yes! How could you..." He regained his composure and remembered with whom he was speaking. "I am still amazed at what you all are capable of knowing and doing... Then you know the story to which I refer?"

Ginger piped up, "She told it to *me* not long ago."

Ivy continued, "After hearing his tale, it finally dawned on me how foolish I had been to bundle everything Becka told me about her family into how I perceived her, herself. And then assign myself a role of such complete unworthiness. Like the gentle-hearted girl from the story said, *'I can't imagine that one such as I, who is so small and insignificant, could be of any help to you in your great journey. I will bind myself to the young man and be his helpmate. For although he is brave and a great hunter, he will need me to become greater than he is.'* Becka is extraordinarily brilliant, determined, adaptable, beautiful---wise even. I had to accept that, as my grandpa told me, I have a few worthwhile characteristics myself and a rich family history of traditions as well. That I could, really, meet Becka on her own terms; that I could be her helpmate in *almost* anything." His audience nodded, smiling. "So, when Becka and I met up again last month, the first thing I had to find out was: if there was any chance at all that I might possibly still have a place in her heart, in spite of having once dismissed her affections so horribly."

Becka chimed in, "Actually he asked: 'If you don't hate me, may I buy you a cup of coffee?' It was a tender and almost romantic proposal... You had to be there."

Ivy finished, "I was determined not to lose her if I had even a whisper of a chance. I bared my heart to her with the story I have just reiterated to you and she invited me on the *Tygress* up to Gothenburg. We spent the next three days alone with each other. When I had to leave on assignment that Tuesday, I left as a proudly engaged man to the most wonderful woman I have ever met! And that's why, as you pointed out, 'I'm here'."

Ginger and John picked up the empty glasses. Vera announced, "Half an hour before we head off to the engagement party! Alfred and I are hosting, and we also insist on hosting your wedding---here if you will or in Sweden if you wish."

Ivy answered at once, "I've been trying to get Becka to accept a date as soon as possible, but she insisted we visit you all before she would commit herself to any date. I'm ready to be married now!"

They all looked at Becka, a little surprised at the turn of events. "I had to have your blessings before I... I just couldn't... even my folks said I should come here and... I idolize you all, more than you know. Your approval is just that important to me."

Ivy assisted, "She *has* said as much on more than one occasion. We humbly ask your blessing and if you are serious about hosting our wedding..." he looked at Becka who nodded, "Is tomorrow or the next day too soon?"

Alfred nodded to John, who nodded to Ginger, who waved for Vera to follow them out the side door. Alfred and John were already heading outside when Vera carried Hana and herded Ivy and Becka out behind the others. Alfred was standing in the sampan and waved Becka and Ivy aboard. Once they were situated he began, "This family has many traditions, but one of the special ones is the recurrence of our being wedded at sea. As the great-great-grandson of our family's patriarch, in his absence, I assume the captaincy of this vessel. Mr. Johannson do you have the ring?"

Ivy did in fact have the ring to match the engagement ring he'd given to Becka. He reached into his pocket and produced a gold band. Alfred commenced, "Rebecca Lara Belle Larrson, do you take this man as your husband, and promise to treat him always with compassion and love, whether you feel like it or not?"

Becka said as calmly as she could manage in a very deliberate voice, "I shall love him as myself, serve him when he requires it, and guide him when he needs it."

"Ivar Viktor Johannson, do you take this woman as your wife, and promise to treat her always with compassion and love, whether you feel like it or not?"

Ivy's grin was nearly a beacon of brightness his joy was so great; he proclaimed aloud, "I shall love her as myself, serve her when she requires it, and guide her when she needs it."

"As the last patriarch of the Livingson traditions, humble mentor to the newest Master of our families," he nodded to John, "and the present Captain of this fine vessel---which is the ever-present reminder that you shall always have further to go upon your journey and must make daily the enormous efforts necessary---I pronounce you husband and wife. Becka kiss your husband. Ivy kiss your wife."

They didn't really need to be told...

An hour later they were being served champagne at a little ristorante several bridges from the Inn. John raised his glass for a toast, they all raised their glasses in response. "May your lives be full of happiness, may your faith in each other be strong, may your children be honorable and wise, and may your love grow ever brighter---your whole life long."

Tears dripped from the ladies' eyes as they all drank to John's toast. Ginger followed with, "To Love and to those who bear it!"

Ivy's eyes were as damp as the others' but he cleared his throat and said, "This day is the happiest day of our lives up to now. We are honored and blessed to be with you and be so cherished by you that you have wedded us together."

Vera had Hana in her lap. She wiggled to be put down on her own feet. She walked around to Becka and raised her arms up. Becka gasped and picked her up. Hana kissed her on her cheek and said as clearly as she was able, "Love Becka."

Ginger and Vera were so proud, their tears flowed anew. Then on top of that performance, Hana reached for Ivy's sleeve and pulled him to her. She repeated the performance saying, "Love Ivy." There was an ovation from the patrons at the tables around their own table in the restaurant. They couldn't help but overhear, although their grasp of English may not have been complete, Hana's actions transcended language. They were so touched by the child's benediction they clapped and cheered. There wasn't a dry eye in the house.

John said simply, "There! Welcome to the family!"

Ivy and Becka were incandescent with joy. Alfred, Vera and Ginger were overwhelmed into a silence that was a palpable embrace. If elation were an energy source they could have lit up all of Venice.

23 April 94   Yesterday Becka and Ivy became Mr. and Mrs. Johannson and Hana blessed them. Vera and I were so proud of our little girl we thought we might come out of our skin and glow like the stars. This is the morning after and none of us expect the newlyweds to emerge from their suite until much later. John and Uncle Alfred are at the market, Vera and Hana are 'reading' a book and I am so utterly humbled that our cousin Becka considered us such a necessary part of her and Ivy's happiness that they came here and were married.

St. Mark's Day is Monday. It's a huge thing here. The rest of the country celebrates the twenty-fifth as Liberation Day, but here in Venice it's St. Mark's Day that everyone celebrates. I asked Alfred about why Venice was so out of sync with the rest of Italy. He explained about their traditions here. St. Mark is said to have personally brought Christianity to Venice during his lifetime. He is therefore the patron saint of this city and his 'actual' relics are even in the Basilica. But the reason *his* day is celebrated with more enthusiasm even than the commemoration of Italy's liberation from fascism is of course: a love story. Once there was a star-crossed love between a noblewoman named Maria Partecipazio and the troubadour Tancredi. In the hopes of overcoming the difference between their social classes, Tancredi went to war seeking glory in the army which would raise him up to the same social status as his beloved. Unluckily, after serving as a valiant soldier in the orders of Charles the Great during the War against the Arabians in Spain, he was fatally wounded. He fell over a white rose bed and all the roses growing in the bed became red from his blood. Dying, Tancredi extracted a promise from Orlando the Paladin to take a blossom from those rose bushes to his beloved Lady in Venice. Orlando kept his promise and reached Venice the day before the Patron Day of St. Mark. He gave the bloom to the Lady and the last message of love from her, now dead, suitor. The next morning Maria Partecipazio was found dead herself, with the red bloom laying over her heart. Since that day, Venetian lovers have used that flower as an emblematic pledge of love. So on Monday you can expect to see red roses in the hands nearly every woman all over the city.

Beat that! Omnia vincit Amor, indeed! How fitting it feels that Ivy and Becka are married and will see all of Venice in red roses just three days after the blessed event. How cool is that?

"The next subcontract from the Pantaleonis is supposed to be along next week," Alfred answered as Ivy and Becka came into the kitchen. "Have some brunch! We didn't know when you two would be down this morning, but there is still plenty ready to be warmed up."

Ginger went to the oven and turned the heat up. Ivy asked, "Becka mentioned that you run a specialty press?"

Ginger smiled proudly, "It's getting off the ground, yes. Between our own families' journals and contract jobs at least we're getting our feet wet..." She went on to describe her vision for Voyager Press.

Ivy looked as if he wanted to ask something but was hesitant to the point of shyness. Becka urged him to ask what he wanted to ask. He explained, "Remember I said that I was handling documentation for Sweden's accession to the EU?"

"Yes, it sounds more exciting than you let on, but yes." Ginger encouraged.

"The thing is this: Some of the packages I have to assemble are manuals, some are guidebooks. There are Reg books that have to be distributed to all the departments on both sides, profiles, annual reports... the list goes on and on. What I was wondering, since you have a print-on-demand system operational, it would be a real timesaver if I could forward someone the electronic files and have them ready for printing in any quantity at a moment's notice. Right now I am at the mercy of a couple offset print firms and their schedules---rush pricing and all that."

Alfred asked, "What quantities are we talking about here?"

Ginger added, "What bindings? Do you require recycled paper for the bodies? What turnarounds do you require? Would orders come only from you, or do they originate from other department heads as well? Do you already have a shipping firm contracted, or would we need to expand our own accounts to insure delivery?"

Ivy was getting more than he'd anticipated. He tried to sort out the questions. "Quantities are variable, from twelve to over two hundred. My current printers use perfect binding and the recycled content is between thirty and fifty percent. The turnarounds right now are fifteen days *at best* from time of order to delivery. All orders are funneled through my group, that is to say myself or one of three others assigned to me. We ship through the same parcel couriers that everyone uses and have accounts with many of them, nothing special though." He sat with his mouth open ready to continue. When he realized he'd run out of questions to answer he closed his mouth. "Oh, I have a couple examples of typical jobs. They're in my bag; I have to send them off as soon as possible... although I understand Monday is a big holiday in Venice. I suppose they'll have to wait until Tuesday to be shipped."

Ginger was keen to have a look at them, as was Alfred. Ivy went up to their rooms and returned with a few A4 sized books and booklets. "These are very typical of our documents. This stuff isn't classified in any way. But that does bring up a subject we might possibly run into..."

That got Alfred's attention. "What are the protocols for becoming an authorized printer for those documents, should your department ever need such services?"

Ivy said candidly, "I don't know. Those documents go to a government authorized press... they never even cross my desk. What I was going to say is that even though none of what I might send your way is 'classified,' strictly speaking, none of it should ever be reprinted accept by direct authorized request from my office. So, if someone at the Council of Ministers, for instance, notices your the print house that produced a certain document and he rings you up directly... that will be one of the few times you get to tell a government official to fu... that is: 'Please, go through proper channels'."

Ginger looked over the construction and content from the viewpoint of format, color, trim and binding. "No problem. And we will likely be able to make your turnaround shorter by half at least; so long as we're not inundated with twenty orders at once for twenty different documents. Even at that, we can still shorten your lead times."

There was a sudden, very loud cracking thud from the sitting room, followed in short order by a most pitiful wailing cry from Hana. The kitchen evacuated as if it were a fire alarm. Ginger was at the sitting room door first and saw Vera holding her hand up, palm to the door, in an obvious gesture to keep them at bay. Hana was sitting up on the floor bawling her eyes out next to a chair laying on its back. Vera inspected Hana's little fingers and kissed them. Hana's sobs came in gasps and slowed.

Vera said, "Hana. Watch." She picked up the chair to right it again, then began tipping it back as if to tip it over. When it reached a balance point she stopped and let it go. It fell to the floor with a crack. Hana's sobs stopped. Vera repeated the demonstration again, this time letting the chair fall toward its feet instead of its back. She repeated it again and actually balanced the chair on two legs. Hana got up and touched it. It fell to its back again. She pushed it up to its four legs once more and went through the tipping demonstration herself. She was still trying to balance the chair when Vera walked to the door and addressed the five faces peering around the edge of the door frame.

"Just a little hard lesson in balance. I could have reached her and kept her from falling, but what would she have learned from that?" It was a rhetorical question. They looked passed her to where Hana was still attempting to balance the chair on two legs. She got very close a time or two but wasn't having the same success Vera had had.

Ginger murmured, "Brilliant. At least she didn't crack her head."

Vera said pointedly, "I *certainly* would have intervened if that were the probable outcome. She needs to know about balance not CATscans. Her head was out of danger; it was her fingers that were doomed in that little experiment. And as you see, she's resilient." She sighed and added, "My heart almost burst from the restraint I forced on myself." She looked at Alfred, "We're too old for this sort of torture!"

Alfred burst out laughing, "This from the woman who survived interrogation under Georgian specialists during the South Ossetian conflict. Hana must be extraordinarily powerful!"

Vera rolled her eyes. "You know *exactly* what I mean Mr. Livingson!"

"Look, look!" John exclaimed. They turned and there Hana stood next to the chair balanced on its back two legs. They all clapped. Hana grinned, then held up her fingers as the chair fell forward onto its four legs once more. Ginger went to kiss them better, just as Vera had earlier. Hana was mollified; she went to another chair and started the demonstration all over again.

27 April 94   It's not exactly the tradition, but John gave me and Hana bouquets of red roses yesterday. I am over thirty and have never received flowers before. I was in tears. Roses are *really* beautiful flowers and smell divine. They are in a vase in front of me while I'm writing this. Have I mentioned lately how much I love my husband?

One might think that after two days of marriage, the bride might be a *little* unhappy that her newlywed husband spent several hours at work instead of with her in wedded bliss doing what honeymooners do. Not our Becka. She was tickled that Ivy and John spent almost all day Tuesday up in the Voyager Press offices setting up an account and making a first run of files Ivy had with him for printing. Ah love.

We girls, on the other hand, went sailing on the *Little Tiger*. It was a warm seventy degrees or so and we went to the Lido and did some early season sunbathing. Here's what I had to work on: Auntie Vera is twice my age, Becka is ten years younger and they both look *incredible*. Then there was Ginger-girl, five months pregnant and wearing essentially the same swimsuits they wore. I was a whale to their dolphinesque figures. No matter how much they complemented me on my figure and health, it was as plain as the growing balloon in my belly that they were being generous. I have always had some pride in my physique, but next to the Swedish Valkyries I felt like a bullfrog. The best I could do was to try and remember myself. My disappointment gradually came into perspective and I was finally able to be objective about my appearance. But I have to admit: that was work!

I realize this admission sounds shallow and that if that's the greatest thing I have to work on, then my life is grand. But let me try and add some context to my ordeal. I didn't want to go sunbathing in the first place, Vera suggested we do whatever Becka wished to do---as a matter of external considering. I didn't want to wear a swimsuit at all; a big hat and kaftan was more on the menu as far as I was concerned. Again, Vera's suggestion won out. I didn't want to be in the middle of the only other sunbathers on the entire seven mile length of sand, nor did I want to have the attentions of several *very* healthy male admirers. I smiled, imagined myself un-pregnant and alluring, and tried to remember myself. I got through it and found out something interesting about myself. I am not what I like and dislike! I can be anything I set my mind to being. That was an amazing experience.

30 April 94   John has been especially warm and tender, thoughtful and supportive the last few weeks. I must be thick to have not noticed until yesterday, but as I look back it appears that he has been just that for perhaps even longer. When I asked him about it he didn't admit to doing anything differently than he had been doing, which made me wonder if either he was fibbing or I have been totally caught up with my own stuff---probably the latter. So I tried to think of some way to reciprocate. First I thought I'd make him a cake. Lame. Then I thought I'd give him a really good back rub and a 'special' night. Then I dragged myself upstairs for the evening, dog-tired and looked in the mirror. Circumstances over-ruled that one. When in doubt ask for advice. I asked Auntie Vera and she said something that seemed so counter-intuitive I laughed when I heard it. She said: 'Say *thank you* every time you notice he has done something nice for you. Always say please when you want him or need him to do something for you. Be delighted when he has taken care of something without your asking him, whether it was for you or not, *or* whether you could have done it yourself or not. And most importantly, smile anytime you notice he's looking at you.'

Like I said, I laughed. She explained that the greatest aphrodisiac a woman has, other than simply being a woman to begin with, is a smile and a kind word. 'We are powerful,' she said, and 'men are like dogs: Feed them, they'll always be at your door. Give them kind attention, they'll follow you anywhere. Then even if you kick them, they'll love you anyway. What you must *never* do is *treat* a man like a dog---they are far more fragile.' So I tried it. Wow, I only *thought* John was being thoughtful and tender before! He's nearly falling over his own feet to take care of me. The hard part is remembering to smile, remembering to acknowledge him in everything...it sounds silly, like I was raised in a barn and never learned proper social behavior. But after a fashion, I kinda was. Peggie and Harvey certainly didn't emphasize the social graces, and my peers... obviously not, and who listens to teachers at school when it comes to personal behavior?

Then I started thinking that what she told me wasn't actually *for John* at all; it was for me! I'm no rocket surgeon, but I figured that much out. It's as difficult as remembering myself, almost. It's certainly a good model for HanaRin. She at least will have the advantage I didn't, as she watches how 'mommy and daddy' act towards each other. And she does watch, everything! Vera admitted that her advice came from MamaKat. She explained that she had to have the same advice given to her after Alfred had at last convinced her that she was the most important woman in the world to him. 'That took me two and a half years to get straight in my head,' she admitted honestly. I just figured Auntie Vera had always been the angel she is now. It never occurred to me that it might have been Uncle Alfred who was the patient lover and she was the thick-headed frump. Even though as I think back on the stories Viola and Portia and even Vera and Alfred have told us, that's exactly what they said in so many words. I really do hear what I expect to hear. More work... oh boy...

"Thank you Johnny; you are so thoughtful." Ginger acknowledged as John came into the kitchen carrying her robe to her.

John yawned and answered, "You are so tightly wound these days. I didn't even hear Hana squeak; you were already out of bed and carrying her down for her breakfast. You are amazing GingerKat."

"Ah, thank you for saying so. I guess my maternal sixth sense is kicking into overdrive. Forgive me for being forgetful, but did Ivy get that authorization from his accounting people he said we needed to have direct deposits?"

A spoonful of oatmeal was still in front of Hana's closed mouth. She was rapidly expecting a different menu everyday. Same old same old wasn't hacking it. Ginger put the spoon down in the bowl and left it for Hana to get herself.

John swallowed his first sip of coffee and replied, "You're not forgetful. He emailed last night to say it was a go." He stretched. "And they pay really well! This contract should allow Voyager to recoup her start-up costs and turn her to significant profitability inside six months. And since we don't have any other profit-sharing employees yet, we're it!"

Hana decided she could *try* another bite of oatmeal. Ginger let her attempt to get that spoonful in her mouth herself. She did. "Oh, what a big girl you are HanaRin! Eating your own oatmeal with your own spoon! Such a big girl!" Ginger praised. Hana grinned and went for another round.

Alfred came into the kitchen and saw Hana feeding herself, he looked to Ginger with a questioning look. Ginger nodded and smiled. Alfred exclaimed, "Is that Hana? That big girl eating by herself?" Hana grinned some more and the last spoonful that had just made it into her mouth nearly fell out again.

Johnny chuckled at the sight; she snapped her head toward him to see if he was laughing at her. He quickly covered by saying, "It was funny when Becka told the story of y'all's trip to Lido. Did she really accept an invitation to a boat party, *then* ask if she could bring her husband?"

Vera came in just then, "Yes she really did. The pitiful young fellow looked as though someone had just shot his dog."

Ginger chimed in, "It didn't help that she said: 'May I bring my six foot four husband, he loves rowing; he was captain of the Swedish Olympic team..."

Hana banged on her empty bowl with her spoon. Vera's eyes opened a little wider, Ginger nodded. "HanaRin! Are you ready for some fruit? Do you want to eat that all by yourself too?" and Vera crossed to the counter and began cutting up a pear into small chunks. Hana did the sitting version of her victory dance, bobbing and swaying in place---the personification of thrilling anticipation. Vera asked, "Alfred darling, shouldn't we have heard about the recovery of the painting for the National Gallery yet?"

Alfred sighed and muttered, "Unfortunately I gave them a fool-proof, absolutely simple plan that trained monkeys could have executed. *But* I didn't do it *myself.* The Scream may remain 'lost' into perpetuity I'm afraid."

John turned a page in the newspaper looking for the crossword for Vera. "Hey, hey! Not perpetuity after all..." He read:

"OSLO, May 3 (AP) – Norway's most famous painting, "The Scream" by Edvard Munch, was recovered today, almost three months after it was stolen from an Oslo museum. Police said the painting, which is on fragile paper, was recovered undamaged in a hotel in Asgardstrand, about 40 miles south of Oslo. Three Norwegians were arrested. The recovery and arrests apparently were made in connection with an attempt to sell or ransom the painting, the Norwegian news agency N.T.B. said. The 1893 painting of a waiflike figure on a bridge was stolen from the National Art Museum in a break-in on Feb. 12, the opening day of the 1994 Winter Olympics in Lillehammer. Over the past 10 days, the police found four pieces of the painting's frame in Nittedal, a suburb north of Oslo, and what may have been cryptic messages that the thieves wanted to discuss a ransom. A few days after the theft, an anti-abortion group said it could have the painting returned if Norwegian television showed an anti-abortion film. The police dismissed their claim. On March 3, the Government received a $1 million ransom demand but refused to pursue it because no proof was offered that those making the demand had the painting.

I'm pretty sure you sent that email about the location of the frame pieces nearly as soon as we left Bygdoy..." John finished.

Another sigh from Alfred, "...not even as efficient as trained monkeys. There you go Vera dear, case closed!"

Hana had already gotten through half the bites of pear in front of her and was looking at the counter, searching for another fruit or *something* to continue her morning's success. Ginger murmured, "Finish the last bites you have there Hana and we'll see how well you can bathe yourself!" Hana had just begun to be able to help with that little chore also and she gave up on the search for more fruit from the counter.

John handed Vera the crossword page then made an announcement, "I have accepted an offer from our IT guys, a gift for our valued patronage---it's a carriage to ourselves, round trip to London on the Venice Simplon-Orient Express. It'll be the first run through the Chunnel that opens Friday. I hope our schedule is clear starting Thursday?" Gasps, and stunned expressions met the announcement. "I *can* cancel. I should have passed it by y'all first... but everyone's been working so hard... I just thought we could use the break."

Ginger and Vera leapt up and hugged his neck. Alfred clapped him on the back, "Excellent! I've had season passes at the Swan Theater burning a hole in my pocket for over a month now; shall I see what's showing?" The ladies squealed excitedly.

Vera and Ginger composed themselves and they both went to bathe and dress Hana. John said, "Uncle Alfred? Maybe we could see all the places..."

Alfred was way ahead of him, "...Already waiting for us to show up. Vera and I made arrangements last year, just on the chance that you and hopefully Ginger would show up at Crooked Island. We thought that at some point you'd like to visit those places. After seeing Mont Saint Michel we realized we hadn't been too presumptive." They sat quietly finishing the bread, cheese and jam, and the last of the coffee.

"I just need to finish up the three jobs on Voyager's plate for the Pantaleonis and Ivy, and we'll be clear for a week and a half. I got the impression from Antoni that this train is very deluxe. Like black tie at meals and that sort of thing..." John mused.

"Uh, yeah. It's that sort of thing." Alfred confirmed. "Let's you and I amble down toward San Marco and pick out a suit or two..." He paused, "On second thought, let's just follow the ladies down there. I'm guessing they'll be excusing themselves for the afternoon in... five, four, three, two..." Vera and Ginger emerged in the kitchen dressed for going out. "..one..."

"Vera and I are going to find a couple outfits for Hana..." Ginger began.

Both men laughed, "You were very close Alfred!" Alfred asked if they wouldn't mind waiting just a moment or two so that John and he could 'stroll' with them to find 'Hana' some clothes. Vera and Ginger knew they were found out.

Vera asked, "Which one of you realized you needed to shop?"

John pointed to Alfred. Alfred pointed at John, as they both hopped up and went to change. In ten minutes they were all walking toward San Marco and deciding on an appointment for lunch at Francesconi's. The ladies found a boutique first and the gentlemen ambled on a little farther until they came to the string of shops along the Mercerie. Fortunately both men were fitted with clothing 'off the rack,' that is to say, suits which only required minor alterations. Their purchases were promised for delivery the next morning and they ambled on toward the cafe keeping an eye out for men's shoes. John hadn't brought any dress shoes; what he wore to the Guggenhiem gala were borrowed from Alfred, and they were a little tight.

They sat at the cafe for an hour before the ladies emerged into the square from the other side, laden with only three relatively small bags. They were seated and the very patient waiter took their orders at last.

Ginger said, "Hana will be able to wear the jumpers we found in almost any situation... very versatile."

John glanced at the three bags of 'things' from as many shops and asked, "Did you have to go to a baby's tops store, then a baby's bottoms store, and then a baby's shoes store? Why three bags?" He kept a very straight face as he asked.

Vera almost giggled, Ginger defended, "No. We found all her things at one shop. These other two bags are just a couple items Auntie and I picked up... just sundries and essentials basically."

Alfred didn't keep his voice low enough when he followed with, "Uh huh..."

Vera challenged, "Well they are!" and she looked at GingerKat, "Although I'm not sure I'd call them 'sundries' per se..."

John uttered, "Uh huh..."

Ginger countered, "And did you two find what you were looking for? I don't see any boxes or bags..."

Alfred took that one. "Because as it happens, clothiers in Venice aren't used to making garments for extraordinarily muscular men; everything we looked at required extensive tailoring and too much time. We had to just leave our sizes with a second hand shop and check in with them tomorrow... The nice lady said she might be getting something in our size then."

Vera and Ginger burst into laughter. John and Alfred exemplified pained innocence all the while. Hana laughed because the ladies were laughing; she looked between Ginger and Vera apparently hoping for some clue as to why it was: girls' laugh time.

John admitted, "Well we did; although I wouldn't call them 'second-hand' per se..." in close approximation of Vera's admission.

Lunch was pleasant and as they gathered their things, Vera

asked, "Would you two carry these back to the Inn for us? We just have a couple places yet to visit... we weren't able to find proper socks for Hana this morning..."

Alfred smiled, "Of course! You sock-hunters, you."

The ladies didn't return to the Inn until nearly sunset. John had almost completed the jobs upstairs in the office and Alfred made pizzas for a buffet dinner. Ginger plopped down on the sofa in front of the fireplace and put her feet up on the coffee table.

"Aaahh... That's a relief." John came down when he heard them come back. He sat at Ginger's feet and rubbed her aching arches and toes. She purred like a kitten. Vera was getting the same treatment from Alfred in the kitchen. Hana toddled between the two rooms, looking down at her brand new shoes: little pink sneakers with bells on the laces. 'Tinkle, tinkle, tinkle' she went back and forth all the while.

"Grab a plate!" Alfred called. "Hana darling, are you ready for your dinner? Uncle Alfred has spaghetti for you... with cheese!" Hana licked her lips in imitation of her mother's expression, and tried to climb up into her highchair unassisted... without much success.

Packages trickled into the Inn the next morning. At first Alfred and John were a little self-conscious that their story about 'second-hand' shop purchases wasn't holding up. Then packages just kept coming from boutique after boutique and it was the ladies' turn to own up to their forays of the day before.

"It's really not as much as it appears..." Ginger explained, "a pair of shoes and a clutch here, a dress or wrap there..."

Vera defended, "It's just that they are sending things along as they come through the back rooms and are sent out for delivery. If they waited and sent it all along at once it wouldn't be so *much*."

That rationale withered as even more items kept arriving and from so many different shops John had to ask. "Did you two buy something at every store you went in yesterday? And exactly how many of these are actually for Hana?"

All pretenses had to be tossed to the wind. Ginger replied candidly, "Yes, just about every single shop had something just perfect for our trip. I just hope the leather luggage gets here before this evening, we really should have everything packed before our morning departure..." Alfred and John rolled their eyes.

Alfred asked Vera, "Leather luggage?"

She remained unruffled, "Yes dear, new luggage. We couldn't very well use the trunks upstairs, they aren't in too good a shape anymore and especially for a trip on the Orient Express where we'll have whatever we take in the cabins with us. That brings up another topic. John, did we hear you to say we have an entire carriage? Meaning *four* cabin suites? We really don't need four."

John nodded, "That's what I was told. I presumed it was due to a dearth of passengers on the north-bound trip. I shouldn't think we'll have the entire coach to ourselves on the return."

"There's the door again..." Alfred announced and went to sign for another set of packages.

When they gathered in the front hall, an hour before they were to be at Santa Lucia station for boarding, they looked every bit like the cosmopolitan world-trippers they actually were. Even Hana had a little pair of chic sunglasses on, which she kept pulling aside to see where she was going. Ginger bubbled, "This is the most fun playing dress-up I've ever had!"

5 May 94 In spite of the whirlwind of recent events, I am more convinced than ever that Auntie's advice is not only sound but seems to work wonders. It's not just for John and Hana, but for my own well-being. I am finding that making each effort to smile and every time I voice appreciation, I am somehow stronger inside, more in command of my world. That seems so counter to what my preconceptions were going into this exercise. I thought people who were *always* so conciliatory and constantly polite had something like a low self-esteem or a profound sense of unworthiness. That they were somehow constrained to maintain a pleasing appearance out of fear that people would otherwise despise them for their weakness and shallowness. At least in this instance, that is so far from the truth it's laughable. It may be that some people habitually manifest as I once perceived, but I am having to re-evaluate most of my historical assumptions anyway. And unless there is sufficient evidence to support any view or suspicion, I'm better off not harboring it.

Then there is the effect it has on Hana. Auntie Vera and Uncle Alfred have always been far more polite and courteous in their interactions with each other. Hana has to have absorbed some of that since it is her environment. That John and I are following suit, at *last* I am too anyway, Hana's environment has become more consistent. I have only noticed little things so far: her waiting to announce her 'demands' until there is a break in conversation for example, or her tendency to want to share her favorite food with whoever is feeding her... Little things. Then there is the possibility that she has always done those sort of things and it's only now that I am noticing. Whatever the effect on those around me, it's good for me and that's a good thing.

We will be on the Venice Simplon Orient Express train for two days and I have never traveled in this realm of elegance other than on the *Anna*, but that's with family not wealthy strangers. It is going to be an interesting experience. We'll see how Ginger-girl copes with it all.

6

Visits

"You're only here for a short visit. Don't hurry, don't worry. And be sure to smell the flowers along the way."
---Walter Hagen

T hey did turn a few heads on their walk to the depot. No one was prepared for the luxurious appointments of their carriage on the Orient Express. The polished marquetry and elegant carpeting rivaled the *Anna* for richness and warmth of refinement. Their personal stewards settled them into their chosen suites and let them know that lunch would be waiting for them in whichever restaurant car they chose to dine in first, and naturally at their leisure. The train pulled out of the station and they followed Hana toward the Cote d'Azur restaurant car, they would sample the delights of the Etoile du Nord and L' Oriental cars before the journey was complete. It was in the dining room that the train made a drastic departure from anything they had yet beheld in any train, plane or yacht. It was whelming even to Alfred and Vera who had certainly been to their fair share of five star restaurants and resorts. A table with a highchair already in place for Hana awaited them. The maitre d' was genial, almost overly solicitous of their wishes. Hana was served a fruit cup and her favorite rice and banana bowl. She at least was feeling right at home. Ginger and John on the other hand were making every effort to achieve an ease of manner neither of them felt.

Vera noticed and confided, "Think of it this way: You are being treated as royalty. Regal behavior is characterized as being the epitome of courtesy, gentleness, humility and confidence. You have each been practicing courtesy and gentleness toward each other for months now. Humility and confidence are byproducts of the work... Be yourselves. You *are* regal."

Alfred smiled with satisfaction as each dish was set before his family. He didn't want to be the one to remind his niece and nephew that they were actually being treated as their genuine 'station in society' dictated; they were nervous enough as it was. What he did instead was to propose a little diversion.

"Ginger, without calling attention to yourself, look over to the table in the corner passed my right shoulder. What do you see?" The others did likewise.

GingerKat made little furtive glances without staring, she remarked conversationally, "I see a couple. They appear to be at ease and in conversation. The gentleman keeps looking at his watch, and the lady has adjusted the napkin in her lap three times now. But their expressions appear calm. Why?"

Alfred observed, "The gentleman is an accountant or financial adviser. He's not so interested in the time as much as he is admiring that new rolex on his own wrist. The lady isn't his wife. She is his paramour and has two young children at home with a nanny. He is trying to impress her and its working. His company is near bankruptcy but he's pretending everything is running smoothly. She is being careful to not mention anything of consequence and she is nearly holding her breath to keep this illusion of extreme affluence alive. Her hands suggest she is perhaps an educator; she gestures as a public speaker is used to doing. Her hair and posture are immaculate, which also suggests she is under constant public scrutiny. His wife is either recently deceased or they have been separated for only a short time. Notice how he can't help but twirl the absent ring on his left ring finger out of long habit. He was a devoted husband, but has no children of his own. The reason they *appear* calm is that they had a 'tumble' in their cabin before coming to brunch. The tension they actually feel is barely under the surface. I won't be surprised if he caresses her rump as they stand and leave shortly."

Ginger and John wanted to be impressed, but remained skeptical. Vera elucidated, "The only way to be certain of Alfred's observations is to somehow interview them yourselves or eavesdrop on them until you have verified his claims for yourselves. I can tell you from experience that Alfred is rarely if ever mistaken when it comes to observation and deduction. His father trained him, Alfie was trained by George Lawrence---and Harry himself trained him. Harry was trained by his great-greatuncle White Feathers; he had no equal when it came to observing human behavior and understanding human nature." Alfred glanced over Vera's shoulder at two gentleman and a lady seated at a table across from them near the window.

"John see the table next to the window? What do you see?" Alfred posed.

John assessed their wardrobe and jewelry, their grooming and posture, then noted their range of expressions. He ventured, "The fellow on the left is with the lady, the gentleman on the right is either his best friend or brother. The lady is used to having her way in everything, which is why her husband brought his friend or brother along on the trip; he needed support. She is connected with the fashion industry, maybe as a buyer or critic. Her husband is in stocks, perhaps a trader or broker. The other guy is a golfer or has some sort of outdoor profession, and he is very attracted to the lady. There is a lot of tension at that table."

Alfred nodded, sincerely impressed. "You are very near the truth of it. What you may not have perceived is that it was the lady who insisted on her brother-in-law's presence on this trip. She has been laying the groundwork for a liaison with him for quite some time. Notice how easily she flirts, but he is sensitized to her innuendos, as is her husband who seems to actually enjoy the interactions as harmless but entertaining. She's in fashion, as you suggested, but it was her husband who found her the position she has, as a buyer for Versace. She's his 'trophy wife' and believes that she is wholly devoted to him because of his wealth. He ordered the most expensive item from the ala carte menu yet he has has only a bite or two and won't touch the rest. He is inwardly as insecure as she is. His brother on the other hand is a professional caddy, has a very well-padded bank account, and is the far more balanced of the two brothers. His ease of manner is genuine and his posture is naturally erect and strong. I like him."

Ginger was now impressed. "How can you *know* these things just from observation?"

Vera responded, "Once you know yourself and become very intimate with your own machine: why you do what you do, what prompts your postures and gestures, why and how you react as you do... You will begin to have a greater insight into the manners and actions of those around you. At some point you will be able to verify your observations and develop those powers of insight even further. Alfred has merely done all of that already, *and* he is *more* than familiar with all the 'flavors' people come in..."

When the couple in the corner rose to leave, Ginger glanced over quickly just in time to see the gentleman run his hand over the woman's rear end as they turned to the door. She squealed excitedly but with her voice lowered, "He felt her up just like you thought!" Alfred nodded and shrugged, as if to say: 'It was inevitable.'

Hana banged on her bowl with her spoon and the maitre d' came over at once. "Will the young lady want to enjoy a sherbet? We have a palette of flavors..."

Ginger smiled and mouthed 'oooh' to Hana. "Perhaps a small cup of peach?"

He replied, "Right away ma'am. May I bring anything at all for any of you?"

Vera asked for a basket of croissants and more jams. John requested a cappucino, Alfred seconded that order. Ginger asked for a second spoon with the sherbet for Hana. Their attendant disappeared into the galley and returned shortly with their requests. When they finished noshing on brunch, Alfred and John chose to stop in at the bar, not for drinks but simply to reconnoiter. They rejoined Ginger and Vera in their carriage before long. John handed Vera three different crosssswords from as many newspapers and she was as delighted as if he had handed her a sack of pearls. Hana was perched on the sofa with her face pressed against the window watching the approach of the Dolomites.

Ginger and Vera worked the first puzzle aloud. Vera commented, "You're very good at this!"

Ginger acknowledged the compliment but explained, "I used to work the New York Times crosswords on Sundays or on plane trips. You've noticed that once you learn the language of the clues, and some of the stock 'fillers,' the rest is just a matter of knowing the trivia or not. Even then there are ways around a stubborn or obscure answer by addressing its parts either vertically or horizontally."

Vera agreed; she had discovered those very techniques. "But I still enjoy them none-the-less, I like to think it helps keep me available to options I otherwise don't usually consider..."

John went over their itinerary with Alfred. "...The Tate Galleries and the British Museum will take up most of one day, I think. Ginger mentioned wanting to see Covent Gardens, which aren't, and some of the parks which are... And I'm pretty sure she wants to do the double-decker bus thing..."

Alfred assured him, "We have rooms at Arran House on Gower Street. It is relatively close to most attractions, like the British Museum, Picadilly Circus or Covent Gardens, and walking distance to Regents Park, a stretch of the legs to Hyde Park and Kensington Gardens, and within reach of the Thames. We can board a bus almost anywhere."

John continued, "Then over to Bath, up to Malvern, Redditch, and Manchester, on down to Stratford-Upon-Avon then back to Victoria Station. Our return is open ended, so if we dawdle, no harm done to the schedule."

Alfred agreed, "Good..." he looked through the doorway to the ladies, "...we will likely 'dawdle' here and there."

The Dolomites gave way to views of the distant Swiss Alps and afternoon tea. Their stewards served while they took turns reciting favorite passages from authors and poets who had both inspired and guided them. As they left the Hauptbahnhof Station in Innsbruck, it was time to dress for dinner in the L'Oriental car. Vera and Ginger took over one of the suites as their dressing room. John and Alfred acquiesced easily; every time their wives sequestered themselves they emerged radiant and refined. This was no exception. The gentlemen waited for them in the Bar car, and before long there was a murmur of voices from the entrance leading from the carriages. Two sophisticated women entered as if from a limousine onto a red carpet. Their poise and grace was such that the very air around them seemed to radiate charisma and nobility. The little girl that walked beside them simply gave them the appearance of actually being mortal rather than divine. John went toward one lady and offered his arm to her and his hand to the child. Alfred imitated his lead and guided the other lady to a seat. Neither gentleman made a fuss about their wives' bearing or appearance, making it clear to the others gathered in that carriage: that was the way they always looked.

They tarried in the Bar car for aperitifs and Hana danced a little to the melodies from the piano since Ginger wouldn't let her climb onto the bench with the pianist. The L'Oriental was easily as opulent as the Cote D'Azur, just differently designed. Hana wasn't too antsy; she just had to be in Alfred or John's lap rather than her highchair, and she went back and forth from lap to lap to lap sampling whatever tidbits she thought looked appealing. It turned out she had a taste for truffles.

"That's our girl..." Vera and Ginger agreed, "...pick something you don't have everyday and eat it like it's going out of style. Here big girl, try this gruyere or camembert."

Ginger was also keeping an eye on their fellow travelers, trying to assess them, not from imagination but from observation and deduction---not an easy task. She checked her observations with Alfred and won a modicum of praise for her sticking to only what she could actually observe and not lapsing into imagination. After dinner, while the others sat in the Bar car, GingerKat wandered to the Boutique and purchased a book: Agatha Christie's *Murder on the Orient Express*. When she rejoined her companions she was thrilled to announce her find, "...And I'll read aloud when we retire... this will be so much fun!" They thought so too.

Alfred pointed out that the train they were riding was even more lavishly upgraded and appointed than that famous train described by Dame Christie. "But the high standards for cabins and cuisine have remained in spite of the march of time. The current owners have certainly rebuilt these carriages with an eye to their history and traditions."

Hana yawned again and John picked her up from Alfred's lap. He carried her to their suite. He had just tucked her in when the others returned and prepared to settle in for the storytelling time. Ginger's voice was lively and kept her audience enthralled in spite of their having read it before and seen the 1974 film adaptation. The mystery was at last resolved and the variant solution, a random act of a stranger, was decided upon to publish to the authorities rather the revenge killing it was. Ginger was applauded for her clear delivery. It was very late when Vera and Alfred went to their own suite for the night.

6 May 94 Auntie is always right; I might as well resign myself to that reality. She said that when we walked into the Bar car, even dressed as we were and exuding confidence, others there might admire us even complement us, but our men wouldn't say a word about our appearance. I figured out why when we arrived for dinner. However extravagantly and beautifully dressed and behaved we were, that was intended to be merely a given---our normal aspect as far as our husbands were concerned. If they *had* made a fuss over us, all our preparations would have been for naught, the effect would have been undermined and exposed as being the exception rather than the rule. Yes, even thick Ginger-baby figured that one out for herself! It is a real surprise to me how much my emotional outlook and even behavior is affected by wearing really, really beautiful dresses and jewelry. It's almost like I become what I imagine a person wearing such things should be. Thankfully Auntie Vera has prepared me to actually be that person. I'm anxious to see if I can manage that transformation in everyday clothes; I'll know, but will anyone else notice---and do I really care if they do or don't?

I know they had all read or seen Agatha Christie's mystery about this train, but I bought it and read it anyway last night. It just felt right to have that added bit of history and mystique since we were on the same train and the descriptions needn't be imagined for once. I enjoyed it anyway, and would do it again. We will be in Paris shortly; I wish we had a little time to see the sights before heading on through the new tunnel to London. Que sera sera. All of life is a visit to an unknown country---the future---what comes, comes. Wherever I go there I am, anyway...

The train had just entered the outskirts of Paris when they were all finally awake and Ginger put away her journal. They postponed breakfast until after what was supposed to be a brief stop at the Gare de l'Est station. The conductor was informed that their inaugural journey on to Victoria Station would have to be delayed by twenty-four hours due to security concerns in Calais: with both the President of France and Queen Elizabeth II in attendance for the ribbon cutting ceremony. The Venice-Simplon apologized profusely for the resultant errors of miscommunication. The company would naturally accommodate their passengers in a hotel of equal luxury. Alfred thanked them warmly on our behalf and said he preferred accommodations at the Hotel Splendid Etoile. A company car was brought to the station and they, along with their luggage, were transported to their hotel. Ginger was elated rather than disappointed. Her feelings were mirrored by Vera, "Twenty-four hours in Paris! where to start?"

"Fortunately it's early." Alfred observed, "I've heard Viola and Portia's stories of Paris enough to know: we have to see Musee D'Orsay, the neighborhood of St. Germaine, Notre Dame and Sainte-Chapelle, we could take a boat tour on the Seine to see other sights like the Eiffel tower, and as you see the Arc d'Triomphe is practically on our doorstep." He pointed through the open window and balcony of their suite.

Hana was dressed in stripes and a beret, the stereotypically ideal little parisian tourist. After breakfast at a nearby brasserie they rode the Metro from near the hotel to the Tuileries and crossed the Seine to the Musee D'Orsay for the impressionist paintings. They strolled to the islands and visited the 'jewel-box' that is Sainte Chapelle, then the imposing Gothic Cathedral of Notre Dame. On the left bank they found a lovely bistro for lunch.

Ginger remarked, "...Even each street has its own sounds and smells. It's like a hundred little countries sharing the space of just a few square miles. And I've never noticed the colors of spring so vivid as here in the little parks and seemingly in every little shop or cafe that we pass." She sighed and Hana imitated her relaxed expression melodramatically. The others chuckled at the performance.

John reminded them of their ancestors' visits to this city. "Of course they had more than a single day to explore, but this is so inspiring to at least make the visit..."

From there they went back to the Seine, selected a tour boat and relaxed from their lunch as Paris came to them. Hana was thrilled to be on a boat again. She scampered from one side to the other more interested in the ducks and other boats than the the Eiffel Tower and monuments. As the sun began to set, they returned to their hotel suite and rejuvenated themselves with baths and showers. Naturally they dressed for the occasion of another elegant meal. Dinner was exquisite in the hotel restaurant. They went to bed satisfied and pleasantly tired from the day of touring.

In the morning the hired car returned them to the station, and once aboard they headed to the restaurant car for breakfast. The outskirts of Paris gave way to the country side and the English Channel drew nearer and nearer. In the afternoon they were again served high tea by their stewards as Kent sped by the windows. By around five o'clock they were bidding their new friends: Nowell and Luigi, the stewards from the train, farewell until they returned for the trip back to Venice and home. A taxi took them to Arran House and they were shown to their suite.

7 *May 94* I can now say I've visited Paris; even though it was only for a day it was memorable. John and I are learning to take the knowledge we are gaining about our own inner worlds and translating that into seeing people around us more objectively. The benefit to me is that I have a lot more compassion for the people that daily cross my path. Their quirks and peculiarities, their attitudes and behaviors are finally, if not making sense, at least understandable to a degree that I have not known before. Take for instance our waitress at dinner last night at the hotel.

She looked like a young woman who was both capable and genial. As I looked closer and listened with sharper ears, it became apparent that she was struggling to maintain her facade of professionalism. Her nails were a little ragged and showed signs of rough use. There were paper cuts on the sides of a few of her fingers. Although her eyes were clear, her lids were slightly puffy, maybe allergies, more likely frequent bouts of crying. She had slight bruises on her forearms just below the inside of her elbows. Her voice was steady but there was a hint of impatience when she was forced to repeat herself to either John or Alfred, the same tone was absent when she spoke to Vera or myself. She couldn't hardly look at Hana without her voice rising in pitch and quickening. When she reached to refill a glass her hand shook slightly, though she certainly looked strong and fit otherwise. She wasn't required to wear a particular uniform and the dress she did wear, although elegant evening wear, showed signs of dried sauce or mud around the hem that would have easily rubbed out with a little damp rag.

With all of that in mind, as we left I asked her if she had settled into her new apartment. She said she had, and without asking how I might have known that. She was mentally as weary as she was physically. I followed with hoping she would find a young man that would share her desire for raising a family. She didn't hesitate to thank me profusely for my kind words of encouragement, that he had been a good mate, but absolutely refused to consider children. It hurt to part after three years together; she had only just finished moving out that morning. I suggested that the couple flights of stairs she was now faced with climbing would have her back in shape in no time. She almost smiled and agreed that just hauling all her boxes up there had nearly done the trick in three days. I complemented her healthy glow and wished her well. Vera remarked to me when we got back to our suite that I had handled that interaction well and the girl would no doubt take heart that there were still caring people in her world, no matter how briefly encountered.

That's the sort of thing that Alfred and Vera have been able to do for years. No wonder they have acquaintances and friends wherever they have been for any amount of time. I am learning how to be in the world but not of it and it's an eye-opening experience to say the least. I am at last beginning to feel like the peasant girl from Auntie Vera's story: guileless and ready to be of assistance.

"I don't know if I can look at another sarcophagi and not viscerally recall how bodies were prepared for mummification..." Ginger remarked as they left the British Museum. The Tate had elicited a similar comment earlier in the day, only regarding how she wouldn't see a Turner painting without wondering how he actually saw the world... poor eyesight and all.

John set Hana down on the steps and sat next to her before they decided where to go next. She was uncommonly quiet, almost introspective and had been since mid-day. John asked her, "Are you hungry munchkin?" She smiled but shook her head.

She stretched out across his lap and Ginger suddenly realized, "Well, of course, she hasn't had a nap all day! What a trooper she's been, not even a pout or a whine. Johnny I'll take her back to the hotel and we'll call it a day."

Alfred and Vera were likewise ready for retreating to the comforts of their rooms. Alfred suggested, "We can order out and maybe catch a rerun of an exciting Cricket match on the telly..." Groans all around washed back on him for that last bit. They tramped up the couple blocks back to Arran House and were assured that there were several take out places at their disposal, and when their dinner arrived it would be brought directly up to them. Hana was already asleep when they closed their door behind them. Vera went to the order out listings; she read them off aloud, "Curry, Sushi, Tapas, Pizza, Fish and Chips, Kabobs... Actually it appears there's everything we like---Any suggestions?"

John voted for tapas or fish and chips. Ginger didn't care so long as someone fed her. Alfred was equally indifferent, but thought sushi would be too battered after delivery to be viable. So Vera rang up a restaurant that had both tapas and fish and chips and placed orders for a decent selection of each. John sprawled on the couch and turned on the TV to find the movies available.

In a moment he was sitting up, "GingerKat? Have you ever seen the *Quiet Man?*"

Vera and Alfred both smiled, "*We* certainly have. That's a classic and we'd be happy to see it for the hundredth time..."

Ginger was game. "If you two can watch it over and over, I can certainly stand to see it once at least."

John checked the schedule, "It's on in... What time is it now?" He looked at the time stamp on the screen, "Never mind. It's on in half an hour."

Ginger said, yawning, "I need to give munchkin a bath in the morning. I think she has a few more teeth coming in. It's even more surprising that she wasn't fussy this afternoon." She sat up. "Vera do you suppose she could have picked up a bug or something?"

Vera looked thoughtful and walked to the bedroom. When she came back she said, "She doesn't seem to have a fever,and her color is good. I think she's just wanting to see everything the same as we do, only her energy has to be replenished with more sleep than we need... She's a trooper alright."

Ginger and John went to shower. When they came back out the food had arrived and Alfred was enjoying putting whatever was within reach into his mouth. "I think I was hungry..." he said still chewing. The movie came on and they all snuggled on the couch.

"Early to bed and late to rise! That's my girl..." Ginger repeated to Hana in the bathtub in the morning. "Would you like to go the park today and fly a kite? Later we can ride on top of a big bus!" She waved her little arms and splashed the bath water like a duck taking to wing. Ginger squinted at the splattering water, "I'll take that as a yes."

"I've never flown a kite," Vera admitted, "and I don't believe that's on Alfred's resume either..."

Ginger and John looked at them in disbelief. "There's something *you* haven't done? Johnny, did you hear that!?"

John made big eyes at Hana, "HanaRin you get to do something today that *only your mother* has done before..."

Ginger was quick to respond. "Whoa there. I haven't flown a kite before either..."

John was thrilled. "Now I *am* excited. We are all going do something we haven't done before---A first!"

It was quite a morning. When they got to Kensington Gardens they located a kite shop to purchase kites for each of them. The young man behind the counter evidently smelled novices and offered a few pointers so that their experience wouldn't be too frustrating.

"These kites here are hand-made and built along traditional lines for leisure flying. You might prefer them to the choices you've made there. Those are fighting kites and require a little more experience and skill..." They accepted his judgement and ventured into the fields where a few other enthusiasts were already holding onto strings and watching their creations cavort in the sky.

It took some trial and error but inside the hour they had all five kites in the air. Hana held onto to hers for all of two minutes before letting go of the string. John chased along the ground after the skittering spool and caught it just as it was about to go airborne. Hana thought that was great fun and coyly accepted her string back again only to let it go once more. The 'Hana Kite Show' had a limited run. John finally caught on to her routine, no matter how innocently she took back the string each time. Alfred, Vera and Ginger were as entertained as Hana at her father's dutiful recovery of the spool each time she let it go. The breezes aloft were strong enough to hold the kites but not too gusty so that they would have had to make continuous adjustments. The sky was unusually clear and the sun on their backs lent them the relaxed feeling of early summer. The grass was a cushion on their bare feet and Hana found a new game in rolling down a little swale near to their patch of park. She climbed up the little incline slower and slower for each new venture.

Ginger spread a small blanket from her backpack onto the ground and Hana laid down for a nap. Her eyes gazed up at the little dancing kites until her lids drooped shut at last. Although they always had food for Hana, they were in need of a bite to eat themselves. Vera walked over to a nearby store and they watched after her until she disappeared inside. She brought back beer and wine, crackers, sausage and cheese. While Hana slept they snacked and talked.

GingerKat saw a young couple crossing the gardens on their way to the Round Pond. They carried model sailboats in the arms. "Ooh, little sailboats!" She clapped. Alfred commented that there were model yachting associations 'over here' and while it was serious business for some, it was just a pleasant diversion for others. Ginger talked John into going with her to see; he didn't need much persuading. They went after the young couple Ginger had first noticed and caught up to them.

"Hello!" Ginger announced and the girl turned to greet her with an uncertain smile.

"Oh, hello. At first I thought you might be one of those Association characters... they can talk your ear off with questions and pointers for your little sailboats..."

The young man nodded with what seemed the agreement from experience. "Are you visiting London for the first time?" he asked genially.

John replied, "Yes we are. That's a handsome miniature yacht you have there. Are there many amateur sailors here often?" They were coming from around a copse and espied a number of 'sailors' chasing around the pond hoping to be where they launched their boats to arrive.

The young woman answered, "Quite a lot actually... 'Spose it has to do with England being an island... a seafaring people... historically at any rate."

Their guides made some adjustments to the sails of their 'yachts' after gauging the prevailing breeze for direction and strength. The girl set hers off first and Ginger tried to keep up with her as she skipped around to where she'd sent her ship. John watched with admiration as the young man tied off the mainsail and foresail of his model schooner. "Most folks don't bother with a two-masted rig... far more iffy if the wind gets up. But I've got her ballast set just right this time, I hope..." and he launched her. The breeze filled her sails and her little jib kept her prow just high enough for her to make her way nicely in the direction he'd hoped.

They walked together, watching the elegant model cut through the calm waters of the pond. He asked John, "Have you ever sailed?"

John admitted that he felt as though he were still a novice but had made the trans-Atlantic passage last winter and recently sailed into the Mediterranean... "The *Anna* is currently moored in Venice. We are just up on holiday. This is really beautiful weather; is it unusual... I have a picture stuck on my mind of London being foggy and gloomy..."

The young man introduced himself as Eddy. He laughed, "It is nice today, and we do get more than our fair share of precipitation. What sort of ship is the *Anna*? That sounds like a brilliant voyage..."

"She's a sixty foot bermuda-rigged trimaran, and yes they were great voyages. I don't mean to pry, and you may ignore me if it's too personal; but did you and... I'm sorry I don't know your lady's name..."

"Naomi," the young man interjected happily.

"Did you and Naomi both already enjoy sailing? Or did one of you drag the other along and get hooked?"

His smile broadened, "Actually, we met right over there..." he pointed to where Naomi and Ginger were lifting her sloop from the pond. "Her father is a long-time member of the association. Which is why she is a very good sailor, but also explains why she has a truck with association types; she knows from experience how obsessed they can be..."

The schooner arrived at their feet and Eddy reached down to readjust her for a diagonal course to the top of the pond. John looked across the pond to see Naomi and Ginger launching her sloop in the same direction. He admired the strategy, probably long established, for meeting up at various points around the 'little sea' as the afternoon stretched on.

Eddy asked, "Your yacht, the *Anna*, out of curiosity what's her mast height?"

John answered smoothly, "Eighty-one feet above the waterline, she carries twenty-four hundred square feet of sail. I've had her up to a cruising speed of twenty-seven knots for hours on end... On a clear day above the Azores I was amazed to see her flying at thirty-two knots. My Aunties were impressed but they have been sailing the *Anna's* sister ships all their lives and have coaxed them up to over thirty-eight on more than one occasion."

Eddy's eyes said it all, "That's great fun! Twenty-four knots! Over thirty! Brilliant. Now that's what I call sailing!" John was a little self-conscious at the admission, but Eddy did certainly revel vicariously in the news, so his conscience was mollified. The young man genuinely, simply loved sailing and sailing ships, nothing more.

Ginger was all grins when they met up at the opposite end of the pond from where they started. "Naomi has invited me to have a go!" She asked John candidly, "Do you think she'll handle just like the *Anna?*"

"One way to find out..." John replied.

Naomi enjoined, "You can't sink her. *Gertrude* rights herself if she begins to heel too hard..." and she pointed out the clever rudder attachment that made that possible.

Ginger set *Gertrude's* sails and tiller for the point Eddy and John had just come from and set her off. She sailed the course straight and true. Ginger admitted, as John had to Eddy, about her sailing experience. Naomi asked all very similar questions as had Eddy of John, plus a few others more natural to a woman's interests. "...*And* your Aunt and Uncle are your shipmates? *And* you have an adopted daughter, with one on the way as well?! You are a very busy woman!"

Ginger was elated that her story had elicited admiration, but she was careful to avoid letting it all go to her head. "Busy, yes; but we're having a truly wonderful time of it all the same. Johnny is such a great and caring husband and father... We are blessed and we know it."

Eddy and Naomi walked back with them to where Hana was still drowsing; Vera and Alfred were stretched out in the sun as well. They introduced their new acquaintances. Eddy and Naomi were invited to make themselves comfortable and share the drinks and snacks they had. The young couple accepted graciously with the caution that they could only stay a little while. Ginger reiterated all she knew of their new friends and Vera asked pleasantly about what they did in the city.

Naomi answered, "Eddy is an engineer with Aleck Associates, a structural engineering company here in London. I am a school teacher... kindergarten. And yourselves? What do you do when not on world cruises?" She asked with a wink to Ginger.

Vera responded, "I am a physician, but do not have a practice at present. Alfred is a master of many trades... mostly he enjoys being a god-father these days." Which prompted Naomi to comment on HanaRin who was still sleeping peacefully.

"She's a cherub to be sure. What a grand occupation..." she announced to Alfred's grinning face.

He replied, "It's the best job I've ever had!"

By the time Hana rolled over and yawned Eddy had informed

John about the whereabouts of the nearest stand for the double-decker buses. Once Hana had made a nice showing of being introduced to Eddy and Naomi, and carefully inspected the great toy boats, the young couple bid them all a good afternoon and went on about their afternoon's appointments.

John and Alfred gathered up their picnic things, disassembled the kites, and led the ladies to the bus stand. Once aboard, they situated themselves on top of a yellow route double-decker and watched the neighborhoods slip passed them. They got off near Trafalgar Square and toured the iconic sights near the river. The tour guide mentioned that a new Globe Theater was under construction on the far bank near the old Bankside Power Station. It was easily seen from where they were. So with a landmark to guide them they walked to the construction sight. A little piece of Shakespeare was rising from Southbank once again and it stood in contrast to the modern buildings of the surrounding neighborhood. They walked across the Blackfriars bridge and visited another of Shakespeare's haunts. The bus came by; they got aboard for more of the tour.

The next time they left the bus was to have dinner at Covent Gardens. A little restaurant perched on the eastern end of the second floor overlooking the street suited them to a tee. Sitting on the terrace, where Hana could toddle about without interrupting other diners, they watched the crowds and traffic, admired the old theater district and dined on a very well produced meal. John had Steak Tartar for the first time---and liked it. Ginger noted in the back of her journal the names and addresses of their new friends, Eddy and Naomi. Her list of contacts entries was growing, from the supply reps for the Voyager Press, their stewards on the train and now the young couple from today's adventures.

10 May 94   John and I met a delightful young British couple at the park yesterday. I heard myself answering Naomi's questions and I couldn't help being as impressed as she obviously was over our travels from the last several months. I didn't mention how long John and I have actually been married, but she made a comment before we parted about how she hoped she and Eddy would be as happily married as we were when they were our age. Age notwithstanding, her comment gave me pause. I'm the first to admit that John and I are very well suited for one another, but that we have begun to build that relationship in such a relatively brief space of time is... well it seems awesome. I'm sure part of it is due to our both working on ourselves, yet still that doesn't cover the breadth of it to my way of thinking.

He and I were both attracted to each other and both of us plunged off the deep end at the same time. The one or two couples I actually know who have done anything similar to that are no longer couples at all. I didn't know George and Belle, of course, to be able to see with my own eyes or hear from her own lips how they managed it. They didn't have a host of family around them, supporting them and guiding them... except for White Feathers, and then later when Harry was born, the voices of their ancestors. How did they deal with their day to day growth together in the interim? They seem to have had common aspirations and compatible backgrounds. They certainly had work and housekeeping to occupy them. But were they really just like John and me?

And speaking of family around them why don't I feel suffocated, as I once would have, with Alfred and Vera near us all the time? To have gone from a lifestyle of essentially solitude to constant companionship and without any niggling attitudes of resentment for being so constantly surrounded... perhaps it's because they are my actual family, perhaps because they are such valuable teachers and guides, perhaps because they are Hana's parents... and why don't I have any resentments about that of all things?! Either I have gained back enough of my conscience to realize the value of certain realities I could not have perceived before, or I am hopelessly brainwashed. If it's the latter, I simply don't care. If the former, more power to Ginger-baby and the future.

WEIGH ANCHOR

The next stop on the tour of England was Bath. The Swindon-Bristol line put them near enough for a short transfer and hop to the White Stone City and their stay at Villa Magdala. It took them no time at all to determine that a section of the Roman baths were open while other facilities were under renovation. A good soak was just what they needed after the time in London. In the morning they opted for a volunteer-led walking tour of the city---very informative and not too strenuous. Since they had plenty of energy still, they took a walk along the towpath next to the canal which led them to a very old and quaint country tavern. Walking tours were the thing to do in Bath, but Ginger's feet and back were either going to get stronger or give out. She and Hana spent a little more time in the baths the next day.

The train up to Great Malvern was pleasant. John led them on a tour of Malvern College and the Girls' College nearby. It was a short sight-seeing venture and before long they were back on the train to Redditch and up to Manchester. The galleries and Museums had their own character in contrast to the places they'd visited in London. Their suite at Britannia Hotel, Manchester City Centre offered an easy walk to Piccadilly Gardens and the train station. It was a lovely stay and they got an earful of Red Devil spirit from the locals. There could be no confusion in which city they were; no matter where they went, Manchester United's victory-hungry fans were everywhere apparent. The trip down to Stratford-upon-Avon allowed for a more sedate pace of activity.

They stayed in central Stratford and were able to see two different performances by the Royal Shakespeare Company in the evenings, after taking all the recommended tours of the Bard's birthplace and town of retirement, during the days. Hana was tickled that the village had the good sense to harbor swans on the river and a butterfly farm nearby. Both of those attractions held her interest far better than the thespian entertainments she mostly slept through in the evenings. Before they left Stratford and headed back to

Victoria Station in London to board the Orient Express for Venice, Ginger and Vera took HanaRin on a tour of the Brass Rubbing Center---something Hana could truly enjoy; and she certainly did. It had been a busy week and a half; their own Inn was going to be a most welcomed sight.

15 May 94   I am so thankful to have Auntie Vera with me. Not that Hana is too much to handle alone, it's just that having another perspective about her wiles and curious solutions to everyday things is so enlightening. Vera doesn't presume to know what Hana is thinking, but between us we can rationalize her behavior so at least she's not as strange as she might otherwise appear. I still don't know what's going on with my seemingly complete acceptance of having Vera and Alfred with us always, but it sure is useful.

I noticed something new about John. I don't think it's new for him, just newly noticed by me. He hardly ever, almost never answers a question or reacts to a situation without having given his response some thought. Sometimes it happens quickly, sometimes less quickly and so it seems more deliberate. Interestingly, and the reason I noticed at all, he is often very accurate in his views and adept in his actions. That's pretty remarkable; I think anyway. That's not to say that he doesn't bump into the occasional coffee table and bang a shin or some such thing, yet that is often very late at night or first thing in the morning when he's fetching Hana or going to make coffee---when his eyes aren't actually open. That part of Ginger-girl that historically is so ready to pounce on inaccuracy or ineptitude has had to take a leave of absence around these three folks. It's just one more thing that should be making me uncomfortable about being around them... but I'm not!

They were greeted by Luigi and Nowell as they boarded and were settled into their cabins. Brunch would be served before long, so they changed for the occasion---which meals aboard the train always were. Hana had become used to her 'touring jumpers' and was a little testy when it was her turn to get all dolled up. Vera consoled her as best she could but Hana was decidedly not in the mood. Alfred insisted on staying with her while they went to the restaurant car.

"It's not the end of the world, and it's not exactly knuckling under to the whims of a child. Let's just look at it as her version of a headache that keeps her from the enjoyment of the theater or something..."

Hana was asleep in his lap by the time they returned from the meal. He whispered, "We read for a little while but she nodded off in no time. Our little cherub is probably going through a growing spurt or something and just needs a bit more nap-time."

She was awake when their stewards brought tea and biscuits later. Playing 'tea-time' was one thing Hana did enjoy; her ragdoll must have enjoyed it too... at least Hana was sure she did. She didn't put up any fuss when it was time to dress for dinner. In fact one would have thought it was a different girl entirely. She ogled her mothers' preparations and preening in front of the mirrors and imitated the postures of turning this way and that, touching up a stray tress, and of course the stately walk each of them evinced as they made their way to the Bar car to meet their men. They tarried in the saloon-sitting room for a while longer than before. The company pianist yielded his seat for Alfred to play a few melodies. His virtuosity was well received by the remaining passengers and he bowed humbly in acknowledgement of their praises.

As before, Hana preferred her fathers' laps to the highchair provided. She was a little put off that there were no truffles or special cheeses. Instead she accepted her own bowl of pureed vegetables and cheesy sauce much to her mother's relief. "She is really acquiring her own tastes and preferences for things. I hope I can keep up with her..." Ginger observed.

Vera responded, "I hope we all can. She is certainly becoming her own little lady!'"

That was even more apparent in the morning when she was awake very early and Ginger, who was the only other person to routinely awake in the wee hours of the morning, was entertained by Hana's inspection of a wardrobe for breakfast---for her ragdoll, not for herself. The 'three' of them were sitting in Ginger's bed reading one of Hana's books when the others gathered in their cabin before breakfast. Hana was very hungry by then and so she and Ginger dressed and headed for the restaurant car ahead of the others. It was scrambled eggs with cheese and oatmeal for the cherub; her mother made do with coffee, bread and jam until the others joined them.

"Auntie? Maybe you can shed some light on something that struck me." Ginger opened. Vera's expression was receptive and Ginger continued. "Why don't I feel suffocated, as I once would have, with you and Alfred near us all the time? I went from a lifestyle of essentially solitude to constant companionship and without any niggling attitudes of resentment for being so constantly surrounded... Is there an objective explanation?"

Vera smiled warmly as she seemed to always do when challenged with some plaint or other from her niece. "What did you come to, yourself?" she replied in response. Ginger recounted her own speculations about the phenomenon just as she had entered into her journal a few days before.

Vera nodded as she spoke, "Those are well perceived resolutions. I might only add that when you were a young girl even though you didn't enjoy the friendship of many girls or boys; you had a healthy imagination. I remember one occasion when you were on your way home from school after your girlfriends had already turned off for their houses, you took a side trip to the woods near the creek. I was very curious so I followed. What I saw was you gathering little branches and stones around in a circle. Then you set your schoolbooks in a little pile for a desk and you played 'classroom' to your imaginary class. I don't know if you were reliving the day's events, or creating a new scenario but you were calm and gentle with 'them' and conducted a seemingly in depth lesson."

Ginger's forehead furrowed struggling to recollect that memory. Something then snapped and her face lit up. "I remember doing that! It wasn't just that once. There was a whole month or two when I was in fifth or sixth grade that I reenacted one particular class from school: Health Science. There were two boys in that class that made it very difficult for the teacher, and so also for the rest of us, to get through any one lesson. I set up a little class everyday before going home to have that class over again but without those two boys in it."

Vera asked, "Why didn't you just go over it in your mind or from the textbook and your notes? Why the whole reenactment?"

Ginger was stumped. Why had she felt the need to actually redo the class in real time rather than simply studying; she blurted out, "Because I wanted to see what it would be like to have the class without those two childish knuckleheads interrupting..."

Vera, Alfred and John waited for her to sort through what she had recovered on her own, knowing any comments they made would be useless perhaps even destructive to her own considerations. Ginger mulled the situation over. Timidly she ventured, "I preferred being alone... but I reenacted a whole class of people... like-minded friends... something that wasn't happening in real life..." Then a light came on for her. "I'm not a loner! I just haven't ever had like-minded people around me... People who wanted what I wanted, or struggled toward the same goals I strove toward!"

Vera asked, "And now you have?"

Ginger beamed and replied as if it weren't a question, "That explains a whole lot!" She shifted gears and became very suspicious of a sudden, "Auntie, how is it that you were able to see so much of what I was doing as a child... you *were* in Tahoe with a medical practice *weren't* you?"

Alfred said, "Let's continue this conversation in our cabins shall we?" John was just as interested in those answers as Ginger and said so. They returned to the privacy of their compartments and Vera deferred to Alfred for the explanations.

"Sweethearts, when Vera and I finally became an item..." he smiled at his wife, "...she was already *capable* of exercising objective reason. There are other potent functions of that center, the higher mental center, which can be developed. You'll remember that it is through the cultivation of reason and impartiality that finer matters are crystallized in our machine?" They nodded.

"Good. Papa Harry found that certain of those 'other' functions, and the avenues to their development, yielded... how shall I say this... ah, certain remarkable results." Ginger and John were rapt; he continued. "You've heard the tales of what Harry and MamaKat were purported as having done, and you saw with your own eyes their final departure..." They nodded in wide-eyed acknowledgement. "Well... Harry trained MamaKat, they trained George Lawrence. He trained his wife Lila; they trained their son Alfie. He trained his wife Olivia and they trained me. As I said earlier, once Vera and I became an item... we were married after a fashion, later... but once we were both certain of our union, I trained Vera." He paused to let that sink in to his listeners.

"One of the byproducts of those personal rigors, through the avenues which Harry was first of our line to uncover and systemize, is what can only be called 'far-sightedness.' There are other functions, but this is the one germane to the topic at hand. The crystallization of higher bodies allows for the development of their own functions. 'As above so below,' you've heard? Just as we have eyes to see far off objects and imagine a path to attain them... whether that is over a topology or through the steps of a process... our higher manifestations have similar attributes. They may seem remarkable, even miraculous, but I assure you it is as 'natural' as twenty-twenty vision is to a regular person without such development."

Again he paused to be sure they realized the import of what he'd explained thus far. John and Ginger both accepted the analogy as a viable rationale for something extra-ordinary.

"You have your cell phone with you. You can call someone halfway around the world and carry on a conversation. Or turn on the TV and see a live report from a foreign correspondent in a far-away land as if it were just outside your own front door. Those activities would seem miraculous to a person from the turn of the century, even in an industrialized nation... more so to a remote villager somewhere less advanced technologically..." That was a given; a simple extrapolation of the obvious. John and Ginger said so. "It was my father's view that those technological advancements were only an imitation of what highly developed people are capable of in reality... he didn't try to relate other of our higher functions to anything not yet technologically attainable, but it's not a far stretch to suspect that technology will one day 'catch up,' if you see what I mean."

Ginger cautiously asked, "Like what other higher functions?"

Vera looked to Alfred and he nodded, "Nothing is forbidden, we just try to avoid that which is unnecessary," he responded to her unasked question. John and Ginger looked from one to the other.

Vera went and opened one of the windows in the cabin. "Ginger, darling, may we use something uniquely yours for a little demonstration? Something that can't possibly be replicated and would be a personal loss to you if it were gone for good?"

Ginger reached for her journal. "This is about as unique and irreplaceable as anything I own."

Vera said, "Throw it as hard as you can out the window."

Ginger hesitated only a second and hurled the book out the window. Everyone saw it flutter out and arc toward the passing ground. When they turned back to each other, there it was laying on the little table between them as it was before she picked it up. John and Ginger stared. No one had moved except Ginger throwing it; it was just there. Ginger picked it up and leafed through it. A page or two was folded over that wasn't before, but that was the extent of the difference. She looked up at Vera. "What just happened?"

"You stated that it was irreplaceable, I wouldn't let something that important to you be lost if I can help it," Vera replied evenly.

"But you didn't move! No one moved... how... when..." Ginger sputtered.

Alfred explained, "Vera did most certainly move. We are on a moving train, and she had to keep her position... beyond that...i t's not movement as we are used to thinking of movement. John, Ginger? You remember being told the stories, or reading in the journals, about Harry or MamaKat 'being in two places at once,' or 'walking through walls'?" They nodded. "And you remember how Uncle Lawrence finally realized what White Feathers meant? And what he said about that phenomena? And then how he explained it to the rest of the family after Oliver and my Grandfather's little demonstration so long ago in Colombo?" Again they nodded. "Did you think they were speaking hypothetically? Or theoretically?"

Ginger responded, "Well, now that you ask directly, yeah. I did kinda gloss right over it as fanciful."

Vera pursued, "And what did you make of Harry and MamaKat's departure? Fanciful, again?"

John responded, "It was just so... so, right before our eyes, and we've seen movie special effects that weren't too far removed from that sight... I guess our credulity just took over and our curiosity shut down."

Alfred smiled, "There you have it in a nutshell. People don't *really* see. And even if they do, as you two obviously did, part of them shuts down to avoid dealing with the reality confronting them---they essentially don't see it! Now, let's perform that little experiment all over again. Only this time I'll throw the book out the window and you two fix your eyes on Vera. Not like you are used to staring at something, but with a softer vision that takes in everything in front of your eyes simultaneously..." Alfred gathered up the journal. John and Ginger relaxed and gazed at Vera. Alfred tossed the book and this time instead of the perception that no one had moved, both of them were able to perceive a shift or phase of Vera's image in front of them, and the book was once again on the table as it had been.

Ginger giggled, "It was like she vibrated."

John added, "...Or shuddered at an incredibly high frequency, like a television screen or fluorescent light does. It cycles at such a high speed or frequency a person will generally take it for a steady state."

Alfred applauded, "Well spotted!" He looked to Vera, "These two have great potential!"

Vera rejoined, "As do all people... They *are* family, Alfred darling, and they *have* been working on themselves. They are possibility personified."

Ginger asked again, "Auntie, I still don't get how you watched me 'holding class' in the woods on the way home?"

Vera smiled. "That is less difficult to explain now. I wanted to see you and I saw you---Where you were and whatever you were doing. 'Conscious wish is the most powerful thing in the world.' I know you've heard that expression. It is as close as can be described how our higher bodies function---through an immaculate Will... such that a wish becomes reality, a foregone conclusion... within certain physical limits..."

John remarked, "It seems that 'physical limits' aren't much of a consideration!"

Alfred cautioned, "Of course they are. They are just different constraints than what are ordinarily perceived. Those constraints allow for some very extraordinary results, but there are constraints none-the-less."

Ginger followed, "But how did you get actual photographs?"

Vera replied candidly, "With a camera." Ginger almost groaned. Vera continued, "People have routines, predictable cycles which we repeat daily. Especially if we are engaged in a 'normal' vocation for instance, or an academic pursuit. Once I knew where you'd be, all I had to do was wait and snap a picture when you showed up. Alfred flew me to Indiana every so often. Or we flew down to Texas and documented whatever John might have been doing at the time... No mystery there. We just happened to know precisely where to go and when."

Alfred added for clarification, "I had an earlier model of the Beechcraft Starship I now pilot. She was a beauty too: three hundred horsepower engines, cruise at two hundred knots and she had a range of over sixteen hundred miles... plenty to get to either destination."

Vera smiled, "She was very comfortable too..."

John asked Ginger, "Has any of this made a dent in explaining why you haven't minded being constantly surrounded since we set sail on the *Anna* last year?"

Ginger contemplated all that had been said. "I think it comes down to something pretty simple after all: I am learning to love. First, you... then Hana *and* you... then you and Hana *and* Vera and Alfred... then... well, I think it's a function of love itself. That and losing so much of a personality that was built from illusion and misperception. I just don't see the world in quite the same way anymore. So naturally, I guess, my attitudes are different, by a lot, than what they once were. Like Auntie just said: No mystery there!"

19 May 94   I'm heading into the last trimester with MirandaLinn, and boy do I know John loves me. He is able to foresee and handle almost everything that I have to take care of during my days. He has either made those tasks easier by being available to help, or has dealt with them himself after getting my input on their execution. Sometimes I think I'd like to stay pregnant interminably, then I get up from a chair and remember how that used to be such a simple thing to accomplish.

After Miranda is born we are thinking about waiting for at least a month or two before climbing aboard the *Anna* and heading for the south seas. Auntie Vera assures me that it is completely dependent on what I feel I can handle and how much attention Miranda appears to need. 'Children are all the same: each one is totally unique,' she told me. I get it. In the interim John and Alfred are training two interns for the press: Valeran and Danielle. They seem to be as capable and reliable as we could have hoped. On days when we have the press up and running to meet contracts, they are here early and stay until the work is done. Alfred and Vera transformed the last room on that side of the Inn; it is now a miniature apartment with kitchenette. Danielle stayed through the night two days ago and had only praises for the opportunity to catch a nap and have a bite to eat right there at the offices.

Being pregnant means having a constant reminding factor. My every movement, every thought and feeling is colored by having Miranda always right here. I told John about having this recurring experience of seeing myself going about my everyday activities now... as if I were my own observer watching from just over my shoulder. He was beside himself with joy and I had to get him to explain why. He told me that one of the things Harry, in the guise of just a guest in his house, told him was that the function of our higher emotional center, the activity of Conscience, was like constantly seeing oneself doing whatever it was one was doing---being both the doer and the watcher... just as I had described: the permanent observer. I had to explain that it was a nearly tactile sensation for me and he grew even more excited. All I know is that I hardly recognize myself with this round belly, but I'm getting used to it.

Still, there creeps into my thoughts from time to time the inkling that

315

I have forgotten something, or that I've missed something somehow important. And for the life of me I can't figure out what it is. I review everything I have done during the day. I recount my obligations and responsibilities. Yet still there is this feeling of missing something...

"If you really want to, I'm sure Auntie Lila will send them to you, or more likely deliver them." Alfred answered.

Ginger was resolute. "And if John's grandfather William kept a journal during his trip with Belle, I want that as well. This family should be as thoroughly documented as we can manage. This is a most remarkable lineage of individuals..."

Vera interrupted, "But GingerKat, no one's going to believe anything written in them, no matter how much you water them down!"

John interjected, "Auntie, it's not a matter of other people believing or disbelieving; how else are our children and our children's children going to know about their heritage? How will Becka and Ivy's kids know? Or Jimmy's kids, if he ever has any... how will any of them know if there isn't some record. Sure Ginger and I can repeat the tales until we are blue in the face, but eventually they will go the way of every other family story: fractured legends and myths, mere shadows of the actual events and persons involved."

Alfred sighed, "That's only too true. All we are saying is that we have an uneasiness about the whole project. It seems that any time anyone tries this sort of thing a whole religion grows around the stories and they are eventually distorted anyway..."

Ginger and John gave that some very considered attention. Ginger posited, "You are probably right. However, even if we only use them as reference material for our children, the project is worth the effort. Our children should know. Besides, what if John or my situations arise again? We absolutely want to have examples of how people are meant to live, and the knowledge that enables those lives to be accessible... just in case."

Vera was next to sigh in resignation, "It's not that we are against the idea; it's just not been done. And frankly, it's a little embarrassing. Papa Harry always made it perfectly clear: 'We are ordinary people. If we show ourselves as anything other than that, we risk much and gain nothing'."

John countered, "Yet, it was White Feathers, Belle, Harry and Kaitlyn who made the point of telling me the stories and expected me to write them down. There was never *any* misunderstanding that I *would* publish them."

Alfred agreed, "I cannot argue that point. All we are saying is that... it's a cause for uneasiness on our part. Even though..." and he put his arm around Vera's waist, "...the structure and exercises could be very beneficial to any genuine seeker who might encounter your books." Vera nodded and brightened a little at the whole prospect of being exposed to the larger world.

She concurred but asked, "Are you planning on distributing the series then? Just like any other set of books?"

John looked to Ginger and she replied, "I know it would be a niche market, there won't be a run on the bookstores to snatch them up or anything, but still..."

Ginger added, "Like White Feathers said to John: A good story is worth telling. And since we are pursuing publishing these, I would really like to add the breadth of other of our family's experiences to them. It just seems right somehow."

Vera volunteered, "I don't think my journals of you two qualify then. They were assembled for your benefit alone... sort of scrapbooks any mother would keep of her children." John and Ginger both agreed and thanked her all over again for her diligence in documenting their lives.

"Now," Ginger began, "...about the other titles Voyager Press might publish; do Valeran or Danielle have friends from among their peers or schoolmates who would like to have their work published? Our press can be a useful stage for aspiring writers of this generation, whether they are in the obscurity of regions of global conflict or from the chaos of society."

John liked that idea as well. "I'll put together a set of criteria for them to go by and they can spread the word through channels they no doubt have access to that no one my age would..."

Ginger suggested, "And what about Becka and Ivy and Jimmy? They probably know people in the same situation. We could perhaps even open our doors to having a one of a kind, *actual* self-publishing press. Set up a rate scale for the 'do-it-yourself' types and *voila* Voyager Press develops a sturdy reputation with an entire generation."

John and Alfred grinned, "Consider it done, Madam Chief President Lady Person..."

Vera mused, "And Children's books? As long as we're all about open doors, couldn't we put together children's books that do a little more than teach colors and letters? What about a focus on thinking properly and reason?" There was an appreciative silence at her suggestion.

Ginger grinned and spoke for all of them, "What a boon to families that would be!"

The next days were a flurry of email writing, conversations with Valeran and Danielle---who loved the ideas---and letters written to Lila and Becka. To Lila for her journals and to Becka to see if she could find any journals from John's grandfather aboard the *Tygress* while they scoured the *Anna's* nooks and crannies. Jimmy was delighted to have a resource for publishing the marketing materials and manuals for his company, and inquiries from his own acquaintances began drifting in as well. Viola and Portia had been wanting to organize and write down all the story ideas they had accumulated for children's books. They had been caring for little ones throughout their lives and had more real stories and ideas for stories than anyone.

Now in addition to their steady contracts, Voyager Press began to make limited runs of pet projects from a wide cross-section of society. In the midst of that there were also poetry books and short story collections coming in from obscure, out of the mainstream, aspiring writers from regions of conflict just as Ginger had originally hoped there might be. Some of them were inspiring, some were informative, but all of them allowed a reader to gain another perspective on their world which they would otherwise never have had.

Valeran and Danielle asked for two more assistants and they already had names to offer as candidates: an Uma and an Henri. They were University students who had taken up residence in Venice, *and* who were disenchanted with the established publishing house they had worked for as interns. John and Alfred interviewed them and were very impressed with their proteges' acumen and good judgement in spotting dependable and skilled talent. Voyager Press now had four 'employees.' Two would be fully vested by September, and the newest help were working to become candidates for vestiture. In addition to the profit-sharing program, John and Alfred added 'medical coverage,' with Vera's permission since *she was the coverage*. Vera also made contacts among the medical practitioners around their Cannaregio neighborhood over the years, so that when they were away from Venice, through her arrangements there could be someone available to deal with any health matters in her absence.

23 May 94   We have put out the word that we are searching for John's grandfather's journals. Becka didn't have any luck looking through the *Tygress* for them, and neither did we on the *Anna*. But now we know why: Auntie Lila emailed to say not only would she be happy to deliver *her* journals, but that she also had Will's! That explained a lot. The *Ananke* will be putting into Venice for a visit by late June, early July! Oh Boy, oh boy... visitors!

John has been transcribing his books, my emended version. We'll still have some editing and decisions to make about the content, but it's becoming a reality at last. In fact, it amazing to me how much of what I'd hoped for over the last half year is coming to fruition. It really does feel like a whirlwind, but each step has been thought through carefully, every aspect of our responsibilities and continued obligations have been deliberated and included in our planning. And to top it off: Hana is practicing a little piano piece and sings with her own accompaniment! She really is a prodigy and a treasure. What floored us about it was that when we mentioned a recital yesterday within earshot of Valeran and Danielle, they insisted on being invited! Danielle said, 'Hana is one of our best assistants, of course we want to celebrate her achievement with you all.' I don't know how much assistance Hana has actually offered them---other than comic relief---but it was a touching gesture and we've scheduled the recital for this Saturday, the twenty-eighth. I'm supposed to play the piece I've been working on as well... it should be a memorable evening.

I mentioned several days ago in these pages that I had an on-going feeling of missing something... I think I've figured out what that something is: Many of my old habits and notions. There is a blank space in me where they used to be---always sapping my energy and causing no end of aggravation. Even though they weren't useful at all, they were fixtures of my inner world and their absence has been duly noted. Hear: Ginger-girl offer a sigh of relief in their passing, realizing what is the vacancy she has been noticing. It's really just as Auntie Vera told me, what seems like ages ago: '...we are trying to use the false personality's structures *against itself*. In that way, we transform whole servings of peas rather than one at a time...' Some of my 'servings of peas' have been cooked and served up to a new manager... Yay Ginger-baby!

"It's not exactly what you think..." Ginger was saying to Danielle, "enlightenment isn't so much a beatific state that separates a person from the rest of the world. It's more of a situation that allows a person to be in the world and perceive its beatific qualities by not being *of* the world any longer... Does that make any sense?"

Danielle liked plays on words as much as the next logophile, but this was a topic for which she was really searching for a clearer understanding. "Yes I do see the distinction, but then why are there all these stories of swamis and gurus and other oriental masters that seem to emphasize the transcendent qualities they have that no one else has?"

Ginger smiled in spite of herself, "Those so-called 'enlightened' people, do they merely take contributions and accept pupils free of charge?"

Danielle replied easily, "My friend Jeanette went to rural northern India and put herself under one of them, yes he definitely expected remuneration for taking her on as a pupil... and I know those that are in the States do as well..." Then a light of comprehension spread across her face. "Are you suggesting they make those claims of more-enlightened-than-thou just to make money? *That* is crass and gross!"

Ginger soothed, "Perhaps some of them actually have something genuinely useful to offer. But if that is so, why can't they support themselves and offer their knowledge without fee? What's the driving force behind their 'school' or ashram, or whatever they call them these days? That's the question someone should ask themselves before blindly following one of these fellows... and, often, signing over their worldly possessions to them. You know?"

Danielle looked disconsolate for just a moment, as if she had been robbed of an opportunity. Then she brightened, "Boss..."

Ginger interrupted, "Just Ginger."

Danielle continued, "Okay... Ginger, how do *you* know how to define enlightenment? That you can make the assertions you have just now?"

Ginger took a deep breath, "That's a rational and just question.

But may I ask you a question first?" Danielle nodded. "What is your interest in this matter? Is it philosophical, or theoretical, or are you yourself looking for some practical guidance to achieve something higher in yourself?"

Danielle had to engage in a bit of introspection it seemed. She finished the bindings they were working on as they chatted and she replied, "I was interested just because of the inconsistencies I have come across in some of the literature available in this genre, but now that you ask... I realize that I actually want to know for myself. Is it possible to make yourself higher through some method? Or is it a matter of putting yourself into a receptive position and hoping the right sound, or smell, or word or something instantly sends you into satori?!"

Ginger replied candidly, "There is a repeatable method. There is no providential satori. It is a path of losing and sacrifice that no one in their right mind would undertake knowing what lay in store for them. It takes every ounce of your energy, all your attention and none of it is for results. Are you sold yet?" she finished with a smile.

Danielle had to smile too. "Oh yeah, that sounds *really* appealing... So why would someone want to start down that path? It sounds awful!"

Ginger answered simply, "Everybody has their own reasons. But masochism isn't actually one of them... One of those fellows who claims to know should just write a book: How to know in order to be able to be and do. But who *could* write such a book, and who *would* read it anyway? People tend to want pat answers, ready-made instructions that yield instant results. It took a lifetime to screw ourselves up; it stands to reason that it would take quite a while to undo that mess."

Danielle accepted that and they loaded another batch for binding after resetting the machine to the new sizes. Valeran had been cutting sheets and feeding the printer during the conversation and Ginger noticed that he had been attentive. She offered a silent word of gratitude that he hadn't joined the discussion as well. It was one thing to field general inquiries but quite another to reveal specifics... 'that would be something for Alfred or Vera to handle... not little old Ginger-girl,' she thought.

Saturday and the evening of the recital arrived. John provided a buffet for their guests. Hana and Ginger were dressed in nearly matching dresses. Uncle Alfred stood next to the piano and introduced them individually. "This evening we have the rare opportunity to attend a recital of accomplishment. Each of these ladies has worked to prepare a piece of music to present this evening, so with out further ado... May I present Virginia Kaitlyn Belle Spelman-Backhouse and her interpretation of *Bridge over Troubled Waters* by Paul Simon."

There was a smattering of enthusiastic applause as Ginger rose, walked to the piano and seated herself at the keyboard. She struck the first few chords, cleared her throat and began to sing the ballad that Paul Simon had once written for Art Garfunkel's voice. Ginger performed the song beautifully. Her voice was clear and compelling; her playing was musical and flowed well... she certainly did it justice. When the last strains echoed into silence, she received an ovation from the small gathering that she wasn't at all prepared to receive. She blushed with embarrassment and a touch of pride in her accomplishment.

Once the applause died down a bit, she announced: "It is my honor and privilege to introduce the star of this evening's performances..." Hana began to grin. "This young lady began lessons when I did and she has exceeded all our expectations of her virtuosity. Accompanying herself at the piano, Hana Nasrin Livingson-Backhouse will now perform that oft-sung lullaby, *Twinkle, Twinkle Little Star.* Miss Backhouse..."

Ginger waved her hand toward Hana and as dignified as you

please, Hana stood and went to the piano bench. Alfred had long before put steps up to it so she didn't need assistance taking her seat. She played out a few bars of the melody, no chords, just the tune itself. Then she began to sing in her little voice. Some of the words weren't yet a part of her 'normal' vocabulary but she tried to enunciate them as best she could. The notes and words came out so sweetly. At last she reached the end and she held her finger on the last key so that it kept sounding after her voice had ceased. The effect was almost professional.

She wasn't prepared for the resounding applause and cheers her family and friends offered instantly. But she climbed down from the bench and stood next to the piano and performed the little curtsy that Vera had taught her. Cameras flashed and there was more applause. Ginger rushed up and lifted her into her arms. She whispered, "That was very well done HanaRin, very well done indeed. Now do you have something to say to all the audience?" Ginger waved for quiet.

Hana said, "Thank you. Now we can have cake!" That little speech was met with giggles and adoring 'aahs.' Hana squirmed to get down and dashed to the table where the cake was waiting. Vera cut her a piece and she then surprised everyone by delivering it to one of the guests. Then she did the same with each piece that Vera sliced, until they all had a serving. Only then did she accept a piece for herself and dig into it with obvious enjoyment. That was a great recital evening. Alfred was coaxed into playing while they chatted and talked sitting comfortably around the music salon in front of the hearth.

The subject Danielle and Ginger had discussed earlier in the week came up again. Only this time it was Valeran who instigated the topic. He asked John, "Is there a methodical approach to finding a higher consciousness in oneself?"

Ginger had already told him about the conversation she'd had with Danielle, so he wasn't so caught off guard as he might otherwise have been. He replied, "Certainly. But it is an excruciating journey. No one would knowingly attempt it. You're better off doing what you're doing now and forgetting about higher things."

Valeran wasn't so easily put off. "Are you suggesting that I am incapable of following such a path, or is it that you don't know the way yourself?"

John wasn't easily baited into a hasty reaction to the query. "Not at all. But if I may ask you a question; is your interest a practical matter of pursuing such a path yourself, or is this a general theoretical or philosophical inquiry?"

Valeran answered, seemingly sincerely, "I heard Danielle and Ginger talking about this very thing earlier this week and I haven't been able to get their conversation out of my head. Yes. I think I would very much like to know for my own benefit."

John smiled, "There are a few very useful books I can recommend to you: *The Psychology of Man's Possible Evolution* by the Russian thinker Ouspensky is one. Another one that could be very helpful is *Views from the Real World*---talks given by an accomplished seeker from the Caucuses---Gurdjieff. Both are collections of lectures with questions and answers by two very well informed gentlemen..."

Valeran seemed to make a mental note of the titles. He asked, "But what about the *Dialogs with White Feathers and other Guests?*" John was taken aback. Valeran hastily added, "I was looking through the Voyager's titles of previously published materials when I came across that one... That was alright wasn't it?"

John assured him that it was completely alright, "It's part of our job to know what we've printed here, of course it's alright. Did you read some of it already?" he asked nonchalantly.

"Actually most all of it, although almost halfway through the speaker changed to a woman and it took me a while to readjust..."

Valeran admitted.

John nodded, "Yeah that should be explained somehow..." He looked to Ginger, "I think those excerpted materials will need your deft editor's touch."

Valeran was now very curious. "We edit manuscripts that come in?!"

Ginger giggled, "Only if they are our own. Otherwise no, we don't edit submissions unless specifically contracted to do so..."

Danielle was now curious. "Valeran, what was the gist of the *Dialogs*...?"

He replied, looking from John to Ginger as he did so, "It's a pretty straight forward discussion of the state of the human condition, from an interesting point of view. Then it presents a rather methodical process for verifying it's own assertions about those views... I thought it was informative and interesting..." He directed his next question to John. "So, who wrote that book, if it wasn't a guy named White Feathers?"

Ginger responded, "John wrote it from his own experience with the man known as White Feathers, a woman named Belle and a couple named Harry and Kaitlyn. *How* he had those conversations is not up for discussion, but that he recorded them in his own journals is without question." Both Danielle and Valeran looked at John with newfound admiration.

"*You* are a writer?" Valeran inquired, surprised.

Ginger fielded that one as well. "Yes my husband is a writer, a very good writer actually. Sometimes a little wordy and overly commafied, but he is definitely a writer. The dialogs you're referring to are not so dissimilar to the the books he has recommended to you already. John would you allow a couple copies to be run of the *Dialogs*? It appears that both Danielle and Valeran have some interest in the subject. Your writings could whet their appetite for actually doing something about their professed desires to seek higher things..."

John accepted that, "Sure. But they really should be edited..." Valeran and Danielle instantly excused themselves and ran up to the Voyager offices to run off a couple copies.

Ginger looked at Vera and Alfred, "They didn't waste any time over that!"

Vera offered, "You handled that nicely. Both of you responded with due caution and honesty. That is the only way to approach most questions of this nature."

Alfred agreed, "Nothing may come of it, but you each were appropriately non-committal about what you could offer. If someone genuinely wishes to pursue this journey, it *really* takes more than a passing desire or fanciful whim---As you both know well! Suggesting that someone *at least* make the effort to read what they can and *then* decide about what they might *actually* wish to do, is a good first step. Besides, how long are those excerpts? A hundred pages? And *Psychology* isn't too much longer than that... Good suggestions."

28 May 94   Hana's and my recital went very well. The best part for me was letting out a great sigh over Hana's response to the adulation of grown-ups over her accomplishment. She was as humble as a child her age could be... She even served the cake to each person in turn! She's a prodigy! The other interesting occurrence of note from this evening was how both Valeran and Danielle were so seemingly interested in finding out about the journey we have been on. Uncle Alfred is right, nothing may come of it all, but it was personally gratifying that someone else---outside the circle of our family---seems to be interested in what John and I have begun to devote our life towards. Not that that is in any way a justification or rationalization for what we decided and are pursuing... it's just nice to know there may be others in the world who are asking those very questions. Will they actually pursue them? Who knows? We'll burn those bridges when we get to them.

I was surprised at how comfortable I was, personally, in responding to their questions and I was *really* impressed at how calmly John responded. We are only babies compared to Alfred or Vera, but they said we responded well also. Of course should either of our young friends actually decide to work on themselves, that will be a different matter entirely from simply answering a few questions. Vera has repeatedly reminded both John and me that we will be good parents... we may be parenting more than just our little girls...

I suppose John was right. I will devote some time over the next several days to editing chores. There will be no sense in having Auntie Lila's or Will's journals if I don't get in the groove and do my job! I am becoming more and more confident that Voyager Press can become a self-sufficient entity with only our intermittent input and support. It's just like the plants in our greenhouse out back: A lot of care and nurturing has to be lavished on them in the beginning, but at a certain point they just do what plants do---they grow and flourish.

7

Gardening

"The foibles that we ridicule must at least be a little bit our own. Only then will the work be a part of our own flesh. The garden must be weeded."
---Paul Klee

"I f there isn't any other way... Then this will have to do," sighed Ginger after examining the their newest binding covers. "I would prefer that they didn't feel as though they were about to snap back closed, but what will be, will be."

John interceded, "We searched and researched for an alternative, but none of the others provided this degree of protection for the leaves of the book, *and* that could be run through our existing binding machines. I thought about purchasing another model, but for one run? It just didn't seem reasonable."

Uma and Henri were being tutored by Valeran that afternoon, and they sighed in relief at John's explanation. The fewer machines they had to master, the better and more productive they could be looking forward.

Valeran offered, "...And even if we did have a second or third, or fifth or sixth binding machine, the choices we would offer potential clients might be too daunting for most of them and scare them off; or worse they'd want to try them all!"

Ginger laughed, "Good point! Okay, the 'mouse trap' binding it is then. Thank you for researching the alternatives though..."

Danielle acknowledged her appreciation, since she had done the lion's share of the search. "At least the paperbacks won't have any rivals in the near future, except for cover art. Ginger, Uma has a background in graphic design. Can I have her take a crack at a few templates or put together a small selection of designs that we can offer to some of our clients who simply have *no clue* when it comes to book covers?"

Uma looked at Ginger expectantly. Ginger was pleased these folks were so capable. "That sounds great. Uma is there a software package you are most comfortable with? We'll order it for you..."

Uma wasn't expecting this level of accommodation, and said so. Ginger wrote out the name of the product and company and posted it on John's 'to-do' board. "John whenever you get to it..." He nodded. Hana came through the door with Mocha in her arms. She set the cat down and plopped down next to her on the floor. Mocha wasn't very energetic, which caught John's attention at once.

"Mocha-baby? Are you feeling alright?" he asked and stroked her head between her ears. She looked back up to him with her eyes half opened. "She looks like she's been drugged or something. Hana darling? Where did you find Mocha kitty just now?"

Hana pointed to the kitchen and said, "Down dere."

John excused himself and went to see if there was some obvious source for the cat's lethargy. What he found was a bowl of mostly devoured catnip from the greenhouse grown just for the cats. Evidently Hana had somehow made a 'salad' for her treasured friend without checking with anyone else. "Well at least it shows compassion and initiative... Poor Mocha-baby..." he sighed.

He went back to the office to order the graphic software and finalize the the books for the month's orders and contracts. Ginger asked, "What was it?"

John smiled, "Too much of a good thing..." and he glanced in Hana's direction. Ginger was equally ready to be done with their first full month's accounting, so she turned her attentions to reviewing and assisting in the number crunching. Uma and Henri were catching on as quickly as could be expected and with that in mind, John asked generally, "We're almost done with the books, does anyone have any questions for us while we're still up here?"

Henri spoke up, "As a matter of fact... Uma and I are hoping that we can each have a copy of the *Dialogs* like Danielle and Valeran have printed. Danielle explained what you said about the other authors of merit; Uma has read *Psychology* before. I'm going to borrow her copy but I'd also like one of these..." and he held up Valeran's bound copy of the *Dialogs*.

John's eyebrows rose, "Sure I suppose so. By the way, maybe I should keep my copy of *Views* on the bookshelves up here..." That whim was greeted with some excitement.

Ginger went to their apartments to retrieve it. When she came back in she mentioned simply, "Just keep our bookmarks where they are. Feel free to insert your own if you wish."

The accounting program was completed. Ginger picked up Hana, and John carried the report and Mocha behind her to the kitchen. Vera and Alfred were tending to the *Anna*: rinsing off her decks, checking on the cats, that sort of thing, and would be back soon. John pointed out the bowl of catnip; Hana made a point of *not* looking at it.

Ginger nodded, "I suppose I'll need to put certain trays of plants out of reach. It just didn't cross my mind that 'the cat' could *possibly* harvest the plants, get out a bowl for them and serve 'herself' up a more than generous helping..." She glanced at Hana who tried not to hear; she just kept tenderly petting poor Mocha---perhaps out of remorse, perhaps not. It was a sign of good faith and her parents were satisfied that the incident would *probably* not be repeated.

When Alfred and Vera returned, Ginger asked their opinion on a topic near to her and John's heart. "What all should we plan to include for a schoolroom-nursery aboard the *Anna*?" That sparked a lively discussion.

Vera led off with, "Bookshelves that actually hold books at sea.

And I suppose it's unavoidable nowadays: a computer."

Alfred soothed, "It's not as bad as all that. Kids growing up now won't remember a time there *wasn't* an internet. It's just a reality of these changing times. Speaking of that, you should probably consider a phonograph, or whatever is today's version of it."

Ginger was jotting down the suggestions as she heard them. "Preferably a reasonable selection of tunes with some uplifting artists as well, but NO lyrics sung by Purple Dinosaurs!" Vera was the only one to know what she meant and she agreed wholeheartedly.

Alfred added to the list, "Steps up to the toilet and sink, plenty of construction toys, drawing boards, loads of pillows..." Vera continued, "Rolls of butcher paper and markers, lots of pillows..."

Ginger interrupted, "I get it; pillows are important... uh... *why?* aside from cushioning falls?"

Vera replied, "Oh, surely you remember being a child! Stacked pillows make forts and houses and caves, they can be thrown without serious injury..." As she listened, Ginger's expression was one of recollection. She hadn't exactly had a 'normal' childhood. 'Peggie never allowed that sort of playing in her house. Only sensible games and sensible toys... meaning utterly boring. That's probably why I spent so much time doing homework or following Harvey through the fields...' she reasoned.

Alfred suggested, "Adding plenty of hammock hooks to both suites in the chosen ama is probably a sound act of foresight. Kids love to hang and swing around, especially when the weather's not nice enough to be on deck swinging around."

Vera added more to the list, "For an infant we'll need to install changing tables on both sides, and something like a basinet for the bathrooms. If you don't want to go with disposables, you'll need some way to wash poopy diapers..." Ginger and John's faces screwed up into sour looks; Ginger remarked, "Disposables."

John suggested, "I can begin making those renovations and additions tomorrow..." Alfred volunteered to assist; John continued, "When the *Ananke* reaches the Adriatic, we could meet her and sail back up here. It *would* be really nice to be on the sea again." Ginger and Vera were thrilled with the prospect of sailing sooner rather than later.

3 June 94 Now all four of our interns seem to be sincerely interested in at least reading about the work. Maybe nothing will come of it. Anyone *can read* about higher things, but they *are* making the effort to at least do that. We'll see.

John and Alfred are making little renovations to the *Anna* for our future voyages that will accommodate two little girls. As a trial run we will sail down as far as Brindisi to meet up with the *Ananke* when she comes for a visit. Either Viola or Portia, I think are usually on that ship, so we'll get to see even more of our family... very exciting. I wonder if Alfred or Vera have given any thought to allowing our interns to reside at the Inn in our absence... at least the greenhouse plants and other daily needs of the place could get looked after. *And* it would be an additional employee benefit... Are there any drawbacks to that idea?

Liability, should something go horribly wrong. Routine maintenance would have to be hired out, unless our crew are even more versatile than they appear to be. The utilities and such will have to be a year-round expense, but they were going to be anyway... at least for the offices and bunk rooms. Parties in our absence. The more people who know that the Inn is occupied by our staff alone, the greater the likelihood that hangers-on and malingerers could begin to infest the place. Inadvertent damages, personal injuries, burst pipes, electrical difficulties or fire, infestations, neglected house cleaning... whew... Okay, We will definitely need to give this a great deal of thought and foresight before anything is done in this regard. We could make a trial run of it in a couple weeks; just to see if it's even a viable prospect. Valeran and Danielle, Uma and Henri are very responsible people, whether they pursue the work or not is moot... I'll speak with John.

Hana is learning that no good deed goes unpunished. She overdosed Mocha the other day with catnip from the greenhouse. She doted on the poor creature for hours afterward. Her centers are awakening gradually, and she is learning about how things really are... this is all good. What a great kid!

Valeran looked to Henri, they both looked to Danielle and Uma. All four looked back to Ginger and John. Danielle replied, "It's a big responsibility. We could try it over your brief voyage to Brindisi and see. None of us have ever had anything larger than a studio apartment to keep up with... since we left home for college anyway." The others nodded.

Uma added, "However, if you leave us lists of responsibilities, contact numbers for emergencies and that sort of thing, it shouldn't be any more difficult than house-sitting---we've all done that at least once or twice. How bad could it be?"

Ginger went over her mental list aloud about 'just how bad could it be.' The four of their expressions widened with the realization that it could be really bad. "But, that's the worst case scenario. In reality, if regular upkeep and sensible living conditions are the standard here, nothing horrible is likely to occur. This old Inn has been here for around two centuries at least; just give her the attention she deserves and all should be well..."

There was a collective sigh and the four of them agreed to the experiment. John thought it was a very good sign that they had trepidation about the undertaking. "A healthy dose of caution is far better than unfounded bravado..." he reasoned to Alfred and Vera later. They agreed with the assessment.

Alfred pointed out, "It's actually a *very* good idea, *if* they are as responsible as they certainly seem to be. And you're right GingerKat, as employee benefits go, this is the deluxe package."

Vera added confidently, "One or two of them will turn out to be a natural housekeeper and will set a good example for the others. I've no doubt there is a latent chef among them as well... They should get on famously." Ginger was very comforted by her Auntie's confident remarks, and said so.

With that in mind Ginger took their interns on a tour of their living spaces. The floor of suites above the offices were an ideal solution. There were admiring comments from each of them as they went from room to room.

Danielle observed, "This is a lot nicer than my flat! And the conservatory is fabulous..."

Ginger took them down to the kitchen and had them look through every drawer and cabinet to familiarize themselves with the arrangements and supplies. "The brick oven is only a challenge if you've never built a fire before. Naturally you won't have to use it if you are uncomfortable with it."

Henri claimed, "My Uncle Gerome runs the patisserie for his wife's family's little hotel in Lyon, I pretty much grew up working for him. His ovens weren't so very different than this; I'm pretty sure it'll come back to me like riding a bicycle. Pizzas or fresh baked breads and pastries are the stuff of life!"

Ginger then took them through the rest of the downstairs appointments. Valeran surprised them by sitting at the piano and playing a lovely piece of popular music. Ginger exclaimed, "Now, I'm even more embarrassed over the recital! I'm so glad I didn't know we were playing to an accomplished audience; it was all I could do to perform in front of people I knew..."

Valeran replied honestly, "You and Hana were great! You have nothing at all to be embarrassed about." The others nodded agreement.

Ginger finished the tour by showing them where the water shut-offs were and the location of the breaker boxes. "That's it. Did I leave out anything?"

Danielle asked, "If our 'experiment' works out as hoped... uh... I hate to bring this up, but I don't know any way except to just spit it out: My apartment lease is up at the end of June. Is there a possibility that I can take up residence here?" She looked sincerely uncertain in asking, but it was an honest and practical question.

Ginger surprised her. "That's excellent! You can get *really* familiar with the place, even gain some degree of 'pride of residence.' Certainly you can move in here." She added, "Of course we'll have to reduce your salary by half..."

Danielle gulped.

Ginger laughed out loud, "Just kidding! In fact, how about the rest of you? Anybody else living month to month in your present quarters?" Three hands went up. Ginger giggled, "Oh to be young again! I wouldn't do it over for any amount of money. Alright; as your leases expire, transition to the Inn and take up residence. This should work out very nicely," she added confidently. "We'll figure out food and such as we go... just the normal stuff of living..."

The next order of business were the orders for their business--- Advertising, scheduling, shipping plans and responsibilities. The accounting for May indicated that they should, as they had suspected, install another set of printers, binders and computers. John had some experience with hypertext and after constant emails back and forth to Jimmy, he set up the Voyager Press website---the first to operate out of Venice. He installed their own servers and acquired a domain. Their established shipping contract was tweaked to accommodate their increased requirements. The informal work schedule they had already adopted from necessity was formalized to a certain degree; with the understanding that modifications were just a part of life.

Alfred and Vera helped the interns become adjusted to actually living at the Inn. While Danielle's lease was up at the end of the month, Uma had been living with her for several weeks already and they were both ready to vacate the cramped flat. Similarly, Valeran and Henri were almost neighbors near the college, and both of them had been on week to week agreements with the student housing authority. It was a no-brainer to put that situation behind them as soon as possible. Before the week was out, there were four new tenants at the Inn. Danielle had no problem sub-letting her flat---she didn't want to be the only one left out of the loop, especially since it was her courage in asking that initiated the transitions to begin with. The full-time residence also offered the aspiring young work students the opportunity to witness firsthand the daily behaviors of far more 'awakened' people than they had known before.

It took Hana no time at all to recognize there were now more adults to look after. At least that's how it appeared. She wandered into their rooms if the doors were left open. In her defense, more often than not she was following or searching for Mocha. The interns accepted their new responsibilities with ease, including keeping an eye on Hana whenever she was around. It was a mutually beneficial arrangement that began to show signs of ever-increasing camaraderie and esprit d'corps that wasn't nearly as present before. With the tighter knit functions of the Press, came a familiarity amongst all the members of the household. It was Danielle, again, who initiated the first in a long series of discussions about the particulars of the work. She and Ginger were with Hana coming back from the vegetable market when Danielle opened the conversation.

"...It's not that I don't see how a person *could* be a collection of many different personalities, or I's; I just don't exactly see it in myself."

Ginger smiled warmly, "That is a very comfortable existence. Are you sure you really want to go any further? It's not as idyllic a reality as you may imagine it to be."

Danielle looked confused, "In what way? I mean yes, I do want to go further. Just how can I think about the concept of multiplicity."

Ginger giggled, "I'm not laughing at you. It's just that I can't tell you how to think about anything. If you want to have a better understanding of 'what is a multiplicity,' to realize it's not actually a concept but an observation of our inner reality, try this: Don't say 'I' for as long as you think you can... say fifteen minutes or so. Go about your usual activities, but refrain from using that single word. Sound straight forward enough?"

Danielle shrugged, "Yeah that sounds pretty simple alright. I'll start now!"

Ginger said simply, "Oops."

Danielle reflected, "Oh, I mean, I'll begin from here on..."

Ginger said again, "Oops."

Danielle composed herself, "That exercise will begin now."

Ginger smiled, "Better."

They arrived at the Inn and went to the kitchen to put away their purchases. John came through following Hana. "Danielle, there's a beeping at your computer; I think you've gotten responses from those clients in Rome."

Danielle brightened quickly, she'd been hoping for confirmation from them. "Great, I'll run up there as soon and I put away these fruits!"

Ginger uttered, "Oops."

Danielle stood stunned, "It just came out!" She appeared to try and formulate the rest of what she wanted to say. "This is not as simple as it first sounded..." Ginger raised her eyebrows and shrugged as if to say, '*Straight forward* and *simple* are two very different things.' Aloud she repeated, "Multiplicity isn't a concept; it's a reality."

When Danielle went on upstairs to tend to business, Ginger informed John of her exercise. John grinned, "It always starts with such stunned disbelief..."

Ginger rejoined, "I tried to warn her: It's much easier not knowing the truth and remaining blissfully ignorant, than starting down the path of seeing what's really going on... But she wanted to know. More power to our Danielle."

Later that afternoon Ginger went up to the offices to print out shipping labels. Uma was at one computer making cover mock-ups, and Valeran was in the next room cutting sheets. Danielle was quietly setting up a print run. She glanced at Ginger when she entered and Ginger asked, "How did your experiment go?"

Danielle let out a sigh. "Sucky. I caught myself saying 'I' when talking to Uma, then when I asked Valeran a question that didn't even need to have 'I' in the phrasing at all, and even when I answered questions that certainly didn't require my adding 'I.' All in all, it was a total failure. I'll try again later, I should get better at it."

Ginger nodded, "That stands to reason; whatever we repeat often we should improve at. However the point of the exercise isn't to perfectly avoid that self-referent but to recognize another reality entirely."

Danielle asked meekly, "Do you mean that 'not saying I,' or rather failing at it, is evidence of multiplicity?"

Ginger nodded and added, "There are other ways to determine that for yourself... *if* you *want* some other ways to see if it's true or not for you..."

Danielle hesitantly nodded. Ginger continued, "Before you go to bed, give yourself a direction to do something different, something out of your usual routine in the morning. Something like: if you always take a shower first thing out of bed, get coffee first instead. Or if the first thing you do is to put on a robe, put on your clothes for the day instead. Do you see what I mean?"

Danielle nodded, "Yeah, I get it. Just a pre-chosen change in my routine."

Ginger smiled and nodded. "Of course it doesn't have to be first thing in the morning, you could tell yourself right now that you're going to do something specifically different when you go to bed tonight, or any of a myriad of commands that you will do something out of your usual patterns. The point is to see if you *even remember* that you intended to do *something* differently at all... *and notice.*"

Danielle said aloud, "I've been meaning to remember to brush my hair out every night before I go to bed... I'll revive that," she looked at Ginger for approval. Ginger was already smiling, "...okay... we'll see..."

Their conversation didn't go unnoticed by either Uma or Valeran, both of whom told Henri when he came up to the office later after his class at school. All four of the interns took on experiments in determining if they were actually exceptions to the rule, or no. Was multiplicity the actual state of each of their inner worlds? They were determined to be the exceptions. At lunchtime the next day, Alfred was in the offices to begin transforming the little 'apartment.' They were going to turn it into a second office space for Uma's graphic work and a station for proofreading manuscripts. Danielle looked as miserable, if not more so, than the other three interns. Alfred was concerned.

"Are you all coming down with the flu or something? You look terrible."

Uma was the first to respond. "The flu would be a consolation prize at this point."

Alfred laughed, "How's that again?"

Danielle whined, "I'm not able to follow through with even the simplest intention. First it was 'not saying I' and failing; now it's several attempts to do just little tiny things differently during my normal day or evening! This is really demoralizing. I'm starting to doubt myself even about what I'm doing in the office!"

Alfred looked sympathetic. "Is that pretty much the story all around?" he looked at each one in turn, they nodded. "This is the state of man: We are many. In order to live with that reality, we use the same name throughout our life, remind ourselves when we look in the mirror that we are still the same person, and effectively ignore any evidence to the contrary---which might insinuate that we are full of constant conflict in our desires and intentions." He looked at a very interested audience and continued. "This is the lie that we were taught from birth, and which has shaped us up to the present. We see what we wish to see, hear what we wish to hear and never doubt our sense of 'individuality.' Your experiences in the last twenty-four hours merely suggest that your presumed unity is *perhaps* not the integral state of being you have always relied upon." Again there were nods of clearer comprehension.

Valeran asked, "But how can we have gone throughout our whole lives up to now and not noticed such an obvious disconnect?"

Alfred was very gentle. "But have you ever *looked* at yourself before from *this* vantage point? Have you ever *sincerely* acknowledged *any* instance that countered your sense of individuality? We are built and conditioned to *not* see such things, and if we happen to... by accident... we discount the observation as the exception rather than the rule. Isn't that your own experience? I'm not superimposing anything abnormal onto your own observations am I?"

Henri replied, "No that's accurate."

Uma said, "Chillingly accurate. But surely this is only with regard to our routines and habits... the same experience wouldn't arise in other aspects of our lives."

Alfred asked simply, "Such as?"

Danielle began to respond, "Like with... our likes and dislikes. Or our convictions, what we love or detest. Those are constants."

341

More nods from the others.

Alfred said, "Fair enough. Valeran, you mentioned the other day that you were really glad that a particular motion in the parliament was defeated. Something I think that had to do with funding for a cause you don't support?"

Valeran acknowledged, "Yes, there will *not* be tax-payer money given to the Italian space initiative. There are far more vitally necessary expenditures that should be directed toward feeding the poor and homeless than wasting money on a dubious venture into space exploration."

Alfred nodded, "I see. Have you taken into account that well over sixty-five percent of the technology we currently use for food stock development, production and distribution is a direct result of aerospace technologies. Or that the infrastructures we rely upon daily have been improved and extended to more people because of the innovation space related activities have yielded? That the problem of poverty and hunger has more to do with education than the redistribution of wealth?"

Valeran rubbed his chin. "I hadn't thought of it that way before. So if there was a movement toward space exploration, there might be a greater emphasis on educating the next generation more thoroughly, and the spin-offs from such a space program might further improve our standard of living? Now I wish that measure had been debated a little longer at least so that a healthier public dialog could have perhaps emerged."

Alfred turned to Uma, "Have you ever tried eating grasshoppers?"

Uma shuddered, "NO, certainly not!"

Alfred responded in mock surprise, "But you *do* like croissants and bread and pastries don't you?" She nodded emphatically. "Will it burst your bubble to know that you've been eating bugs your whole life then? At least in other parts of the world, in other cultures, there is the recognition and acceptance of eating insects, and without camouflage or subterfuge as in the West..."

Danielle yielded to his points, "But love is a constant... isn't it?"

Alfred replied sincerely, "What is love? Can you define your terms? I don't want to respond inappropriately to something so close to your heart as it were."

She reflected a moment then described a feeling that arose from one person towards another, or even several others. A sense of connection and of beneficial relationship. Alfred acknowledged, "Have you never loved a person for a long time then one day looked at them as if they were a stranger... feeling nothing at all for them after all?"

Each of them admitted to that very experience or something very similar. Alfred continued, "I repeat: We are many. We are composed of thousands of I's, each claiming to be the whole. Each has its own desires and aversions, its own likes and dislikes. Our attitudes aren't ours, we have picked them up from those around us: we are suggestible, pulled this way and that by whatever is around us at the moment. We are influenced by what others think, our convictions are subject to change, our loves are ephemeral, and our identity is based upon the lie: that we are one."

He was genuinely pained by their downcast expressions following that announcement. "On the other hand. You are wholly entitled to forget I said any of this, or that you experienced what you claimed to have experienced. In a few days you will have forgotten that any of this took place at all and you may boldly and happily continue with your lives as before. No harm, No foul. Really! I know I speak for Vera, and for Johnny and Ginger when I say: we are very proud to have you in our business and our lives. Nothing changes that for us."

Sighs around the room suggested that he was right to have added that last. Danielle said meekly, "But I can't abide knowing that

I'm not who or what I thought I was..." Without exception, each of them in turn said something to that effect. She continued, "How did *you* deal with this realization?"

Alfred laughed out loud. "I'm not the one you need to get answers from on that score... I'm something of an anomaly in our little family. Ask Ginger or John, or Vera. They can actually answer that question from their own experience. *That* would be far more useful than what I have to say about it."

Henri queried, "An anomaly? In what way?"

Alfred took a deep breath, "Let's just say I wasn't raised 'normally.' What I *can* say is that it only matters what *you* decide to do with *your* realization: forget it or make the efforts to change. There *are no other* alternatives."

John came in and announced, "The new machines have arrived! Any volunteers?"

Alfred said, "Danielle and these other fine people have a few questions for you and Ginger when you have a chance. I'm afraid I am insufficiently prepared to assist them," and he went downstairs to begin bringing up the crates and boxes.

John replied to the room in general, "That seems highly unlikely."

Once all the equipment was set up and made operational it was dinnertime. Ginger and Vera called up to the offices from the courtyard. "Friday Night Pizza Night at the Inn! Come on down when you get cleaned up for dinner!" That was greeted with relief and echoes of appreciation from all of them. The interns were nicely dressed as if it were an occasion for celebrating. Furtive glances from one to the other, or toward a member of their host family were made all through the meal.

Finally Uma said, "I for one refuse to forget what I have discovered of my mechanicalness. I realize I have been reading about this path longer than the others, but that of itself certainly didn't make much difference when it came to taking one *practical* step forward. I wish to change. Will you teach me how?" Before John or Ginger could respond, Danielle made a similar announcement. Then Henri described his disgust with what was becoming clearer to him of his fractious inner world. Valeran was eloquent in his request: "My inner world is crap, but I don't know how to shovel it out even if I had a big enough shovel to start the cleaning. Please teach me."

Ginger answered, "John and I are only a little ways down this road. We have seen much and have made some headway towards our own aims. What little we have we will share. What we understand we will attempt to communicate. That being said, you must understand this: we can only point the way. *You* must each make the journey; *you* must each make the efforts necessary. It is only through the strength of *your own wish* that will keep you on the path. This is a path of sacrifice and loss, of renunciation and re-evaluation of all that you have held dear---your dreams, your likes, desires and plans. Like the song says: 'you will walk down that lonesome road all by yourself.' To turn back or give up will be more dangerous than you can know--- For you will have seen much and those visions will haunt and torment you. There is no magic wand, no special incantation, no secret or hidden vital bit of data to at last obtain. All will be plainly presented and simple to verify, but verify it you must! *You* will do the *work*."

John added, "Now *that's* what I call a great sales pitch..." They all burst out laughing at that. "Who wouldn't want to go on now?" When they composed themselves again he continued, "Your first task, and one which shall always remain before you in your every endeavor, is this: Believe nothing; not what we say, not even yourself. Verify everything. Only through repeatable experiment and experience can you truly 'know' anything of value for yourself. Only *that* knowledge can be inalienably and truly yours."

Vera said quietly, "We study the structure and functioning of a system whose very presence forms existence itself. It is ubiquitous and pervasive. It is the fabric of reality. It is our own inner construction and we are a microcosm of all that exists. Any of us can and will offer guidance and direction, instruction and data, but as Ginger said: it is you, yourselves, who will do the heavy lifting in your inner worlds."

Alfred smiled, "So who's ready for dessert? Cake and ice cream coming right up!" Hana toddled after him immediately---just in case there was a miscalculation in their actual resources no doubt.

9 June 94 'By teaching others you will learn yourself.' I read that in the back of *Views.* Boy is that the truth! Danielle asked a few questions innocently enough, and before long at all I was offering the results of my meager efforts and knowledge in answer to her needs. I am learning a lot about myself in the process. Thinking, *really* thinking is a challenge. It seems to come easier for Johnny. He is asked a question and after a moment's silence he comes forward with responses and answers that I am still marveling at. Like when Uma asked him how to understand 'free will.' I was still trying define the concept in my mind when he said that 'will' as it is generally understood is just one I's desire overpowering some other set of I's and their desires. He added that free will is actually the function of a fully realized individual, that it is only a hope or in most cases only a dream for the rest of us. Will is the expression of individuality; so a multiplicity---a person remaining in relative sleep-wakefulness as most people are---cannot have any idea what it *actually* entails. Then he said a remarkable thing: At the same time, we all have the seeds of will sown in us as humans. Learning to go against our mechanical nature by struggling with our habits and mindless routines--- *that* is the beginning of developing will, developing *intentionality.* He made it sound so clear and simple. I wondered why I hadn't thought to say that at once.

He told me later, when I said how much I appreciated what he told Uma, that it didn't occur to him that he was explaining anything that wasn't patently obvious. I muttered something about being a blind idiot then by comparison. He elaborated that nearly all the noble concepts we as humans value are generally only functions and properties of the master, of higher mental center. That the higher emotional center is a gateway of sorts and substantiates our experience of compassion, of love, of loyalty and other virtues. But it is from the master that we ultimately gain license to possess those qualities. I am an idiot. I hope the people who love me will take care of me when I start to drool and swat at imaginary flies.

"We're not avoiding you, we just have some renovations to make to the *Anna*. What is it that is worrying you just now?" Ginger asked.

Danielle blushed a little, "Just that I am feeling so inept! A week ago I was confident of almost everything I did. Now I'm uncertain whether or not I'm even completely dressed when I leave my room in the morning..."

Ginger put her arm around her, "Come with me, Okay?" Danielle looked over her shoulder to Uma and Valeran who were in the office also.

Valeran waved for Danielle to go, "We'll get by for a little while without you... just don't take a holiday or anything..."

Ginger spoke as they walked to the docks. "I know precisely what you mean."

Danielle looked imploringly back to her.

"Really. And I don't mean I used to feel that way and it got better; I mean right now, all the time."

Danielle stopped suddenly, "I find that hard to believe. But for the sake of argument---*How can you stand it*?!"

Ginger offered a little shrug of resignation. "I surrendered to the realization that what I once perceived as my strength of confidence was based on ignoring as much as possible anything to the contrary. In lieu of the blinders I have worn all my life, I'm learning to face what comes with the determination to do what I can, the best that I can. I am prepared to fail. I promise *that* hasn't come easily to me," they continued their walk.

Danielle remarked, "It's so debilitating. I'm convinced my self esteem is built into that feeling of confidence I've always had. With it's absence, I feel like a nobody: ineffectual, insignificant and wholly unworthy to be among regular people, let alone maintain my position at the Press..."

Ginger wanted to laugh but fortunately didn't. "Try this one on for size: I was such a success in publishing, that I was sought out by every major house and courted with incentives to make a girl's head swim. *I chose* the position as managing editor for Boundary Press in the States. I called the shots when it came to *who* we published, *what* we published and *how* that material would be handled. I had a corner flat in New York City, a *very* healthy bank account, *all* my traveling was on an expense account, *and* an exquisite new model sportscar. I went to Texas for just a routine signing and possible development of a promising writer. And everything about my world began to crumble.

I arrived late in the afternoon one day at the end of *last November* and didn't leave that person's house for almost two weeks. In that time I listened to a story about *my own life*, and the lives of the family I'd never known---it so happens, I was stolen from my mother as a child---I fell in love and married. Like you, I began to learn about myself things I wasn't enjoying learning and then a month after *that* I had an adopted daughter *and* found out I was pregnant. I have been consistently surrounded by individuals who are as far above me in development as I am above a cat. I have had to purge and re-purge who and what I thought I was and am. I have had to toss out just about everything that I once relied upon for my inner stability and self-esteem---sound familiar yet?

And to top it off: John and I are now supposed to assist you and Uma and Valeran and Henri to learn what we have only *begun* to claim as our own." They were nearing the *Anna*, and Ginger added, "Did I mention all this has transpired since last November... that's seven months ago the twenty-first of this month!"

Danielle's mouth was hanging open and she appeared not to notice it. Ginger reached over and raised her chin with a finger. They both smiled. Danielle said quietly, "I really don't have much to worry about do I?"

Ginger did laugh now. "I have given myself license to worry, or be angry, or pitch a fit, or even indulge in self-pity if I so please. However, the condition I've put on myself is that: I must schedule it. Saturday mornings are for being angry..."

Danielle observed timidly, "This is Saturday morning..."

Ginger chuckled, "Yep. It's surprising how *poorly* I follow that schedule, or any of those other 'well-deserved' activities any more. I'm just not who I once was... It's *so* unsettling!" she winked.

Danielle had to smile at last, the genuine smile of insight and understanding. "Thank you Ginger; that *really* helped." She hadn't seen the *Anna* before and she finally focused on the yacht in front of her. Her mouth fell open again.

Ginger commented, "Being a mouth-breather is very unbecoming sweetheart."

John called out from the bridge, "Welcome aboard the *Anna Virginia*!"

Ginger gave Danielle the nickel tour. Her young protege was duly impressed with everything about the *Anna*, which certainly delighted Ginger. "We love her. Right now we are in the process of refitting this ama as a kindergarten and nursery." She patted her very round belly. "I'll be back to the Inn after while; I promise."

Danielle beamed, "Take your time, boss. Everything will be fine and dandy when you get there."

Ginger remarked, "It appears it's fine and dandy right now..."

Danielle giggled and headed back to the Inn.

John asked, "What was that all about?"

Ginger said off-handedly, "Just a little peptalk, girl-to-girl. Now what have you gotten done? Or are you just laying low?"

11 June 94   Aside from installing shelves and hammock hooks, steps in the bathrooms and drawing boards in the cabins, the rest of our refit work has been provisioning the rooms with kiddy things and painting. I have completed the first two volumes of edits to John's journals and am halfway through the final one. I'll be ready to go with Auntie Lila's when they arrive. They emailed yesterday to say that they were approaching Suez and would be earlier than they anticipated. John and Alfred put up the *Anna's* sails again and furled them. We are planning to leave for our little excursion the day after tomorrow. We would have left tomorrow but Alfred wants to see the World Cup finals. Italy is playing Bulgaria, and Sweden is up against Brazil; Alfred may have a little wager or two with our vegetable vendor over Italy's chances.

Our apprentices are immersed in going over and over the octave structures---when they're not in the offices or at class that is. Fortunately the structure speaks for itself, and they do have John's *Dialogs* to guide them through a lot of it and answer outstanding questions. They'll be fine for the week we're away. Hana is certainly excited about the junket. She came aboard yesterday and it was all Vera and I could do to coax her to come home again. The playrooms are a definite success already. I'll load the week's provisions tomorrow and transfer our personal effects. John wants to also experiment with our ship-to-shore office setup and work out any kinks in the system... Have I said lately how much I love that man?

"And you know these books are promised for Tuesday, and these over here are supposed to go into pre-production as soon as you can get to them..." Ginger was going from room to room in the offices with the interns following her and grinning. "What's so funny?" she said at last.

Valeran replied, "It's just that it's so rare to see you hovering like this. We'll be fine. Go enjoy!"

Ginger conceded, "Yes. Thank you. Okay. We'll be back..."

"On the nineteenth or twentieth!" Uma announced, "Yes, you've told us."

John was at the door grinning like an idiot. "It is entertaining to see what you'll probably be like with our daughters on their first overnight stay with friends..."

Ginger retorted, "You mean when they are *twenty-five* and leaving the house for the *first time*? No, I should be over it by then..." He laughed, and went in front of her down the stairwell.

Alfred and Vera were playing with Hana on the bridge when they arrived aboard. John called out, "Let's weigh anchor! Auntie please raise the jib and we'll get this road on the show."

Alfred threw the mooring lines to the decks. The breezes caught the jib and pulled the *Anna's* prow away from the dock. In half an hour they were heading through the lagoon and toward the gateway to the Adriatic. She caught a wind coming off the shore; her mainsail filled and both foresails ballooned out. She was skimming across the water again and the crew was thrilled to be at sea once more.

"I think we've timed this to meet the *Ananke* the morning after we make Brindisi. The weather is supposed to hold like this... fair and warmer for several days at least." Alfred observed. "Now then, who's ready for brunch?"

Hana went to her 'highchair;' the hammock-chair she loved to sit in whether it was mealtime or not. Ginger lifted her into it and attached her tray. With a squeaky toy in front of her, she was completely content to watch Alfred make the meal. They were making for Pescara, and once they were well away from the Venetian lagoon the maestral winds from the west caused John to trim sails as they flew down the coast on a prolonged starboard beam reach.

13 June 94   It is great to be at sea again. The *Anna* feels more like home than anywhere I've ever been... even the Inn which I love dearly. I'm exempt from piloting on this trip, not because I can't but because they won't let me. Sigh. I'm consigned to inside until we are anchored. No one is taking any chances that I might suddenly bang against something while on deck... and I'm pretty sure they're not worried about *me* being bruised. This must be how royal women are treated---everything is managed for them---practically no freedom at all. Sigh.

I only have two months of this left to go; I can handle it. My breathing is shorter, I have to pee more often, my back and feet hurt more, my belly and breasts sometimes feel as if they'll pop, and getting up from or into chairs should be classified as an Olympic competition. At least MirandaLinn is enjoying herself. She must be; why else would she spend so much time doing flips and bouncing off the walls except to entertain herself---and there are times I could swear she's in two places at once, or has all fours pressing in the same spot... The only time she's still is when I sing... which I've taken to doing often. I'll hum a little tune or sing songs with Hana... anything to have a respite from the circus in there. Curiously, since we set sail she hasn't been as rambunctious... maybe it's an affinity with the sea, maybe it's something my body is doing while I'm shipboard. Whatever it is she's a little more sedate.

This entry sounds like a lot of whining, but I'm not actually unhappy. I am just telling it like it is as I face each moment... after moment... after moment. Hana is in the port playroom with Vera, John is at the helm, Alfred is sitting quietly out on the prow leaning back on the forestay. Idyllic. The sun is warm, the winds are blowing with gentle strength. It's like what John said about traveling through the Kiel Canal---the *Anna* is a magic carpet ride. There are clouds building castles in the sky down south in front of us. Beautiful.

Oh, Alfred broke even on his World Cup wagers. He said it's a toss up between Italy and Brazil at the top, but he's got money on Sweden over Bulgaria for the third spot. I think he and Vincente, the grocer, have all of a cup of coffee wagered between them... Uncle Alfred just likes the thrill of rooting for a team with something at stake since the States don't seem to be able to field a decent team. I'd like to say 'I get it'... but I don't.

"Johnny? What's the name of that character on Star Trek that is some kind of genius, but has a problem socializing?" Ginger called loudly from a sofa seat nearest to the aft helm.

John's hair was longer and it was blowing in the wind. 'He might not have heard me...' she thought. John looked over at her as if to say, 'huh?' She called out her question again. He smiled, "Lieutenant Reginald Barclay... The actor Dwight something from the A-Team show."

Ginger rolled her eyes. It was so frustrating to have a name on the tip of you tongue and not get it out. "Yeah him! Thanks..."

John called back, "Are you working a crossword or something?"

"No. I was just thinking about some of the episodes we used to watch. I hate it that the shows I enjoy seem to end just when they're getting really good... I mean Deep Space Nine is a nice continuation, I just miss the adventures and crew of the Enterprise..."

John nodded. "In that case, what was the title of the episode about the aliens who only spoke in extended metaphors?"

"Darmok!" Ginger shouted instantly, "That's one of my favorites."

John grinned, "Darmok and Jalad at Tennagra, and the tale of Gilgamesh..."

It was Ginger's turn, "What was the episode when Picard lives a lifetime in a few hours?"

John looked up at the sails whistling a tune that Ginger couldn't hear, but she knew what the melody had to be. She first heard it played by Kamin on his Ressickan flute. John called out, "Oh!? With Eline and that flute... 'Inner Light'!"

Ginger clapped, "Well done Batai! Your turn..."

John pondered his choices, "How about the one where Worf and Troi are married?" Ginger didn't even have to think hard, "That was a great one, 'Parallels.' How about the one with Olivia d'Abo as Amanda from Kansas?"

This time it was John's turn to respond at once, "'True Q'... She was in one of the Conan movies. Alright, try this one: Which episode has Picard and Dr. Crusher accused of spying on an alien world?"

Ginger beamed, "That is one of my all-time favorites. When they finally reveal their hidden feelings for each other because they can read each others' minds---'Attached.' If you remember that one then you should remember when Beverly Crusher was the commander of the USS Pasteur... and was the *ex-wife* of Picard..."

John sighed, "And that brings us back to your plaint earlier, just when it starts getting really good they take it off the air. We just saw it; the final episode: 'All Good Things'."

Ginger shouted, "TaDa!"

John took a bow to port, "Thank you, thank you," and a bow to starboard, "Oh you're too kind, thank you..." Ginger clapped for him each time and laughed.

"Ooh! I've gotta be careful; belly laughs can be hazardous to my health these days..." she winced. Vera and Hana had come up to the bridge and caught the last bit of the episode challenges. Vera stepped over to Ginger's side and put her hands on Ginger's belly, Hana imitated her.

"I remember the last trimester vividly. You are being very stoic, all things considered," she soothed. Ginger smiled a pained but optimistic smile.

"I'm doing fine. Just a couple months to go... Just don't believe everything you read in my journal... it's not as bad as all that."

Vera's expression was all skepticism, "I know it is, and you *are* being truly noble about it. If it were really easy, men would have figured out a way of carrying children by now..."

Ginger laughed out loud again... and again she had to wince. "I'm pretty sure I just peed myself..." She let Vera help her to her feet and she went below. Hana bounded out to stand at the helm with her father. She held one of his pant legs and put one hand on the wheel. She was the picture of a proud captain... just in miniature and cuter. Vera's delight was transparent. Alfred returned to the bridge and began preparations for a late lunch.

"I always feel like such a kid again when we get around my folks; I am really looking forward to the next week or so."

Vera replied, keeping her eyes on Hana, "I know exactly what you mean. Truth be told, I've begun to feel that way when I'm with Hana. Do you know what she wanted to play this morning? Publisher! She had all her little dolls at stations and each of them had a job to do. I was just the paper cutter. She drew a cover for her book and wrapped it around several pages with pictures and lines that looked like text, then presented it to me. I was also the customer."

Alfred grinned, "What was her first title?"

Vera giggled, "*Mocha the Cat*. It's a treasure. I am definitely feeling younger the more I play with her."

Ginger came back up. "Ah, fresh underwear for the third time today. A girl just can't change underwear enough, you know. Mmm, that smells good. Monte Cristos?"

"And here's the first one just for you..." Alfred handed her a plate. "Chips, pickles and orange slices are there," he pointed.

"Thank you kindly sir; I am just famished. Why I am certain I haven't eaten for at least two hours!" Ginger drawled her best Scarlet O'Hara.

Vera observed, "As it should be. Little meals all the time is best for you at this stage. Let alone that's about all you can handle at one time anyway..." Ginger sighed and set her plate on a side table, then maneuvered onto the sofa.

John called out, "There are dolphins off the starboard bow!"

Alfred dropped what he was doing and rushed out to the foredeck, "I waited up there all morning to see some of them. Now I'm certain they just waited for me to get hungry..."

John clipped a harness line to Hana's belt and she toddled up to where Alfred was sprawled on the prow. He set her on his lap and they watched the dolphins dance out in front of them. Hana was entranced. Her mouth was agape and her arms were up pointing and clapping at the graceful creatures gliding as fast as the *Anna* sailed. They wove back and forth, sprang into the air, some of them even came back abreast of the prow where they sat. Hana wanted to reach out and touch them... and she tried. Mocha skittered out from the bridge and went up to sit behind them. Even the cat was fascinated by the water ballet ahead of the yacht.

One of the new devices Alfred added to the *Anna* before they left on this little trip was a mast-mounted video camera. Ginger and Vera watched them on the monitor while they were watching the dolphins. Vera commented to Ginger, "I suppose her next book will be about dolphins. She is mesmerized."

Ginger nibbled on her sandwich and gazed at the screen, "The only other ones I've seen up close were the ones that escorted us out of the Caribbean. They are almost magical and so smart!"

Pescara was just an hour or so away when John suddenly called forward, "Look off to port, about ten o'clock."

Alfred and Hana ducked under the jib and Alfred pointed, "See over there munchkin, that's a Cuvier's beaked whale. Isn't it pretty; all pale and mottled. You can tell they're Cuvier's; see their dorsal is almost all the way back by their flukes. Ooh, there are two more... wait, six whales. Now *that's* a sight to behold."

Vera came up from below and out to the prow with a few pairs of field glasses. "Here you go..."

Alfred and Hana held their binoculars and looked at the whales up close and personal. Hana hooted and waved to the pale beasts surrounded now by *her* dolphin pod, cavorting and seemingly entertaining their larger brethren. What appeared to have been six were actually *many* more. The others had been deep diving, when they *all* surfaced once again their numbers were closer to *twenty---very* unusual, even rare. Ginger made a note in her journal about the unparalleled occurrence. Fortunately Vera snapped several pictures as well to document the occasion.

The lights of Pescara shimmered across the marina and music from the ristorantes drifted over the waters to the *Anna* where she was anchored for the night. That would have been a beautiful sight, but all hands were below. Ginger and John's Next Generation trivia exchange earlier prompted Ginger to pull out their video collection of all seven seasons.

Vera chided her, "...And you said you didn't see many movies!"

Ginger retorted, "Next Generation is... was a serial on TV. There *are* Star Trek *movies* and I saw them in the cinema, but that's about the extent of my movie-going..." She was cuing up the second of her favorite episodes, "Oh, and I saw the three Star Wars movies as well..." She sat back on the lower salon sofa and reached for the giant bowl of popcorn John had made for her. "Aah, paradise!"

The others *said* they were just keeping her company. But it was surprising how long they had to wait for Vera before they were *allowed* to take it off of pause when *she* had to go to the bathroom... *Just* keeping her company.

357

14 June 94   There was a pod of what appeared to be twenty Cuvier's beaked whales being escorted by a really big group of dolphins. None of us had ever seen anything like it before. It was amazing... of course I only got to see them through the bridge windows, but still it was a sight to behold. We'll be in Brindisi this evening. I feel like a queen bee---bloated and consigned to stay in the hive while everyone else does all the work. It may sound like a privileged position, but not from my vantage point. Which makes me wonder how Vera made it through Turkey and into the Kurdish territory with Viola and Portia when she was this size; she's an amazing woman, of that I am certain.

Vera and I are stretching and doing as much 'exercising' as I can manage these days. I am determined to keep my spirits up and my energy level as elevated as is possible... but it's difficult.

"I have a surprise for you sweetheart..." John announced as he poured coffee.

Ginger put away her journal and looked up expectantly, "What sort of surprise? Have you figured a way to carry MirandaLinn for the rest of her gestation?"

He chuckled, "Not quite, but it is along those lines. You looked so disappointed yesterday when we were whale-watching and you could only see them through the windows..."

"Yeah..." she responded, now more interested.

John continued, unable to keep a secret for very long, "Alfred and I have rigged a harness for you to be able to go aloft!"

Ginger squealed with glee. Hana climbed up the steps from below and heard her mother's excitement. She clapped and squealed also, without knowing what was the purpose. Clapping, squealing and hopping with joy didn't need a good reason.

"When can I go up?" Ginger asked expectantly.

"That completely depends on you. I suppose after we're under way and the sun is higher would be a good time."

Ginger was tearing up. "I don't know why, but this has really made me so happy. Thank you all for taking such good care of me!" She wiped her eyes with a burp rag that was always next to Hana's highchair. "I've been really struggling against self-pity... Thank... you for... being so... thoughtful... and loving me..." She was nearly incoherent.

John sat next to her and hugged her. "GingerKat, I'd carry Miranda if I could. I'd do anything for you. I love you so much." Ginger sobbed even louder. Hana wasn't sure what to make of the seeming reversal of emotions. Ginger saw her face and tried to laugh.

"Mama's really happy, darling one. She's just confused inside." Hana looked skeptical.

"Remember when you fell down in the chair, because it was out of balance?" Hana shuddered a little, she remembered. "You were very surprised and your fingers hurt, but you also watched MamaVera show you how the chair could balance? Remember?" Hana nodded uncertainly. "You had two emotions then, like Mama has now."

Whether she comprehended the similarity from the example or not, she smiled and put her head on her mother's lap. That prompted more tears from Ginger. She kept smiling though and the catharsis of the experience washed through her. 'If something so simple and really insignificant as this can send me into roiling emotions, how am I going to get through the next two months without going insane? Hang in there Ginger-baby... It's just hormones. Rule your world! You can do this!' she told herself.

Hana spotted Mocha sitting on the back of the sofa and climbed up toward the cat. Mocha waited until she was nearly upon her before leaping to the deck and bolting through the far companionway. Hana giggled and took chase, but to the opposite side where she stood looking like a little spy trying to be invisible next to the opening. Sure enough there came the cat. Hana pounced and the cat surrendered at once. It was a long-standing treaty they had: Hana wouldn't crush the cat and Mocha wouldn't claw her up... too much.

Vera and Alfred followed not far behind Mocha up the steps from below, "It must be morning; the cat has started her laps for the day!" Alfred chuckled.

Ginger pushed herself up off the sofa and hugged Alfred, "Thank you for rigging a harness for me to see the sea today!"

Vera smiled at Alfred's expression: not *too* overwhelmed but definitely affected by Ginger's appreciation. "You're very welcome, boss. John and I are your faithful servants..." he murmured. Vera stroked Ginger's hair.

"Shall we get some stretching in while your faithful servants get the ship underway and breakfast made?"

Ginger nodded and let Vera help her down to a sitting position on the floor. Hana let go of the cat and joined them. Anything that looked like playtime and was at her level demanded her participation. While they stretched and 'exercised' Ginger asked, "Auntie? How *did* you do all that you did when you were this big?"

Vera confided, "Alfred and the girls kept me in the bridge the first few days on the yacht as well. There is a real concern about adjusting to the new physical center of gravity and getting your sea legs back... no one was willing to just pass that over lightly. I just decided to take everything in stride, so to speak. And like you I was determined to keep doing whatever I was able to do."

Ginger understood that much. "But what about the aches and pains, the swelling, the shortness of breath... having to pee all the time? How did you adjust?!"

Vera chuckled, "One step at a time. One longer exertion at a time, until I was confident of *what* I really could do and *how long* I

360

really could endure. You'll find strength inside yourself you may not have suspected you really have... How is your balance today? Are you getting used to the sea again?"

Ginger admitted, "I hadn't even paid attention... how pitiful is that? I've been more inclined toward self-pity than self-awareness. Thank you Vera."

They were both reaching across their outstretched legs and if anyone didn't notice Ginger's 'bulge' they wouldn't have suspected that she wasn't any more or less physically capable as the woman in front of her. Hana made them both look like stiff mannequins; she was as limber as cooked pasta. The smells of toasted bread filled the cabin.

"Here you go! Hana cherub, let's get you into your highchair..." said Alfred. Hana bounced up and held her arms up to be lifted into her chair. Alfred picked her up and growled as he 'ate' her little belly; she squealed and squirmed in glee. "Okay munchkin... nutella, jam or butter?"

She pointed to the brown jar and said, "mutella!" He spread a dab on her muffin and set it on her tray. "Poached eggs and muffins for our ladies," he laid out their plates on the table. "...and a breakfast sandwich for the captain... I'll be right back."

The morning was brightening and the few clouds to the east lent themselves to a picture-perfect-postcard of a sunrise. Pescara dwindled in the *Anna's* wake as her full sails pulled her down the coastal waters of the Italian shoreline. "Here you are captain, a bite to go with your morning coffee. Do you need a refill?"

John took a bite and handed his mug to Alfred, "Yes please..." he mumbled.

He took a deep breath with each bite and gazed at the wonder of the new day. The world poured into him bringing new life and energy with each draught of air and vision. A streak of sunlight illumined the helm just as Ginger looked out at him standing there.

It took her breath away and she said softly, "He's magnificent..."

Vera followed her gaze. "Indeed. We *are* two *very* fortunate women, and *they* are two very fortunate men!" She looked back at Ginger, who smiled broadly at her comment.

"Absolutely!" she rejoined.

Hana pointed at her fathers outside and declared in her high voice, "Angel Daddy, Angel Daddy!" They both looked again and it did, really look as if there were a halo around Johnny and Alfred--- they positively glowed. Alfred handed up the fresh mug and was captured in the brighter glow around the helm. For a moment they were both enveloped in a shaft of the rosy dawn light.

"Now that's how to start a day!" Vera announced triumphantly.

Ginger swayed a little back and forth high over the deck in the redesigned harness Johnny and Alfred had prepared for her. She gazed at the far off coastline and around at the sea floating by beneath the ship. She was once again overtaken by the sensation of being on a magic carpet speeding noiselessly over the sea.

Johnny called up to her, "Here comes a partner for you!" Alfred was raising Hana in her own specially fitted harness up to her mother.

"Hello there little bird!" Ginger called to Hana. Hana grinned, wide-eyed at the world around her. 'She'll never forget *this* experience,' Ginger thought.

Aloud she said, "Welcome to where the clouds live HanaRin..."

They swayed in unison as the ship gently rocked below them. One or the other would point off toward something only they could see from that vantage. Time nearly stood still as they 'flew' along above the sea around them. Ginger wasn't likely to ever forget this moment either.

When they were lowered back to the deck once more and each of them regained the use of their legs, they clipped onto the harness lines and took a stroll around the decks. For Ginger, especially, it was invigorating to be out and about again. "Care to take a turn at the helm? Boss?" John asked as they passed nearby.

Ginger and Hana mounted the helm platform and took hold of the wheel. "For a little while anyway..." she answered.

They reached Brindisi in the late afternoon. The *Anna* made harbor before the *Ananke*, as expected. Alfred got up from the nav station. "They're about forty miles out is all. We timed this pretty well." His excitement was contagious. After John had furled the sails he raised two sets of signal flags. Ginger looked up at the messages.

She read, "Heaven-on-Earth. This-Way." She looked around the harbor. "We might get some visitors with that advertisement!" she chuckled.

Vera put out the deck chairs and table on the foredeck. "Come on, have a seat..." she called. "I have something to talk about before our family arrives."

They ambled up and gathered around the table. She continued, "Among the family, only Viola and Portia are aware of Hana's origins---and they are absolutely sworn to silence. Alfred and I intend to keep it that way. You two are her parents and that is that. Whatever anyone else may suspect about it is immaterial. Alfred was very careful, as was I, to keep our pregnancy from *any* possible 'viewing,' if you catch my meaning. It was an extraordinary effort on our part, not just because of the ever-constant exertions required, but because no one has *ever* even attempted to mask *anything* like that before. I'm telling you this because you need to know... It wasn't like: just not writing or calling your relatives for a while, it was *work*. We would *really* prefer that that those efforts weren't made in vain. That you two figured it out is laudable; if anyone else were to discover the truth of it, it would be miraculous. There is a reason for this... I'd like to be able to share that as well, but you'll just have to trust us on this one."

Alfred added, "It may seem like it was a strange use of our energies, but please humor us in this request. Perhaps someday it will become plainer, but we can't say anymore about it than that."

John and Ginger accepted their earnest appeals at face value. Neither of them wished to pursue what Alfred and Vera were clearly unwilling to elaborate on. Ginger said only, "Hana is *our* daughter; just as MirandaLinn is *our* daughter." It was clear from her expression and her stress on the 'our' that everyone at the table should understand her meaning: whatever they were restrained from admitting privately or publicly, the truth of the situation was simply that Hana and Miranda were *all of their* children, regardless of birth.

Vera and Alfred nodded solemnly. Alfred acknowledged simply, "We are honored by your faith in us."

John was gazing over Alfred's shoulder. "There are some tall sails coming over the horizon!" Ginger grabbed the field glasses laying on the table and peered at the approaching ship.

"It's the *Ananke!*"

Within the hour the yachts were tethered and the reunion had begun. Viola was first across and embraced them each after the other. "Ginger, you look positively divine!" She caressed Ginger's belly. "And I really think you're taller than when I last saw you! How is *that* possible!?"

Ginger giggled. That remark sounded precisely like what a doting aunt might say to a growing child she hadn't seen for a long time. It had only been three and a half months and Ginger was certainly no longer a child. "I have been five-ten for as long as I can remember..."

Vera stood up with her back to Ginger, "Viola, who is taller?"

Viola reached for a book that was on the table and set the spine across the tops of their heads. Alfred and Johnny looked at the result also. "Well what do you know about that?!" Alfred exclaimed. "Vera have you shrunk? Ginger's exactly your height... and you've always been five-eleven in your bare feet!"

John interposed himself with his back to Vera. "Alfred, I am six, one. Auntie comes to my mid-forehead... doesn't she still?" Alfred looked intently.

"Yep," he remarked.

Viola just grinned, "What? Did you think I was slipping or something? Ginger's taller!"

Lila and Olivia came aboard. "Hello MamaKat!" they called. More embraces, more comments on her radiance and stature. When George and Alfie came over they said the same.

Ginger surrendered, "Okay, okay. I wanted to keep it a secret... Johnny has installed a rack in our cabin and has been torturing me every night!" Chuckles and giggles met that, especially when Johnny shrugged and nodded.

"It's just some good clean fun..."

"I'll just warm the foods and bring out the cold platters... Welcome to the Adriatic!" Alfred called over his shoulder. Alfie followed him to the galley.

Alfie commended, "Well son, Johnny and Ginger certainly look healthy and sound. And Vera and yourself are the very pictures of happiness."

Alfred grinned, "They are doing really well---Better than anyone could have hoped. John is an ideal father and husband. He has mastered more than he realizes. And Ginger isn't far behind in any way that's important."

Alfie added quietly, "Mama is far more excited about her and dad's journals being turned into a book, or books, than she'll ever let on. John and Ginger have given her another cause for joy and it's been wonderful to behold."

His son confided, "The same was true for Vera when she presented them with her formalized scrapbooks... Vera has been on cloud nine. The long night of these last decades has given way to a glorious new day for all of us."

"Amen to that, son; amen to that," Alfie confirmed.

George and Lila were carrying over wrapped presents when they returned to the foredeck with platters. Vera, Olivia, Viola and Ginger were in a tight little circle on one side of the table. Hana bounced from person to person, all over the deck... her harness line was constantly being lifted passed whoever was about to be entangled next. She clung to legs, hugged necks and chased around after Mocha.

"Here are a few things for the mother-to-be..." Lila announced.

Ginger's expression was passed beatific; she was radiant. Tears moistened her cheeks, "Thank you so much... and MirandaLinn thanks you too." Her hand went to her belly and she gulped. "She's doing cartwheels I think."

The first package she opened were a collection of five leather-bound notebooks, tied together with a faded red hair ribbon. Lila announced, "Ally wore that ribbon in her hair to keep her curls up under her hat when we had to tone down our appearance in certain country sides." Ginger put her fingers to the once velvety cloth and held the bundle close to her heart.

"Thank you. I'll cherish this," she whispered.

She set it them in her lap and began to open the next package. Hana grabbed at the loose wrapping paper and gathered it up into her arms like a shopping find. Vera whispered to Viola, "That'll show up in her playroom before the evening's out. Tomorrow we can expect 'books' made from it."

Ginger peered into the open box. "What is this?" She lifted up a satin bag that jangled. The noise had Hana's attention at once. Ginger pulled it open and held up a string of bells.

Lila said, "Those are Tiger bells; they're supposed to be good luck and are also handy for always knowing where your children are..."

Hana eagerly accepted having the string of noise-makers tied around her ankle. As a location device, they worked like a charm. Ginger found two more little bags like the first and set them unopened on the table. "Now what else is here?" she muttered into the box. She lifted out a large fabric covered box. Lifting the latch, she opened it for all to see. Gasps circled the table.

Lila explained, "Those are a part of my mother's dowry when she married my father. Like the boxes I gave to Olivia and to Vera, they are the last of my family's gold and jewelry." She reached inside and selected out a tangle of golden bracelets inside. "This was one of my mother's favorites..." And she fitted them over Ginger's hand to her wrist. She turned to Johnny, "These are also good for always knowing where your wife is..." That got chuckles all around.

Olivia pushed the last box toward Ginger. "This is from Alfie and me. Like MamaLila, we wanted you to have something of us with you always."

Ginger carefully pulled away the wrapping paper. Inside the little brown box was something wrapped in tissue. When she pushed away the tissues, she held up a silver penknife. She looked up at Olivia questioningly. Olivia smiled, "MamaKat gave that to me the day Alfred was born. She said, 'It's amazing what can be accomplished with just a bit of metal and some creativity,' I was as skeptical as you probably are just now. I treasured it because it was hers... until a few years later I discovered the truth of her cryptic statement. I'm sure you will also in time."

Ginger was in tears again as soon as Olivia told her it belonged to MamaKat. It had a loop with a little cord through it for fastening it to one's person. George said, "Mama wore it around her neck more often than not... Belle gave it to her after my sisters were born..." Ginger just stared at the shining thing dangling in front of her. She slid the loop over her head and patted it where it rested on her chest.

With all the voice she could muster she whispered, "Thank you."

Viola observed, "Things in this family don't necessarily always get handed from parent to child per se. Like that pebble at your neck... Fate moves along strange and unforeseeable paths to reach it's many resting places."

Lila smiled proudly at her niece's comment, "You are so right sweetheart. So right..."

Stories were shared. Johnny and Ginger explained the progress made at the Press; Alfred and Vera told about the young interns and their first steps of development. The Livingsons brought everyone up to speed about developments with the GFHAS which had most recently occurred. And as Vera anticipated, Hana gathered all the wrapping paper and dragged Viola to her playroom to make books. Vera told the others about their whale and dolphin sightings from yesterday. Ginger assured them she had been dutifully making entries in her journal.

"Oh that reminds me. Are Will's journals here also?"

Lila nodded, "George would you please fetch them from the bridge?" He left and returned presently.

"Uh, I took the liberty of making a preliminary transcription..." and he handed over a couple floppy disks as well.

Ginger beamed, "Thank you so much! That was *very* helpful."

Lila admitted, "That went over well..." and she reached into her pocket. "Here are the disks for my journals. I wasn't sure if you would want to do *everything* yourself or not. It also gave me the chance to make a few 'marginal notes,' you might say..."

Ginger was just as pleased at this as she had been before. "At least my sitting around time will be more productive over the next couple months."

Alfred was as giddy as a child all evening. Vera caught some of his enthusiasm and began giggling at things for no apparent reason. John and Ginger were captivated to say the least to see their mentors and friends so ebullient. Ginger asked Vera about their 'change,' "Did you two dip into that Amsterdam stuff?"

Vera really giggled at that. "No..." and she lowered her voice, "When Alfred is around his folks he just becomes a little puppy again and I totally enjoy watching him. He just feels so young around them. In fact, that's the way I feel about their company as well."

Ginger accepted that easily. "Well no wonder. John and I always feel so young around any of our family... no offense."

"None taken. For Alfred and myself it's... well... you know, it's just so encouraging, and actually I think it's a relief to be with them... they do have a lot of years behind them. Although to be fair, like Lila says: it's the miles..."

Ginger giggled, "I do understand a little. I have begun to feel older around our interns at the Press. There's only maybe seven or eight years between us... But I really see how it's more accurate to think in terms of mileage. I feel that too... in my small way at least." Vera squeezed her hand.

"Our experiences are subjective, therefore we have different perceptions of time and age. That's why we *know* very *poignantly* that 'time is the uniquely subjective phenomenon,' we live it in more ways than one."

The next morning John looked for Hana before he went up to the galley; she was in her playroom. She had three new 'books' ready for binding. She held them up for him to see, one by one. He made a serious inspection of each and offered a suggestion here and there. She nodded solemnly in return. "Do you want to help me make Mamas' breakfast?" Hana hopped up and was completely ready to undertake other grown-up tasks.

Viola was in the bridge salon when they came up the steps. "Good morning," she said. "I thought I'd make coffee over here... Do you have a minute or two?" she asked uncharacteristically. Hana ran and hugged her legs then climbed onto the sofa next to the galley and stood at the end ready to supervise the meal.

"Sure. What's on your mind?" John replied and opened the fridge in search of eggs and butter.

"It's about Portia..." Viola began and hesitated. John set the carton and dish on the counter and waited, looking at her. "She's trying to decide whether to leave with Papa and our mothers or stay on with me..."

John's mind raced; he sorted through all the possible implications of the words he'd just heard. His face was a mask of concern. "Why have *you* decided to stay on?" was all he thought to ask as his mind continued crunching.

Viola straightened her shoulders, "I'm not done yet. Neither is Portia, but she's made up her mind, I think..."

"Did she say so?" he pursued.

"Not in so many words. But neither did she want to come on the *Ananke* and see the Mediterranean... and she loves the Med..."

He followed up with another, "And Oliver, Lena and Mia *have* actually said they *are* going to leave?"

"Not in so many words. But they have already transferred all authority for the society to the *Ananke*, and they aren't planning for this year's tours..."

John sat down next to Hana. Viola sat with him. He began respectfully, "Auntie? Do you also suspect *when* they are planning to leave?"

She bowed her head; and for the first time he'd heard of or seen, she began to tear up and her voice was soft and almost inaudible. "Right now. Today. We left and the *Hannah* was anchored off Colombo and I just know when I... we get back there I'll be alone on her for the first time in my life..."

John's heart sank. He put his arms around Viola and stroked her hair. "Is it at all possible you've misunderstood anything... anything at all that has convinced you of this... this parting?" Viola couldn't speak. She shook her head.

He sat up taller, took a deep breath and looked out the windows across the harbor. "If this is so, and if you will consent, please consider the *Anna* your home for as long as you wish."

Her sobs erupted then; the loudest sound of sadness he was sure she'd ever made before. In between spates of gasps and moans John asked, "Does George Lawrence know or suspect?"

She nodded and muttered, "He and Lila are planning to go too; when we get back... I think..."

John was numbed by the revelation of events. "Alfie and Olivia?"

"They asked me to stay on the *Ananke*, and they are going to talk to Alfred and Vera about living aboard as well..." she looked at John in a conspiratorial expression.

He understood implicitly. "Alfred and Vera will stay wherever Hana is. *That* is without debate..." She nodded, knowing it was so. "Hmm. So there will be two of the sister ships without sufficient long-range crews. And almost half of our family is all that will remain..."

He looked calmly into Viola's eyes and dabbed at them with the kitchen rag he was still holding. Hana had climbed into her lap and simply laid her head against her chest.

He continued, "That our family has chosen to depart is a personal matter of their own and we can only admire and be inspired by the lives we have been privileged to be a part of. The personal losses we each must inevitably feel shall have to find salve in their immaculate examples. The practical nature of going on ourselves now faces us and we must make decisions which both honor their memories and are consistent with our ongoing needs and aims." Viola was already breathing easier and was looking at John with renewed respect.

"In three months, after MirandaLinn is born, we will sail to Colombo first; separate crews to take the *Hannah Belle* to Gotland, or San Francisco, or wherever you decide you will want her dry docked and renovated..."

"Gotland I think..." Viola whispered.

"Alfie and Olivia will need at least two more aboard *Ananke* to keep her a viable cruising yacht... perhaps Ivy and Becka or Jimmy might be interested... those commitments will have to wait, but we *will* need their assistance bringing back two yachts. Has Alfred or Vera been involved with the society in the past?" Viola nodded; he finished, "I will approach them about offering more of their time to its governance. What else will you need from me?"

Viola hadn't known what to expect from John when she chose to open her heart about this. She looked into his eyes and patted Hana's head. In a voice that began to sound like her own again she answered, "You know Johnny? I haven't heard your own voice before... you sound a lot like grandpa Harry. I like it: Compassionate, practical and well-considered..." she squinted to look deeper into his eyes, "...is Harry *in* there?" she whispered.

John burst out laughing; her comment caught him so off-guard. "No... I don't think the greatest Livingson has secreted himself away in my mind or soul... it's just me and my meager attempts to handle what must be dealt with, with what I have available to me."

She grinned at his humility, "Spoken as a true Livingson... I'm not so sure..." Hana clapped. This was more to her liking: laughter and smiles, banter---and maybe someone would *actually* start breakfast now.

Viola rose, "Hana and I will get the food started. I hear Alfred coming up; you'll probably want to be taking a turn on the deck with him..." she winked and John turned to the companionway, "Good morning Uncle Alfred!"

Alfred returned an uncertain smile. "Hmm, Viola at the stove and Johnny letting her... What's on your mind?"

"May I have a word, maybe outside?" John waved toward the bridge exit on the starboard side of the helm... away from the tethered *Ananke*.

15 June 94   I haven't stayed in bed this late this many days in a row since I was five years old and sick with epizootis or something. I could get to like this. My GreatAunts made wonderful gifts of very special things to me when they arrived yesterday. Vera confided in me that Grandmother Ronia made it clear that between Becka and I a substantial dowry should be amassed for ours and our daughters' good futures. They certainly did their parts, between the real values and the unquantifiable values of their gifts my girls and I are the most wealthy women on the continent at the moment. Viola seemed a lot quieter than I remember her being. I'm almost certain I saw a tear trickling down her cheek as Olivia and Lila made their presentations... curious. I must ask for time to have a talk with her.

Alfred and Vera were behaving almost like adolescents when the *Ananke* arrived. Vera told me the reasons for their regression. It's just what I have been feeling around our interns: like I have lived a lot longer than I should feel at my age... or something like that. We'll spend another day here in Brindisi, at least, then head back up the coast. I hear Hana coming toward the door... For a little girl she can certainly put her feet down!

"May we come in? We brought breakfast..." Viola whispered through the slightly open door. "Hana's getting Vera up and dragging her over as well. We might need to have some girl talk this morning..."

Alfred and Johnny sipped their coffee. "I should have seen this coming. Grandpa almost said as much in Lillehammer, but I shrugged it off as just musings..."

"Be that as it may, what do you think about dry-docking one of the yachts in Port Isabel? That would leave her accessible to the Caribbean *and* Atlantic." John put forward again after Alfred absorbed the news.

He winked, "I don't know that Mama and Papa will need more than one other aboard. I spent a bit of time with Euell while we were there... I think it might be time to fit the *Ananke* with Elco electrics and a couple powered winches will save weary arms when raising the mainsail."

John grinned, "That's timely. Where do *I* get in line for those modifications to the *Anna*?"

Alfred chuckled and added "I wouldn't be at all surprised if Oliver and Grandpa haven't already built a warehouse for the *Hannah* at the plantation."

John thought a moment, "Viola didn't say so, but if that's the case, then..."

Viola repeated the story of the partings to Ginger and Vera. Ginger remarked, "I *thought* you were more subdued, but you seem more your old self now. What gives?"

Viola smiled confidently, "I just finished unloading on Johnny. You know I think there is something of Harry in that man. Your husband..." then she turned to Vera, "...and your nephew is becoming quite the remarkable man. Compassionate, keenly insightful, humble... I'm liking him better every time I see him. He eased my mind, even over missing Portia..."

Vera squeezed her hand. "...the unkindest cut of all... You will always have a home with us, wherever we are." Ginger seconded that.

Viola laughed again, "It's good you agree, Johnny has already made that clear as a sunny day!"

On the foredeck Johnny elaborated, "...we can keep to our hopes to travel to Sri Lanka then on to San Francisco. By a year from now we can put in at Port Isabel, gather up or get rid of whatever is remaining to be dealt with of my Texas properties. What do you think?"

Alfred looked over to the *Ananke*, "I wonder what kind of school marm Viola will turn out to be?" and he grinned, "Our girls won't lack for an interesting education, I'm thinking. Then it'll just be a matter of where they might like to take degrees and in what discipline?" John cocked an eye at his uncle.

"This from the professional student without a sheepskin?"

Below, Ginger made an effort to roll out of bed. "So you *are* a part of our little family on the *Anna*? Or must I turn Alfred loose on you?"

Viola cackled, "I'm here to stay! But if you *want* me to permanently disable Alfred and cause Vera no end of discombobulation with me..."

Vera giggled, "Not necessary... besides, we are trying to set good examples for our little cherubs these days."

Ginger, with Hana's help, was dressed oddly for the day. "Alright punkin, but I may have to take off the wool stockings in a little while..." Hana nodded reluctantly as they all went up to the bridge for something sweet. John and Alfred came in from the decks as they entered.

Alfred held out his arms and Viola threw herself into his hug. "Welcome home Auntie Sweetheart. We've been needing a shot in the arm of pure ornery!"

Her laughter was muted with her face buried in his chest. When she held him at arm's length she said, "...maybe just in time at that?!"

John reiterated what conclusions they were able to come to, while the ladies did the same in turn. Ginger pointed out, "This is so much better than just freaking out and running around like headless chickens for days until someone sorts through the facts..."

Viola interjected, "I *wondered* how the rest of the world did anything! Headless chickens... stark imagery..."

John and Ginger looked at Viola. Ginger posited, "Auntie? Are you serious? You've never heard that expression? Really?"

It was Alfred, Vera and Viola's turn to stare blankly. Viola replied sheepishly, "You didn't just make it up!?"

Everyone held their own innocent blank looks as long as they could stand. It was Alfred who cracked first. Between the sighs, giggles and outbursts of louder laughter, it was only Hana who was actually still in the dark about the cliché.

John remarked, "This *is* going to be interesting..."

Alfred went to the nav station and typed out emails to Ivy and Becka and copied Jimmy. He asked aloud, "Do you suppose I should copy Nils and Carl as well?"

Viola shrugged; Vera nodded. Alfred kept typing. When he rose again he announced, "Viola, sweetheart..."

Viola shuddered, "I don't know how long I can take being called 'sweetheart.' Do you four talk like that *all* the time?!"

Ginger giggled, "Force of habit. Is 'wench' better?"

Viola nearly peed herself with laughter. "'Sweetheart' will be fine..."

Alfred continued, "Will you take some time today to bring Vera and me up to speed? I'd really rather that there be no gap in administration..."

Viola countered, "I've been handling most everything for months and months... well, Portia and I have anyway... Your grandfather and Papa have been involved in speaking engagements since before the Caribbean."

Vera reached for her hand. There was no reason to think that the void left by Portia's decision would be soon healed or filled. That's just the way of the heart. Viola's heart was no different, regardless of her disdain for her own mortality. At the same time no one was going to sidestep the matter to cushion the reality for her. Life is.

In the afternoon, after the Processione del Calvallo Parato had left the seaside blessing until the next year, the elephant in the room had to be addressed. It was Vera who opened the dialog with, "Did Portia mention her own reasons for leaving at the same time as her parents?"

Lila replied as calmly as if it had been the topic of conversation for the entire day, "She has always been more attached, to some degree, to her father and mothers' example than Viola..." she smiled to her niece. "It wasn't too much of a surprise, even with Viola's support and love through the years, that when her parents' absence was imminent..."

George interjected, "...To stay here and continue decade after decade isn't the fabulous fountain of the Alexander Romance to some. To actually overcome most of our limitations necessitates our setting certain boundaries upon ourselves instead; it is a personal matter for each person to grapple with themselves."

Lila looked at each of them in turn and continued, "We have seen wonders, made extraordinary efforts, observed the world change and change again. We are, as Oliver and the twins were and Harry and MamaKat before them, ready to relinquish our part in this family's story."

George smiled, "You have, no doubt, determined what to do in response to our absence... That is the key, after all: Always determine a palette of responses and you'll be prepared for what comes."

Lila took his hand, "No one can rival Harry and Kat for flair.

We'll just say farewell and leave it at that..."

They stood up; said farewell to them all and were simply gone. No glowing, no meteoric soaring into the sunset, they vanished like smoke in the wind.

Alfie turned to his son, "The Ananke is all yours now. Olivia and I are going to accept Ilsa and Carl's invitation to take up residence in Gotland... Am I correct in assuming that you wish to have her dry docked in the cove?"

Alfred nodded, "Until she has a full crew again; yes sir."

Olivia smiled, "I *thought* you and Vera might remain with the *Anna*. Jimmy and his father will be in Venice before long at all to escort us home. You likely have an email to that effect..."

Alfred went in to see if he had indeed received a response from his previous emails. Sure enough, there was Jimmy's reply outlining what his mother had just explained: 'He and his father were with Ivy and Becka already enroute to Venice on the *Tygress*. Another day in Brindisi and they would join them heading back up the coast.'

Ginger was tickled that she would see Becka again so soon... and the *Tygress*. Vera and Viola shared her enthusiasm for seeing Becka. Olivia was anxious to see her great niece as well *and* to meet her new husband. "Is he everything she hoped and deserves?" she asked.

Vera and Ginger wanted to respond instantly but thought perhaps Alfred and Johnny had heard their praises of Ivy enough already. "Let's take a launch into Brindisi, shall we? We can talk at that little patio ristorante at the beach..." Viola and Vera led the way as the four women embarked in the *Agate* for their 'talk.'

Alfie asked, "What brought that on?"

John answered evenly, "Ivy makes Thor look like a mama's boy, and they know we're tired of hearing it. Becka did just fine in lassoing that fella for her own." Alfred's father laughed heartily, not so much at the news but from the expressions they wore relating that little tidbit.

"We have a case of beer on the *Ananke*, we might as well enjoy keeping Hana company while the ladies are away."

20 June 94   The Inn is full. Viola is settling into her newest role with the Gotland Society, and Becka is pregnant! Jimmy *says* he's seeing a lady, who happens to be running a rival business. Johnny and Alfred are sensitizing themselves to being the only men on the *Anna* when we sail this September. Vera and Viola have been taking Hana for walks and sailing. Our little girl will be a sailor in no time. The *Hannah Belle* is actually already dry docked in Colombo, just as the *Ananke* will soon be in Gotland. Ilsa and Eva are so excited at the prospect of a grandchild through Becka they are being rather merciless to poor Jimmy about his reticence in settling down.

Johnny is going through his grandfather's journals while I am focusing on Lila's. It was truly a stroke of kindness that they have already been transcribed into a digital format. Our interns were a little intimidated by our family at first, but now they are inundating them with questions and discussions about all they are learning. That gives John and I the time we need to work on our newest projects. Speaking of that, I am only half way into the first volume of the expeditioneers trip and I can't begin to say how understated Lila was about their journey. I am now convinced, as if I weren't already, that the Livingsons weren't just unparalleled seekers, they are singularly adept practitioners of higher consciousness and functions. Putting aside any discussion that: as of now eight of that family have *chosen* the moment of their departure from their corporeal existence. What I can't help but marvel at is how completely *ordinary* they have striven to appear in *nearly* every other situation of their lives. Ordinary in the sense of not playing superhero---which any of them might easily have done.

They have been aiding humanity not by leading directly but but nudging and guiding through indirect channels. For instance, when

George and Lila chose to pursue finding the proof of 'one human family,' and published their preliminary findings, they didn't stop there. Their lectures over decades fell on the ears of those who took up the banner: Cavalli-Sforza, Bodmer, Gould, their students and others. Science is only now mapping, genetically, what Lila and George insisted upon at the beginning of the twentieth century... 'one world, one people.' That's just one thing. The *Hananh Belle's* voyages laid the practical groundwork for the GFHAS to engage like-minded individuals the world over in effective humanitarian activity. The operative word there is *effective*---organized, coordinated and international, like the offshoots such as Médecins Sans Frontières, et al. Even Alfred and Vera were instrumental in bringing the plight of missing children to the forefront of cultural awareness through their methodical and far-flung endeavors searching for John and me.

To say that John and I have big shoes to fill is an understatement. Harry's charge to us was the dissemination of objective knowledge without the baggage of the millennia of traditions generally inherent in other historical 'ways.' It's a tall order but I am now *certain* we are not alone. There *have* to be others out there, very likely as ordinary-seeming as our family, who are equally capable of providing objective guidance for those who seek. But, maybe like all other things we've encountered, that 'objective' knowledge is in fragments and not the comprehensive mathematical model we depend upon. We'll see.

"You were hardly gone any time at all. We fulfilled five orders, shipped them off and spent the rest of our time trying to assemble these charts and diagrams. I think we finally figured out the spacing..." Danielle held up her copy of the inner octaves map. Ginger noted with satisfaction that not only had Danielle laid out the vibrations neatly, but had drawn in the cards where they should go as well.

"...And has this been useful?" she asked casually.

Danielle's expression spoke for her, "Is it helpful?! Where else would someone see in mathematical precision the organization of their own inner world!? This is more than illuminating it's most practical. And with the hints and statements given about how everything works, it's no wonder the work is called the work. We decided each of our inner worlds looked more like a game of fifty-two card pick-up than this nicely organized structure..."

Ginger chuckled, "You're not alone there. Not by a long shot." Uma and Valeran sat quietly as Danielle described their activities over the few days' absence.

Now Valeran spoke up. "The scary thing is that if a person just found this 'map' and somehow understood it's significance, they might be inclined to think they were already properly organized internally. Henri almost did. It took some real personal sincerity to acknowledge that this is a *guide*, not a snapshot of the de facto state of things. I think it's safe to say we all now realize how fu... uh... messed up we are."

Ginger couldn't help but laugh. "I think those were close to my very words about myself..."

Uma asked, "Boss, have you seen the La Maddelena church?"

Ginger had been waiting for this for some time, "Yes Uma. Are you referring to the symbol over the door?" Uma nodded. "There *is* a striking similarity between the interlaced triangle with the circle and the eye in the middle to the enneagram... but please keep in mind that the *diatonic nature* of the world *we* know isn't reflected directly even in *that* symbology. It's just a curious coincidence that this Inn, which is a haven for objective knowledge, is a hundred feet from the church of Mary Magdalene sporting that interesting, seemingly evocative, esoteric symbol above the door. But that's all it is: coincidence."

Uma wasn't so easily deterred. "Boss, the enneagram is supposed to have come from some hidden source. Whether it was from the sufis, or hermits in Tibet, esoteric Christian-Gnostics, the Essenes... or whoever, why is it so important to know where that was? Or who it was from?"

Ginger took a reasonable approach to responding, "Alfred? Can you come and answer a question?" He got up from the computer in the other office and came in to where the interns were.

"What can I do you for?" he asked. Ginger gave a recap of her observation and Uma repeated her question. "I see. Good points all around. What might be useful to include in your deliberations is this: geometric shapes are combined for the oddest reasons... that the symbol over the door to La Maddalena has the all-seeing eye in the middle is just more of the same... a recombination of interesting symbology and fragmentary at best. The practical underpinnings of any symbol must be useful; else it remains a hollow collection of geometric shapes."

He mused a little more about the subject. "The enneagram is so rich in possibilities that it has been cited for everything from: personality determination and animal totems, to harmonic stability and a bunch of other stuff... which is what people tend to do with everything they don't actually understand. What is missing in all of this is any objectivity. Why? Because the world *isn't in even sevenths* as is portrayed in the symbol, and the three forces are not naturally united in modern man. Hence the aspect of diatonicity, which the symbol only indicates but doesn't show directly, is *completely absent* in any discussions outside of objective circles. Does that help at all?"

Uma had a follow-up, "So, whether this symbol is really ancient or is a modern invention is actually immaterial to its usefulness?"

Alfred nodded, "Simply put? Yes. Because it leads to the view of a pervasive and ubiquitous octave structure with both inner and outer manifestations---that it *does* perform the function of an objective vehicle for both understanding ourselves and the world of which we are a part."

Valeran had to add, "So taking a geometric symbol at face value is just as futile as taking symbolic writing like fables, parables and poetry as literal."

Alfred nodded, "Well put." Ginger thanked Alfred for helping and apologized for the interruption. He winked, "Yeah I hated that..."

Danielle returned to her initial observations. "But this discussion has a lot to do with what I was going to ask about the overlay of playing cards on the three scales of inner octaves. Did someone actually know what they were doing when the deck of cards was invented? Or was it an amazing coincidence?"

Ginger called out before Alfred got too far away, "Uncle Alfred here's another one for you..." He turned on the spot like a dancer and sauntered back.

"Uh huh, What's up?" Danielle repeated her question; Alfred nodded calmly as she did so.

He replied, "Great question. I don't know. I wasn't there. Next question?" Danielle looked crest-fallen so he continued, "Whether it was or wasn't preordained isn't really relevant to its usefulness. Just like the case of the enneagram's origins: a nine pointed symbol that represents the law of seven *and* the law of three. We know it is actually a stylized construct that points to the diatonic, a pathway to understanding the underlying structure of existence---we can verify the practicable nature of the construct without having to vet its origins. Is it necessary to know the origins of a recipe for bread to make bread? Or know who first made a chair to sit in one with confidence? Or who first cultivated domestic plants in order to grow them successfully? There are myriad distractions along the journey... it is through the development of discernment that we are able to keep to our aim and not become hopelessly sidetracked by those distractions. Does that help?"

Danielle accepted his response and asked, "Does everyone ask these questions when they start this path?"

He smiled, "People often place undo emphasis upon the irrelevancies of certain aspects of origin. Partly because they want to be a part of something ancient and greater than themselves---that by appending a long history to something somehow stands as a validation of its veracity---so that it can be approached without question. The odd and paradoxical thing about *that* is that many people presume ancient peoples were somehow less informed scientifically than we are today. So why would an ancient source for something be deemed some how *more* virtuous than a contemporary source? Claims made of antiquity for the origins of the enneagram, or for a deck of playing cards for that matter, may or may not be valid---What is imperative is that it be useful for our work."

Danielle pursued the matter only a little further. "What do *you* think about either of those two things' origins?"

Alfred sighed, "Just as a matter of record: my family has known of and used each of those artifacts for countless generations---but more importantly they have always only been vehicles of knowledge, not objects of worship..." Danielle was at last mollified.

Alfred added, "In the end it doesn't matter what I think about anything... it's what you each determine through your own experience that has any merit and real worth."

Valeran and Uma thanked him also. Valeran added, "Henri asked about this but since he's not here, I'll ask in his stead: What is a good working definition of self-remembering?" Ginger was delighted to actually have given that some thought.

She replied, "Even though it sounds like, from the word itself: 'remembering,' that it has *all* to do with memory---it doesn't. It would be better if there were a hyphen inserted between the 're' and the 'membering.' Because that would at least be more indicative of what's taking place. It is the experience of assembling our centers as they were designed to be assembled: re-member-ing. The resultant state of consciousness is the gateway to objective self knowledge and ultimately to impartiality. Self-remembering *can* happen randomly, accidentally throughout our lives. It can *even* be elicited from a forced trauma of some sort. *But* depending upon accident isn't very reliable. Nor is carrying a two-by-four around with you to every now and again smack yourself in the head. Developing self-remembering through exercises intentionally undertaken is not only more reliable but it is repeatable and therefore can obtain objective results. The other struggle then is its other connotation---to actually remember to remember... Does that help?"

Valeran grinned, "If I don't repeat it word-for-word to Henri, you'll be answering that again..." Ginger assured him that was just fine.

Uma still had one last thing to contribute. "'To know, in order to be able to be and to do.' That's how it goes, right?" Ginger nodded.

Uma continued, "So recreating the structure mathematically and studying the systematic processes inherent inside of it... is that the 'to know' part?"

Ginger replied, "That *is* knowledge; *using* that knowledge... *experimenting* with the repercussions and implications of it... *that* is what leads to understanding and gradually *being able* to be a real 'normal' human being."

Uma smiled. "Good! Thank you Boss!"

Ginger added again, "You know you don't have to keep calling me 'boss'."

Uma was still smiling, "I suppose that's true, but it just feels right to me somehow... it's respectful."

Danielle offered a sigh of relief, "It has been very difficult for me not to call you 'Boss,' ever since you said to just call you 'Ginger.' If it's alright with you I think I'll go back to: 'Boss'."

Ginger responded, "Just avoid mechanicalness and habit, and

you can call me anything."

25 June 94   Alfie and Olivia left with Carl and Jimmy on the *Ananke* yesterday. Ivy and Becka are staying on for a while in Venice. I think Ivy is fascinated by our little setup and how well our interns work together. Anyway, he's not due to make another trip to Brussels for a while so they prefer to stick around here. Becka has voiced her wish to be here for MirandaLinn's first day on earth, and I told her how much I would like that. What I didn't tell her was that I was really hoping Grandmama Ronia and Olivia would be here also. It would make the occasion so 'right' somehow.

Hana has made friends with one of the other girls at the playground and her mother and I are arranging 'play-days' for them. Tomorrow's playday is supposed to be here. Her name is Antonia and her daughter is Regina---she's a little cutie. Antonia's husband, Timon, is an engineer working on the MOSE project: Modulo Sperimentale Elettromeccanico to keep the Venice Lagoon from such devastating floods. I don't even pretend to know more about it than that. Anyway, Antonia met him 'on the job,' so to speak. She worked for the engineering firm that produced the scaled prototype for demonstration, and he was the liaison from the Venice Water Authority. They married a few years ago and then Regina came along. Antonia resigned her position for the indefinite future.

Viola has taken over the kitchen as her domain. She is a *really* good cook, just like her Uncle Jean. Like John, she's convinced cayenne is an ingredient, not a spice or condiment... so most of her dishes are chemically hyperactive to say the least. All Vera and I know is that we aren't allowed to do any more than assist... and I was just getting the hang of the culinary arts. I suppose I'll just have to put myself under her tutelage.

Alfred was such a help the other day. While Henri was at class, the others backed me into a corner with questions I wasn't sure how to answer to their satisfaction. Alfred certainly did. And I found out something myself: the Livingsons have had something like the 'cards' for ever. I just presumed they adopted their use at some point; I didn't have a clue that they might have been the genesis for what we all take for granted as a normal deck of playing cards... who would have?!

"This is our Aunt Viola..." Ginger introduced her family as she walked Antonia through the Inn.

Viola took her hand cordially. "It is a pleasure to meet a fellow engineer, and one who has dealt with the issues of tides and currents as well... Delightful. We must find time to talk shop sometime."

Antonia replied demurely, "Timon is the working engineer in the family just now... but I would like to compare notes. Ginger has told me that you have spent years in naval engineering on humanitarian projects, but aren't you a physician as well?"

Viola nodded shyly.

Antonia admitted, "I am no where nearly as accomplished as to have pursued two professions---but in engineering we should have much in common."

Next was John and Alfred who were busily designing the best way to introduce electric winches and perhaps a twin electric drive for the *Anna*. They smiled, exchanged warm greetings and went back to their deliberations. Becka and Ivy were with Vera in the courtyard sailing paper boats in the fountain basin with Regina and Hana. They stood when Ginger brought out Antonia.

"This is my cousin Becka and her husband Ivy," more handshaking all around. "And this is Hana's Godmother, my Auntie Vera." Vera hadn't heard herself referred to as Godmother before and she rather liked it... it was suitable and respectful at the same time.

Vera smiled, "It is so good to meet you! Regina is a darling. I think she and Hana have actually come up with a new game here..."

In fact Hana and her friend did indeed seem to have made a game of sinking the paper boats with alphabet blocks before the fountain water-logged them and sunk them anyway. Ginger took Antonia up to the Voyager Press offices next where she introduced the staff.

"Valeran and Danielle were our earliest partners," more handshakes, "And not long after we were fortunate enough to take on Uma and Henri."

Antonia asked each of them about their interests, and to the men: why they chose Venice as a home... pleasantries between transplanted Venetians as they all were. Ginger offered her new friend a selection of titles if she so chose. Antonia selected one of the Pantaleoni artbooks with great appreciation for the opportunity. They wandered back downstairs and sat down in a corner of the courtyard for tea and cake. The girls toddled off to the piano and could be heard making 'music' through the open doors.

Antonia asked, "Timon and I are hoping for an opportunity to travel soon. Have you and John done much traveling yourselves?"

Ginger thought quickly, 'Where to begin? Does she need to hear everything?'

Aloud she replied, "We sailed to Brindisi last week to visit relatives. We aren't going anywhere very far away until after this one is ready to crew for us..." She smiled and rubbed her belly.

That was sufficient for Antonia. She was more interested in talking about *her* family's hopes of travel than actually hearing about Ginger's. Antonia began telling about her husband's family in Monaco, how they were so proud of him when he graduated university and took up civil engineering. She told about her own family in Milan, her sisters and one brother. The afternoon waned and Antonia kept up a fountain of information regarding everything from her favorite recipes to how often they visited their families--- not nearly enough to her own sense of 'justice.' Ginger smiled, nodded, and made a comment or two when Antonia took a breath. At five-thirty she announced they would have to be leaving to prepare Timon's dinner.

"This has been so delightful! You must bring Hana to our house soon so that we can return the favor. And please ask any of your family to accompany you... I am a very strong advocate of family activities." She gathered up Regina and they headed for the front door. Vera assured her that she looked forward to coming for the next play-date, and they were gone.

"Whew! She doesn't have too many outlets for adult conversation! I'm sure she was *very* happy to have a friendly ear..." Ginger sighed and sprawled in an armchair. "I'll get Hana's dinner ready in just a moment... Antonia was draining."

Vera dimpled, "No hurry at all. In fact, please let me get it ready and you can do the shoveling... how about that?" Ginger was grateful and ambled to the kitchen.

Viola asked Ginger, "Have John and Alfred considered dye-sensitized solar cells in addition to the wind generators? There's a company just across in Suisse that is leading the way for Europe in making low cost panels..."

Ginger shook her head. "They are up in the offices, I think, you might check up there..."

Viola handed Ginger the wooden spoon, "Please just keep stirring this. I won't be but a minute; I don't want them to go off on a tangent without considering these," and she was off.

Vera came in with Hana in tow. Hana climbed up into her highchair while Vera went to select the array of the menu Hana was sure to eat, "Here we are munchkin. You start with the orange pieces, and I'll get your beans and rice ready." Hana nodded her approval of the plan.

Ginger surrendered the stirring chore for the 'shoveling' task, even though recently Hana had begun to hit her own mouth with food still on the spoon more often than not, *and* she was determined to keep practicing. Peas were easy targets for her fingers, as were finely chopped green beans. Every meal was an event.

8

Weeding

"Prejudices, it is well known, are most difficult to eradicate from the heart whose soil has never been loosened or fertilized by education; they grow firm there, firm as weeds among stones."
---Charlotte Bronte

"Johnny, I want to lounge in a cool pool of water all day long. Does that make me a hippopotamus?" Ginger asked and splashed at John and Hana. All the womenfolk had begun to retreat to the shallow waters of the fountain basin as the mid-days grew uncomfortably warm.

"That's a loaded question. Tigers like water too; I think you're more feline than water horse," he answered tactfully. Even under their sunglasses and broad-rimmed hats, the ladies' satisfaction with his answer was apparent. Alfred and Ivy winked in approval to Johnny.

Viola asked, "Weren't the solar panels cheaper from Switzerland? And were they helpful about calculating your requirements?"

Alfred answered, "Yes and yes. John and I will sail the *Anna* up to Gotland and help Nils and Carl install them the same time we retrofit the electric winches and drives."

Ivy piped up, "Could you use another hand on the trip? I'd love to see how one of these trimarans sail."

While Alfred and John accepted his offer, Becka whispered to Ginger and Viola, "Ivy just doesn't want to be the only man left here for a couple weeks at least."

Viola cocked an eye at him and sighed, "Too bad..." Vera and

Ginger seconded that emotion.

Becka beamed and continued aloud, "So will you fly back to help me sail the *Tygress*? Or will I have to hire one of these women to crew for me?"

Ivy assured her that was precisely what he'd do. Then aside to John and Alfred, "My wife is a very capable woman, but single-handing a yacht while pregnant isn't going to happen on my watch."

Vera asked, "When is this going to happen? Ginger's going to pop in less than two months; do you have enough time?"

John replied, "We *were* going to slip out quietly, unnoticed, in the morning, but that plan got shot down. Care to see us off?"

Ginger insisted, "And you will just fly back with Ivy if there is *any* chance at all that you won't be back in time!"

Alfred assured them all that, barring bad weather, the whole round-trip including the refit should only take thirty days. "That'll put us back here by the first of August at the *very* latest. Good enough?"

Ginger smiled, "And if I go into labor prematurely, you'll fly! Good enough?" she retorted.

John grinned, "Good enough then."

29 June 94   The men left this morning to refit the *Anna* in Gotland. Fortunately, both Viola and Vera have given me a qualified assurance that MirandaLinn doesn't appear to be in any hurry to come out before her due date. It is a blessing to have two doctors at Becka's and my beck and call.

There has been a rash of orders flooding into the Press lately, even eight *new* publications. Uma's cover designs have come in very handy on several occasions in the last month; she's tickled to have made herself so invaluable. Since they are all working on themselves and are all together most of the time, walking into the office is a very interesting experience. For one thing they seem to be toiling in slow motion some times, at other times they might go an entire day without saying a word aloud. Then there are the times they get caught up in a round-robin of reciting passages they all know. It's really a marvel to witness their efforts. Becka has taken to spending time with them for long stretches of the day as well. She said it was inspiring and personally useful to participate in their work.

It's almost time for Hana's play day with Regina. I think I'll take Antonia up on her invitation to bring along Becka and our Aunts---Safety in numbers. Hana and I are practicing new pieces on the piano; we may be ready for another little concert-recital in a week or so. I should encourage Valeran to have a go as well.

My back and butt are sore so I'll cut this entry short.

"Boss? Will it be alright if we take some time off? Not all at once, but in shifts?" Valeran asked at dinner the next evening.

Ginger didn't have to hesitate. "Certainly. Make out the schedules and I'll sign off on them. Where do you think you'll head first? If I'm not prying..."

Uma answered first, "I have a wedding to attend; I am one of the bride's maids..."

Henri said, "And I promised to help my family with sorting through my grandfather's estate, finally. He died six months ago and we still haven't gotten to his things yet."

Valeran said, "I don't have anything really pressing. I'm just used to taking a tour or something in the summertime..."

Danielle spoke up, "...And I have agreed to go with him. If..." and she turned to him, "...you are still planning on seeing southern Spain."

"Yes ma'am. That's what I am hoping to do..." he replied.

Viola asked, "Then before anyone packs a backpack, would you all be willing to give me a crash course in the operations? Everybody else seems to know how to run things up there... I'm starting to feel a little left out."

Uma grinned, "I'd be happy to! And I won't give you any false sense of security by saying, 'there's nothing to it,' because there *is*..." Viola was satisfied.

Danielle brought around their tentative holiday schedules the next morning. Out of the blue she asked, "Boss? Can I ask my sister to come for a visit?"

Ginger was beginning to think that none of them had any family outside of the Inn. She explained her myopic notions to Danielle. She laughed, "Yeah, like seeing your teacher at the shoe store or something. It's a wake up call that they have actual lives outside the classroom." Ginger chuckled in agreement. "I just want Norah to see this place and meet you all and everything. We have always been close; we email everyday but it's not the same as being together."

"I completely understand. I look forward to meeting her. When might you have her come? We still have three rooms available for her... or she can of course stay with you... whatever you wish," Ginger responded.

Danielle answered carefully, "Well, actually, I was hoping she could come before I go off to Spain with Valeran. I'm really hoping she'll decide to go with me; she's been thinking about it. Maybe this weekend?"

Ginger nodded, "...And just between us girls: Are you and Valeran... I mean..."

Danielle giggled, "No *we're* not... Actually I'm thinking Norah might..."

Ginger's eyebrows rose, "Ah. Say no more. Wink, wink, nod, nod. I hope it works out."

"Valeran has said often enough that he's not looking for relationship, but stranger things have happened." Danielle sighed.

Ginger whispered, "Neither was I and neither was Johnny seven and a half months ago. Stranger things had *not* happened to us before..."

Valeran passed by them in the courtyard on his way to the kitchen. Their instant affectations of innocence aroused his curiosity. "You two are terrible conspirators. What's gives?" He asked casually and pulled up a chair. "Something to do with the holiday schedules? Did I ask for too much time? Is it because *both* of us will be away too long? No, that wouldn't cause those expressions... You're talking about girl things. Let's see..."

Neither woman had said anything nor given up their looks of incomprehension.

He continued, "It's not the work; that elicits much different expressions. It's not the shop; again too business-like for your faces. That leaves: babies, fashion or... relationships!" He seemed satisfied with his deduction. "Who's the poor sap under consideration?" Again neither of them let on anything. "Oh my... Okay, who am I getting set up with?" They were silent. "Come on ladies! No: warning? No: by your leave?" He rose and looked pained. "It's not fair, you know, I should have some say in it... I'm not a dress to be decided who would best wear me out..." And he plodded on toward the kitchen.

Ginger and Danielle looked at each other at last and burst out laughing. Valeran put his head back through the door. "Not even a hint?"

Ginger answered evenly, "How long have you been *convinced* everything is about you?"

He winced, "Touche. Forget I said anything."

Danielle lowered her voice, "See what I'm up against!? Norah doesn't stand a chance."

Ginger soothed, "Que sera, sera. A fellow can't follow a girl around unless she's walking away from him. Think about it."

A light went on behind Danielle's eyes. "Aah... I think I see... it's always what we don't think we can have." And she stood up ready to go back to the office. "You know Boss, you're pretty smart." Ginger smiled gratefully just as Valeran came back through. Danielle made sure she was ahead of him as they went back upstairs.

Ginger wondered, 'Now does she really think she's pushing Norah at him, or is she going to trap our poor sap for herself after all... Dani-girl, know your heart...'

"Is that the holiday chart?" Vera asked as he brought out two cups of tea and set one in front of Ginger. "Have they kept someone here at least?"

Ginger turned the page for her to see for herself. She looked at the calendar, "That's pretty equitable. Even in their free time they seem responsible." Ginger giggled.

Vera cocked an eye at her, "What's so funny about that?"

She briefly outlined her talk with Danielle.

She sighed too loud, "For her sister!" she lowered her voice, "Her appreciation for his finer qualities can't have gone unnoticed by everyone else...y ou've seen her looks, haven't you?" She called, "Viola. Would you come out to the courtyard for a moment?" She turned back to Ginger, "Viola's been here the shortest time... I'm sure even she's noticed."

Viola came out of the greenhouse with Hana in tow and made her way to the courtyard wiping loose soil from her hands as she came. "What's the racket about?"

Vera tried to frame the question fairly, "Which of our interns is in danger of a relationship?"

Viola didn't hesitate, "You dragged me away from playing with Hana for that?" She made a mock sigh of exasperation, "The best I can tell: Henri really admires Valeran, but so does Danielle; Uma is attracted to Henri... but she seems to realize the hurdle she must leap. And Valeran seems to be the densest male of twenty-three I've encountered in a long while. Does that about cover it for you? Why, has something changed? Are the holiday schedules a mess?"

Vera held up the calendar for her to see for herself. "Hmm, that's pretty good. Has anyone noticed that the wedding Uma is attending is in Henri's grandfather's village? And did Danielle mention that her sister Norah is her twin?"

Ginger gasped, "So that's how she's playing it!"

Viola rejoined, "Playing what?" Ginger repeated the scenario over again. "I see. Clever girl. Ah... Valeran, poor sap..." Viola sighed and glanced up to the office. "This should be mildly interesting..."

2 July 94   I am so thankful I am not twenty-something again. Besides working on themselves, our partners have also been engaged in vying for one another's attentions. Johnny tried to warn me when we hired Henri and Uma... But wait on that; let me describe them first. Valeran Daane is tallish and what we used to call gangly---kinda puppyish. His shoulders are probably broader than they look, but because he stoops a lot, who can tell. He doesn't smile overmuch and his dark brown eyes makes his expressions a little vacant seeming. He's skilled and intelligent... of our interns he's the only one with a master's level degree. Then there's Henri Rast: French mother, Swiss father. He's even slighter of build than Valeran, but his posture and carriage are impeccable, so he looks almost the tallest. He has wavy dark hair and I've seen him grin once. He speaks eight languages fluently and is just finishing his undergraduate degree. We are really hoping he continues at the press after graduation this autumn.

That brings us to Uma Favri. She's also finishing her undergraduate degree, also as a linguist. She's introspective and wears glasses. She keeps her thick curly, almost kinky, hair pulled away from her face. Although she stands as tall as she can, she's a head shorter than I am. Her eyes are nearly violet; her mother is Swedish which may explain her fair skin for a native Venetian. Uma's got a lovely figure but she has only ever worn really baggy clothes since I've been around her... so who would know but by chance. Of our four interns, she's the one who had read up on the work long before she came here, and she is also the one with the sharpest critical mind. Then there is Danielle Soranzo, whom I just found out has a twin sister, Norah--- who just finished graduate school in Munich. Norah is coming today, so we'll see if they are actually identical or just look-a-like fraternals. Anyway, Danielle is a girly-girl on the outside and a true skeptic on the inside. Her mother is eastern European and gave her daughters her fair hair and freckles. The thing that first catches anyone's attention about Danielle is her cat-like walk and very feminine curves. She keeps her hair in french braids and is the only girl I know who wears silk skirts and army boots... at the same time. Fashion aside, she has a great mind for business and is an excellent office coordinator. We *really* hope she stays.

Hana likes them each equally, as do the rest of us. Naturally I'm a little closer to Danielle, not just because of our similar natures, but because we talk more together than I do with the others. There's a ruckus downstairs... maybe it's Norah...

Laughter and squeals came wafting up from the great room downstairs. Viola and Hana were already in the kitchen and went to answer the door. Danielle had been listening for the knocking, knowing her sister would be there early. So Norah was herded to the kitchen first and Hana climbed back into her highchair so she could oversee the visit. Ginger came in and introduced herself. Danielle giggled, "Boss, you know me already," and she turned toward her sister, "This is Norah."

Ginger smiled uncertainly, "That takes care of the 'is she identical' question..."

Viola added quickly, "Appearances can be deceiving. It's in their mannerisms and tone of voice that twins generally distinguish themselves." She turned to the girls, "My mother and her sister were *absolutely* indistinguishable because they intended to be that way. But they were a very rare exception."

Norah offered, "Dani and I are very different. I am not too fond of boots and I can't sit at the computer for hours on end..."

Danielle concurred, "That's true enough, but beyond personal preferences, we *do* tend to behave similarly just not identically."

Norah sat down, "Speaking of sisters," and she turned her attention to Hana, "Are you looking forward to being a big sister?"

Hana grinned and nodded---still getting over her: 'you're still new to me' stage of acquaintance. Vera came down with Uma behind her. "More ladies at the Inn! We probably won't see the gentlemen for a while then."

As if to counter any preconceptions, both Valeran and Henri came into the kitchen. Henri offered, "Viola, may I assist with breakfast?"

Viola made a wink to Vera and Ginger, "Certainly, how nice to have such capable assistance," and they proceeded to make preparations while the others sat with coffee and chatted.

After introductions Valeran asked, "Has your sister mentioned our trip to southern Spain?"

Norah replied, "Yes, she did, but I haven't heard what are the firm dates for the trip yet?"

Danielle took down the schedule on the wall, "The eighth through the sixteenth are the first choice, but when Henri and Uma get back from their holidays there's another window in early August. Right now we don't have any runs scheduled, but that can change. We all want to be here for the baby's birthday..." she pointed to the circled day on the calendar, the twentieth of August.

Norah looked undecided. "I started sending out resumes in April, but I still haven't had any valid nibbles." She tried to sound enthusiastic for her sister's sake, "It probably wouldn't hurt anything to tour southern Spain while I wait." She sorted through her responsibilities out loud, "I've moved my things to mom and dad's new house in Verona until I settle into a job... Sure, I can do that."

Valeran outlined the itinerary he had in mind while Uma and Vera had a quiet discussion about her upcoming wedding participation. "The maid of honor was a roommate from my first year in college, she and the bride-to-be were the only friends I had. We all kept in touch after they transferred, so this will be a reunion of sorts."

Vera asked, "And where is it again?" as if she didn't know.

"Lyon. They just graduated from Lumière University. My only real dilemma is the bridesmaid dresses they've chosen aren't what I would choose to be caught dead in... the colors are fine, but the style is *very* revealing!"

Vera chuckled, "...the sacrifices we must make. At least Henri will be in the vicinity if you need moral support." She raised her voice, "Henri? Isn't your grandpapa's estate outside Lyon?"

He nodded, "He wasn't much of a pack rat, hopefully now that the rest of the family has collected their inheritances, there won't be much to dispose of... hopefully..."

Uma looked up wistfully, "I wish that were all I was going to do, at least I could wear comfortable clothes."

Henri added almost frivolously, "Or you could drop by the estate before the wedding and get a pep talk, you know: build up your confidence from hearing the praises of a friend..."

Uma looked thoughtful. "That is predicated on my looking halfway decent in what appears from the pictures to be not much more than a glorified petticoat."

Henri offered a wolfish grin, "I'll chance it."

Uma insisted, "I'd be demanding something that sounded like

praise, not apathy or pity."

He looked hurt, "You wound me. I can be sincere *and* supportive... Besides who's to say you won't look brilliant?"

Vera seconded that, "You know, I have a dress or two that fits that description. Let's you and I play dress-up this afternoon, shall we. I do know a thing or two about transformations..."

Viola enjoined, "She's just wanting to be presentable, not a femme fatale."

Uma giggled, "As if that were possible! You really have to have something to work with first... I'm no Cinderella by a long stretch... more like the awkward step-sister."

Vera concluded, "We shall see about that."

Ginger tried to listen in on both conversations while also monitoring Hana's meal. She was successful in preventing Hana from dropping cheesy eggs on Mocha's head, but she missed parts of both chats. Valeran excused himself to fetch a guidebook. Danielle and Norah waited until he was out of earshot to whisper, "I'm so glad you're coming..."

"I'm so glad you invited me. Why *did* you invite me? Don't you trust yourself alone with him?"

"That's not the issue; I don't think he knows I exist in that sense..."

Ginger offered, "Stranger things have happened..."

Norah was willing to assist any way she could, "I like the look of him, and he seems really smart *and* sweet..."

Danielle replied in a hushed voice only her sister could hear, "Uh huh, too bad men don't just have a switch to turn them on and off."

"Breakfast is served!" Viola called toward the doorway for Valeran to hear. "Buffet style this morning ladies and sir..." They dished up what they pleased and settled around the large table.

Valeran passed the guidebook to Danielle and Norah. Henri asked Viola about her choosing to stay in Venice. "I don't mean to pry or anything..."

Viola answered, "Actually it's because I was invited. That and my folks passed on recently. I just like being around my family I guess."

He accepted that easily, "You do have a remarkable family here. That's one of the reasons we all have committed to staying with the Press. These folks are great."

Norah asked Ginger, "Danielle said that you practice a self-awareness method or something? But you all seem pretty normal to me... I halfway expected to find her in a commune or something."

Valeran laughed, "Yeah except for biting off chicken heads during full moons, everyone here is very normal."

Danielle responded quickly, "He's kidding. It doesn't have to be a full moon..."

Henri nearly had orange juice coming out his nose hearing the absurdity and snorting so hard. Vera handed him a another napkin. "Thank you. That caught me off-guard. Danielle! You do have a sense of humor after all!" He cackled.

She straightened up, "Who said I didn't?"

He corrected, "No one. It just really caught me off-guard is all."

Ginger responded to Norah, "I suppose calling it a method for self-awareness is as good as anything else. We're just trying to keep our noses above water... 'in the cesspool but not of it' sort of thing."

"Interesting turn of phrase," Uma conceded, "I like that. It's descriptive and very much what it often feels like to me."

Norah pursued, "Well, whatever it is, I haven't seen Danielle so calm and collected since we were children." She looked at her sister, "You're doing *something* right. I could stand more 'calm and collected' myself. This has been a hectic year so far."

Danielle explained, "Norah was engaged to be married and the guy ended it abruptly, just when she was almost finished with her degree and the date was set for after graduation."

Consoling sounds of sympathy arose from them all. Norah was matter-of-fact about it. "So I poured myself into circulating resumes and going to interviews, but like I mentioned before... still waiting for viable offers."

"What positions are you seeking?" Viola asked innocently.

Norah replied, "International Business and Development. It's a mouth full, but essentially I am trained and ready to work for anything from volunteer organizations and humanitarian NGOs to staffing for Departments of State."

"Really..." Viola was very interested now. "And what salary range are you anticipating? Is that too personal? People can be silly about money."

"I'm not. I have surveyed the field and am just asking for the starting base salary. Even at that, I should be able to house and feed myself properly," Norah admitted.

Vera and Viola exchanged glances. Vera asked, "Did you happen to bring a copy of your resume with you on holiday? Or can you email it?"

Norah put her napkin down and leaned over to her duffle. "I've got copies... Here you go. Do you know someone who knows someone? Or anything like that?"

Viola looked over the page, "Uh huh, something like that..." She passed it to Vera who did the same and asked, "You said here that you spent six months with a group in Sri Lanka; which organization? What were you doing with them?"

Norah recited pertly since it was part of her interview preparation, "It was a dual purpose operation to both establish funding for, and train beginning entrepreneurs in, grant applications, tax law, and business modeling and planning. It was through an arm of SCI India under the auspices of the GFHAS. And *that* was the closest I've been to anything remotely prestigious in this field."

Viola asked simply, "Do you suppose you could supervise several on-going projects at once? That is to say, how are your managerial skills? Do you delegate effectively? You're a people person or you wouldn't be in this arena..."

Danielle offered, "Norah ran three tutoring programs all the while she was in university. She managed them until she sold the operations to a education resource company last year." Norah nodded.

Vera asked, "Would you like to take a look at a few established programs and offer some feedback on any ways you might notice how they could become more effective?"

Norah looked askance at Viola and Vera. "Sure I guess. But I am just a recent graduate without much experience to speak of... Yeah, I'd like to take a look at some actual programs. Lord knows I've had my share of virtual ones during the last couple years."

Viola said, "Lovely. Perhaps a half hour or so, once you get settled in... we don't want to horn in on your visit with Danielle... I'll set up on the terrace. Okay?"

Danielle and Norah looked at one another. Norah replied, "It's not a problem..."

Danielle rejoined, "I'll tag along; if that's alright?"

Viola acknowledged, "The more the merrier," and she excused herself to set up her laptop and bring up the programs. Vera announced that she and Uma had some girl-time to spend and they left the kitchen. Ginger looked at Valeran and Henri.

"Since Henri helped with preparation, I suppose it's down to me and you to clean up..." she remarked to Valeran.

"Happy to do it!" he chirped back amused at the morning's

happenstances.

"Good!" announced Danielle and took her sister's duffle over her shoulder. "Let me show you my suite... It's great!" Norah followed her upstairs and got the tour of the Inn in the bargain.

Becka passed them going up as she came down, when she reached the kitchen, "What did I miss?" she asked Ginger.

Ginger wiped Hana's face and hands. "Norah arrived. Uma is playing dress-up with Vera, and Viola may have found a trained assistant for the Society. And Hana got most of her breakfast in her gob instead of on the floor..."

"It's too bad I had to 'give up' so much of my time in the bathroom retching then..." Becka admitted.

"Aw, sweetheart, was it the dinner last night?" Ginger sympathized.

"The desserts..." Becka corrected. Henri and Valeran said they were very sorry, but it was plain that occasional morning sickness wasn't a part of their histories. "Is there anything left of breakfast? I definitely have an empty stomach..."

Ginger and Becka sat and chatted while Hana followed the men up to the office looking for Mocha. Ginger brought her wholly up to speed on the text and subtext of the morning's events. Becka remarked, "This place is a lot livelier when the women are in charge!"

Ginger chuckled, "Perhaps. I want to see what Uma looks like in a gown. Are you in?"

Becka swallowed another bite of muffin, "Right behind you boss."

Ginger rolled her eyes, "Don't you start with that too..." and Becka giggled knowing Ginger was self-conscious about the title.

They knocked on the door. "Just us girls," Becka called.

The door opened and there stood Uma in a slinky black dress

without her glasses. "Holy..." Becka gasped. Ginger added, "Wow."

Uma blushed to her toes. Vera grinned, "See you don't have to take my word for it, if you won't believe a mirror!"

Uma muttered, "It's damn uncomfortable, but these contacts Vera had available are great..." and she stared at her reflection in the mirror some more.

Becka volunteered, "It'll be more uncomfortable for whoever sees you: Women will be green and men will want to serve your every whim. You are gorgeous! Now may I play with your hair just a little?"

Uma surrendered, "Oh sure, I've gone this far..."

Becka fetched combs and a brush from the bathroom. "This won't take any time at all... My you do have a thick head of hair."

Uma commented, "That's why I just pull it back; it's a lot to keep up with every morning..."

In ten minutes, in her bare feet, Uma was persuaded to accompany Ginger to the office. 'Just to look over some cover suggestions,' she said. Valeran and Henri looked as though they'd never seen a woman before. They actually fell into each other following her and Ginger to the next office to look at book covers. Uma was as calm as she could manage through the ordeal. When they returned to the refuge of the apartments, Uma broke out into peals of laughter.

When she got her breath again, "Okay. I'm not hideous. I get it."

Vera was as pleased as she could be, "Darling you are what you wish to be. I spent twenty years as a frump and no one, not even my dearest auntie could persuade to be otherwise. One day I just decided to be a woman again. It's just about that simple."

Uma retorted, "Then I'm overdue. I'm twenty two and I've been like this all my life."

"Yes, I'd say you are certainly overdue." Vera agreed.

Becka and Ginger next wanted to hear how Viola's interview with Norah was going. They excused themselves, spotted Hana at the offices door and took her along upstairs to the terrace. Norah was saying, "This program looks really familiar..."

Viola kept her innocent expression. Then it dawned on Norah where she'd seen it before. "This is from our textbooks! These are the GFHAS operations in..." she pointed to the monitors, "...Bangladesh, Ethiopia, South Africa, and this one's in Nicaragua... How do you have such in-depth accounting of those?"

Viola had hoped to not have to go there. "I kind of run them right now. Two of my cousins aren't up to speed, and two are on sabbatical. That just leaves me..."

Norah's jaw dropped. She whispered in awe, "*You* are the Gotland Freedom and Humanitarian Aid Society?!"

Becka chimed in, "And doing a bang up job of it too!"

Viola continued, "So you think you might be able to help out? Maybe as an executive assistant director plenipotentiary adjunct, or whatever you want to call yourself?"

Norah was still recovering. Viola misinterpreted her silence, "It's a non-profit, so I can only offer you a salary in accordance with the by-laws. Is a seventy-five thousand a starting salary in the field? I haven't done any research... ever... about other organizations. I've only ever been inside this one..."

Norah slumped back in her chair, incapable of speech. Danielle offered, "I don't think she expected a job offer... and definitely not an executive position..." She looked at her sister who stared blankly back up at her. "Norah dear... Is this the sort of organization that you were sending resumes to?"

Norah finally gathered her wits. "I'm sorry. This was just a shock. You people just seemed like kindly, normal, ordinary folks just trying to be helpful... Not *THE* family that runs the largest, most prestigious NGO on the entire freaking planet!"

Ginger and Becka replied quickly, "We're from the poorer side of the family. Viola's the woman in charge."

Now Danielle was becoming more than impressed, "Norah, what does that mean, the largest NGO on the planet?"

Norah stated, "A non-governmental organization is a private organization that pursues activities to relieve suffering, promote the interests of the poor, protect the environment, provide basic social services, or undertake community development... internationally. The GFHAS is the grandfather of them all; the bloody United Nations goes to *them* to get things done. Even though they're not a for-profit organization..."

"Which we're not." Viola emphasized.

"...their operational budgets surpass Japan's GDP in volume and worth," she concluded.

Danielle answered, "Oh, I see. They're really big..." she looked at Viola, "I mean *you're* really big..." The ladies all laughed. Danielle amended, "Not that *you're* big... I mean you run..."

Viola held up her hand, "I get it. No harm, no foul. Yes, we are pretty much everywhere. Well, Miss Norah, are you going to help out?"

Norah smiled, "That's the best offer I've had all year!"

"Excellent, then if it's alright, would you consider extending your visit a few days to get up to speed on these few programs?" Viola hoped.

Danielle answered for her, "Well yeah!" Norah nodded enthusiastically.

Viola added, "Just one more thing. We keep a pretty low profile. Please don't advertise your affiliation with us... people seem to go missing when there are billions at stake. It would be nice to have an assistant that doesn't get kidnapped... or worse... I'm just saying."

Norah nodded, "We studied a few of those cases. A word to the wise is sufficient. I just work with the chef at the Inn as far as anyone else need know."

Viola smiled. "That's a relief."

7 July 94   John, Ivy and Alfred are in Gotland. Norah, Danielle and Valeran are packing for their excursion to southern Spain. Hana has used the toilet and given herself a bath by herself, and she's convinced she's a big girl now... I think so too. Vera and Viola have split their time between the Press and the GFHAS activities when not tending to chores around the Inn. Henri is finished with university for the summer; Uma has begun to wear girl-like clothes more and more. In her words, 'just to get used to them before the wedding in Lyon...' Okay, if that makes it better for her sense of continuity, fine. And then there's Ginger-girl.

I am content. I don't know what the future holds nor do I have any apprehension about it. It's not even troubling me that in these last days of my pregnancy John has gone on a trip to take care of the *Anna's* refit. I don't have anything pulling me one way or another; I don't feel anything pushing me to do something I'm not doing. What I don't yet know about myself I know will surface in time and I'll deal with it dutifully. Yet I don't feel apathy, nor do I feel disconnected from the people around me. Everything just is what it is, and I am just who I am. I wake up to every morning like it's a new start and not just a continuation of yesterday or the rest of my history. I sing quietly to MirandaLinn all the time it seems. I am accustomed to what the present state of my body allows me to do and what is a challenge for it. And if anyone had tried to describe this emotional and physical condition to me, say even four months ago, I don't know if could have comprehended it. The world is alive around me and I am a part of that life. I notice little sounds and recognize them for what they are. I almost see breezes as they drift along on their way to somewhere else, each one trying to touch as much of the world it can as it passes. There is an aroma from almost everything too; like every little thing is vying for recognition. And there is the sea: eternal, vast, with a voice that calls to the air and sky in a constant chant of reflection.

I am compelled to perform every task I undertake with all my attention and ability. Not because I think I should but because it seems I've forgotten how else to approach it. I'm losing the grasp of what it is to be interrupted in an activity. The people around me, whether here at the Inn, at the market, at Hana's playground or just passersby as I go about my day... are all more solid, more really significant. Everyone has their own motivations, their own desires, worries, fears, joys and pride which they wear on their faces and in their postures, in their movements and words. And all of them are worth attention, have some ineffable quality that calls out to be noticed... even cherished.

I can't breath too deeply these days, but every breath is vital and precious. I can't move with the agility I am used to having, but each motion is more deliberate. I don't have energy for the unnecessary fidgeting or idle tensions my body had for so long become accustomed. There is something small and intensely strong inside me, besides MirandaLinn. Yet that something is still fragile and must be carefully protected it seems. More and more of myself is bound up in that something... as if who I am is relocating to a new residence inside me. I often watch myself as if from across the room, or above my head, or walking backwards in front of me, observing me without judgement... just viewing for its own sake.

"Whatcha writing about?" Danielle and Viola stood on either side of Ginger where she sat in the courtyard with Hana at her feet serving tea and cake to Mocha and special doll-friends.

Ginger looked up and smiled, "Just jotting down some thoughts and observations about being here and now. What are you two up to today?"

Danielle looked to Viola before speaking, "I wanted to ask you if it would be practical and alright to invite Norah to live here permanently..." she hurriedly added, "she can stay in my suite, I'll get another bed moved in there... she can pay her own way..."

Ginger looked up at Viola, but answered Danielle, "I thought it was a given that she would? I am getting dense I guess." She looked to Danielle, "Norah can certainly have a room or apartment to herself. In fact why doesn't she settle into the suite next to Viola..." she pointed up to the apartments above and across from the Voyager offices.

Both women grinned, Viola remarked, "Now was that so bad? I told you our Ginger girl wasn't the ogre you imagined!"

Ginger would have doubled over in laughter, if she could double over, as it was her belly laugh erupted and she sighed heartily on the heels of it. "Oops, time to change underwear again..." She made to stand and caught herself, immobile for a minute as the two women held her arms. "Oooh, that took my breath away. I'm pretty sure that must have been one of those braxton-hicks contractions you warned me about."

Viola's face was a mixed mask of concern and confidence. "Let's try that again, only let us help you up, alright?" She glanced at her watch just as a precaution and noted the time. They helped her up and she thanked them.

"Hana, Mama will be right back," and she moved toward the courtyard door and the staircase beyond.

Danielle asked, "Is that normal?"

Viola nodded assuringly, "Almost all mothers-to-be have false contractions sometime during their pregnancy. I'm surprised she's made it this far along without them." Becka came out of the office door above them. Viola called up to her, "Would you wander around to Ginger's rooms and see if she needs any help changing?"

Becka shrugged and nodded. Vera followed her out of the door and asked, "What's up? Is Ginger alright?"

Viola calmly replied, "Braxton-Hicks have introduced themselves today. She's fine. That first one was," and she glanced at her watch, "four minutes ago..."

Vera nodded knowingly and went after Becka to the apartments. Danielle asked, "Do false contractions come in anticipated intervals? Is that why you told Vera when they were?"

Viola looked at Danielle appraisingly, "You don't miss a trick, do you? Not generally, so if there is a pattern emerging, and if her water breaks... well the show will have begun and MirandaLinn may be planning an early debut."

Danielle looked up to the apartment door. "Oh my..."

Viola added confidently, "But it's probably just a preview. A woman's body tries to prepare her for the main event with little previews like this. It's perfectly normal."

Becka and Vera came out together behind Ginger. Ginger called, chuckling, "And for my next trick I shall waddle back downstairs! Underwear changing performances are scheduled throughout the day... we'll be here for a six week run..." Vera smiled to Viola and gave an okay signal with her fingers. Viola gave out a slight sigh as if she'd been almost holding her breath.

Norah and Uma came in the front door and went to deposit a couple bags of produce in the kitchen. They were chatting as they passed the open doors. Uma said, "...they were looking at you not me..."

Norah countered with, "Trust me, I've been ogled by the best and worst of them... they were not looking at me!"

Danielle went to the kitchen door, *that* sounded interesting. "Who was ogling Uma?"

Uma rolled her eyes, "No one was. They were watching Norah

bend over the lemons and oranges. I saw them."

Norah riposted, "That may be, but when you reached across the cabbages for the carrots and radishes, you should have seen them trying to get a better vantage of your hips and chest at the same time... it was almost comical. Don't you go to that market all the time? You haven't noticed the way they look at you before?!"

Uma remained wholly skeptical. Danielle and Becka offered, "They probably don't even recognize her as the same woman."

"Uma you *really* appear *very* different without your baggy clothes and glasses."

"Really different..."

Uma surrendered and brightened, "I am just in disguise is all. I can go back to being unnoticed easily enough."

Becka giggled, "Our own Mata Hari! If you were six inches taller you wouldn't find it so easy to slip in and out of disguises..." she commented trying to slump and look shorter.

Viola said wistfully, "Ah the burdens of pulchritude. Gone are the days..."

Vera almost spat in disbelief, "Viola Belle! There is no way you are going to stand there and tell me that you no longer notice the stares of admiring men when you walk down the street! You're the same beauty that made Anna and me look like little girls on the beach at Waikiki!"

That piqued the other girls' interest. Uma asked, "What? When was this?"

Vera and Viola suddenly went mum and blushed slightly. Ginger was standing behind them all with one eye on Hana and an ear for the conversation. "I'll tell you. It was the day before Vera's sixteenth birthday. She was on Oahu with my mother and our family gathered in Kaneohe Bay. Anna and Vera sailed with Viola and her sister Portia around to Waikiki beach to ostensibly 'learn to surf.' Vera and my mother wore these daring, for the time, two-piece Catalina swimsuits that reveled their femininity to their best advantage..." The younger women looked at Vera as if she was somehow suddenly very scandalous. "When all of a sudden Viola and Portia took off their over shirts to reveal French bikinis---absolutely unseen on those islands before. Needless to say they ruled the beach that day: free lunches and drinks, free surfing lessons, tanned and tall males at their beck and call..."

Danielle looked at Viola and Vera more closely as she asked timidly of Ginger, "Dare I ask? When was that?"

Vera shrugged, "You three are nearly part of the family anyway..." she sighed, "Johnny's father threw a wonderful sixteenth birthday party for me in Hawaii 1949..." There were gasps. Uma stared. Norah and Danielle looked between Viola and Vera like they were strangers.

Uma's mind raced, "You were sixteen in 1949... You are sixty-one?! You can't be! You look younger than my mother and she's forty-five this year..."

Then their attention was bent on Viola as it dawned on them that Vera had once referred to her as her great aunt. Norah whispered, "Viola? How old were you when that took place in Hawaii?"

Viola let out a deep breath, "I'll save you the higher math; I was born in Manilla Bay on the yacht *Hannah Belle* April eighth, 1911..."

The women in the room fell silent.

Uma ventured, "You two are pulling our legs... This is just impossible! For one thing you both look the same age: barely forty, if even that, and both of you are more physically capable than any of us are now at twenty... and I'm not even going to make a big deal out of how *no* sixty or eighty year old looks like a freaking playboy bunny the way you two do in swimsuits... We're not blind, you know!"

Viola and Vera remained quiet. Ginger mumbled as she went back to her seat near Hana, "Have it your way... we're just saying..." Vera and Viola followed her out.

The girls looked at Becka; Uma said sarcastically, "And I suppose you're ninety?"

Becka laughed out loud, "No I'm really twenty-one, married and pregnant."

Norah followed with, "How can this be? *Seriously*! There's not a gray hair, any real wrinkles, except for laugh lines, let alone nothing's drooping or anything... What is going on here?"

Becka replied candidly, "Good clean living, no worries, a lot of work without anticipation of results or reward... Just normal ordinary women."

Danielle asked, "And the Boss?"

Becka confided, "She's thirty-one this year, and she is obviously pregnant and may not say so, but could use all our support over the next couple months. This is her first, and from what Vera and Viola have said---their both doctors you know---labor with the first child is usually the toughest."

Uma asked, "But we thought Hana..."

Becka nodded, "She and John adopted her when she was nine months old. Alfred and Vera rescued her from a bombed out village near the Turkish border. Lucky girl..."

The young women gathered up snacks and went into the courtyard; they surrounded the marvelous ones with Hana still playing in midst of all of them. No one said a word for quite a while. Uma said to no one in particular, "I think I like wearing feminine clothing... These contacts are a pain in the ass though... uh, you know what I mean." Muted chuckles circled the little group. She added, "It is an honor to live and work with you three women. I hope we three will measure up to your example of humility and grace."

It was the first time Uma had made such a heartfelt and sincere acknowledgement in front of anyone and Ginger responded, "Humility, I'm learning. Grace? I *can* pee myself with dignity now!" The silence was broken and their laughter tinkled and echoed off the tiled walls of the courtyard like little bells or a sprinkle of rain. Valeran and Henri came out of the office and stretched.

Valeran announced, "Alright that gets the Press up to a holding pattern for several days. Thanks for the help Henri."

He answered, "Don't mention it. It was the least I could do to be shut of you for a whole week!"

Valeran snickered, an odd sound coming from his tall frame. "In that case, I suppose you expect me to make lunch today?!"

Ginger called up, naturally overhearing them just above her, "Save your effort, my treat at Cafe Florian for lunch today!" A smattering of clapping met her offer. "Now all I have to do is get up..."

Five women were instantly at her elbows; in an second she was on her feet. "I feel I have the strength of six women today!" More chuckles and knowing winks. "HanaRin, pick which little friend you want to accompany you to lunch; we're going to town."

Hana looked up, then down at her company. She seemed to have to explain to the others why this one particular friend would be going and the others must stay. Vera asked, "Why that one Hana?"

Hana looked up as they walked to the door and whispered, "She's not feeling well; needs me close."

'Aahs' met that admission as Valeran and Henri held the front doors open for the ladies. Henri said quietly but loud enough to actually be heard, "I feel like a bodyguard for Victoria's Secret models on holiday..."

Valeran remarked in kind, "Tough job, but somebody's gotta do it..."

Norah and Danielle took one of Valeran's arms apiece, as Uma gently held Henri's arm. They looked to be the proudest fellows on the streets. Becka and Viola hovered near Ginger, while Vera held Hana's hand as they walked. "Just a pleasant stroll around our town..." Ginger commented, as she gazed at the colors, the people passing, the breezes through the alleyways and the sparkling ripples on the water beneath the bridges they crossed.

10 July 94   The refit certainly took no time at all; John called to say they were setting off in the morning for the trip back to Venice. I'll be ready to have him back in my arms again where he belongs. Fortunately he's tall enough to reach over this belly of mine. I know Becka is anxious to have Ivy beside her again, that's not a guess, we talked about our attachments to our mates just yesterday. Valeran and the Soranzo sisters are off to Spain on holiday. Danielle actually said she'd keep and eye and ear out for any business they could bring back with them. Remarkable. Henri and Uma are plugging away in the offices even though there's only half day's work at a time just now. I think it's an official excuse to be near each other without making any special effort to show their affections otherwise... I don't know that, but if I were her...

My false contractions come and go when they will without warning, with no rhyme or reason than I can see. Labor is going to be a new adventure if these are only a mild foretaste of things to come. Hana is rapidly becoming more a little girl and less a toddler. At dinner last night she had already pulled her highchair out of sight... we found it in the pantry... and put a cushion from the sofa in her chair to sit at the table just like everyone else. Now we need to focus on asking for things at the table, not just crawling across it to fetch things herself. One step at a time. Yet to her credit she didn't *actually* put her hands or feet into anyone's plates.

We got little sprinkles the last couple days, Vera and Viola assure me that this isn't the season for excessive amounts of rain and that the *Anna* won't have to contend with anything nastier than bright sunshine on their return trip. I must have wondered aloud about it, or looked oddly at the what little fell here; I know I don't have any anxiety over the subject. Everyone around me seems to be treating me with kid gloves, or maybe I just haven't noticed their explicit considerations until now. Which ever it is, I am content... even happy. Am I getting funnier? That's another thing I've noticed lately, unless everyone else has a lowered threshold for humor, they certainly seem to find even my absent comments worth a laugh or chuckle... Again, maybe I just haven't noticed before.

"Where's Henri?" Becka came into the piano room and asked. Hana went on practicing uninterrupted and Vera didn't look up from her crossword.

Ginger replied, "Isn't he in the office? It's only eleven. They usually don't knock off until one or so..."

"No, I just checked there. Uma hasn't seen him either..." Becka said as she looked toward the front door. Viola passed by the doors on the other side of the courtyard and Becka went to the kitchen to ask her. "Viola have you seen Henri?"

"Yeah. About this tall, wavy hair, piercing eyes, lithe build..." Viola replied without smiling.

Becka rolled her eyes, "I mean today. Did he say where he was going?"

Viola peeled a banana, "Nope. Not to me. What's up? Has he been trying on your clothes or something?"

Becka looked exasperated, "Ha ha. No he was going to show me how to run the bindery; I'm putting together a book for Ivy before he gets back..."

Viola asked, "Why don't you ask Uma to show you, or Vera or me for that matter..."

Becka replied simply, "Because *he* said *he* would this morning. You know, following up on what we say we'll do and all... they're work students first and foremost..."

Viola looked passed Becka over her shoulder, "You can ask him where he was..." and she inclined her head to the courtyard; Henri was just entering the piano room. Becka hmphed and strode to the other room.

"...so I thought that before I lost my nerve, I'd just buy it. What do you think?" Henri was asking Vera and Ginger when Becka walked in.

She asked, "Buy what?"

Vera waved her over to see the little box he was holding open for them to see. Becka gasped, "That's beautiful... Does she know you're proposing?"

Henri shrugged, "If she does, she's a mind-reader. I laid in bed last night trying to explain to myself all the reasons I shouldn't ask her to marry me... Then I had a long bout of questioning my motives and what was driving me to desire this so much..."

Viola joined the little circle, "And you decided you're an idiot that you haven't made any effort toward this until now..."

Henri looked quizzically at her. "Yeah! How did you know?"

"Just a shot in the dark... I think even Hana has been wondering about your sanity though..." Viola retorted.

Uma came down the stairs and entered just then. "Who's crazy?"

Everyone fell instantly silent and Henri looked as if he'd been caught without his clothes on. Uma folded her arms, "What gives?! Out with it..." They just stared silently back at her; she looked at her reflection in the french doors to the courtyard... "Do I have my shirt on backwards or something?"

Viola gave Henri a nudge in the small of his back and he

stumbled forward a step then went to one knee before Uma. She stared down at him with a questioning expression, "Are you alright, Henri?"

He took a deep breath; Hana stopped practicing her scales and dashed to see what everybody was looking at. She stood behind him looking at the little box behind his back.

Henri began, "Uma, I am not very good at many things, and I'm almost an idiot when it comes to expressing myself honestly..."

Viola whispered to Becka, "Oh great start Romeo, just throw up on her shoes while you're at it..." Becka swatted her.

Henri was still talking, "...Here's what I know: You are one of the most accomplished, talented and skilled women I have ever met, and truthfully, I was hoping to always have you as my closest and most respected friend..."

Uma wasn't catching on to any of this, "How nice of you to say so..." she rolled her eyes. "But?"

Henri continued, "But... No, I mean... yeah... But I don't think that's going to be good enough anymore. Uma..."

She was getting a little testy, "Yes... Henri..."

"I love you more than anything. I can't think of life with out you, and I must know if I stand any chance at all of ever having you feel that way toward me!"

He rapidly spilled the words from his mouth as if he didn't hurry she'd lose patience and walk away. Uma's face was a blank mask, an enigma.

He continued, "Even if your feelings toward me aren't as strong as mine for you, I give you my heart and all that I am... I will simply serve you, if you'll allow it."

She unfolded her arms and knelt to look him in the eye. "Henri, this is a little unexpected isn't it?"

Hana, still standing behind him, shook her head side to side.

The rest of the onlookers chuckled and Uma accepted that others noticed things better than she did.

"Henri, I didn't decide to wear girl clothes to er ce you, nor did I exchange my glasses for these contacts for any reason other than to explore what these other women have and I have been ignoring: being feminine."

Henri shook his head and looked like he was going to say he never thought she had... she continued before he could speak.

"But if I *ever* thought I'd hear you say what you *just* said, I would have rushed to this moment in stiletto heels as fast as I could run, if that's what it would've taken." She took a deep breath, "I love you too, Henri. Always have, always will... And what happened to your right arm? Is it broken or something?"

Viola cackled with delight... "Uma is a treasure! She's my kinda girl..."

Henri brought his hand from behind his back. "Uma will you marry me?"

Uma's face was like a candle in a dark room. It was as if a light inside her suddenly burst from her eyes unable to be contained any longer. "Marry you?!" she exclaimed, and Henri immediately thought he'd completely messed something up.

She tossed her head back and dragged him to his feet with her so that they were standing once again. "Henri I will marry you. But on one condition..."

Relieved, he spouted, "Name it!"

"Today. You marry me today! I'm not letting you rethink your position for a moment." She demanded.

Viola laughed even louder, "I can help with that... Becka give me a hand with that sampan on the wall." She and Becka carried it to the courtyard and set it on a channel of the water issuing from the fountain. "Alright you two... Into the boat!" she commanded. Henri and Uma did as they were told.

"This is the third wedding to be performed in this little vessel. The first were Ginger's great-great-grandparents, the next was Becka and her cherished husband Ivy. You are constrained therefore to realize that what is united here stands united for all time." They nodded, looking into each other's eyes. "Good. As the eldest of the Livingson family remaining, and therefore the present captain of this my grandfather's boat, I ask you: Uma, will you love this man at all times whether you feel like it or not?"

Uma nodded, "I will... I do."

"And will you Henri, love Uma at all times whether you feel like it or not?"

Henri answered with a full voice at last, "I do and I will."

Viola said, "Put the ring on her finger then," and she put her hands over theirs, "Before these witnesses, under the sky above and and the waters below us, you have been two and are now one." She leaned toward Uma and whispered, "This is the part where you kiss him..." and she inclined her head as if nudging Uma toward Henri's face.

Henri bent down his head, as Uma lifted her face and their lips met. Hana clapped and danced around the boat and the women watching dabbed at their tears. When the newlyweds came up for breath, they were met with applause and smiles of congratulations. They just stood there, hand in hand, grinning like children at Christmas.

Viola announced, "Now go and put this boat back on the wall you two. This has always remained as a symbol for lives together, that you will have to make the necessary efforts every day that passes to strive towards greater unity both together and as individuals. Do you understand and accept the challenge?"

They answered in near unison, "Yes ma'am!" and carried the sampan back to its place of honor on the wall of the great room.

Vera whispered to Viola, "That was very well done Auntie, very well done..."

Viola embraced her niece and replied, "Thank you Vera honey, that means an awful lot coming from you... Thank you."

Becka put her hands on her hips and announced, "Now Mrs. Rast, if you will excuse me, Mr. Rast promised to show me how to use the bindery machine this morning... and it's already afternoon!"

Uma nearly split a seam laughing, "Henri! I heard you promise her... keep your promises! I'm not going anywhere." Henri happily led the way to the offices and made good on his word.

Ginger asked, "Vera? Should we take everyone for an afternoon wedding feast to that little place we took Becka and Ivy?"

She answered, "Precisely what I was thinking. Uma dear, let's you and I have a little chat shall we?" Uma nodded, not knowing what on earth Vera had in mind. They went upstairs.

Viola and Ginger looked up at the rooms around the courtyard. Ginger mentioned, "They can have the double room there..." she pointed, "...tonight, and we'll arrange proper apartments for them tomorrow..."

Viola replied, "Good by me, Boss!"

When they were all assembled again in the front hall, Vera walked down the stairs in front of Uma. Henri kept trying to see passed Vera but without luck. Vera stepped aside and Uma was standing there alone. Her hair was french braided, and she wore a simple cotton dress that did for her what the sea shell did for Venus in Bouguereau's painting of her birth.

Their silence at her presence surprised her, Uma said shyly, "Is this alright?"

Henri walked forward, offered her his arm and said, "Uma Favri-Rast you are a vision of womanhood. Even the air was still in your honor."

Viola rolled her eyes, "Whew! You go boy..."

15 July 94   The *Anna* is entering the Mediterranean on her way home. Uma emailed to say that Henri's family adore her. Danielle and Valeran were stunned at the news of their friends' marriage. They are spending a lot of time in the offices since we were nearly inundated by orders and submissions two days ago. Viola is bringing Norah along at a pace that's comfortable for both of them. Norah admitted that she hasn't even told her own parents about whom she works for... just that she is employed at last with an humanitarian organization. Vera and I started watching all of John and my collection of Next Generation recordings. After the first night, word spread fast, and now it's a house activity to gather in front of the screen and watch an episode every other day. Hana's not sure whether she wants to be Dr. Crusher or Jordie... she really likes the visor that Danielle made for her. We are planning our piano recital the night after our men return. I have been preparing a special song for Johnny; I hope he likes it.

I'm going to have to keep this short. I can't find a comfortable position in which to write.

"...And even when the bride walked the aisle, most of the men in the audience were still staring at Uma!" Henri related proudly.

Uma defended, "It was more embarrassing than I can say. Thank God we had *our* little ceremony here with just you all around us..."

Viola whispered to Vera, "See what you've done! You've created a lethal female weapon..."

Vera countered in a hushed voice, "She was always a femme fatale, I just pulled away the curtain is all..."

Henri was saying, "...show them what my mother gave you from the estate..." Uma held her hand up where everyone could see. Henri continued, "That ring was my great-grandmother's, given her by none other than Albert Grimaldi... Albert I of Monaco... before he was the ruler of course. She was a beauty, and when my mother saw Uma for the first time she wept and pointed to the portrait of my great-grandmother. They really do bear a striking resemblance..."

Uma demurred, "What's a girl to do?"

Ginger shifted in her seat on the sofa again. "HanaRin, would you hand mama that pillow there?" Hana picked up the cushion and shoved it as hard as her little hands could push into the gap between Ginger's lower back and the sofa. "Aah, thank you cherub."

Norah kept looking at her phone at every odd interval. Viola noticed and asked, "Did your paycheck bounce? Are they cutting off your service?"

Norah laughed, "No. It's just that it's almost seven in Afghanistan and I'm certain the field director said he'd call back by now..."

Viola replied, "Humphrey has a little difficulty with punctuality. If someone didn't remind him, he'd miss every flight and phone call he's ever had. Give him another hour then call him again. You'll get to know our people as well as your own family before long." Norah tried a smile.

Vera asked, "Valeran? Danielle said you were going to look into how to modify the website to add publications on a monthly cycle... Is that happening?"

Everybody looked at him. Valeran gulped. "Uh, well, I asked one of my former classmates who does that for a living now, and he sat down with me for several hours to explain what was entailed. I think I can do it, but I'm going to have to have John looking over my shoulder for the first go around. One thing my friend emphasized was how badly I could fu... uh... mess things up if I didn't pay attention to the sequence he outlined. I'm not confident of doing it on my own."

Danielle looked at him with newfound admiration. "Val, that's the first time I can remember you didn't just rush right into doing whatever you thought 'was so simple even a monkey could do it without training' attitude. Who are you and what have you done with my Valeran!"

Norah looked at the ceiling. "Jeez!" she exclaimed, "Please don't start another cycle of barbs and veiled insults! You two are driving me nutso! The whole trip it was arguing about how much tip to leave, or what time to set the alarm in the morning, or who saw the most surrealist paintings---and Picasso was born in Malaga, he didn't live in A Coruna until he was ten years old!" her exasperation wasn't lost on anyone within earshot.

Viola muttered to Vera, "Here we go again... get ready to get the boat..."

Danielle turned on her sister, "Val was also right most of the time, I was just being argumentative because of the way he stared at you on the beach."

Norah retorted, "...Stared at me! You need eyes in back of your head sis, because Prince Valiant here only had eyes for your pretty... for you during the whole trip. I was starting to feel like a fifth wheel before we got out of Italy!"

Valeran kept trying to interject something but Henri put his hand on his arm to stifle his compulsion. Danielle came back with, "If you hadn't encouraged him I wouldn't have been so annoying...y ou could have at least worn a bra or an undershirt *sometime* during the trip!"

"Me! Did you even take underwear? Or were so sure you wouldn't need it?" Norah blasted right back.

Danielle was nearly beside herself, "You gave him the soft sweet voice, and barked at me. You always expected he would carry your bag and I had to carry my own. You couldn't have mentioned how thankful you were that you'd finished graduate school any more often... I think the owners of the hostels know how long and how successful you were in school... And your poor stupid sister just barely got through her undergraduate! Uhrgh!"

Norah opened her mouth to respond but Viola stopped her. "Before this breaks out into a full-fledged mud wrestling match, may I know one thing?"

Danielle gathered her self, totally embarrassed at her outburst. Norah shivered at being, to her way of thinking, unjustly accused. Danielle replied as civilly as she could muster, "What would you like to know?"

Viola looked at Valeran, "Mr. Daane? How long are you going to let Danielle flap in the breeze?"

Valeran looked at the faces now turned toward him. "Uh..." and he looked at Danielle, "I didn't notice what Norah was wearing or not wearing. I did notice that when you ask a question your nostrils flare slightly, and when you are ready to eat you shiver a little, and when you reach for something you always reach to push up your sleeve whether your wearing sleeves or not. When you walk your shoulders are back and your eyes are alive, when you sit down it's almost like slow motion, when you yawn you make a little noise like a hawk in the air, when you look at me you make my heart pound like it's going to tell everyone how much I love you..."

Viola clapped, "Now that wasn't so hard, was it?"

Danielle and Norah, and the other women for that matter, dabbed at the tears in their eyes. In a soft voice she had never managed before, Viola asked Danielle, "Well, don't you have something to say to your sister?"

Danielle threw herself across the short space between them that had a few moments before been a no man's land. With her arms around her sister's neck she whispered only what they could hear between them. Norah held her at arms length, "I think you have another apology to make..."

Danielle looked at Ginger and then to Valeran. "I'm sorry I suspected you of such hurtful things. I'll be better, I promise."

Viola waited a moment and prodded Valeran. "That's your cue, Prince..."

Valeran's gaze had never left Danielle's eyes. "Dani? Marry me. I can't take this day in and day out anymore. But don't pity me, say yes only if you can really love me."

Danielle's face was priceless, "I can, I do, and I will; any other conditions?"

Valeran was visibly relieved and raised his shoulders as if relinquishing any other considerations. The sampan was brought out again. Again, Viola presided over an impromptu ceremony. Again they adjourned to dinner.

25 July 94   Everyone is back home now. John, Alfred and Ivy had no mishaps or poor weather. But that's not the greatest news: Grandmama Ronia and Auntie Olivia returned with them on the *Anna* and will be here for MirandaLinn's debut!!

Our living arrangements have been reorganized to the new couples' satisfaction and the daily rhythms of the Inn have returned to a more sedate pace. Ronia and Olivia are getting a good picture of how the Inn functions at near full capacity. The men were delighted that the personal tensions in the offices had abated... and I think they were relieved that it all transpired while they were away. Hana was the most glad to have her fathers home; she still climbs on their laps at every opportunity. I think it's to physically restrain them from 'disappearing' again.

With our partners now paired off, Alfred and Vera, even Viola suggested that their work on themselves might accelerate. By the same token Ivy was rapidly fulfilling the niche for Valeran and Henri. Such is often the case when two or more people are striving toward similar objectives... of course that also means that they will likely encounter more of themselves than they were previously willing to look at on their own. Being the same age as Danielle and Uma, Becka was a great role model and was happy to allow herself to become an example for them. The three women were becoming thick as thieves. If they each can maintain sincerity with themselves perhaps it will all advance without too many recriminations... we'll see. All I know is that the Press is running smoothly and growing.

Our little welcome home recital went splendidly. John enjoyed my musical gift to him so much that I played the songs over again so he could record them. In our apartments at least, the strains of *Unchained Melody, Can't Help Falling in Love With You* and *Dream a Little Dream of Me* are a constant background. It may sound a little self-centered for me to admit this but I really am glad he recorded me... it's just one more way for me to step back and look at (in this case: hear) myself from outside myself. He naturally recorded Hana's renditions of her first song and also this last one: *Puff the Magic Dragon*. I wonder about how she interprets the words she sings. They aren't all a part of everyday conversation, and then there is how she verbalizes them, or more aptly mashes them up. I certainly remember thinking for the longest time that the words to the national anthem included the question: 'What are gallantly steaming?...' Such is the nature of communication and miscommunications.

"Just a few weeks to go! How are you doing today MamaKat?" Ronia asked as Ginger came into the kitchen.

Ginger's smile was easy, "Grandmama we are great! It's even better having you and Olivia here. I feel so supported and loved... I can't tell you how much." She set the kettle to boil for more tea.

Ronia commented, "I really like your young partners. They are so bright and courteous and... young."

Ginger nodded, "Young yes, but growing and working hard. They have been a constant source of delight."

Ronia idly stirred her tea cup, although she didn't take sugar or anything else in it. "Ginger, I have been so looking forward to spending this time with you. I've thought of everything I'd want to tell you, how much we love you... have loved you for so long... But now that I'm here and see you and Johnny... how happy you are... how well-adjusted... how capable and strong... I just can't recall what I was so concerned about that I thought so needed saying. Does that make any sense?"

Ginger listened and smiled, "It really does. I think it's a little like what I *plan* to tell Hana about something she's just learning. But when she encounters it, she is so curious and explores and experiments so much with it that I find anything I was going to say won't exactly map onto how she's actually experiencing that thing for herself..."

"You are a very perceptive woman GingerKat. I don't think I could have explained it any better. Thank you. Anna would be so proud of you!" Ronia reflected. That brought tears to Ginger's eyes in a flash. Ronia added gently, "You don't know this, but you and your mother are alike in some very uncanny ways... not just your appearances, but how you approach your world, how you sort through whatever challenges you... even certain of your mannerisms recall her to me as if she were sitting here in front of me. I am so thankful you took a chance on Johnny and he loves you. You deserve all that and more."

Vera and Viola had waited quietly at the door, hoping their presence wouldn't interrupt this special moment for two special women. Ronia saw them in the corner of her eye. "Don't you think so Vera? Viola you certainly spent plenty of time with Anna when we were all in Gotland and then while you were in California..."

Vera went and sat next to Ginger, Viola took a seat across from them both. Vera began, "It's true. I haven't made an issue of it... well, because you are you and Anna was Anna... But oh my yes! I can almost hear your mother's voice in yours. It's all I can do sometimes to hold my tongue, and remember to call you 'Ginger'."

Viola had a different take on it. "Portia and I are *so much* like *our* mothers it's disturbing. Even though you and Anna weren't able to be together, I can assure you that the more you become who you *really* are... the more you will know exactly *who* your mother *really* was. I can't express it any better than that."

The other ladies nodded an confident agreement. Ginger just kept dabbing at her eyes. "Thank you," she voiced quietly. "I think I actually know what you mean. Over the last month or so I have begun to see myself as if I am hovering around myself: seeing myself doing whatever I'm doing and also being me doing it. So I think, after a fashion, I am seeing what your describing... a little at a time."

Ronia grinned. "You are an amazing woman." Viola and Vera added only, "So true, so true."

Ginger went to stand, and there was a gushing of water on the floor beneath her chair. She looked down in mid-movement. Vera was already up and out the kitchen door calling for Alfred and John to "Bring my obstetric and neonatal equipment to the apartment! Stat! Put out the mattress cover and sterile sheets on the bed. Start the air filters in all our apartment's rooms. Viola will walk her up, while she's doing that, everybody scrub. Move!!"

It was somewhat startling to everyone save Viola and Alfred just what an *incredibly* commanding voice Dr. Masterson-Livingson actually had.

Viola was around the table as if she transported, her voice was as gentle as a flower petal while her energy was as focused as a laser. "Ginger we are going to walk very slowly up to your room..." She looked to Ronia and pointed with her eyes to Hana, "...Hana's going to wash her hands and put on a cute little gown so that she can come help mama. How does your pelvis feel just now? Overly warm? Any cramping yet? Do you feel that your belly has dropped lower?"

Ginger was helped to a standing position and answered simply, "Uh huh, yep... Oooh, yeah that's either a contraction or a cramp from standing too quickly..."

Viola was far stronger than Ginger would have ever suspected. Viola was behind her going up the stairs and Ginger had the distinct feeling that she was being lifted by the elbows all the way up. As they slowly made their way to the end of the balcony corridor and the apartment, Viola asked a few more questions.

"Did you have any bloody discharge in the last twenty-four hours?"

Ginger uttered, "No."

"Good, and any more Braxton-Hicks over the same time?"

Again Ginger managed, "No..."

"Good. We're almost there. We'll go to the bathroom first. I'll clean you up and we'll get you into a gown. Then you can sit back in bed and focus on the labor that's coming on now. Vera and John have everything ready for you. Alright GingerKat? Do you understand?"

"Yep." Ginger squeaked.

As they entered the apartment doorway, Alfred and John stood aside. The living room had been instantly transformed into a neonatal nursery. Ginger looked at all the equipment and paraphernalia, "Wow, where did this stuff come from?"

Viola's soft voice answered, "We've had it stored just next door for a few weeks, there's no reason you would have noticed." She raised her voice in the direction of the bedroom, "No spotting, slight tenderness, mild cramping; set up to u/s her cervix... I think I'm going to win this bet after all..."

Vera responded calmly but with authority, "I set up a saline drip; the ultrasound is ready at your elbow," and she helped Ginger onto the bed.

Ginger asked, "This looks like you all anticipated an early labor... Ooh," she winced. Vera waited until the little contraction abated, looking at the clock on the wall as she did. Ginger continued, "What is the bet Viola talked about?"

Viola came in, gowned, and answered, "All your lab tests and ultrasounds hinted at a multiple birth but were inconclusive. Our women only saw one baby growing, but that's not foolproof... Look at Hana Nasrin. Alfred and Vera completely kept her off the radar so to speak. Now, your contractions will come more frequently in just a while and they will become gradually more intense. Vera and I have delivered enough babies to populate a small nation, you're doing just fine."

Vera commented, "I'll take a moment to catch up our family on the particulars... and yes it does appear that you were right... Alfred will be tickled---he thought so too. Be right back..." and she slipped through the room to the door and left Viola setting up the drip and proceeding with the ultrasound.

Viola gave a running commentary of all that she did. Partially to give Ginger something to distract her slightly, partly for information's sake. She spread lubricant across Ginger's 'waist' at her pelvis and right up over and around her belly in spots. "Alright now let's take one last peek shall we?" Ginger looked up on the monitor. Viola pointed, "There is one big ole head... she's getting herself into position nicely." She went to a couple other spots. "There!" And she scanned in a small radius at the new location. "*That* young lady is her..." and she carefully followed the image along it's spine as far as she could. "...I'm going with sister on this one. No wonder we didn't notice before... They've been dancing a tango... but they do not appear cojoined..."

Ginger muttered, "So, I'm *supposed* to be as big as a house... that's a relief *right?*"

Viola chuckled, "Thats what ultimately gave it away. Vera had her suspicions too, but truly you could have had one ginormous amazon... And yes that's good. Your water breaking a couple, few weeks early cinched it... It's far more common for first time mothers to be early with twins than with one big baby."

Ginger winced again, but uttered not a sound. 'Okay girls this is the big show... we've been working toward this moment... I'll do my part with as much grace as I can manage and you two do yours... Deal?' She was slightly startled by the whisper of an echo in answer to her mental petition...

Aloud she said after the contraction abated, "It's a good thing John and I chose such a long name..." Vera came back in and nodded. Ginger continued, "...Anna Sonia Isabelle and Anna Miranda Linn have agreed to do their part."

Vera looked to Viola who shrugged; she asked, "GingerKat? Did they tell you that?" Her voice was even. There was no hint of skepticism or incredulity, just curiosity.

Ginger replied in a increasingly ragged voice, "I heard some agreement to the deal I just proposed... my part is to lead by example."

Vera and Viola looked with new wonder at each other and to Ginger. John carried Hana into the room. Becka, Olivia and Ronia crowded just inside the doorway, ready to hop out of the way should it be necessary.

Hana was grinning at them all, "MamaKat having kittenses?"

Ginger looked up at her and smiled even though this next round of contractions wasn't anything to take lightly, "Um hmm..." She relaxed a bit, "Do you want to sit over here on this stool and be ready to welcome your sisters?" She waved her hand to the tall stool above and near her head. "PapaKat will be just here across from you, okay?"

John followed her directions and set HanaRin on the stool where she composed herself and sat quietly. John went round to the other side and took up a similar position. Vera and Viola were alternating in checking dilation on either side of her, and the other women took up positions against the wall opposite the foot of the bed, leaving plenty of room for Vera and Viola to maneuver. Ginger was nearly in a sitting up position with her knees up and feet on the bed bracing against a pair of blocks that her aunts had installed for that purpose. Her pelvis was elevated off the bed sheets and several linen sheets were folded and laying beneath her hips with a couple towels directly beneath her.

"Ginger's eyes squinted and her breath was rapid and deep. The sounds of the piano from downstairs came in through all the open doors and she smiled. "Uncle Alfred is a darling man... how very thoughtful of him to play for our girls..."

The ordeal lasted through the morning. There was a brigade line to the kitchen from her room bringing ice chips, tea, crackers, whatever was called for. Alfred played without ceasing, Hana sat and watched without blinking, John kept up a soothing soliloquy in Ginger's ear, while Vera and Viola monitored, encouraged, chatted and praised. The partners were the couriers, messengers, kitchen staff and orderlies. Ivy kept Alfred company and supplied with food and drink. The afternoon began to wane.

As Alfred began Mozart's piano Concerto Number Twenty-one, there was a shrill cry from upstairs, a little while later a second cry erupted nearly louder than the first. Ahs, Ohs and clapping that sounded like rain on a tin roof spattered around the Inn. The Annas were at last among them. Hana came dashing down to his side and delivered the news personally. "PapaRed! Anna Sonia Isabelle and Anna Miranda Linn are here! They're here! Come and see. Come and See!"

He lifted her up into his arms and carried her back upstairs. Vera met them at the door to the apartments, a little bedraggled but bright and contented. She nodded happily and ushered Hana and her husband into the rooms. Ginger was holding court, an Anna in the crook of each arm. They were small little wrinkled footballs, but they were their newest little angels. Ginger positively glowed---actually illuminating the room. She said in a voice that had a tinge of weariness in it, "Please, let me introduce the youngest Livingson-Spelman-Backhouses." She turned her head to her left and gazed down at the cherub, "This is Anna Miranda Linn..." Alfred bowed deeply. "And this..." she inclined her head to the seraph on her right, "...is Anna Sonia Isabelle. Ladies this is your Papa Alfred..."

Viola and Vera, as well as all others looking on, held there breath as Alfred approached, took John's hands into his own and gripped them tightly. He moved closer to the bedside and looked down at the angels. For all the world it really appeared as though they turned their heads toward him as he spoke. "Welcome at last young ladies. We have been looking forward to having your acquaintance for some time now..."

Each of them actually opened their little mouths and made the tiniest of noises, like the sounds of mewling kittens or of whimpering newborn puppies. A wave of gentle applause went round the room. Ronia came forward and announced, "Well done Virginia, very well done indeed."

What no one else in the room heard, save John and Ginger were the praises and commendations from the faint voices of Anna Spelman, Robert and Izzy Backhouse... The young Backhouse's tears weren't out of place and no one could have guessed that they were at last in a brief but most poignant family reunion so long overdue.

Ginger asked, "HanaRin, would you go and fetch MamaKat's journal please?" Hana skipped out the door and returned in a moment to place it next to her mother's hand. She picked it up and opened to the place she'd last left her pen. She read aloud as she wrote:

2 August 94   Earlier than expected, and more beautiful than imagined, our lives have been increased two-fold by these two girls beside me. Our family has been the strength in our resolve to be the best we can become and now we shall endeavor to do the same for all of our children. Mine and John's parents made it very clear in the few moments we had with them, that our family is far more enduring than they had ever hoped or imagined and gave us their last blessing before leaving for good. They waited for this moment with only a slim chance of ever achieving it. We shall always revere their unparalleled devotion and faith in us. Welcome: Anna Sonia Isabelle and Anna Miranda Linn. Your sister Hana Nasrin, and your parents, Alfred, Vera, Viola, Johnny, and Ginger will always strive to do right by you and the promise of life and love you bring.

She closed her journal, and handed it to Hana. She received it with a grin and returned it to where she found it. Ronia said, "I think I can speak for all our absent family in saying: You and John have fulfilled our greatest hopes for a bright dawn after decades of a withering night."

Becka and Ivy came near and reached out to the twins. They were followed in turn by everyone in the Inn.

At last Viola asked, "I don't suppose you're as hungry as we are?!..."

Ginger laughed out loud, and winced, "Ravenous!"

Viola left to fetch a few items of food, Vera leaned close to Ginger's ear and whispered, "We have never witnessed such poise and grace in the midst of tremendous effort. Your family is exceedingly impressed and... in awe. By the way, I put in a couple extra stitches..." She glanced over to Johnny. "You'll be your old self again in a matter of weeks..." she winked.

Ginger giggled, "Honestly... I don't think my old self even exists anymore."

Vera caught her breath and a tear ran down her cheek. "Yes, boss, the world itself has been changed for the better today." She straightened up. "Now let's see just how hungry our girls are after their ordeal..." She arranged pillows to accommodate each girl on either side of Ginger's breasts and let nature take its course. The twins nuzzled into position and Ginger let out a surprised gasp. Vera grinned, "The novelty will wear off in time... but yeah... it's something isn't it?"

Ginger looked down at each of the suckling infants. "Thankfully your mother is a cow!" She and Vera laughed out loud just as Viola came back in with snacks and juice.

"You're not alone in that. Our women have always been udderly endowed..." Viola punned to groans and giggles. "I for one would like for once use these jugs for something other than eliciting stares."

Ginger sighed, "You know I think that can be arranged..." she looked up to Vera, "Any other volunteers?" Vera's face couldn't have been more innocently thrilled.

Viola inserted, "If you hadn't caught us off-guard, we'd be ready now... But remember it's your milk that gives them the best of what they need for a while. We will certainly be delighted to take up the slack though."

There were little noises of squeals and gasps at her chest. Ginger asked, "Is that bread and jam and cheese I smell? Aah, manna from heaven..."

The rest of the women in the Inn made trips up to her room all through the rest of the evening and into the early hours of the night. Uma, Danielle and Becka all moved as a group. The gentlemen sat in the courtyard with brandy and cigars, lounging and joking, chatting and grinning. John and Alfred got more than they bargained for of consoling attentions.

Ivy's comments summed them up, "Two men on a yacht full of six women... for weeks even months? We certainly hope you still know how to talk about something other than relationships and pretty things when you return to manly company..."

Alfred and Johnny grinned. John proposed another toast, "To remembering growling and grunting..." They all chuckled and drank.

The few women in earshot, when they passed by on errands of their own, couldn't help but giggle as they eavesdropped on the ramblings of their men. They dutifully passed along what was said and alluded to when they inevitably returned to the apartments upstairs and tended to the new mother and all her girls. Hana didn't leave the room all night. Vera and Viola were sure she was in the pink of health and so set up a hammock for her near her sisters.

In the morning John brought in a tray of tasty things for his girls to rummage through for breakfast. Hana truly felt like a big girl being tended to just like Ginger. "The doctors said it wouldn't be a bad idea to give your legs a stretch sometime to day... just to get your joints and muscles used to moving again..."

Ginger drowsily said, "I'll start by going to the bathroom again..." and she slowly rolled to the side of the bed and accepted his arm. The twins were swaddled and laying in a crib at the head of the bed where Hana could keep a watchful eye on them. "Okay..." Ginger uttered tensely, "That wasn't so bad... one foot in front of the other GingerKat..." she coached herself.

That afternoon she made several laps around the courtyard balconies. As she passed the offices she asked about the daily things she usually checked on routinely. She was wearing a long linen robe, Vera had braided her hair, and her steps were becoming more sure and steady with each lap. The partners just marveled.

Danielle asked, obviously impressed, "Boss, is there anything you can't do?!"

Ginger replied, "Sure, I can't imagine my life without all of you..."

Her staff was noticeably touched. Becka overheard the exchange from the courtyard. She turned to Ronia and Olivia, "MamaKat is in the building!"

The two women replied in so many words, "Hope has sprung eternal."

J. L. LAWSON

Manuscripts Currently Published by
J. L. Lawson

---The Donkey and the Wall Trilogy---

Book One: An Honest Man
Book Two: The Thief
Book Three: The Tiger

---The Curious Voyages of the Anna Virginia Saga---

First: Weigh Anchor
Second: Harbor
Third: Storms
Fourth: Locks & Gates
Fifth: Tidal Bore
Sixth: Beyond the Littoral
Seventh (final): Red Sky at Night

www.ingramcontent.com/pod-product-compliance
Lightning Source LLC
Chambersburg PA
CBHW020829030726
47496CB00001B/159